The Bell Cannon Affair

by Dean Whitlock

BOATMAN
PRESS
Thetford, Vermont

Cover illustration and design ©2021 by Maurizio Manzieri

Published by Boatman Press, LLC, Thetford Center, Vermont

This is a work of fiction. It represents many months of thought, research, writing, and rewriting. If you like it, please tell your friends. Thank you.

A bad-luck crewman with one last chance to redeem himself, a deported physicist whose secret project killed dozens, the physicist's genius daughter – it's 1878, and the steam liner *Isle of Lewis* is about to depart New York for Glasgow. No other ship will take them, but the *Lewis* can't afford not to. As passions rise on board, she steams eastward into a maelstrom of stowaways, shysters, dissemblers, spies, and a raging hurricane, with the mystery of the Bell Cannon at its eye.
Steampunk, Gaslight, Mystery, Thriller, Adventure

ISBN-13: 978-1-7355514-3-2

2nd Edition

A stunning story of a quest for truth which will change all the lives it touches . . . an impressively compelling read. —*Children's Bookwatch*

A fast-paced, heartwarming adventure. —*Kirkus*

Skillful, evocative writing, a uniquely drawn setting, and richly developed characters mark this fiction debut for fantasy fans. —*The Midwest Book Review*

Those who look to fantasy for well-imaged situations and settings will find an ample supply in this one, which can be readily enjoyed by newcomers to Whitlock's world. —*Booklist*

Other books by Dean Whitlock

The Arrow Rune
Finn's Clock
The Carver's World Series:
>   Sky Carver
>   Raven
>   Fireboy

Iridescence and other stories
The Man Who Loved Kites *(a chapbook of the novelette, also in Iridescence)*

For Sally

Prologue
The Final Test

Tereza Skovajsová tapped the tuning fork against the heel of her hand, held it to the tertiary bell, and listened intently. The bell hummed gently, but she could still hear a wavering double frequency. Still slightly sharp. Carefully, she turned the knurled head of the tuning bolt on the twelfth resonator. The waver slowed and the frequencies joined into a single, sweet tone. Tereza imagined that time itself had slowed by a tiny bit of a second, bringing the world closer to harmony. She smiled and moved on to the thirteenth resonator.

The segmented barrel of the apparatus was made up of five concentric, bell-like reflectors, growing progressively narrower and deeper along the length of the central core. The widest, at the bottom, was eight feet in diameter and two feet deep, with forty-eight tunable resonators around its rim. The final reflector was only a foot in diameter, with sixteen resonators, but it was five feet deep, reaching out to the very end of the copper-and-quartz impulse shaft. The entire apparatus, including its mushroom-shaped cast-iron base, was fourteen feet long. The blocky power supply – a rank of tall crystal-and-foil Leyden jars, black ceramic insulators, and coiled copper wiring – added to the appearance of mass.

In truth, the reflectors – or bells as the Americans preferred to call them – were thin shells, cast in bronze and polished to within one-hundredth of an inch of her father's design measurements. They shone, even under the broad lean-to roof of his combined laboratory and testing emplacement. One soft tap from a finger, and they hummed in a minor chord, almost like the echo of distant church bells. The Americans—those few who knew about it—called it the Bell Cannon.

Tereza disliked the name. It was too warlike, too aggressive. Her father's apparatus wasn't intended to attack or siege, only to defend, and it looked it. She held the tuning fork to the bell, delicately turned the tuning bolt with slim, sure fingers, and heard a matching beauty come into its voice. Her father and his assistant were working nearby, but she paid them no mind, totally absorbed in her task.

"Tereza." Her father's voice intruded. She ignored it and finished tuning the resonator.

"Tereza," he repeated, more firmly. "General Burton and the Secretary will be here soon. It's time for you and your mother to leave."

Tereza looked up, startled. "But it's not yet 2:00, Papa. They aren't due fo—"

"For another hour. Yes, I know, my dear, but—"

She frowned. "But I haven't finished tuning the final quadrant on the tertiary bell."

He grimaced, a typical show of irritation, and cleared his throat. "I realize that, Tereza," he told her sternly, "but I will have to finish the job for you. It's something I need to do myself, without distractions." He tried an empty smile on her. "After all, I can't have you here with a soiled smock and grease on your fingers when the Secretary of War arrives, can I?" He ran the tip of his index finger along the side of her nose. "Grease on your face, as well, I might add." He smiled again.

She did not see the humor. "I can easily finish this before he and the general are due, Papa. Even if they arrive early, we will hear them, and I will disappear out the far door."

"The carriage, however, is out the front door, and you can hardly expect your mother to 'disappear' with you. She is a lady, not a schoolgirl."

Tereza's frown deepened. "I will be seventeen in June."

"And so *you* are too old to act like a schoolgirl," he went on, voice rising. "Now, please put down that tuning fork, empty the tools from your pockets, collect your mother, and go."

She clenched her fists. "I am not acting like—"

"Go," he repeated, holding out his hand for the tuning fork. "Please. I do not have time to argue. This is too important. This means my career. My life."

"And mine!" She slapped the tuning fork into his palm, followed by everything else in her apron, just to make her point: a trio of small wrenches, a screwdriver, pliers, and a large spanner that she knew she had no use for but had felt good in her hand. "There!"

She turned, head held high, and strode toward the doorway.

Jakub Skovajsa sighed and followed her as she stalked down the viewing line. She walked as stiffly as a stork, and he realized he was doing the same. It had become another battle, distressingly frequent in the past year. *Sakra!* he thought. *Damnation! Why must we always fight like this? Why now, when I need to remain clear-headed?*

His wife looked up from her book and glanced at each of them in turn. One eyebrow rose, along with a corner of her mouth, but she managed not to smile outright.

"Eliška, it is time for the two of you to leave," he said.

"Of course, Jakub," she replied, closing her book and rising. Her full skirts slid loose from the chair seat and swirled almost calmly into place. "You must prepare without us here to worry you."

"Yes, thank you." As always, her easy grace and good

humor calmed him a little.

Tereza had marched straight past her mother to the doorway. They both watched her go out, pointedly slamming the door behind her.

"Don't worry," Eliška said, "she will not stay sixteen forever."

"And thank Heaven for that," he murmured. "She is so helpful, and yet so . . . so . . ."

"So much like her father, Herr Professor? She looks like you. What else can you expect?" Eliška let herself smile fully, and Jakub could not help but smile back.

"I hope I am not quite like that," he said.

"Headstrong, yes. Absolutely sure of yourself, yes. Full of tantrums . . ." She cocked her head. "Not so much anymore."

"So there is hope for her?"

"And still some for you." Eliška leaned forward and pressed a light kiss on his cheek. When she pulled away, she was no longer smiling. "Be careful, Jakub," she said quietly, glancing past his shoulder at his apparatus. "I know the prototype worked perfectly and the early tests went well, but still, this time, at full power, it will be so much more . . . *kräftig*. Potent."

He reached for her hand, then realized he was still holding Tereza's tuning fork and tools. Eliška smiled again and wrapped her gloved fingers around the back of his wrist. "Get to work, Doctor Professor Skovajsa. Show your American friends what Bohemian genius can do."

"Thank you, my dear Mrs. Skovajsová." He bowed his head to her and watched her slim back as she left, indulging himself in a moment of grateful affection.

Then he pulled out his pocket watch and snapped open the case. There was just enough time to finish adjusting the resonators. He knew Tereza could probably have helped, but the coming test was too critical. He would not trust even her delicate touch on the tuning bolts. He closed the watch and slipped it back into his vest pocket. She was headstrong, yes, but it was his own fault. He had indulged her. The fact that she was brilliant should have made no difference. He would not let himself be angry at her now. He strode back to the apparatus, calling for his assistant.

"Hoeffler! Where are you? Check the dynamo. Be certain that lazy fireman doesn't let the pressure fall in the boiler. Double-check the charge on every one of the Leyden jars. And don't bother me! Let no one in, not even if it is President Hayes!"

&

Three-quarters of an hour later, the Bell Cannon was almost ready. Stimulated by a series of electrical pulses from the power supply, the reflectors would make no sound. At least, none that a human ear could hear. Instead, they would cause the very aether to resonate. That unseen and unweighable stuff between the atoms of the air, aether had properties that Jakub and a few other devoted natural philosophers were only beginning to catalog. Though it lacked mass, aether had presence and could exert an almost electrical force when made to vibrate at the right frequency and in the right direction.

The reflectors, or bells, did both, providing resonance and vector to the natural aether present everywhere. Any person in the path of that constrained pulse of aether would be penetrated, his very innards set vibrating. Only the most delicate part would feel the effects: the brain, that perfect engine of personality, mentation, and action. The power behind the heart. All thought would dissolve under the invisible onslaught, and the body would stop dead.

Jakub had begun at the top, tuning each resonator on each reflector in turn, even the ones Tereza had already tuned. Just to be sure. Now, with the ladder pulled aside and the apparatus aimed to its highest elevation, there was only the bottom reflector to finish.

Jakub took a moment to wipe his face with his handkerchief and check his watch. Luckily, Secretary Lowell was noted for his tardiness. There would be time to finish and tidy up. He reached for the next tuning head.

A carriage rattled up outside the entrance.

Sakra!

"Hoeffler," he muttered. "They're early. Delay them."

Hoeffler was standing on the far side of the power supply, checking each of the Leyden jars to make sure they were at maximum charge. "Yes, sir, Just as soon as I —"

"Now!" Jakub barked.

"Yes, sir. I'll do what I can."

He set down the amperage meter and hurried toward the entrance, wiping his hands on his vest. Jakub tried to focus on the resonator under his hand, but he couldn't block out the muted sounds of Hoeffler's voice, a faint reply, an argument. He realized suddenly that the other voice was Eliška's. She hurried through the doorway, followed by a very agitated Hoeffler.

"I'm very sorry, Professor," he said. "She wouldn't—"

Jakub silenced him with a curt wave. "Eliška, what can be so important?" he demanded.

Eliška was staring into every corner of the lab, as though hunting for something. "Tereza's not here?" she asked.

"Tereza? You took her home." Jakub felt stupid the moment he said it. "What's happened to her?"

Eliška threw up her hands. "Moping somewhere, I suppose. She complained the entire way. 'I've worked my whole life on this, Mother.' She went up to her room, and when it seemed too silent, I went to look. She was gone."

Eliška sighed and gave Jakub a worried smile. "I was certain that she would be here, all in your hair."

"Well, she's not, though she's hardly had time. I suppose she might turn up any minute." Jakub ran his hand down his chin, smoothing his short beard. "Well, no harm done yet. I'm sure you're right that she's merely sulking somewhere. After all, this experiment has indeed run though the course of her entire life. But now I must..." He half turned, gesturing back to the waiting resonators.

"Of course. I'll go at once and leave you to it. How much time?"

"Ten minutes at most," Hoeffler said, frowning anxiously.

"I'll search for her on the drive back," Eliška said. "She should be home, safe, not hiding in the woods, pouting like a two-year-old."

"She is safe, no matter where she's hiding," Jakub reassured her. "Tell her I will come as soon as the test is completed, and describe every detail."

Eliška flashed him another smile and hurried out.

"Nine minutes, sir," Hoeffler said.

Jakub smoothed his beard again. *Seventeen years. Almost every waking hour since 1861, and all to be decided in nine more minutes.* He took a breath and focused his thoughts.

"Then let us finish in nine. Check on the fireman, then wait by the doorway and let me know the minute you see the Secretary's carriage."

It was actually eleven minutes before Hoeffler cried out, and the extra minutes had allowed Jakub to tune all but the sixteenth resonator on the bottom bell. That took but a moment more. He was at the doorway, hands wiped, hair and beard smoothed, a small smile on his lips, as Secretary Lowell stepped down from the carriage.

The party was larger than Jakub had expected, which

was already more than he'd wanted. He had planned at least two more private tests before inviting visitors, but General Burton, his only certain sponsor, had made it clear that the Secretary needed a viewing now if Jakub hoped to see more funding. Reluctantly, Jakub had agreed. But now the general and the Secretary both had brought an aide – Major Martins, whom Jakub had at least met, and a Mr. Striker – and following in a second carriage was Senator Clement, who had brought Senator Rice. Clement, like the general, had been one of Jakub's sponsors since the beginning. Rice, though, was a stranger; a potential ally, perhaps, but it meant being overly polite and conscientious when what Jakub wanted was simply to show the Secretary what the aetheric resonator would do.

"Clement has told me only the tiniest bit about your Bell Cannon, Professor," Senator Rice said, shaking Jakub's hand with the usual lengthy and violent American greeting. "I'm no scientist, but all of this talk of ether has me confused. Does it put people to sleep?"

"It's aether," Jakub said, barely maintaining his smile, "and it is not an anesthetic." He withdrew his hand and marshaled his thoughts, trying to think of a simple explanation that this florid politician would understand.

General Burton saved him. "Why don't we just run the test and watch what it can do, Senator. Seeing is believing."

"Excellent idea," Secretary Lowell put in. "I'm afraid I'm on a schedule this afternoon."

With a sigh of relief, Jakub directed the men to their seats and quickly pointed out the apparatus, the power supply, and the thick insulated cables that led out back to the dynamo and the steam engine that turned it. They could easily hear the whine of the first and the chuffing of the second. Hoeffler took his place at the side doorway, where he could yell out to the fireman or step to the

Leyden jars, as needed. Jakub himself engaged the gear that opened the shutters. Warm April sunshine filled the workroom-turned-viewing-stand.

The men exclaimed when they saw the subjects of the test; the targets of the so-called Bell Cannon. Chained to stakes at twenty-yard intervals that stretched out to half a mile away were dogs, horses, and people.

"Condemned prisoners," General Burton told the others. "Murderers, deserters, the worst. Instead of hanging, they will give their lives to the service of their country."

"What if it doesn't work?" Rice muttered to Clement.

Burton heard and smiled. "Then they'll be hanged. But it'll work."

Jakub turned his mind from their chatter. With a signal to Hoeffler, the two of them began turning the cranks to aim the apparatus. The column of gleaming bells tipped down and swung to the right, until its narrow end was aimed down the long line of targets. The prisoners were blindfolded. The dogs stared uncomprehendingly; a few barks sounded along the line. The horses nibbled at the grass.

Hoeffler went back to his post. Jakub raised his hand, and Hoeffler raised his. The steam engine ran faster; the whine of the dynamo rose an octave. Jakub watched the Leyden jars. The coiled wires on top began to redden, then glow. When they were all golden hot, he closed the heavy two-armed switch between the apparatus and the power supply. The apparatus jerked almost imperceptibly. The bells hummed for just a moment, a hum that quickly soared up the scale, through an instant of auditory pain, and then seemed to disappear. Only a faint tingling remained, hovering an inch inside the ear.

Jakub frowned. That moment of pain, that tingling – they weren't right. He gripped the handle of the switch, ready to yank it down, to cut the connection and halt the test.

"What happened?" Rice whispered to Clement. "Did it break?"

Jakub let go of the switch. Of course it didn't break. Senator Rice would soon be convinced.

The dynamo strained, and the coils on the Leyden jars dimmed as they shot a pulse of energy into the apparatus. Then again, and again, each pulse building in unfelt intensity. Twenty yards out, the nearest horse lifted its head and neighed. The dog began to snarl, tugging back on its chain. The prisoner jerked to attention, shaking his hooded head.

"More power, Hoeffler." Jakub tried to sound unconcerned.

Hoeffler turned and signaled outside. The dynamo whine increased again. The coils dimmed. And Jakub felt it again, that instant of pain, the tingling inside his ears. The dog howled and tore at the iron chain with its teeth. The horse reared, shrieking. The prisoner began to wail and gibber like a man being burned alive.

Sakra! It was supposed to be instant! Painless!

"More power!" Jakub yelled.

As Hoeffler leaned out the door to signal, one of the Leyden jars exploded. Shards of foil-coated crystal flew in all directions. Jakub felt a sharp pain on his cheek. Hoeffler turned back and ran toward the power supply. Another Leyden jar exploded; suddenly Hoeffler's face was covered in blood. He stumbled over the power supply, fell against the wide, bottom bell. And screamed.

The inside of Jakub's head rang. He staggered back, hands clamped over his ears. They did no good. A shrill disharmony rang in his mind, and with it, the cries of the other men; cutting through all, the crescendo whine of the dynamo. Another Leyden jar exploded. The bells began to vibrate, visibly pulsing as charge after charge poured through them. Warping. Crimping. The tertiary bell cracked, then tore asunder. A foot-wide plate of polished brass flew against Jakub's forehead.

Sound, sight, knowing – everything went blank.

Chapter 1

The Last Chance

With six feet of dirty open water still to go, Ewan Gilmore leaped from bow of the Brooklyn ferry to the South Street ramp. Ignoring the outraged yells of the dock crew, he sprinted up the slope to the street and slipped into the traffic under the elevated train.

A string of rail cars rumbled by overhead, shedding soot and cinders. Wagons and cabs rattled along the cobbles or stood by the granite curbs, their horses adding fresh piles of dung to the gutters. Hand carts and barrows filled every little gap, and people crowded the sidewalks, all in a hurry to load, unload, or get somewhere else. Ewan dodged through them as quickly as he could, heading down toward the Battery. A spray of stinking water and fish guts came flying from an open doorway toward the mess in the gutter. Ewan ducked back just in time, then jumped past ahead of a second volley. He checked his uniform quickly as he ran, making sure an errant drop hadn't spotted the dark blue jacket or tartan waistcoat. It wouldn't do at all to show up smelling of fish. Or worse. He hopped over an errant pile of manure and hurried on.

A horsecar swung in from Fulton Street, but the conductor didn't look the type to let a fellow grab a free ride on the landing, even someone dressed in a clean uniform and the natty gold-lettered cap of the Scots-American Line. Ewan let the car pass him, then jumped the gutter and grabbed onto the handrail at the rear, swinging back along the stanchion to cling to the rear railing. He hung low, where no one on board could see him. Two blocks later, the car turned onto Wall Street. Ewan grinned. Things were going his way again. Finally.

It was sheer luck he'd been moping at home in the family's Brooklyn apartment when the telegram from the Scots-American Line terminal arrived. Usually he'd have slept on board and been up early, readying to receive the first passengers for the departure this afternoon. But not this time. It was September 14. The summer's fares had fallen off, and eastbound passages were always light for steam liners on the Atlantic. Immigrants came west, leaving steerage almost empty on the passage back to Europe. Now, with the weather getting cool and stormy, even cabin passengers were in short supply. There was no need for a full complement of stewards. The newer ones were left behind.

Not that he was new to the line, just that this had been his first summer on the *Isle of Lewis*. Ewan had started his apprenticeship at age 15 on one of her sister ships, *The Isle of Uist*, working as a steward in steerage, a messy, noisy, low-paid job. The next year, he'd moved up to cabin class, and at 18 he'd moved up to the deck crew. Last year he'd split his time between the ropes and the bridge, learning semaphore and the flags, handling the wheel under the watchful eyes of the quartermasters and the third officer, heading up the ranks toward officer. Or maybe to oiler, machinist, and engineer. Or to purser and dockmaster. But everyone started at steward. Where some got stuck.

Now 21, Ewan was back down to steward, and through no fault of his own. He was determined not to get stuck. He had to make this departure.

Another block down Wall Street, the horse car slowed. Traffic closed in. Ewan heard music ahead and leaned out to see what was blocking the way. He caught a glimpse of tall hats, braided coats, sign boards, brass horns – some kind of march spilling off the sidewalk and halfway across the street. Drays, hacks, and carriages were jammed in the gap. A shabby gent on the horse car, leaning out for his own look, noticed Ewan. All mustache and red cheeks, with a face as round as his derby, he swung his cane at Ewan's head.

"Get along there, yob! Go walk with the rest of your kind!"

"Eat your hat!" Ewan shouted back, dodging the cane. He jumped clear, scooted across the street, and ran up the sidewalk, cutting down William Street to Exchange Place to avoid the tussle, then back up to Broadway. He was halfway across the avenue before he noticed the steam car out of the corner of his eye. It was coming right at him on rubber-capped tires, silent as a brisk wind. The driver looked terrified. He didn't even try to sound his whistle or turn the tiller, he just screamed. Ewan dove for the far sidewalk, and the damned thing *wooshed* by an inch behind his heels. He hit, rolled, and came up standing against the far wall with his cap in his hand and grime all over his coat and trousers.

"Get a horse, you geekin' bampot!" Ewan yelled, but the steam car was too far gone already, scattering pedestrians in its wake. Cursing, he brushed himself off as best he could. Then he was off again, jogging down and over to West and finally up the last fifty yards under the El to Pier 10 on the Hudson River, where the *Isle of Lewis* lay alongside, leaking a steady fog of gray smoke from her single blue-and-white-striped funnel. She sported two masts, both fully rigged with a square course and topsails and a big fore-and-aft spanker, but the sails were all furled. Steam did the work unless she had plenty of sea room and a strong breeze behind her.

Carriages and cabs crowded the near end of the pier, where the ship's plumb bow almost kissed the roadway. The *Lewis* was trim – her beam a pleasant fifty feet wide –

but she reached back three hundred and fifty feet to her taffrail, almost the full length of the pier. A row of portholes and a lower row of deadlights curved along the length of the hull, showing off her pleasing shape. She was no greyhound, but she rarely missed her scheduled 12-day passage.

A third of the way down the pier, cabin-class passengers were presenting their tickets to a pair of stewards at the head of the midships gangway, then parading across the weather deck and into the long deckhouse, to clamber down the companionway to their cabins on the saloon deck. Porters bearing trunks and valises trooped after them, along with knots of well-dressed, happy friends. More waving groups clustered at the edge of the pier, calling goodbyes. Aft of the funnel, the few steerage passengers were filing up their own narrow gangway, across the deck and into a smaller companionway. Porters were bringing aboard last-minute crates of fresh food. A pair of officers stood on the port bridge wing, watching. The deck crew stood by the lines, ready to cast off.

Ewan felt the same thrill he always did just before departure. The dingy city air seemed fresher, the light brighter, the cares of the land already left behind. He wove through the press of carriages, ran past the crowded midship gangway, and joined the thin line of steerage passengers. There were more than Ewan expected, including a large group of mismatched men, all carrying black cases of various sizes. Given the odd shape of the largest, it had to hold a tuba.

Ewan chuckled. His mother, it seemed, had managed to book an entire band. They were holding up the line, but his uniform and a steady stream of *pardon-me-sir-ma'am* got him quickly to the companionway. Then it was down two decks to steerage, squeezed in above the hold, where big oil lamps hanging from the center beam cast a stark yellow glare on ranks and ranks of narrow berths ranged along the curving hull. The widely spaced deadlights piercing the steel plates of the hull added spots of glare but little real light.

The passengers were already staking out small territories, single men forward, families amidships, and single women aft. There couldn't be more than a dozen so far. Ewan went forward, looking for Donald MacLeod, the second steward, and found him helping an old man and his wife lift their small satchel into the end of a lower berth.

"What are you doing here?" MacLeod demanded when he spotted Ewan.

"I got a telegram to report on board right away," he replied.

"Not to me, you didn't," MacLeod said.

"Then where?" Ewan asked, as politely as he could. MacLeod, like most of the crew, had little patience to spare for him, but it didn't do to talk back the same way.

"Don't know and too busy right now to care. Check with the chief." MacLeod hurried forward.

"And a good voyage to you, too," Ewan muttered, hurrying aft again.

He went back up the companionway as far as the saloon deck hatchway, only to discover a roughly dressed man on the landing, trying the handle.

"I'm sorry, you can't go through there, sir," Ewan said, pointing to the large sign that clearly stated *Crew Only*.

The man stepped back and mumbled something in a foreign language, Italian maybe, but maybe not. The drooping brim of his battered hat shadowed his features.

"No passage," Ewan said, rattling the latch to show it was locked. He pointed down the companion ladder. "Go this way to steerage. See. This way." He jabbed his finger several times in the right direction.

"*Si.* Yes. Tank-a-you," the man muttered, shouldering a large burlap sack and slipping past.

Ewan waited a moment, then turned the latch again and slipped through the hatchway. It really was supposed to be bolted from the other side when passengers were on board, but the steerage stewards found it too useful a shortcut and usually unsealed it when MacLeod wasn't looking. You just had to know how to work the latch. Ewan grinned and hurried forward along the passageway, past the waiters station and the barber's cabin and the tiny infirmary to cabin class.

Chief Steward Tormod Morrison was at his usual post at the foot of the companionway, greeting the cabin-class passengers as they came down. He saw Ewan and flashed him a sharp frown that clearly meant *Slow down and stay quiet!*

Ewan waited, fidgeting, until the chief had said a few more words to a sporty couple who looked lost. As soon as they were headed in the right direction, he turned to Ewan.

"What are you doing here?" he demanded.

Ewan started to explain, but the chief cut him off.

"Doesn't matter. I know you're not with me this passage. Go check with the purser; she'll know what's up."

"Yes sir!" Ewan gave a snappy salute, but the chief had turned away to snag a gentleman who was just slipping past him. Ewan pelted toward the companion ladder.

"Slow down!" the chief barked, not even turning.

Ewan ignored him for four steps, but was forced to stop completely at the landing to let a well fed couple with two dogs and two heavily laden stewards get past him. The stewards both gave him glares. He didn't care; he wasn't a steward any more. That was the only thing this could mean. He'd moved back up to deck crew.

Ewan almost laughed out loud. Since June, he'd been sailing under a cloud. His father, Murdoc Gilmore, second officer on the *Isle of Uist*, had run the ship at full steam onto Tor Beg rock, off the coast of Donegal, less than half a mile from the Inishtrahull lighthouse. The night had been cloudy, with no moon, but even a drunk could have seen the light. His father still swore he hadn't been drinking. Ewan still didn't know whether to believe him.

But seventy-five passengers had died in steerage, and two crew members asleep in the fo'c'sle. Ewan had been right beside them only minutes before. He'd been woken by a full bladder and had gone to the head, one deck up and aft of the companionway. The collision had thrown him hard against the bulkhead, but he'd been able get out with no more than a bleeding forehead and a few bad bruises.

You could say it was a miracle so few were lost, and his father's quick action after the collision had been one reason why. You could also point out that a dozen ships were lost on the North Atlantic each and every year. But any loss of life was too much, and the *Uist* had been a total loss, too. The Scots-American Line had had only four ships as it was. Now the line was scrambling to meet commitments and make the payroll, while trying to scrape together the heavy charter fee for a replacement ship so they could resume their weekly sailing schedule. To make matters worse, the press had made hay with the story and ticket sales were down, even in steerage. And it was all his father's fault.

Which made it Ewan's fault, too, in the eyes of most of the crew. He was a Jonah, bad luck, a man to bring an ill wind aboard. It was no wonder he'd been put on shore as soon as the summer season ended. Yet here he was, back on board, with another chance to make his own place in the Scots-American Line. And back on the deck crew.

The purser's cabin was in the deckhouse, just aft of the companionway. Ewan swung round the railing and through the door in one swoop.

"Aunt Nellie, did you send me the telegr—?" He skidded to a stop. The purser was Nellie Gilmore, his father's oldest sister. She didn't mind if he sometimes called her Aunt instead of Purser, but only when they were alone. First Officer Sorley MacKay was with her, and so was Ewan's mother.

Lilla Gilmore, née MacKay, had come to work for the line right out of school. The Gilmores were a sept of Clan Morrison, the owners of the line, and the MacKays were an allied clan. Lilla had made wise use of both connections, advancing from clerk to ticket agent in short order. Now she was the chief booking agent for the line's Manhattan terminal. She should have been in the terminal building now, dealing with latecomers and lining up passengers and cargo for the next passage.

"Thank goodness you got here in time," she said. "Here, get changed quickly." She pressed a bundle of clothing into Ewan's hands.

Ewan stared at the clothes, dumbfounded. These were street clothes. Topped by a derby. Landlubber kit. He clenched his hands, almost shaking with disappointment and anger.

"I'm not going with the ship?" he demanded.

"You're going," Sorley MacKay said. "Get changed and listen."

"You can step into my berth," Aunt Nellie said. "Leave the hatch ajar. We'll explain while you're dressing."

More confused than relieved, Ewan went through the hatchway into the small berth behind the purser's office and began to change. His spirits sank deeper with each piece of uniform he doffed. He felt as if he was shedding his proper skin.

"Do you remember in the news last April, about the deaths down in Maryland?" Aunt Nellie asked. Ewan muttered a yes. "You remember the professor, Skovajsa, the only one who lived?" Ewan grunted, donning the new trousers. "Well, your mother's sold him a ticket."

Ewan shoved his other foot through a pants leg. "Right. What's that got to do with me?"

"Do you want to sail with the ship or not?" MacKay demanded.

"Or course I do!" Ewan snapped, only just remembering to add, "Sir."

"This is your one chance, Ewan Gilmore," MacKay said. He used the full name deliberately. There were so many Morrisons, Gilmores, MacKays, and all on board, it was common practice to use both names to show who you meant, but not face to face like this. He was making sure Ewan understood that the family connection could only go so far.

"We had a hard time convincing the captain," his mother said. "If the First Officer here hadn't spoken up for you, you ken, you wouldn't be aboard."

"Fine then. I ken. Thank you, Ma'am, Sir," Ewan said, struggling with the thin, black tie. "But you still haven't told me what I'm to do."

"Skovajsa's failed experiment, whatever it was, made a lot of people upset," his mother said.

"It made them frightened," Aunt Nellie put in, "and no one likes to admit they're afraid. All the deaths gave the *radgies* an excuse to be angry instead. There were calls for a hanging."

"Wasn't there already a trial?" Ewan asked. He pulled on the waistcoat and started in on the dozen, small buttons.

"An inquest," she replied, "and Skovajsa was found innocent, all right and proper, but that didn't satisfy the mob. They wanted someone to pay for making them afraid. The professor went into hiding, but now, supposedly for his own safety but mostly because the judges are too much a parcel o' cowards to face down a mob, he's been ordered to leave the country. Well, no other line would have him. They're afraid they'd lose half their passengers."

"They're afraid they'd lose their ship," MacKay said. "No one knows exactly what Professor Skovajsa did, only that he managed to kill the Secretary of War and one of the highest generals in the Army, along with two Senators and a platoon or more of soldiers. The Army won't admit how many."

"Rumor has it he was testing some kind of weapon," his mother said, "but nobody knows what kind or how it works. Or where it is now."

"Or how big it is," MacKay added. "The latest papers say it could be as small as a suitcase."

"That's just *mince*, of course," Aunt Nellie said, "but the more the Army says not to worry, the more frightened and angry and *dafty* everyone else gets."

Ewan stared at the derby in his hands, then down at his steward's cap, lying on Aunt Nellie's bunk beside the small, neatly folded stack of his uniform. That waistcoat was made in the clan tartan. That tie was blue and white, the line's colors. That cap had gold lettering. The derby was dark black, with a plain black band. Everything was black. Just like any *dafty* on the street would wear. He went back into the office, still holding the derby.

"Put on the hat, Ewan," his mother said.

Sighing, he obeyed.

She eyed him critically. "Nellie?"

Nellie nodded, smiling. "He looks first rate," she said. "A regular swell."

If it was meant to reassure him, it failed. "Why this?"

he demanded. "You still haven't told me."

"You're to shadow him, Ewan," his mother said. "His life's been threatened, and you're to make sure he comes to no harm."

"You're to make sure no one even tries anything," MacKay added. "These are too-close quarters. Imagine the scene in the saloon if he showed up for dinner and someone recognized him. Someone frightened, with a quick temper."

"Then why'd you sell him a ticket?" Ewan demanded.

"We can't afford not to," his mother replied. "The Army's paid for an entire cabin."

"You'll be better placed as a passenger," Aunt Nellie went on. "You'll be right across the passageway, and no one will suspect if you join him in the saloon and on deck."

"And watch by the door when he takes a bath, too, I suppose," he muttered.

"If you can do it without being noticed, yes." MacKay made it an order. "This is a serious business, sailor. Are you able to treat it that way?"

Ewan met his gaze. "Yes. Yes, Sir. If it's what the ship needs, it's what I'll do."

"Good!" Aunt Nellie said. "You'll need to get below now and wait for him. Make his acquaintance quickly."

"Does the chief know about it?"

"Not yet. I'll go down now."

"And I need to get back to the terminal," his mother said. She handed him a new, handsome valise. "Here's a change of clothes. And a hair brush. Practice using it."

"I'll be at the bow when we drop lines," MacKay said, "and I'll be on the bridge this evening if you need anything."

"Wait," Ewan said as they all started to leave. "Is he traveling under his own name? Or is all this on the sly?"

"On the sly," Aunt Nellie said. "He's to use an assumed name and travel quiet—"

A high-pitched steam whistle shrieked outside, coming from the direction of the street. It shrieked again, then again, coming slowly down the pier toward the ship.

"Now what the Devil's name is that?" MacKay said.

Chapter 2

A Botched Arrival

They followed MacKay out onto the deck and up the port-side ladder to the bridge wing. From that vantage, they could see over the heads of the passengers and well-wishers. The thick jam-up of carriages on the pier was being parted by a blunt, black steamcar, sounding its whistle and bell. Blue-uniformed coppers stood on each running board, ordering everyone to make way. A second steamcar followed, and then an even thicker press of men on foot, brandishing notebooks and sketchbooks and yelling at the passengers inside.

Professor Skovajsa had arrived, and so had the press, in force.

"So much for a quiet arrival," MacKay remarked. "What's his assumed name, P.T. Barnum?"

Lilla Gilmore looked calm, but Ewan could tell she was mad as a badger. "Herr Schmidt," she muttered. She turned and stalked down the ladder, gripping her skirts with one clenched fist.

"I'd better go down, too," MacKay said, but Aunt Nellie stopped him with a firm hand on his sleeve.

"No," she said. "Don't make the *fraca* any bigger than it is already. Go explain to the captain. Ask him to please come onto the bridge and just watch, as though this sort of *bucker* happened at every departure. Ewan and I will go down to meet Professor Skovajsa."

The first officer crossed the bridge to the wheelhouse and disappeared inside. Aunt Nellie turned to Ewan.

"Remember what he said, Ewan. This is your chance

to remake your name with the crew and the captain. Your only chance. The captain was all for picking another man, but MacKay went out on a limb and vouched for you."

"You mean the captain thinks I'm a Jonah, too?" Ewan gripped the bridge railing with both hands.

"No, but he'll do whatever he thinks is best for the ship. Right now, that means keeping the crew happy."

"It's not bloody fair, blaming me for what my father did!"

"It's not just that, and you know it," Aunt Nellie told him. "Trouble seems to dog you."

Ewan turned on her, seething. "Is that what you think? That everyone's right?"

"*Haud yer wheest!* I said 'seems,' didn't I? And don't forget where we are. On board, I'm not your aunt, I'm the purser. And on this voyage you report directly to me. I expect you to address me as an officer."

Ewan glared at her, but he raised his hand to the brim of his derby and muttered, "Aye, aye, Ma'am." He couldn't help resenting that she was still in uniform, with a proper cap and all.

"That's better," she said. "And, no, I don't believe you're a Jonah. But even you have to admit you've been cursed by a bad string of coincidences."

Ewan couldn't argue. On his very first passage on the *Lewis*, she had lost her propeller when the pin sheared. Down it went, in 300 fathoms, beyond the reach of man or woman. They'd been forced to sail the rest of the way to Glasgow, arriving four days late. On the passage home, one of the topsail hands had fallen from the yard while taking in sail during a rising gale. He missed the deck and fell into the water instead. He'd never even come to the surface. The next trip, two of the passengers had gotten in a fight during a card game. One pulled a knife, and a waiter had been slashed in the tussle. Then the butter had all gone bad six days out, no small thing when the line bragged about the quality of its meals. Then one of the two stewardesses had been found with a married gent in cabin class and spent the rest of the passage in the brig. Then three in steerage had died of consumption on one single passage. None of it had anything to do with Ewan, except that he was the new crewman, and his father had sunk the *Isle of Uist*. After that, he'd been blamed for everything.

"So you've got good reason to make sure nothing happens to Professor Skovajsa, or anyone else on board, don't you?" Aunt Nellie said. "That's why I wanted you. That and the fact that you're smart, you look good in a suit, and you deserve the chance, no matter what the crew might think. Now show me I'm right. Get below and make yourself a chance to bump into the professor."

"Yes, Ma'am," Ewan said. Her words made it a little easier to swallow his frustration. "Does he know to be watching for me?"

"He knows we'll have someone close." She glared out at the to-do on the pier, where the coppers had formed a cordon between the leading steamcar and the clamoring reporters. "I daresay he's smart enough to realize it's you. Whether he has the sense to is another question."

Or the sense to keep it quiet, Ewan thought.

The rear door on the steamcar swung open and a man in a plain dark suit and a low topper climbed out. He was pale and thin, with a salting of white in his mustache and goatee. Ewan guessed this was the infamous Professor Skovajsa. The sketches in the papers had made him look more foreign and almost starved. He certainly was gaunt, but apart from that he looked normal enough, not like the sort who'd murder a couple of Senators and a Cabinet member.

Ewan caught himself; it had been an accident, not

murder. The professor was simply a victim of his own mistakes. Like Ewan's father. Ewan looked at Skovajsa in a new light, trying to decide if it was better or worse.

The professor turned back toward the steamcar and held up his hand. A girl stepped out onto the running board and took it. The reporters' shouting swelled. She winced, glanced at them once, than stared straight ahead, her face pale and drawn under the brim of a simple, tied hat. Clenched in her left hand was a blue parasol, closed tight. She held it in front of her chest, like a shield.

"Who's that?" Ewan asked.

"His daughter, Tereza Skovajsová," Aunt Nellie replied.

"Skovajsová?"

"It's how they say it for the women."

The girl stepped down beside the professor, and it was easy to see the resemblance: dark hair, broad forehead, pointed chin, slight frame. And the way she stood: stiff, brittle even, in her very plain clothes and practical hat. She was still wearing a calf-length skirt; that meant she wasn't eighteen yet, though her drawn face made it hard to guess her age.

"You never said he had a daughter."

"I thought you knew. She was in the reports. The mother died in the accident."

"I'd forgotten," Ewan admitted. In truth, he'd only skimmed most of the stories, looking mainly for information about the weapon, or whatever it was the professor had been building. Now he vaguely remembered the daughter. "I guess I'd thought she was younger."

Aunt Nellie smiled. "Seventeen now. She had a birthday a few weeks ago. Does the task suddenly appear more interesting?"

"She still looks sixteen," Ewan replied.

Aunt Nellie's smile thinned. "She could be your best excuse for staying close to her father. Just don't let her be a distraction."

"Don't worry," Ewan replied. "What's my story? I mean to the other passengers, when they ask who I am and where I'm going and all."

"Stick as close to the truth as you can," Aunt Nellie said, "otherwise it's too easy to trip up. Say you're with the line, going to work in the Glasgow terminal. Booking agent, like your mum. Then right away turn the questions around and ask about them. And keep asking. Most passengers love to talk about themselves. It comes with the money, I suppose. Now give me a minute to speak to the chief steward, then come on down, before they beat you there."

Ewan sketched another salute and crossed the bridge to the other side of the wheelhouse to go down the starboard ladder. The deck there was empty, and the deckhouse shielded him from view of the pier. Hurrying aft, he went down the carpeted stairs in the saloon companionway, startling a pair of waiters hauling trays piled with pasties and scones for tea, then went forward on the starboard side, past the kitchens and bakery, now rich with the smells of the evening's supper. Halfway along, he nearly collided with a gentlemen coming out of the steerage companionway. It was a young man in a fine suit and derby, with a bright leather valise and an overcoat.

"Pardon me, sir," Ewan said stepping back quickly. "I didn't mean to bump you like that. Can I help you?" He was thinking that cabin passengers gave tips at the end of the voyage, and this one looked to be worth more than a few dollars. Then Ewan remembered he had a valise and overcoat, too. He was one of the tippers. He squared his shoulders. "Ewan Gilmore," he said, bowing like the

British passengers did. "Have you lost your way?"

The young man looked flustered. "Well, yes, I do seem to be a bit lost. I thought I remembered the layout from my last trip, and . . . Excuse me, how rude. Reed. Derek Reed." He grabbed Ewan's hand and gave it a quick shake. "I came down past the saloon, you see, trying to avoid the line, and thought this door led on to the cabins, but . . ." He ended with a grin and a shrug.

Ewan took him for a bit of a dandy, and a scatterbrain to boot. There were two passageways running forward from the saloon to the passenger cabins, one on either side of the engine-room well, which filled the center of the hull amidships, from the weather deck right down to the bilge. Whichever side you went, all you had to do was go straight.

"The cabins are right down this way, Mr. Reed," he said, pointing forward.

The young man looked but just stood there. "Ah, good. Just fine. Please, you go on ahead. You look in a hurry. I'll follow along. Get the lay of the land again, you see."

Ewan was already leaving. "Sure. Take your time." He tried hard to stroll, not run.

He came out at the foot of the first class companionway, to see Aunt Nellie still talking with the chief steward. She noticed him, said another few words, then turned and went up the ladder with no more than a polite nod.

"Well, *Mister* Gilmore is it?" the chief said.

Ewan ignored the chief's stress on *mister*. "Yes, that's right, Mr. Morrison," he said. "Which cabin, please?"

"You should be showing me your ticket," the chief murmured, "like a passenger, right?"

"Right," Ewan muttered. He fumbled in the pockets of the overcoat until he found it.

The chief made a show of reading it carefully. "Cabin thirteen, Mr. Gilmore. Berth two. It's the next to last cabin on the starboard side. That's the right-hand side going forward."

"Thanks, I'll remember that," Ewan replied, pretending to smile. The forward cabins heaved the worst in any kind of sea, and berth two was an upper bunk, which didn't help. On the other hand, the forward cabins were usually the last to be booked. "Is the cabin full?"

"Not yet, but there could be late-comers. Please use your assigned berth."

Only until we're underway, Ewan thought. "Which cabin is Herr Schmidt in?" he murmured.

"Twelve, directly across the way. Now get along. There's passengers coming."

Ewan hurried forward, glancing back once. There was no sign of the professor yet.

The cabins were ranged along the outside of the hull. Right at the bottom of the companionway steps, the center space was roomy enough, though busy now with the flurry of arriving passengers. Just past the first two cabins on either side, a wood-paneled bulkhead surrounded the shaft of the number two hatchway, forcing traffic into narrow aisles on each side. Like the engine well, the hatchways stretched down through both passenger decks to reach the hold. A cabin door opened onto each of the aisles, then the space opened up again to reveal the rest of the cabins. The thick butt of the foremast rose through the middle of the forward space, which stretched to the paneled wall enclosing the forward hatchway. It, too, was flanked by narrow side aisles, which passed by two more cabins and led to the passenger heads and two bathing rooms. Beyond the final bulkhead lay the fo'c'sle, which housed the deck crew.

Ewan made his way through another mill of

passengers to cabin thirteen, just off the narrow aisle on the starboard side. It was one of the smaller cabins, with only six berths. Berth number two was just to the right of the door. There was no sign of cabin mates yet. Ewan threw his valise and overcoat onto the plaid blanket, checked himself quickly in the small mirror over the washstand, ran his fingers through his hair, reset the ridiculous derby, and hurried back out.

The main area at the foot of the companionway was even busier now, with passengers still coming down and others trying to head back up to the weather deck for the departure. But the companionway itself was temporarily blocked. The professor had arrived.

He and his daughter were standing at the bottom, talking to the chief steward. A couple of porters had their bags, and two more were leaning on a large steamer trunk that by rights should have gone into the hold. Ewan was amazed they'd managed to wrestle it around the turn in the companionway. He hung back in the aisle, waiting for them to come his way.

Instead, the sport he'd run into earlier came ambling up to him.

"Hello again, Mr. Gilmore," the young man said. "Is your cabin through that way, too?"

"Yes, it is, Mr. . . ." Ewan tried to remember the name. ". . . Reed."

"Yes, I'm right toward the bow, I'm afraid," Reed said. "That's what comes of booking last minute, I suppose? How about you?"

"Cabin thirteen," Ewan said, trying to be polite and still keep an eye on the professor.

"Why, that's my cabin, too!" Reed exclaimed. "We'll be traveling companions."

"Yes, I suppose so," Ewan said.

"Excellent! Are you heading back on deck? May I join

you? Come along while I drop my valise."

Ewan tried to think of an excuse, then decided he had a better chance of approaching the professor after he and his daughter were settled in their cabin.

"This way," he said, leading Reed up the aisle, which was barely wide enough for the two of them. They hadn't gone three steps before the door to cabin five swung inward, freeing a whiff of lilacs, and someone stepped out. Ewan had a moment's glimpse – trim bonnet, blonde ringlets, startled face – and plowed right into her.

Chapter 8

Meeting with Strangers

Daisy MacLaren was just stepping out of her cabin when someone in the aisle bumped into her. She gasped and started to tumble sideways, but a strong hand grabbed her arm and steadied her. The man who'd bumped her stumbled backward, looking just as flustered as she felt. A bright blush made freckles stand out all over his face as he stammered an apology.

Mr. Steady Hand, seeming extremely concerned, asked, "Are you all right, miss?" He was a nice-looking fellow, in his early twenties she guessed, perhaps a year or two older than his still-blushing companion.

"I am, thank you," she replied.

His concern transformed to a pleasant smile. "Good. Good." He let go of her arm, a bit reluctantly Daisy thought, tipped his hat, and said, "I must apologize for both of us. If I hadn't been—"

"Not at all," Daisy said, straightening her sleeve. "I should have been watching where I was going." She turned to the freckled man and smiled. "Please, think nothing of it."

His eyes were an interesting hazel green, though he was too embarrassed to meet hers directly. "As long as you're all right, miss," he said, belatedly tipping his hat. He had an interesting accent too, she noticed; American, but from where?

"I assure you, I'm fine," she replied. "I have never known a gentler assailant."

Her quip had the desired result. He blushed again but

finally smiled back. Then, with a quick glance over his shoulder, he began to edge past her. "Since you're all right . . ."

Mr. Steady Hand was standing in the way. "We're on our way to our cabin, you see," he said, not budging an inch, "but perhaps we'll run into you again on the voyage."

"Undoubtedly, though not so literally, I hope," Daisy replied.

She found them both amusing. The *Isle of Lewis* was hardly a large ship; they couldn't possibly avoid seeing each other again. The question was, would they seek out each other's company? She wondered who they were and where from; brothers or friends or merely cabin mates by chance? She wished she could ask their names, but without a chaperone, introductions were out of the question. On the other hand, nobody on the ship would know anyone else, and they couldn't spend ten or eleven whole days ignoring each other. Oh, to be a girl again, untrained in etiquette and able to introduce herself. No longer; just two months ago she had turned eighteen, happily put up her hair, and outfitted herself with a complete wardrobe of women's clothing. Once they reached Edinburgh, she would officially be Father's hostess at the consulate.

As if on command, the cabin door opened and Father stepped out.

"Good afternoon, gentlemen," he said. "I hope everything is all right."

"Everything is fine, Father," she said, touching his hand. "I'm afraid I was clumsy and walked right into this gentleman. Luckily I didn't injure him." She stifled a smile as the fellow blushed again.

"It was entirely our fault, sir," Mr. Steady Hand said quickly. "We were in too big a hurry, not thinking that a cabin door could open at any moment."

"And I stepped right out without pausing to check,"

Daisy said. "No one is to blame."

He father smiled. "No harm done, obviously." He gave a slight bow. "Colonel Robert MacLaren."

Mr. Steady Hand bowed back. "Derek Reed, sir, of Louisville, and this is Ewan Gilmore, of the Scots-American Line."

That explained the accent, at least. Gilmore, looking again down the aisle, turned back and bowed awkwardly.

"Pleased to make your acquaintance, gentlemen," Father replied. "As you have probably realized, this is my daughter, Margaret Adelaide MacLaren."

Daisy curtseyed. "Of Bel Air, Maryland, now on our way to Edinburgh. Are you really with the line, Mr. Gilmore? How exciting! Do you have a home on land, or do you wander forever on the sea, like the Ancient Mariner?"

"Brooklyn," he said. "Right now I'm on my way to Glasgow to work in the Scots-American terminal there."

"His family owns the line," Reed said. "I'm hoping he can get us seats beside the captain at meals."

Gilmore looked flustered again, though not quite so red. "I'm afraid Captain Morrison takes most of his meals in the wardroom. The deck officers usually stand in for him in the saloon. I'm sure you won't have any trouble getting a seat by them," he added. "Just arrive a bit early and sit near the head of the starboard table, by the piano."

"Thank you," Father replied. He turned to Mr. Reed. "I met a Major Reed from Louisville during the war," he went on. "Hugo Reed. He was in banking, if I recall. Or perhaps coal-mining. Any relation?"

Reed appeared a bit ruffled. "Ah. Uh, yes sir. He is my father. He would be very pleased you remembered." His tone suggested to Daisy that Mr. Reed, *fils*, was not at all pleased.

The feeling-out would have gone on, but another

gentleman came into the aisle, leading a largish group.

"Excuse me," he said in a somewhat Germanic accent. "May we pass through, please?"

"Of course, sir," her father said. "Gentlemen, we'll speak more later, I'm sure. Daisy, watch your feet." And he closed the door. She understood his meaning quite clearly – stop running into young men.

"Right. We're going this way," Gilmore said, rather brusquely. He tipped his hat again, grabbed Reed's arm, and pulled him up the aisle.

"We'll look for you on deck," Reed called.

Rather than squeeze past the newcomers, Daisy followed the gentlemen.

"I'm so sorry to have blocked the way," she said over her shoulder to the German gentleman and the young woman beside him, obviously his daughter.

He waved his hand. "It's nothing," he said. "We are sorry to have disturbed your conversation."

They came out of the aisle, and Daisy slowed to walk beside them. "We should have removed to the deck. I'm very excited to watch the departure. This is my first time on an ocean liner. I've been on steamboats on the Chesapeake before, but this will be quite different."

He stopped in front of cabin twelve. "I daresay it will. It has been sixteen brief years since I came here, but so much is different on ships now. Times change quickly, yes?"

"Yes, very. Well, I'll leave you to settle in." She nodded, making a point to include his daughter in her smile. The girl seemed extremely shy. She clutched her closed parasol as though she could hide behind it.

The gentleman bowed. "Perhaps we shall have the pleasure of further conversation later. I am Profes— Herr . . . *Sakra!*" he muttered, and said something to his daughter in a language that did not sound German.

His daughter replied with the single, quiet word, "Schmidt."

The gentleman made a face. He bowed again and said, "I am Professor Jakub Skovajsa."

&

Tereza couldn't believe it. "Father! Not—"

"No," he snapped. "It is too ugly. It will not do." He turned back to the stranger. "And this is my daughter, Tereza Skovajsová," he said, as though she had not even spoken. "We are very pleased to meet you."

The stranger obviously knew who they were but hid her surprise in a bow.

"Miss Daisy MacLaren. I am certainly pleased to meet you both, professor," she replied.

She started to say more but stopped herself and nodded once more to Tereza. "I hope we might meet again on deck while the ship sets sail. I would enjoy the company of another young woman. There seem to be few of us on board."

Tereza forced a nod in reply. Father brightened visibly.

"Yes, you are kind, very kind." he said, then babbled on. "I'm sure Tereza would be pleased to join you, yes, Tereza? She has been very, ah, preoccupied of late. To leave home, you know, on top of . . . everything else. It has been . . . tiring. Yes, tiring." He glanced at her; she could only glare in reply. "Yes! We will both join you, as soon as our luggage is settled."

"Then I will look for you just forward of the gangplank on the port side, where we all came aboard," she said. "Until then, *adieu.*"

Tereza watched Miss MacLaren walk away. The French, the parting smile, but mostly her light step as she slipped easily past oncoming passengers brought on a wave of envy that threatened to swell into anger. The shrill whining that hovered constantly at the edge of her hearing grew louder. It had been almost unbearable in the police car, with its constant whistle and bell. Tereza gripped the parasol, wishing for silence, fighting the whine, trying to think of something else.

"Are you all right, my dear?" her father asked.

Immediately, her anger shifted to him. How could he babble on like that? *Pleased to join her?* As if they could be pleased at anything! She turned toward him, seething.

"Why must you —?"

Father immediately held up his hand. "Not now," he muttered.

Tereza bit off her words, and the whining threatened to become ringing. She closed her eyes, controlled her breathing, tried counting primes backward from nine-hundred-ninety-seven, and barely managed to hold herself together. Eyes averted, she stood stiffly outside the cabin until the porters had settled the luggage, accepted Father's tip, and hurried off. By then her anger had ebbed and the whine was merely a whine. She stalked through the narrow doorway and across the short length of the cabin to stare out the small porthole in the outer wall. The gray daylight seemed harsh beside the walnut-paneling and dim amber glow of the two electric globes flanking the vanity.

"Well," Father said. "It's small, but at least we don't have to share it with other passengers. When your mother and I first..." His trailed off, voice cracking. "Well," he managed, trying to sound jollier, "that was almost exactly twenty years ago. Much has changed." He cleared his throat. "This is just one more change."

"Father, please." She finally turned to face him. *Please don't push me at every smiling face that happens to act friendly. And whyever did you tell her our real names?*

That's what she'd been meaning to say, despite the attempt at a smile in his voice. But he wasn't smiling. His face was still so thin, so pale. He was on the verge of tears. Again. Always. And that triggered another flare of anger. She was the one who'd been awake all through the worst of it. She was the one who'd sat by his bed in the hospital, wondering if he'd spend the rest of his life inert, unhearing, half dead. She was the one who had heard Mother die. And now, to spare him, she couldn't let herself cry. Immediately, she felt guilty for the thought.

Six-hundred-nineteen, six-hundred-seventeen, six-hundred-thirteen.

"Please, stop worrying about me," she said. "It doesn't matter if we keep to ourselves during the voyage. We don't have to rush into . . ." She waved her hand vaguely. "We shouldn't foist ourselves upon—"

"Now, now. This Miss MacLaren seems friendly enough," Father protested. "She made the first advances. All that *povyk*. . . that *bother* out there—" He waved his hand toward the porthole. "—it's over. Here on this ship, we've already left it behind."

"No. We haven't. Everyone on board has brought it with them."

"Then we will make them forget!" They glared at each other. "We must show them that it is over, that we have left it! We will not lock ourselves up like criminals. We will unpack quickly, then we will go back out and find Miss MacLaren, as she so kindly invited."

"You do realize she recognized our names immediately?"

"And it made no difference! She, at least, is willing—" A quick triple rap at the door broke in. "*Sakra!*" he muttered, and turned to answer it.

It was a steward, his cap at a jaunty angle, a bundle of cloth under his arm.

"Good morning, sir, miss," he said. "I've come to hang the curtain for you, if you don't mind."

"Of course," Father said, "we will just—"

"No need to leave, sir. Just plop yourselves on the nearest berth, and I'll be done in a trice." He was already inside, squeezing past Father, lifting a corner of the curtain toward a ring set into the ceiling. Tereza found herself in the way and tried to squeeze to the other side of the porthole, tight against the washstand.

"Just you sidle port-ways onto that lower berth, miss, and you'll be no bother," he said, almost leaning over her to clip a curtain hook onto a wire that ran from the ring, through another in the center of the ceiling, to the opposite corner of the cabin. "And if you're needing anything at all, ask for Ranald. That's me. Or, if you're needing something in the ladylike way, you can ask for the stewardess. That's Margaret. Peggy once you get to know her." He paused an instant in his work to flash a wink and a smile at Tereza.

She could only stare back, but it didn't matter. He was already turning away to hang the next loop of curtain, talking to Father now. Several loops later, he was done. The cabin had been divided neatly in two by a diagonal curtain woven in the same tartan as the curtains flanking the porthole and the blankets on the six berths. The effect made Tereza dizzy.

Five hundred eighty-seven, five hundred seventy-seven, five hundred seventy-one . . .

The steward swept the curtain open from the center to each end. "There you are," he said. "Your own private berth when you need it." He turned to her father. "How's that, sir?"

"Fine, just fine," Father replied. "Thank you."

"Quite all right, sir. Are you needing anything else?"

"No, I guess not. Tereza?" He peered at her.

She shook her head. *Five hundred and three, four hundred ninety-nine . . .*

"Then I guess I'll be going, sir." The steward stood where he was, smiling.

"Yes." Father blinked. "Oh, yes." He fumbled in his coat, found some change, and pushed a couple of coins into the man's palm. "Thank you."

"At your service, sir. Just ask for Ranald." He breezed out the door, shutting it with a smart snap behind him.

The sudden silence was a gift. Tereza stopped counting and realized she was still holding her parasol. Her hand was aching. She set the parasol down beside her on the berth and stared at her valise, a green lump almost lost in the shadow and pattern on the berth across the narrow isle.

"Well, I suppose we should unpack," Father said. "Then go up on deck?"

She heard the slight question in his voice but had lost the will to argue. "Yes, Father. Of course."

&

Daisy thought she had recovered from her gaffe rather well. She just wished she knew a few words of the Bohemian language, so she could have said goodbye properly. It hadn't been German at all, though the professor was said to have studied at Leipzig as well as in Prague. Tereza, on the other hand, had grown up in the States, so perhaps a simple American *goodbye* would have been best. Daisy frowned. She would have to be quicker witted than this once she and her father reached Edinburgh and took up residence in the U.S. consulate. The official language there was English, but there were Scottish dialects to learn, as well as Gaelic. She was determined to master them. She wanted to help make her father's tenure as Consul shine.

She glanced back at the doorway from the deckhouse – she reminded herself to use the proper nautical term and call it a hatchway – and saw Mr. Steady Hand came out. He spotted her, smiled hugely, and joined her by the rail.

"Hello, Mr. Reed," Daisy said. "You've lost your traveling companion."

"Temporarily," he replied. "He'll be joining us any minute."

"Good. I have dozens of questions about the ship and the line." And she knew it would be better to have a third party at hand, to avoid any appearance of intimacy.

Daisy's mother had died almost fifteen years ago, so she lacked the close womanly advice that might have helped in such matters. She had met enough young men in her family's social circuit to guess Mr. Reed's general interest, and a well-meaning aunt had warned her about young gentlemen travelers, but it was broad daylight and they were hardly alone. She also thought he seemed genuinely friendly, if a bit awkward. She was pleased to note that, so far, he acted no more forward than was polite, standing an appropriate two feet away, steady hands under control.

"Look at that!" he exclaimed, suddenly noticing the crowd on the pier. "I wonder what it's all about?"

Policemen were standing by both gangways, keeping back a slew of spectators. Only ticket-holders were being allowed to pass.

"I believe it's the press," Daisy said. "We have a celebrity on board."

"Really? Who's that?"

Daisy remembered Tereza's reaction when her father had used his real name. The press had made them more notorious than famous. Some passengers might not be pleased to hear the professor was on board, but she decided she would trust Mr. Reed to act like a mature adult. If nothing else, she would learn his true character. She lowered her voice.

"Professor Jakub Skovajsa and his daughter, Tereza," she said.

"Really?" he said again. "The one in the papers? Who killed the Secretary of—?"

"*Shh!*" Daisy shot him a frown. "Let them have a few moments' peace. It'll come out soon enough, I'm sure."

Derek stared at her a moment, puzzled, then caught on. "Ah, of course. The price of infamy." He gestured at the milling reporters." I imagine the poor man can't wait to leave all this behind."

Daisy shook her head. "The publicity, certainly. The tragedy, even more. But they are being forced to leave their home as well, the land where Mrs. Skovajsová is buried."

"Hm. Yes, that does cast a harsher light on it," Derek said. "Sad, isn't it."

"Sad indeed, Mr. Reed."

Her father arrived then, and Daisy let him lead the conversation. He was very good at drawing people out, and she learned quickly that Derek was twenty and in college – William and Mary – but was traveling to Scotland to spend the year at St. Andrews University. Studying the classics, although, he added with a poorly concealed sour note, his father expected him to join the bank when he returned. His favorite subjects were history and poetry. The romantics specifically, Byron in particular. Whom he quoted. Daisy hid a smile. Young men could be so overblown.

Several more minutes passed while Daisy kept her eye on the hatchway. More late passengers boarded. A small launch swung in at the end of the pier and unloaded a dozen or so ragged people, mostly men, who were escorted up the steerage gangway by a quartet of large, uniformed officials. She asked a passing steward, who said they were rejects being shipped back to Europe by the immigration office at Battery Park.

Like the professor, in a way, she thought, and she wondered if the Skovajsas would be coming out for the departure after all. The professor might simply have been being polite.

But five minutes later he appeared, with a reluctant Tereza in tow clenching her blue parasol. Daisy discretely pointed them out to her father and described her chance meeting with them.

"Very good," Father said. He stepped forward as the Skovajsas approached and introduced himself and Mr. Reed.

Daisy nodded again to Tereza, and was pleased to receive a small smile in return. The smile died quickly when a photographer on the pier began aiming his camera at them.

"The hubbub here certainly is distracting, isn't it," Daisy remarked

Her father picked up the cue immediately. "It is at that. Why don't we go around to the other side of the deckhouse?"

"A good idea," the professor said. "We have no one to wave to, in any case."

The two fathers led them around the front of the deckhouse to the starboard rail, which gave them a more relaxing view of the ships at the next pier.

Derek tried to engage the professor in conversation. "Skovajsa is an interesting name. Hungarian is it? No? Well, it's a fine day to be sailing." Then, with a glance at Daisy, "Sad, too, of course, to be leaving friends and ... and family behind. But I guess that's the way of it with voyages. At least it's not raining. Quite warm actually, for mid September. Warm sun, clear skies."

Daisy rescued him by asking Tereza how she liked their cabin.

Tereza shrugged. "It will do."

"It is quite fine," the professor said. "The steward has hung a curtain so we each have a half of the cabin. Tereza has the sink, with cold *and* hot water from spigots!"

"We have the same arrangement," Father said. "And the spare berths provide plenty of room to spread out. Soft bedding, extra pillows; it's quite comfortable actually."

"If one can ignore the never-ending pattern in the curtains," Daisy said.

"Now, now," her father replied. "That pattern is the line's tartan."

"Speaking of which, there's Mr. Gilmore," Daisy said. He was hanging back under the shadow of the bridge, acting almost as shy as Tereza. "Do you think he's spotted us, Mr. Reed?"

"No worry," Reed said, "I'll fetch him," and he strode over, calling, "Gilmore!"

A dozen heads turned their way, then quickly turned back. Daisy suppressed a sigh.

Reed returned with Gilmore in tow and made the introduction to the Skovajsas, being sure to add that Gilmore's family owned the ship and the line.

"My uncle's family," he protested.

"I thought you said your father's," Reed replied.

Gilmore blushed. "No, my father's not ... He's an officer."

"And rather high up, I daresay," Reed remarked. "Mr. Gilmore has agreed to get Colonel and Miss MacLaren a seat at the captain's table."

"The officer's table," Gilmore corrected, sounding more and more flustered.

"It seems the captain prefers to dine in the officer's wardroom," Daisy explained. "The other officers bear the brunt of our landlubberly assault in his stead."

"That's one way to put it, Miss MacLaren," Gilmore said, smiling again.

"Perhaps you can get invitations for all of us, Mr. Gilmore," she suggested.

"And a tour of the ship!" Reed put in.

"Excuse me," Tereza said suddenly. Daisy was surprised to hear her speak, and even more surprised to see the sudden show of interest on her face. Her dark eyes had come back to life. She leaned toward Mr. Gilmore. "Do you think you could get the first officer to show us the engines?"

"Yes! Wonderful idea, Tereza," the professor said. "We must see the power plant!"

Gilmore looked taken aback. And before he could muster a reply, a bell rang shrilly behind them, immediately followed by the ship's horn, which let out a long, bellowing wail from its mount on the front of the funnel. Tereza gasped, dropped her parasol, and clamped her hands over her ears. As the bell rang again, she swayed and began to topple.

Chapter 4

A Forced Departure

Ewan watched in shock as Tereza began to keel over, stiff as a board. The professor, right beside her, seemed frozen. Ewan grabbed for her arm but missed. Derek lunged forward and caught Tereza around the waist.

"Careful there, Miss!" he said. "A deck makes a hard cushion, you know."

He straightened her up but she began to fold at the waist.

"Steady, now!" he exclaimed, trying to shift his hold to her shoulders. Thrown off balance, he stumbled, and they both almost went down. Ewan braced Derek's side.

Daisy took Tereza's thin wrists. "Tereza, can you hear me? Take a breath, a deep one. You're all right. Just keep breathing."

Meanwhile, the professor stared past the front of the deckhouse, where the ringing sound grew louder. The chief steward appeared, ringing a hand bell.

"All visitors ashore!" he called. "Departure in fifteen minutes! All visitors ashore!"

The professor suddenly unfroze. He laughed sharply and wiped his face. Only then did he notice his daughter's condition. He muttered something foreign, snatched up the parasol, and crowded in beside Daisy.

Great, Ewan thought. Next the colonel will pull out a horse pistol and fire a few shots, just to make sure everyone notices the professor's on board.

"I'm sorry," the professor mumbled. "So sorry. This has happened before with loud noises like this, unexpected, the surprise and the noise together. The trip here in the steam car was . . . difficult. Tereza was almost— I'm sorry you had to— *Zatracenĕ!* Can he not stop that ringing?"

The professor turned, glaring at the chief's back as he walked aft, repeating the all-ashore. Ewan wondered why the professor was so bothered by the bell. It was the horn that had startled Tereza.

Just then, her eyes fluttered open. She took a breath, then jerked her hands free as the bell rang again. "Father? Are you all right?" she asked, staring around for him as though nothing at all had happened to her.

He turned to her quickly. "Why, yes, yes, I'm fine, Tereza. I'm just fine. It's you who have us all worried."

"Indeed," Daisy said. "Are you sure you're all right now, Tereza? Would you like a drink of water? Or to sit down?"

She shook her head. "No, I'm fine. Really, I was just startled."

"It's enough to startle anyone, Miss," Derek said.

She suddenly noticed him, standing right behind her. They both took an awkward step apart. The professor handed her the parasol, and she clenched it close to her chest again.

"The horn will sound a lot as we back out of the slip," Ewan warned. "Whenever we pass another ship in the channel, too. Just so you know."

She managed a thin smile. "Thank you, Mr. Gilmore. It won't happen again."

Ewan wasn't sure he believed her—her wide eyes always looked startled—but she took another breath and more color returned to her pale cheeks. She lowered the parasol.

"I don't suppose the horn can be heard down in the engine room," Daisy said. "Can it, Mr. Gilmore?"

Ewan cursed silently. He'd hoped they would forget about that.

"This wouldn't be a good time," he said. "Things happen fast down there when we're getting underway. Mr. MacLeod would order us all to get out and never come back, only not that politely."

"I take it Mr. MacLeod is the chief engineer?" Colonel MacLaren asked.

"Yes sir," Ewan answered, "and he's a bit testy about his precious engine."

"As he should be," the professor said. "That engine must keep running smoothly day and night for the next week-and-a-half. Without it, where would we be, eh?"

"We do have the sails," Ewan said, remembering the disaster of his first passage. "But it's pretty slow going, I admit. You pray for a trailing wind."

The professor laughed again. "Sails! By rights they should be completely unnecessary. We have the technology to make better engines, engines that won't fail. Ships with two engines and two propellers. Ships that cannot sink. We are simply unwilling to pay for them."

"What would your Engineer MacLeod say to that, I wonder?" Colonel MacLaren asked.

"If he is any kind of an engineer, he will agree," the professor replied. "Now more than ever I look forward to meeting him to discuss the engines."

Ewan swallowed another curse. Keeping the professor out of trouble was turning out to be a lot trickier than he'd thought. But he smiled and said, "I'll see what I can do, sir."

"Me, too," Tereza insisted.

"And I should love to accompany them," Daisy added.

Ewan had blessed the lucky collision that introduced him to Daisy, the perfect excuse to fall into company with the professor. Now he wasn't so sure it had been good luck. MacLeod could hardly stand having a gentleman invade his dark hole. And a woman? Pretty or not, Ewan could imagine the explosion.

The horn sounded again for the ten-minute warning, and the chief steward made another round with the bell. Everyone had been on edge, expecting it, but everyone still jumped. Ewan was ready to make a grab for Tereza, but she took her father's arm, and together they kept each other upright and in the real world. Daisy provided a distraction by asking Ewan about the sails, ventilators, lifeboats, and every other little thing. Meanwhile, the professor wanted to know what powered the winches and the capstan, and why the sails were still handled by sailors instead of engines. Ewan thought he would go hoarse with all the answers. But the distractions worked; when the horn sounded the five-minute warning, Tereza grimaced but stayed in tight control.

Things got very busy then. The stewards herded the last of the visitors off the ship. The deck crew pulled in the gangways and made them fast, then loosed the spring lines and hawsers. A pair of tugs that had been standing by for the last half hour edged closer, black smoke billowing from their funnels, sounding short bleats on their shrill horns. Mr. Frasier, the wardroom steward, appeared in his kilt and sash, bagpipe cradled under his left elbow. Slow and stately, he walked to the bow, where the ship's bronze signal cannon sat in a sliding carriage. The bosun and two deckhands joined him.

Daisy made to follow, but Ewan stopped her. "Sorry, Miss MacLaren. Passengers aren't allowed forward of the mast there. That's crew country. If you put one toe over, they charge you a three-dollar fine."

"Three dollars?" Daisy exclaimed.

"Yes, miss. And they hold you hostage till they get it. It's all in good fun, though," he added quickly. "It goes to the seamen's general fund, for those who get hurt or sick."

"I note there's no mention of that in the handbills," the colonel said. "Not an oversight, I suspect."

Ewan grinned. "No sir."

"I suppose that guarantees at least one hostage each trip."

"Usually more, sir," Ewan said. "Young women seem to forget the rule."

The colonel chuckled. "I hope you'll avoid that temptation, Daisy. I warn you, I won't pay the ransom."

"I should hardly be so silly, Father," Daisy replied.

There was a last, long blast from the *Lewis's* horn, and a gentle vibration began to swell beneath their feet. Captain Morrison walked out to the very end of the portside bridge, while Mr. Frasier, up in the very eye of the bow, began to play the pipes. At the same time, the bosun and his two deckhands began to load the small cannon. The crowd on the pier cheered, and many of the passengers cheered back, waving madly and tossing paper streamers that the stewards were handing out. The vibration deepened and grew, and the *Lewis* began to ease backward toward the river. The pier crowd cheered again. Tereza and the professor clutched each other's hands. Ewan had never seen such a sad pair of faces. The professor wiped a tear from his cheek. Tereza turned her back on the city and began walking toward the stern, pulling her father with her. Ewan stayed close behind, and the others followed. She led them all the way past the stern deckhouse to the taffrail, where the big Stars and Stripes flapped just above their heads. Directly beneath them, the propeller churned the water as it pulled the ship past the end of the pier and into the Hudson River.

Now the tugs came alongside, one near the bow and one near the stern, on opposite sides of the ship. Signaling to each other with their horns, they eased their fat, padded prows against the iron plates of the *Lewis*'s hull and began to turn her downstream. The propeller slowed, stopped, lay quiet a moment, and then reversed. The water roiled into dirty billows. The ship lost her sternway and began to slip forward. The cannon in the bow boomed, startling everyone and echoing off the facades of the city. The buildings on the New Jersey side of the Hudson appeared to slide slowly sideways. The horn sounded again as they moved into the main channel and joined the busy river traffic. The tugs veered off, whistling farewells. The cannon boomed again. The skirl of the pipes drifted back to them along the full length of the ship.

"Look, Tereza," the professor said. "We are underway. Leaving America." His voice broke slightly, but he squared his shoulders and pointed back at the pier they had just left behind. "Look, we may never see this sight again."

Tereza kept her back turned on the city and her eyes fixed resolutely forward. Without replying, she took his hand again and began to walk toward the bow. Ewan shook his head and followed.

"How sad," Daisy murmured, close on his heels.

"Quite so," Derek replied. "You'd think she would linger for the very last glimpse of her mother's resting place."

"*Shh!* Not so loud," Daisy whispered. "It must be terribly hard for her. Perhaps she's right – the best thing is to keep looking to the future.

"Hm. And hope it will be better," Derek agreed. They walked in silence a few steps, watching the stiff backs of the Skovajsas. "Still, I sure wish I knew what the professor did that caused all this fuss and bother."

"Let's hope that's all behind them, too," Daisy said. "Perhaps a quiet voyage away from every other thing will help them begin to forget."

"I suppose it will," Derek said. "There's not much to go

wrong at sea."

If only you knew, Ewan thought.

Tereza led them as far forward as she could. They clustered at the rail just aft of the foremast shrouds, watching New Jersey and the harbor islands slip by. The horn sounded frequently as the *Lewis* passed inbound ships and overtook slower craft, but Tereza stopped flinching. Neither she nor the professor said a word, but Daisy had apparently decided to handle their share. She exclaimed over every landmark, referring to some guide book she had read. She also asked about incoming ships and wanted to know what their flags signified. Ewan, kept busy answering, was glad when they entered the Narrows and the sea breeze picked up, bringing with it the first exciting hint of the ocean. Despite the sun, the air was suddenly much cooler and smelled of salt instead of coal smoke and city. Everyone exclaimed about it, except Tereza, but her eyes brightened, and she seemed to actually be paying attention to what lay ahead, instead of pretending to ignore what they were leaving behind.

They passed the quarantine islands and came out into the wide expanse of the lower bay, bounded by low marshes and high dunes. Frasier stopped playing his pipes, to scattered applause from a few of the passengers, including Daisy, and made his stately way back into the deckhouse. Tereza suddenly turned and led them across the deck to the opposite rail, moving with such silent determination that the passengers there quickly made room. She stared through the wide opening at the mouth of the bay onto the even wider Atlantic and all that lay eastward. Everyone fell silent for a moment or two.

Then Daisy asked, "Why are we still going south? Shouldn't we be turning out and up toward the northeast."

"Sandbars," Ewan explained. "We have to stay in the channel." He pointed at the spit of land at the lower end of the bay. "We'll bear east about halfway to Sandy Hook there, and then east-nor'east when we're out in the ocean proper."

"So that's Sandy Hook!" Daisy exclaimed. "Yes, I can see the lighthouse and the fort." She dipped a hand beneath her coat and pulled out a small telescope.

Her father chuckled. "She insisted on having her own spyglass for the voyage."

"And I was right, wasn't I," she said, snapping it open with a smug smile. Then she tried to focus it on the Sandy Hook light. "Oh, dear," she said. "I hadn't realized we were already rocking so much. This was much easier on the veranda at home."

"It'll rock a lot more soon," Ewan said, "but you'll get used to it."

"I'm sure I will. I don't get seasick, not even in a Chesapeake storm."

I've heard that before, Ewan thought wryly, but he kept it to himself.

"Oh!" she said. "There's a line of signal flags showing at the fort. I wonder what that's all about. Look, Tereza. They're very colorful." She offered the telescope to Tereza, who hesitated, but then took it with a faint thank-you. "Would they be trying to signal us, do you think?" Daisy asked Ewan.

"It's not very likely, Miss MacLaren." He scanned the waters inside and outside the Hook. "There might be a Navy ship coming in."

Just as he said it, a rocket went trailing up from the fort and burst high above the lighthouse. The explosion was only a faint pop at that distance, but the bright flash and cloud of smoke were clear against the blue sky. Ewan looked back at the bridge. Sure enough, both Captain Morrison and the first officer had their telescopes trained on the fort. Then the quartermaster came out of the wheelhouse with his semaphore flags. And the captain didn't look any too happy. He said a few words, and the quartermaster signaled that they had seen the message. Some of the other passengers noticed and began pointing at the fort.

"I guess I'm wrong," Ewan said. He peered at the distant flags, trying to make them out. They came down too soon, and a new set was hoisted. The captain took a long look at it and lowered his telescope, frowning. He snapped another few words, then turned and aimed the telescope back over the stern toward the Narrows. The first officer gave a command to the men in the wheelhouse, and the telegraph bell signaling the engine room rang clearly through the doorway. Ewan could feel the changing vibration as the engine slowed. The *Lewis* answered smoothly, her graceful lope slowing to an ungainly wallow in the low cross swells coming in off the Atlantic.

"What's happening?" the colonel asked. "Can you tell?"

Ewan watched the quartermaster's final signal.

"Yes," he said. "We're waiting for another passenger."

"Another passenger?" the colonel exclaimed. "Out here? How?"

"A boat, I suppose," Ewan replied, but he was wrong again.

"Oh!" Tereza exclaimed, peering aft through Daisy's little telescope. "I see it! Father, it's an airship!"

Chapter 5

La Grande Entrée en Scène

As the airship slowly drew nearer, Ewan recognized it as one of the West River Air Ferries that had been operating between Manhattan and New Jersey for the past few years. With two large propellers and a bank of batteries, continually recharged by a pair of lean dogs on treadmills, they were faster than the water-bound ferries. But they were also expensive and couldn't handle heavy weather. Many days they never came out of their hangars. He couldn't imagine what had tempted the pilot to carry someone out over the bay in pursuit of a steam liner.

"I can make out two people in the front seat," Tereza said, peering though the little telescope. "There may be another one or two behind them."

"At most, if there is also luggage," the professor remarked. "It's making good headway, too good to be fully loaded."

If this is good headway, Ewan thought, *I'll stay on the water and go by steam.*

The *Lewis* had turned into the East Channel by the time the airship finally caught up. Captain Morrison steered directly into the wind, rang the engines to dead slow ahead, and the airship took position directly above the stern deckhouse. All of the passengers hurried back to watch what would happen next. Daisy and Tereza slipped to the front of the crowd – the gentlemen all showed courtesy to two young women – and Ewan kept in their wake.

The airship dropped a line, and one of the deck crew

secured it to the stern capstan. There wasn't much space there, just a few feet from the second saloon skylight to the capstan and a few more on back to the deckhouse, but it was one of the only places on board that didn't have a web of shrouds, stays, and other rigging filling the air above it. There was only the mizzen boom, now hauled over to port. The airship winched itself down to the height of the mizzen mast, then dropped a long rope ladder. A pair of sailors grabbed it and braced themselves against the deck by the starboard rail. As the ship rose and fell in the small swell, they let the ladder rise to arm's length, then pulled it back down, like human springs.

"You'd never get me climbing down that," one gentleman exclaimed loudly over the general chatter.

A leg appeared in the hatch on the bottom of the gondola, followed by a second leg. The crowd went silent, all heads turned upward. A man in a sharp suit descended as nimbly as a sailor on the shrouds. Ewan was impressed; the fellow had it right, with a foot on either side of the ladder, to avoid swinging like a pendulum. And he somehow managed to hold onto his hat at the same time. He paused just above the sailors, waiting for the lift of the ship, then smoothly dropped past the last four rungs to land firmly on the deck without a hint of a stumble. He doffed his hat – a very modern low bowler with a jaunty brim and a neat brush at the knot of the band – and bowed courteously to the assembled passengers. They erupted into cheers and applause.

The first officer was waiting to greet him, along with the chief steward and Aunt Nellie. The newcomer went right to her and presented a pair of tickets with a flourish. He was lean and black-haired, sporting a trim mustache and a dazzling smile.

"Pierre-Alexandre Serge Henri, *comte de* Beausoleil," he announced. "Thank you so much for waiting. I am very sorry to have discommoded everyone with such a tiresome delay."

"That's quite all right, count," Nellie said. She gave the tickets a cursory glance and handed back the receipt. "You've given your fellow passengers a wee diversion to start the passage. I'm sure not a one will begrudge you a few minutes' delay."

Except Captain Morrison, Ewan thought. The *Lewis* was no greyhound of the sea, but the captain made every passage a race against his own best time.

And now a second man was coming down the ladder, having a much harder time of it. He had both feet on the same side, which made the ladder swing away from him, till he was almost on his back. His hat fell off and tumbled to the deck. He struggled to find the next rung, hunting madly with one foot, clinging desperately. One of the women cried out when he lost his grip and hung by one hand for a moment. But he was made of stronger stuff than anyone guessed. He stopped bothering with his feet at all and lowered himself hand by hand into the grasp of a second pair of sailors, who had rushed forward to help the first two.

Once on deck, he brushed them off curtly, straightened his short jacket, and marched over to the count.

"My valet, Larousse," said the count, expressing both sympathy and apology. The valet bowed stiffly without a word. "His family has served mine for generations. I'm afraid I try his loyalty very much today." The count said something in French and gestured back toward the ladder, which was rising into the belly of the gondola. Larousse nodded and went to stand by the sailors, again without a word.

"Poor fellow," Derek murmured. "Struck dumb by fright."

"Or perhaps he's a mute," Daisy said. She walked across the deck and held out Larousse's hat, speaking to him in French.

He looked completely taken aback for a moment. Then he muttered something barely audible, snatched the hat, jammed it onto his head, and turned his back on Daisy to peer upward.

"He's a rude devil, isn't he!" Derek exclaimed.

"He's just watching for the luggage," Ewan pointed out. The ladder had been raised, and now a trunk and a valise appeared, lashed together and tied to a line. Daisy watched as it descended in jerks, twisting in the wind. A sudden gust pushed the airship sideways. The luggage swung her way, twirling wildly, and the knot let go. The luggage dropped. There were shouts, screams. Daisy jumped backward, into the arms of the count, who spun her to the side, and the two bags thudded onto the deck right where she'd been standing.

Into the moment of absolute silence that followed, the count said calmly, "*Par bonheur* the luggage was made in France, and is completely undamaged. You also I hope, *mademoiselle?*"

He opened his arms and Daisy stepped back. "*Complètement, monsieur le comte,*" she replied, bowing. "I was made in America."

There was a great burst of relieved laughter from the crowd. The count bowed deeply in return, then gestured at his valet.

"Larousse, clear this baggage away before someone trips over it. *Emportez les baggages. Allez vite, s'il vous plait.* It has provided enough excitement for one day, I think. Excuse me, please, mademoiselle. I must finish my business with the officers and see to my cabin. Perhaps we will have time to talk again this evening. *Vous parlez Français, il me semble?*"

"*Un petit peu, monsieur*," Daisy replied. "Too little, I fear, to carry on a long conversation, but I do look forward to making your acquaintance properly later."

Derek muttered something.

"What?" Ewan asked.

"Nothing," Derek grumbled, and Ewan hid a smile. A count would be stiff competition for Daisy's attentions.

Meanwhile, he had to get back to his guard duties. The colonel had made his way through the crowd and was talking with Daisy. Tereza was standing stiffly beside her, watching the airship, which had closed its hatch and was letting out its tether. But there was no sign of the professor. Ewan scanned the crowd for the professor's top hat. There were plenty of gentlemen who still wore the same style of low topper, and almost all of them were in black suits as well. The professor was a bit shorter than average, though, and Ewan glimpsed him beyond some taller heads, in the shadow of the number nine lifeboat. He appeared to be talking to someone even shorter. Ewan made his way forward past the skylight and had almost reached them when he realized the gentleman couldn't be the professor. Not unless the professor was starting a shipboard romance. His arm was linked with that of a dumpy, pale woman in a drab outfit. Then the gentleman raised his head to look across the deck, and he clearly wasn't the professor, just another man with a similar build, beard, and coloring.

Ewan swore and scanned the crowd again but still didn't see the professor. He did notice a small knot of passengers, heads together, punctuating their conversation with glances aft toward Tereza and Daisy. He began to make his way back toward the capstan, carefully studying every face under a top hat. Most of them were looking up now. The airship was literally at the end of its rope. At a double beep from its tiny horn, the sailors released the tether from the capstan, and the airship bounced higher, pushed backward by the sea breeze. It spun slowly, released a pair of sails that swung out on booms from the sides of the gondola, and quickly receded toward the shoreline. The passengers began applauding again, only to be drowned out by a tremendous blast from the *Lewis's* horn. Ewan saw Tereza stiffen, and her hand went to her mouth. Daisy quickly took her arm. He hurried toward them.

Tereza was white as a sheet, eyes half closed. Daisy was still holding her arm, and Derek was chunnering away, apparently trying to bore her out of her shock.

Ewan butted right in. "Excuse me, Miss Skovajsová, do you know where your father's gone? I can't see him anywhere."

It worked better than he'd wanted. Tereza snapped back to the here and now, but she looked terrified.

"What do you mean? He was over by the rail." She looked frantically in every direction. "He was with Colonel MacLaren. They must still be together."

But the colonel was beside the saloon skylight, talking with First Officer MacKay.

"Maybe he's gone into the smoking cabin," Ewan said.

"He doesn't smoke," Tereza said, sounding even worse. "He hates it."

"There he is!" Derek exclaimed, pointing. "Under that life boat!"

"No, that's just someone built like him" Ewan said. "I made the same mistake."

Ewan was beginning to feel as worried as Tereza looked. It didn't seem possible that the professor would leave Tereza alone on deck, even with Daisy and the colonel as chaperones. Not without saying something at least. He was odd, but surely not that odd.

With the airship gone and the count on his way below,

the other passengers were drifting forward. Tereza was rooted to the deck, her lips pressed into a thin, white line. Ewan continued to scan the faces passing by them. The *Lewis* was back on course, and the swells were growing higher. The Atlantic beckoned.

"You're shivering, Tereza, and the breeze is picking up," Daisy said. "It will be much cooler on the open waters. We'll go to your cabin and wait for your father there."

"But what if—?" Tereza suddenly ran to the rail and leaned out, searching the water behind them. They hurried after her. "What if he's fallen in?"

"Someone would have noticed," Ewan said immediately. "The deck was packed. He would have cried out."

She grabbed his hand. "But—"

"Look! There he is!" Derek cried.

"Where!" Tereza frantically scanned the ship's wake.

"At the very end, behind the little cabin there. Under Old Glory."

They looked up and there was the professor, standing at the taffrail beneath the billowing U.S. ensign, deep in conversation with another man. Ewan felt a surge of relief, followed by a bigger surge of irritation at himself. He should have kept better watch.

"There, you see?" Daisy said. "He's perfectly fine." She linked elbows with Tereza. "Let's go see who he's talking with. Maybe it's another scientist. Don't hurry. Never let a man know you're worried about him, not even a father. Let them think they can take care of themselves."

Tereza, grim faced, controlled her pace.

"That was a jest, wasn't it?" Derek mumbled, as he and Ewan followed more slowly.

"I think she meant to jest, but I'm betting she believes it," Ewan replied.

"Well, pride goeth before destruction and all that, but I think most men can," Derek said. "Take care of themselves, that is."

Ewan wondered.

When they reached the taffrail, Tereza let go of Daisy and grabbed her father's arm.

He looked at her, startled. "Ah, Tereza. There you are. Did you see the airship depart? Those sails, you know, are really quite worthless. I was telling Mr. King here – Oh, excuse me. Mr. King, permit me to introduce my daughter, Tereza Skovajsová. Tereza, Mr. Hamilton King. He has flown in an airship! Oh, and these are Tereza's young friends."

He introduced them all hurriedly, then plunged on about airships. Mr. King, it appeared, had flown only once, at a fair in Buffalo, New York, in a short jaunt above Lake Erie. Ewan thought that hardly made anyone an expert, but King wasn't shy about relating every detail he could remember, which mostly involved how unafraid he had felt through the entire flight. The professor wanted to know about the shape, the motive power, the gas in the envelope (as he called it), how it was steered, how it went down after getting up in the first place, and more. King had very few answers. He did know that there were two propellers, that the pilot steered with a tiller and two pedals, and that the batteries were charged by a trio of men pedaling a mechanism similar to a bicycle.

"Without the wheels, of course," he finished.

The professor then went on about how much power three men could generate, and what that implied about the size of the batteries, how long the pedalers could maintain the charge, and how far they could go without resting.

"Some day," he proclaimed, "airships will cross, not just a Great Lake, but the Atlantic Ocean. It is only a matter of improving the batteries and finding a more reliable means to recharge them. I wonder . . ." He trailed off, eyes fixed on the speck of the receding airship.

The *Lewis* meanwhile, had cleared the channel; they were now on the Atlantic proper, heading east by northeast at 12 knots, on the first leg of the route that would take them two thousand nine hundred and ninety-seven miles to Glasgow. The deck vibrated to the deep hum of the engines. The salt water roiled beneath them, churned into a long, frothing wake by the *Lewis's* twenty-foot-tall propeller. The Stars and Stripes flapped above their heads, pointing back at the land they were leaving. Ewan took it all in with a surprising sense of pleasure. They were alone at the taffrail, the professor and King were getting along famously, Tereza seemed to have relaxed, and not a soul, at the moment, was looking at them in surprise, worry, or threat. This bodyguard duty was irritating, but it had its rewards. He wondered if the rest of the passage would be like this. He wondered if it would be his last passage. But he shook that thought off. It was good place to be for now.

"I need to return to our cabin and prepare for supper," Daisy said, proving that nothing good lasts forever. "Besides, the day has cooled considerably. I, for one, need a heavier wrap."

She was right. The sun was dipping toward the thinning silhouette of Long Island, on their port quarter, and the breeze was chilly. The professor suddenly realized that Tereza was shivering and became fatherly. He took his leave of King with a promise to continue the discussion after dinner, if not during.

"A fine gentleman," he remarked, as Daisy and Derek led them forward in search of the colonel. "Though not a trained engineer, he is possessed of a quick and perceptive mind."

"What is his profession?" Daisy asked.

"I must admit, I never found out," the professor replied. "I'm afraid I overwhelmed the conversation, as usual. Forgive me, it is a failing. Tereza will chide me in the privacy of our cabin, I'm sure."

"No, Father," she murmured. "I'm growing used to it."

"As did your poor mother," he replied, patting her hand. "You are too good to me."

Grief was so plain in his voice that Ewan felt like an eavesdropper. Everyone fell silent.

The colonel was standing in the warm lee of the funnel, watching for them. Daisy spotted his wave and went over. Derek fell in beside Ewan.

"Heavens, she's a bright and lively one, isn't she," Derek said.

"Be careful," Ewan said, grinning, "her father's a colonel. He probably keeps his revolver close at hand."

"Oh, not likely," Derek protested. "He's retired, he said so. Besides, I . . . I haven't been brazen, have I?"

Ewan almost laughed at the worry on his face. "Not brazen, just obvious."

"Really? Obvious? Do you think so? Dang!"

Derek was a picture of proper reserve as they made their way down to the cabins, where Ewan and he discovered that they had another cabin mate. A valise lay on the lower berth by the porthole, and a second, larger case was slid underneath. The owner was not there, but the valise was lettered clearly: H. Hamilton King, Esq., MI, MHA, PsD.

"Well, how about that," Derek said. "He's a man of letters. I wonder what they stand for?"

"Too Lazy to Spell," Ewan replied. He went to the sink and quickly washed his hands and face. "I need to check with the chief steward," he said as he toweled off. "About . . . about seating at supper. If I'm to get you and

Daisy at the same table."

Derek broke into a huge smile. "You can really do that?"

"I'm sure of it. But you wait here." He gave Derek a critical glance. "You might want to shave."

"Do you think so?" Derek ran a hand over his chin. "It has been a couple of days, I suppose."

"The barber's cabin is in the port passageway, just past the companionway – the stairs."

"Oh, I'll do my own, if you really think it—"

"Definitely," Ewan said, and he hurried out before Derek could change his mind. He didn't need to see anyone about seating; they simply needed to be first at the table, and once you claimed a seat, it was yours for the passage. What Ewan did need to do was make sure he managed to meet up with the Skovajsas. Nellie would kill him if he wasn't sitting right beside the professor.

The passageway was almost empty, which was not unusual. Cabin passengers made a point of dressing for dinner and supper. Ewan lingered outside the Skovajsas' cabin, but after three passengers went past him to the bathrooms and then passed him again on the way back to their cabins, he began to feel conspicuous. Stewards kept coming and going as well, answering calls from passengers who had forgotten their shaving soap or needed fresh towels or didn't know how the electric lights worked. A couple of them gave him glares. Ewan moved into the outer passageway and waited by the companion ladder. But that was no better. He decided it was better to keep moving and went back forward past the MacLaren's cabin.

As he came out of the narrow passageway, someone disappeared into the one on the opposite side. He glimpsed only the train of a skirt, but it looked a lot like Tereza's. Ewan hurried across for a look. Yes, it was her, alone for some reason. He didn't call out; the last thing he wanted to do was startle her into a swoon. He walked as quickly as he could without running.

He reached her on the first step of the companionway. "Miss Skov—?"

He never got past the first syllable. Tereza gave a little cry, spun, and jabbed him with the point of her parasol. Pain jolted through his gut, all the way out to his fingers and toes. Ewan's vision went white. Stiff as a board, he toppled backward to the deck.

Chapter 6

A Shocking Moment

When his eyes cleared, Ewan was flat on his back, in pain, with Tereza's face hovering just above him. She didn't look nearly as concerned as he thought she should. He started to get up, groaned, and decided it could wait a moment longer. It felt like every joint in his body had been bent backwards.

Her eyes narrowed. "Are you hurting?" she asked, with a lot of interest but still not much sympathy.

"No, it's nothing," he lied. "I just slipped and bumped my head." Come to mention it, his head was pounding.

"Oh, no, Mr. Gilmore. You didn't slip. I'm afraid I shocked you."

"You what?" Ewan made another effort to rise, but the pounding only grew worse.

She took him under the arm. "I shocked you," she explained, helping him to his knees. "With my parasol. It has an electrical capacitor in the handle. It's Father's design, a modified Leyden Apparatus. For self protection. It was my . . . my mother's."

"That's wonderful," Ewan said. "I suppose she used it all the time."

"No, I don't think she ever had need to." Tereza gave a heave and got him to his feet.

Ewan swayed against her. The pain was less, but now he felt woozy. "And you just carry it for sentimental reasons?"

"Hardly!" she exclaimed. "Father received threats! We were yelled at! I . . . I . . ."

In the space of those few words, Tereza went from composed to angry to the fragile-seeming girl he had first seen.

"I thought I might need it," she murmured. "I thought Mother would want me to . . . to have it. And use it. If it came to that." Tears formed in the corners of her eyes. "I didn't mean to, really. It just . . . happened." She stepped away from him and wouldn't meet his eyes. "Please forgive me, sir. I won't bother you any further."

She started to climb the stairs.

"Wait!" Ewan said. "Don't go. I know you didn't mean it. It was entirely my fault. I shouldn't have startled you like that."

She stopped and looked at him from the corner of her eye.

"You're sure you're all right?"

"Absolutely fine," he lied. "Here —" He bent, biting back another groan, and picked up her parasol, which she had set on the deck beside him. "I believe you're right, your mother would want you to carry it."

She came back down slowly, step by step, and carefully took the parasol by the handle. "Thank you, Mr. Gilmore," she said. She knelt and picked up his bowler, which he hadn't even noticed had fallen off. "And you'll want this, I'm sure."

Not really, he thought, *but I suppose I need it*. "Yes, thank you."

He took it and she smiled.

"Ha-hum" A gentle cough brought him back to the passageway. An older mean and women were standing right behind him, waiting to go up the companionway, as were half a dozen other passengers and two stewards.

"Are you all right, miss?" one of the stewards asked, stepping a bit too close to Ewan. "Or will you be needing more help to move along, *sir*?" It was Ranald Morrison, pushing his long nose into places it didn't belong. He'd been on the *Lewis* for ten years and had never advanced to the deck crew. Instead he had plans to be the next Chief Steward. He'd also made it plain he had no use for Ewan Gilmore.

Ewan flushed and jammed the bowler onto his head.

"I don't need any help," he snapped. "I just tripped. Miss Skov— Miss Schultz here was kind enough to help me up." He addressed the group behind Ranald. "Sorry for the bother. We're going now." He turned and started painfully up the stairs.

Tereza matched his pace. "Thank you for not telling." Ewan shrugged. "It's supposed to be Schmidt, by the way, not Schultz."

Ewan blushed again. All he had done so far to protect the professor was make a spectacle in front of the other passengers.

"In any case, everyone knows who we are by now. We're much too obvious to hide behind false names. Besides, Father would have nothing to do with Schmidt. Far too Prussian. So you may call me Miss Skovajsová." She paused, then added quietly, "Tereza would be all right, too."

"I doubt your father would have anything to do with that either," Ewan said, though he was surprised by how pleased he felt by the offer. Pleased, but also embarrassed. "I'm just a watch dog, you know, here to make sure no one tries to hurt him. Or you."

"I thought so," she said, "but you made it obvious when you called me Miss Schultz. No one else would have known to make that mistake."

Of course. They'd been introduced as the Skovajsas. Ewan sighed. He was making a real hash of his job.

"Is you uncle truly the owner of the line?" she asked.

"Only if you go back a couple of hundred years," he

admitted. Her face fell. "But I can still get you seated by the first officer," he added quickly.

"That's Miss MacLaren's wish," she said. "I'm hoping to see—"

"To see the engine room. Yes." Ewan sighed again. "I can get you in, but you'll have to figure out how to charm Mr. MacLeod if you want to stay long enough to see anything."

She brightened immediately. "Oh, thank you! I will charm his hat right off!"

With that smile, you just might be able to do it, he thought.

They reached the open deck and moved to the rail. The sun was already setting, and bright stars were showing in the East. Ewan started to point out the North Star and the dippers, but Tereza beat him to it. She named Castor, Pollux, Vega, Arcturus, and a half-dozen others, too.

"If we had Miss MacLaren's telescope, I could show you the twin stars in the handle of the Big Dipper," she added.

"Maybe later tonight or tomorrow evening," Ewan said. "Right now we should fetch your father and go right to the saloon to grab the best seats."

"He said he would meet me there," Tereza replied, "but you're right. He's probably there by now, wondering where I am. I told him I was going to Miss MacLaren's cabin. Actually, I just needed to get out alone for a minute, and he wouldn't have let me go unattended. He worries so much since . . ." She took a breath. "Since the accident. Every little thing sets him off, as though it were happening over and over again."

She shuddered, and Ewan realized Tereza was having the same fits of memory.

"Well then, it's a good thing you're here to help him get through them, isn't it," he said. "We'd better get down there and put his mind to rest."

It drew a faint smile at least. "Yes, thank you."

She took his elbow, and a shiver coursed up his arm to tickle his chest.

Must be from that shock, he thought.

&

Daisy smiled and suggested it was time to collect the gentlemen and venture to the saloon.

Mrs. Curmidge wrinkled her broad nose. "I suppose you're right, my dear. Reverend Curmidge will be finished with his cheroot by now, one would hope. I could never understand the attraction men find in that noisome habit. At least the ship has the courtesy to banish them to their own little smoke hole." She heaved a plump sigh and hoisted herself from the settee. "This parlor is rather a cozy little space, isn't it? Who'd have thought the Americans – let alone the Scots – would have set aside a cabin just for we ladies. I imagine we shall spend a great deal of the voyage safely ensconced here. You did bring your embroidery, I hope."

"I did indeed," Daisy replied, for the second time, "though I plan to spend some time each day walking the deck."

Mrs. Curmidge *humphed*, a surprisingly deep and derogatory sound from such a small, unremarkable woman. She was shorter even than Daisy and many inches rounder, with an equally round face that could have been seen as cherubic except for her constant scowl. She was dressed in unrelieved gray: dress, shawl, bonnet, and scarf. Her husband, the reverend, seemed much more pleasant. They were returning to England after a Methodist convocation of some sort in Western Pennsylvania, and Reverend Curmidge said he was almost sorry to be leaving without the chance to see more of the country. Mrs. Curmidge, on the other hand, made it clear she couldn't wait to be "out of this wretched frontier and back in civilization."

"Thank Heavens this is a British liner," she said now. "At least the food is reputed to be good."

She presented her arm to Daisy and directed her out into the companionway.

Reverend Curmidge was already waiting there, at the top of the stairs down to the saloon. The smoking cabin shared the same deckhouse with the ladies' cabin and the saloon companionway, but it had a separate entrance, facing the after deck. The reverend's short walk through the sea air had done little to blow off the scent of cigar smoke that clung to his jacket. Mrs. Curmidge sniffed disdainfully.

The reverend smiled pleasantly through a trim beard stained with nicotine at the left side of his mouth. "There you are," he said. "I wondered if all that velvet upholstery hadn't swallowed you two right up." He chuckled.

Mrs. Curmidge *humphed*. "It's hardly that luxurious, sir, though certainly more civilized than the leather-lined den you've just wafted from."

Daisy suppressed a smile. The two seemed determined to outdo each other in being opposites. "Shall we go down?" she said.

"Certainly," the reverend replied. "Lead on."

Just then, Tereza entered from the deck, close on the arm of young Mr. Gilmore.

Mrs. Curmidge's sniffed again.

"Well met, friends," Daisy said quickly. "How nice to see you two together."

Miss Lawson's stress on "together" broke through Tereza's surprise at the sudden meeting. She was suddenly very aware of Ewan's arm beneath her hand. She quickly let go and shifted an awkward half step away.

Miss Lawson continued smoothly past the strained silence to introduce them all.

"Pleased to meet you, miss, and you, young man," the reverend said, with a polite bow to each.

"Surely," Mrs. Curmidge murmured, with only the slightest nod. Her small eyes flicked from Ewan to Tereza and bored in. The scowl remained on her face. Tereza dropped her eyes and barely managed an answering nod.

"We should hurry down or we shall be seated in the very stern," Miss Lawson said.

"Not to worry," Reverend Curmidge replied. "Your father went on ahead. I was assigned the duty of chaperone, he the task of claiming seats near the captain."

"Bravo, Father!" Miss Lawson exclaimed. "He spoils me at times, but only for the best of reasons. Come, Tereza, Mr. Gilmore, let's not keep him on duty a minute longer."

She offered her arm to Mrs. Curmidge and deftly turned her toward the stairs.

"After you, sir," Ewan said to the reverend.

"Thank you, young man," the reverend replied. He offered his arm to Tereza. "May I assist you, Miss?"

Tereza didn't see that she had a choice. "Thank you," she murmured, taking his arm.

He smiled warmly. "Careful on these steep steps now. They keep moving."

Tereza forced herself to relax but still could find few words to say in reply to his polite questions. She had never felt easy around strangers, and the past months had made it even harder. So many strangers, so many strained words, uncertain smiles, false attempts at comfort when the only comfort she'd wanted was to see her father awaken. She'd escaped into his books, notes, and formulae, reading and rereading them, writing her own notes in the margins. The recent weeks had been even worse, with his journals packed away and out of reach, first on the road, then in the courtroom, then among the throngs in Washington and in New York.

Stop it! She told herself. *That's over, left behind. For the next ten days you're on this ship, with these few people. Father's getting better. At least, he's trying.*

They reached the bottom of the stairs and stepped through the glazed and paneled double doors into the saloon.

"Here we are then, miss," the reverend said. "And well in time for supper."

"Thank you, sir." Tereza managed a slight sideways smile, dropped her hand, and turned away, pretending to study the room. She was very aware of Ewan, standing just behind her.

Colonel MacLaren was defending an empty block of seats at the head table, but it was hardly necessary. There were empty seats at all six of the long tables running three to a side down the length of the saloon. Father was with the colonel, watching the doorway worriedly. His expression relaxed when he saw Tereza, and he waved. She wished he hadn't. It made her feel conspicuous, and even more aware of Ewan.

Derek Reed popped out from behind Father. "Over here!" he called.

The buzz of conversation dropped for a moment and glances turned their way. Tereza wished she could disappear.

Miss Lawson calmly ignored Reed and the stares. She escorted Mrs. Curmidge to the table to introduce her and the reverend to the rest of the party. The chatter at the second table resumed first, Tereza noticed, led by the strong voice of the purser, who sat at its head. Tereza remembered the woman was also named Gilmore and wondered how closely she and Ewan were related. The arrival of Mr. King distracted her. Father invited him to sit with them, which meant a bit of reshuffling.

"Oh, no worry, we'll move," the woman beside Mr. Reed said quickly, hauling her startled husband down to the fourth table before anyone could protest. Then the couple who had been sitting very quietly beside them followed, as though the foursome were old friends. The table had not been filled; they could simply have moved down a seat.

Rats deserting the ship, Tereza thought. She glanced at Father, but he was listening to King's effusive apologies for being late and didn't seem to notice the empty seats around them. Ewan, on the other hand, was staring intently after the departing passengers, as though trying to memorize their faces. Tereza suddenly felt a little less exposed. She hoped he would sit beside her.

"Pardon me, *mademoiselle*. Is this place taken?"

It was the Count de Beausoleil, of course; who else would use French? Daisy suddenly found herself wishing she had carried a fan. The thought irked her; she didn't need to hide behind fripperies. She summoned her French vocabulary.

"*Non, monsieur le comte, ce n'est pas occupé. S'il vous plaît, assiez-vous là.*"

She knew that the idioms weren't precisely correct, but she also knew that, when dealing with men, style trumped accuracy every time.

He smiled warmly. "*Merci beaucoup, mademoiselle.* I'm afraid I was *très gauche* this afternoon and did not properly introduce myself. Please forgive me and allow me to redress my gaffe now."

"*Ce ne fait rien*," Daisy replied. "I myself was so taken aback by the events that I forgot to offer my own name." She knew she was being very forward – Mrs. Curmidge's scowl was so deep her eyes had almost disappeared in the folds of her cheeks – but they were, after all, on board an ocean liner, with no mutual acquaintance to introduce them. Daisy pressed on. "I am Margaret Adelaide Duvray MacLaren."

She introduced her father and the others, and was pleased to see that Tereza had gotten over her shyness enough to greet the count in schoolgirl French. Derek, on the other hand, barely nodded. The count treated them all as equals, bowing to the ladies first, then nodding to each of the men.

"Please let us sit," he said to the company, but in a manner that took in the entire table. "*Madame* Curmidge, I would pull out your chair but, *hélas*, I see they are bolted to the floor. Permit me to rotate it for you."

With a pleasant smile, he swiveled her chair out so she could sit, and would have swiveled it back, but she brushed him away.

"*Humph.* I can manage it myself, Mr. Count."

"Of course," he replied. "But, please, there is no need to address me by ancient titles here in the middle of the sea. *Après toys*, we share the same table and fare, yes? 'De Beausoleil' will suffice."

The other women were all seated by then, and the gentlemen took their places in a great mutter of *after-yous*, bumping knees as they swiveled into place. The count, who had managed to seat himself between Daisy and Mrs. Curmidge, slid smoothly into place without mussing the crease in his trousers. He directed the flow of conversation just as smoothly, drawing out each member of the small company, even Mrs. Curmidge, if only so she could contradict her cheerful husband on the subject of what she called, "the Pennsylvania wilderness." Daisy studied him as a good model for the role she would have to play when hosting for her father at the consulate.

The ship's bell sounded faintly from the bridge, and was repeated by the lookout on watch at the masthead. Six bells. Seven p.m., Daisy recalled from her research. She glanced at Tereza, but both of the Skovakjas were listening to Mr. King and didn't seem to have noticed. As the lookout's faint call of *all's well and lights burning bright* drifted down to them, the first officer entered the saloon and stopped at the head of the table.

"Good evening, ladies," he said, his rich voice cutting easily through the chatter. He sat quickly. "Please stay seated, gentlemen. The chairs are comfortable but too awkward to stand on ceremony. I'm First Officer MacKay. I apologize for the captain's absence, but he prefers to stand the watch when we are still so close to shore. The shipping lanes are crowded here. I will do my best to fill in for him. Shall we say grace? Reverend Curmidge, perhaps you would do us the honor?"

The entire saloon fell silent, except for the shuffling of shoes and rustling of the ladies' laced cuffs as the passengers bowed their heads and clasped hands. Daisy was suddenly aware of the rhythmic *thrumming* of the engine; the smooth lift, sway, and drop of the swell; and the constant vibration in the deck, her chair, the table, and everything else on board, herself included. Bottles lined up on the side table tinged together in an almost melodic rattle.

The reverend cleared his throat and spoke a blessedly few words about the food to come – so few, in fact, that there was an awkward pause after his *amen*. Then everyone realized he had finished and the many conversations resumed.

"*Eh bien, ce fut bref,*" the count murmured. Well, that was brief. "*Ici, en haute mer, j'avais redouté une longue tirade recommandant nos âmes à Dieu.*" Here, at sea, I was dreading a long tirade recommending our souls to God.

Daisy replied in French: "*Oh, no. The reverend is far too cheerful for that.*"

"*Good. Let's hope his wife is never called upon to say the grace. It's to the Devil, I fear, that she would send all our souls.*"

"What was that, Mr. Boo-so-lay?" Mrs. Curmidge asked.

"The count – excuse me, *Monsieur* de Beausoleil – was merely saying that he hoped the meal would live up to such a gracefully expressed blessing," Daisy replied.

The professor began to cough, a sound suspiciously similar to stifled laughter.

Tereza, actually smiling, handed him his water glass. "Careful, Father. Take a sip."

King, sitting on the professor's other side, seemed to snap awake. He slapped the professor's back. "Lift your arms, sir! Lift your arms! Open the airways wide!"

He slapped again just as the professor was taking a drink. Half the water spewed out, but half went down the wrong way, and the professor began to cough in earnest.

"Oh, my goodness!" one of the other women exclaimed. "He's choking."

"Hit him again!" a gentleman called.

There was a general hubbub, but the professor covered his mouth with a napkin, waved an arm to fend off King, and cleared his throat with a final long cough. A waiter rushed to his side with more napkins and a dry setting. People kept talking loudly.

Suddenly, the skirl of a bagpipe sounded above them, outside the near skylight. Everyone fell silent, except for the last thread of a sentence, spoken from one of the far tables.

". . . be rid of him, at least."

Chapter 7

In the Ladies' Cabin

The pipe tune continued alone for a long, strained moment. Ewan scanned the group at table six, trying to spot who had made the comment. Every face was stiff as stone.

The first officer broke the tension. "Professor Skovajsa, I hope you're fully recovered. Would you like some wine?" He signaled to the wine steward.

"Thank you, Lieutenant." The professor cleared his throat again. "But, please, serve the ladies first. It was merely a bit of water in my esophagus."

King began a blustery apology, but the professor cut him off. "It was an accident, friend King. No harm done."

King's slap had been an accident, Ewan thought, but what about the unknown fellow at table six who wanted to be rid of someone? Was he just a loudmouth, or was he planning another accident? Had he even meant the professor? He glanced toward Aunt Nellie, who was talking with two gentlemen at her table. She caught his eye for a moment and made a slight shrug.

At least she knew he was keeping an eye out – when he wasn't staring at Tereza, he sheepishly admitted. In fact, he couldn't make himself ignore her, but he did make a point of looking at every face but hers as the dinner got underway. No one seemed to be paying particular attention to the professor. If anything, everyone was trying very hard to avoid even a glance at the head table, as though they, too, were trying not to notice a particular someone.

The arrival of the first course was a welcome distraction. Stewards and crew never ate in the saloon. Oh, they got plenty to eat, but only the steerage menu: oatmeal, oatcakes, bread, duff, beef broth, kale, neeps and tatties, and plenty of hot tea, with treacle if you liked it sweet. Plain, filling, repetitive. By the end of a passage, you were starving for steak and a piece of fruit. Now, right in front of him was a dish of fruit salad, and when the waiters cleared that away, shelled oysters in a bone-white plate with little hollows in place of shells. And smoked cod dressed with herbs and a side dish of some kind of white pickle sauce. And wine to go with it, because the fruit wine apparently was only for drinking with fruit.

But there was Aunt Nellie again, catching his eye with a slight shake of the head, hand over the top of her glass. Ewan put down the wine and drank water.

After the fish came quail on a bed of rice, with tiny boiled quail eggs arranged in piles on the plate. You needed half a dozen to get a mouthful. And instead of kale there was chard cooked with leeks and splashed with wine vinegar. And then came lamb, legs of it, surrounded by roasted potatoes and sprouts, which was when Ewan realized he had been taking too much of each course.

He wasn't alone; one of the people at the second table lurched from his seat and hurried out, napkin clenched over his mouth.

Mrs. Curmidge sniffed. "The wages of excess."

"Oh, I think rather he looked green about the gills," Reverend Curmidge protested. "Poor fellow. Seasickness is a scourge that strikes good and bad alike."

The reverend's earthy good humor was a surprise to Ewan. This was the man he had mistaken, from behind, for the professor. Seen from the front, they were nothing alike and they sure didn't act the same. He didn't even act like a minister. His wife played that role enough for two.

"I myself am never seasick," Mrs. Curmidge stated.

"*Eh bien*," the count remarked. "It is good to know you are one of the fortunate of those groups."

"*Fortunate* is indeed the right word," the professor remarked. "It is more a matter of luck than strength of virtue. One is either born susceptible or immune. Would you not agree, Officer MacKay?"

"I wouldn't say *immune*," MacKay replied. "In my experience even the strongest of stomachs can be turned inside out in a heavy swell and a cross wind. A ship will pitch, roll, and yaw on a confused sea." He demonstrated by moving his hand. "Then, out of nowhere, a rogue wave will quarter the swell, with a twist and a kick and down she slides, rail under and nearly on her beam ends. It's the surprise that brings up breakfast."

"Please!" Daisy exclaimed. "You'll give us all *le mal de mer* with tales like that!"

Ewan couldn't help smiling. Most of the stewards bet on which passengers would succumb, but there was a strict, unspoken rule among them never to encourage it. They had to clean up the mess.

MacKay apologized, but Daisy, eyes twinkling, lifted her chin. "I'm not sure that's sufficient, sir. You must promise us a smooth voyage with none of those 'confused' seas."

"Believe me, Miss MacLaren, I would if I could," MacKay said. "All I can promise is the fastest crossing possible, to lessen the chance and shorten the agony, should it befall you. The well-being of all our passengers is the chief concern of every member of our crew, and I don't say that lightly. We drum it into every head, from the very first, don't we Mr. Gilmore?"

Caught by surprise, Ewan felt his stomach twist, as though the ship had run into one of MacKay's rogue waves. "Yes, sir. Absolutely. It's, uh, in our blood, I guess you'd say."

"Like getting seasick, I suppose," Derek said, and, in the face of their confusion, added, "I mean you're born with it. Or not. The concern, you see."

"Let us hope not 'not,' *alors*" the count said with a chuckle.

"Let us hope those with *not* don't stay long with the line," the colonel said.

"I'd certainly *not* be sailing with them," the reverend added.

"There are *not* any on this ship," MacKay stated, joining in.

"Gentlemen, desist!" Daisy exclaimed. "Your word play is worse than the waves!"

"Isn't there a cure?" Tereza asked.

"Only time, unfortunately," MacKay replied. "After a day or so it usually goes away on its own."

"'Usually?'" Tereza pressed.

"There are those who can't shake it the entire trip," MacKay admitted. "For them, there is no cure."

"Don't be so sure," King said, laying a finger alongside his nose, as though he were keeping a big secret.

"Yes, don't be too sure, Officer MacKay," the professor agreed. "Science has more to offer than you might suspect."

MacKay nodded to them. "If so, you'll have plenty of eager patients queuing up." He smiled at Tereza and then at Daisy. "I hope none of us here have to join the queue."

"If it stays like this, we shouldn't have much trouble," the reverend stated. He lifted his glass. "A toast to fair weather and calm seas."

"Hear, hear!" Derek exclaimed, and the rest echoed him.

Ewan took a small sip of wine, but he knew better than to hope it would do anything to appease the sea. The *Lewis* was still well inshore, but she was bound steadily northeast toward the turning point off Cape Sable, where they would bear more northerly onto the great circle route to the Irish Sea, ten days away. By tomorrow evening at the latest, they could expect heavier swells. Sooner or later, and more likely sooner, the wind would rise, and with it MacKay's confused seas. Then it would be all hands to the chamber pot.

But not this evening. The courses kept appearing, the waiters kept filling the wine glasses, and by the time the pudding arrived, the conversation was much louder and merrier. Afterward, some people left to take the air on deck. Others went up to the ladies' cabin or the smoking cabin. A group of gentlemen at table four began a card game. A few mixed couples moved to the settees at the stern end of the saloon, where a curving bookcase served as the ship's library. The count pointed out the piano, bolted to the deck inside the starboard entrance to the saloon, near the bar and the head of their table.

"Do you play, *mademoiselle* MacLaren?" he asked.

"Only a little," Daisy replied.

"Don't believe her," the colonel said. "She plays quite passably, and sings even better."

"Then please honor us with a selection," the count requested.

"Yes, do! Please!" Derek chimed in. "I – We should all be most grateful." He stood and swept his arm back toward the piano in a theatrical flourish, face flushed with wine.

"No, really, never believe a father," she protested.

MacKay stood and offered his arm. "I was about to excuse myself to return to the bridge," he said, "but I would be glad of an excuse to stay for the length of a song."

The reverend clapped lightly, and King joined in. Mrs.

Curmidge sniffed.

Daisy glanced at the woman's scowl, and her own lips quirked upward in a slight smile. "Well, I suppose I can't refuse, can I," she said, rising to take MacKay's arm. "But I warn you, 'passable' is the best you can hope for."

She played swell, to Ewan's ear, hardly missing a note, and her voice was pretty, too; a bit light maybe, but she could hit the notes and knew the words, and that was more than he could say for himself. On the second verse, MacKay joined in with a rich baritone. They made a fine duet, until Derek went over to the other end of the piano and tried to sing along. He had a voice like his last name – reedy – but he sang with gusto, and everyone applauded when the song was done.

Daisy was forced to play a couple more tunes after that, but then MacKay really did have to leave. The reverend and King used the opportunity to excuse themselves and leave for the smoking cabin, and the professor, or maybe Tereza, decided it was time to turn in. Besides the card players, they were the only ones left in the saloon, and Daisy joked that her playing had driven everyone else away. Only Mrs. Curmidge seemed to agree.

Ewan saw the Skovajsas safely to their cabin and then went up to check with Aunt Nellie. She was in her office, working on some papers at her tiny desk.

"How are they?" she asked.

"Fine," he replied. "Couldn't be better, in fact."

She raised her eyebrows. "And you're enjoying yourself a wee bit, I see."

He smiled. "The food's good."

"And the company."

He shrugged. "I think they've forgotten about visiting the engine room at least." He hesitated, then went on, trying to voice what was really bothering him. "I'm not sure I'm really cut out for this. It's hard to believe that someone would want to do them harm. Sure, there was that muttering at dinner, but . . ." He shrugged again. "Everyone forgot about it once the food came out. I feel like I could be doing something more useful."

"Such as?"

"Quartermaster? Steward at least. Waiter even. Part of the crew."

Nellie shook her head. "Ewan, you are part of the crew. Doing an important job."

"Only you think that!" he protested. "Everyone else is sneering behind my back!"

"Let the *dafties* sneer," she replied, frowning. "MacKay's behind you, and so is the captain. Remember, you wouldn't be on board at all if it weren't for the trouble following Professor Skovajsa. You heard just a bit of a grumble this evening from some bampot, who I'm sure has no intention of matching word to deed. It's not the grumblers you need to worry about, it's the quiet ones, biding their time. Or the frantic ones, all smiles till something goes wrong and then they strike out in panic. That's when you need to be at Skovajsa's side. Do you ken?"

Ewan sighed. "I do."

Aunt Nellie smiled wryly. "It's not an easy job, I know. You're trying to keep alert every minute, waiting for something that never happens, but the last thing we want is for something to happen. You ken that, too, I hope."

Ewan took a quick walk around the deck to settle the big meal and clear out the fumes of the wine, but once in bed he still tossed and turned for at least an hour, thinking of Tereza mostly. He tried to see her objectively: young, awkward, moody, a bit odd, actually. Pretty enough, but so thin. Of course, she'd been through a lot, but there was more to it than that. And more to what he was feeling than just a prettyish face. She appealed to him, and he didn't know exactly why, and maybe that was part of why. He fell asleep before he'd really made up his mind.

Sometime after midnight, Derek and King returned, smelling of whiskey and cigars, waking him with exaggerated whispers and stumbling tip-toe steps on a rolling ship when they were too tipsy to walk a straight line on solid ground. He had no sooner fallen back to sleep when both of them started snoring. And then his bladder reminded him about all the wine. Ewan put his head under his pillow, clenched his knees, and tried to get back to sleep, but it was no use. Admitting defeat, he rolled out of his berth, pulled on his clothes, and slipped out into the passageway.

The water closets and washrooms were at the forward end of the cabin section, in a central compartment that was just a few steps from his cabin door. Ewan stumbled to the nearest stall and was somewhat amazed at how long it took him to empty his bladder. *Another reason to avoid the wine*, he thought. *Thank you, Aunt Nellie.*

Fumbling with the small buttons on the fly of his new dress pants, he opened the stall door just in time to glimpse someone disappearing into the narrow, shadowed portside passageway leading aft. It took Ewan a second or two to realize it was the professor. He gave up on the last two buttons and hurried after, silent in his stockinged feet.

By the time he reached the end of the passageway, the professor was already halfway up the companionway and moving quickly. Ewan called softly, but the professor didn't respond. Ewan wondered where he could be going. The seas weren't any heavier, so he doubted it was seasickness. Could he be meeting someone? Who? And why?

Ewan chided himself for being so suspicious. *It's Aunt Nellie's fault*, he thought. *She's got me looking for trouble everywhere*. But he didn't call again, and gave the professor time to reach the top of the stairs before following. If he was meeting someone, Ewan wanted to see who it was before showing himself.

The moon had set. When Ewan reached the top of the companionway and peered out onto the deck, the professor was hardly more than a shadow. Suddenly, the ship's bell sounded five times – two-thirty. The professor started at the sound but kept striding aft as the lookout repeated the bells and called the all's-well. Ewan crossed over to the starboard exit and paralleled the professor down the deck, catching glimpses of him though the open areas between the deckhouses, ventilator, and funnel. Except that the professor didn't reappear on the stern deck. Ewan waited a minute, then slunk to the door to the smoking cabin and listened carefully. There wasn't a sound. He crept back to the saloon companionway and peered in, listening again, but the only sounds came from the kitchen below, along with the smell of baking. The door to the ladies' cabin was right there at the top of the stairway down to the saloon, so Ewan poked his head in, just to be sure.

It was pitch dark inside, the lamps extinguished, the round deadlights heavily draped. The light from the companionway didn't reach into the corners; the plush chairs and plump settees were no more than vague black forms in the general gloom. Ewan took a step farther in, and his stockinged foot dug into something firm on the carpet. He touched it again, feeling its contours with his toes. It gave a little in places, but was bone hard in others.

It was a body.

Chapter 8

The Wrong Corpse

Ewan raced out on deck, his first thought to wake Aunt Nellie, but there was the bridge wing looming overhead, and on it the dark form of the officer of the watch. It was James Gilmore, the second officer, his first cousin and Nellie's eldest son. Ewan blessed his luck – he and James had always got along. He hurried up the ladder.

James didn't question Ewan's report. He left the third officer to watch the bridge and got a hooded lantern from the wheelhouse. He moved quickly, but to Ewan it seemed he was strolling.

"You're sure it's Skovajsa?" James asked as they strode down the deck to the ladies' cabin.

"It has to be," Ewan said. "I followed him all the way from his cabin."

The light of the lantern proved him wrong: The dead man was Reverend Curmidge.

Ewan's heart raced again, this time with relief. Then he felt ashamed. He had no right to be happy when someone had died.

James set the lantern on the table. "Fetch the doctor, purser, and chief steward," he said.

"The captain, too?"

"Not yet. He'll be up soon enough. Let's make sure we have a full report."

Ewan woke Aunt Nellie first, then Doctor Gifford, snoring in his berth amidships on the cabin deck, and finally the chief steward, already stirring in his tiny cabin by the Glory Hole at the very stern in steerage. Voices were already muttering in the cramped steerage berths as they hurried back up to the ladies cabin. Ewan wondered how many minutes it would take for everyone on board to know.

Aunt Nellie was already there, and Doctor Gifford arrived a minute or two later. Gifford had been among the gamblers in the saloon, and he appeared to have kept on drinking. He rubbed his face, knelt shakily, and turned the body onto its back. Still shaking, he bent down to listen to Curmidge's heart.

"Well, there's no doubt he's dead," he muttered. He tried to close the corpse's mouth, but the jaw wouldn't stay shut. After three attempts, he gave up, heaved himself to his feet, and stepped away.

"Any idea how he died?" James Gilmore asked.

Doctor Gifford looked down at the body. "Heart attack?" he ventured.

Aunt Nellie took the lantern and knelt to inspect the dark Persian weave more closely. "There's blood here. See, it's still wet. And, there, the back of his head is soaked with it."

"Here's his hat!" Ewan scooped up the low topper from beneath one of the plush chairs. It was dented askew, and the brim at the back was torn.

"He must have fallen and hit the chair, then," Gifford said. "Too much to drink, a largish wave, and over he went."

"But why was he here in the ladies cabin?" Nellie wondered.

"Well, perhaps his wife forgot something and sent him up to find it," Gifford suggested. "Yes, that must be it." He pulled a large handkerchief from his coat pocket and mopped his brow.

Nellie swept the light of the lantern around the room. "I don't see anything, a bag or fan."

"She wasn't carrying a fan," Ewan said, "and she would have left her bag in the saloon if anywhere. She went right back to her cabin after supper."

"You have sharp eyes, Ewan, and a good memory," Aunt Nellie said, with an approving nod. "We'll ask her, but first we'll have to tell her. Chief, would you accompany me?"

"Of course," he replied.

"And Ewan," Aunt Nellie went on, "it'd be better if none of the passengers knew you were following Skovajsa, or the reverend for that matter."

"Following? Skovajsa?" the doctor asked.

"I'll explain later," Aunt Nellie said. "You stay here and make sure no one disturbs the body until we can shift it. Ewan, get back to your cabin ahead of Chief Morrison and me. Quietly."

Ewan went. She was right, of course, but it irked him. He felt left out, and no amount of seeing her side made it feel better.

The plan didn't work anyway. The crew all knew the details by the next watch, and it only confirmed their opinion that he was a Jonah. Ranald Morrison had a jab ready next time they crossed paths.

"Nice job on the reverend, Ewan Gilmore," he murmured. "Did you trip him or cosh him?"

Then he was gone up the passageway.

Ewan tried to ignore him and focus on who really had done the job. He didn't believe for a minute that Reverend Curmidge had tripped and banged his head hard enough to kill himself. He'd been steady as a tree when Ewan was following him. Besides, there wasn't a drop of blood on any of the chairs or the edge of the table above Curmidge's head. Ewan had checked. Then there was the hat. The more Ewan thought about it, the more likely it seemed that something hard had come down on it, to tear the brim like that. If Curmidge had fallen, the blow would have come upward.

But who would have had reason to kill Curmidge? The only one on board who'd shown any dislike had been his own wife. On the other hand, everyone had reason to dislike the professor, even to fear him. And from the back at least, the two men were almost twins.

The news of the reverend's death swept over the ship like a cold fog. Passengers who had barely just met drew together like neighbors and spoke in whispers, heads close. From each group, a man or couple went to the purser's office to ask how "poor Mrs. Curmidge" was doing and ferret out as many details as they could. Rumors went one way and then the next: heart attack, stroke, dead drunk, choked on a biscuit or a drink. One or two suggested robbery and murder. And in every group, at one time or another, the name Skovajsa was mentioned. After all, the two had dined together that very night.

To the passengers, the professor was as big a pariah as Ewan was to the crew. By the time Captain Morrison appeared in the saloon after breakfast to lead the Sunday service, table one was empty but for the Skovajsas, the MacLarens, Derek Reed, and Ewan. King's excuse was liquor; he was still snoring in his berth. And poor Mrs. Curmidge stayed in her cabin, sobbing loudly enough to be heard clearly throughout cabin class. Everyone at the table was quiet as a shy mouse, and the Professor and Tereza looked on the verge of tears. Ewan guessed it reminded them too much of Mrs. Skovajsová's death.

The captain didn't look pleased as he stepped to his place and opened his bible. After the call to worship and a hymn, still scowling, he recited pieces from the service for burial at sea.

"Behold, thou hast made my days as it were a span long, and mine age is even as nothing in respect of thee. A thousand years in God's sight are but as yesterday, past as a watch in the night. We shall not all sleep, but we shall all be changed, in a moment, in the twinkling of an eye. Then shall be brought to pass the saying that is written, Oh death, where is thy sting? Oh grave, where is thy victory? Thanks be to God, which giveth us the victory. Therefore be ye steadfast, always abounding in the work of the Lord. Amen."

The passengers echoed, "Amen."

Captain Morrison raised his head and glowered at them. He was a tall man, broad-shouldered, and full chested. His face was large and weathered, framed by a trim, white beard and mustache. He'd gone to sea as a boy, served in the Royal Navy, captained both sailing ships and paddlewheel steamers, and the years of experience showed in his stance. Ewan felt himself shrink under his gaze.

"We have lost one of our passengers, the Reverend Harold Arthur Curmidge. Last night, he tripped and fell and struck his head on the edge of a table, perhaps caught off balance by the roll of the ship. The ship's doctor has told me that the impact probably killed him instantly, but he was alone in any case, with no one to go for help."

He paused and swept his frown across the passengers, as if to make sure they got the point. "It could have happened to any one of us. God's eyes spend little time on the open sea, but his hand rests heavy here. Every crewman on this ship, from the barber and doctor to the chief engineer, first officer, and me, understands that well. Our single purpose is to cross this ocean safely and deliver you to the quay alive – all of you, regardless of your past or your reasons for traveling. We judge no one; that is God's duty. I, we, the Scots-American Line, would do nothing to imperil a single person on board. The sea has dangers enough, even on a calm night, as you all have now seen. Do not add the imaginings of rumor and gossip to the list." He let his frown make the point. "Let us pray together the Lord's Prayer."

Another hymn followed, then the benediction, and then, while Frasier piped a slow recessional from the top of the companionway, the captain retreated to the seclusion of the bridge. The Skovajsas quickly fled to their cabin. Meanwhile, the other passengers rejoined their clubs to whisper about what the short sermon had meant. To Ewan it was clear enough: Leave the professor alone.

Miss MacLaren, it seemed, felt the same way. "That was well said! Poor Mrs. Curmidge has anguish enough without the foolish suggestion that the reverend was drunk—or worse, that foul play was involved. Do you think she would welcome visitors?"

"I suspect it's a bit soon, Dear" Colonel MacLaren replied. "We hardly know her."

"But that's the problem," she stated; "she hardly knows anyone! She is alone in the middle of the ocean with no one to turn to for comfort. We have dined with her, and she and I spoke at great length in the ladies' cabin. We are the closest to friends that she has. What do you say, Mr. Gilmore? What is the custom on shipboard?"

"I've never been on board when a passenger died," Ewan said, ignoring the last, terrible minutes of the *Isle of Uist*, "but I've seen one injured. And, yes, some of the other passengers stepped up to lend a hand for the rest of the passage."

"There, Father, you see!" Daisy replied.

They were strolling forward along the passageway and she dropped her voice as they reached the door to the MacLaren's cabin. "Listen. She's quiet now. I do hope she's fallen asleep."

As if on cue, a faint sob reached them. Mrs. Curmidge was in cabin 14, just beyond the Skovajsas. It was one of the smaller cabins, but now Mrs. Curmidge was alone in there, and Ewan thought it must seem very empty. Her reaction surprised him, he had to admit. She seemed a hard, tight nut of a woman, a *crabbit,* hardly the sort to feel much grief for anything, let alone show it, even for her husband.

Miss MacClaren sighed. "It breaks your heart, doesn't it?"

"It does indeed," Derek said. "I suspect the reverend was all the good humor she had in the world. With that gone, she has lost her only reason to feel any joy at all."

Or maybe she enjoys feeling so bad, Ewan thought. *It gives her something important to complain about.*

Miss MacLaren flashed Derek a smile. "Such a generous thought, Mr. Reed. Perhaps you would like to join Father and me when we pay our condolences."

Derek grinned foolishly. "C-certainly," he stammered. "I-I would be delighted. That is, honored, if you see what I mean. Hardly delighted under the circumstances."

"We understand completely, Mr. Reed. We shall be her friends now, in her hour of need. No one should suffer the death of a loved one alone."

Her voice rang with determination, but the wind was blowing harder and the seas were rising. The ship lifted suddenly on a steeper wave, then teetered into the trough. She grabbed Ewan's arm, her smile falling as the deck fell beneath them. Ewan held her steady as the *Lewis* returned to a more even pace.

"All right now?" he asked, watching her face with concern. There was a hint of green in her cheeks.

She swallowed. "Yes, fine, thank you, Mr. Gilmore." She let go of his arm and smiled bravely. "Well, that was exciting, wasn't it."

Chapter 9

Wretched & Entranced

By mid day, the seas were even higher. At Daisy's urging, the Skovajsas had re-emerged from their cabin for the morning tea. Now she stood at the rail with Tereza, Reed, and Gilmore, watching the play of the waves that lifted the bow and foamed along the ship's side as it dipped through the trough into the next rising wave. It remained exciting at first. The freshening wind tugged at the ribbons on Daisy's small, well-tied hat. The sun flashed on schools of whitecaps as they surged from the peaking waves. The *Isle of Lewis* surged with them. Then it grew disconcerting – not in a frightening way, but down in the pit of her stomach. Each rise became a swoop, each dip a plummet, each surge a lurch. Her throat seemed too full. Her eyes found it hard to focus on things nearby.

When the ship's bell rang four times and Ewan said, "Two o'clock, dinner time," she had to swallow very hard to still a sudden surge in her innards. Her mid morning bite – no more than a cup of tea and a scone – had tried to make an exit.

"Are you all right, Miss MacLaren?" Gilmore asked. "You look a bit pale."

She waved a wand dismissively. "Oh, no, I'm fine. It's just a bit . . . brisk. Perhaps we should go inside."

But the minute she turned from the rail, her breakfast made another attempt. She turned back quickly and drew in a gulp of the cold wind. It settled her for a moment.

"Are you quite sure you're all right?" Reed asked. "You do look a bit green about the gills."

The description made Daisy square her jaw. She would *not* be seasick. "It's nothing, really," she insisted. "That last wave just caught me by surprise."

The next one surprised her again: swoop . . . plummet . . . lurch. Her stomach fell into the trough; her breakfast tried to stay at the peak. An icy sweat ran from every pore on her body.

"Excuse me," she gasped. "I think I'm about t—"

She threw up.

Over the rail at least, and the wind swept the mess sternward, leaving her clothing remarkably clean. Poor Reed, standing downwind, was not so lucky. The vomit blew through the open railing and spattered his trousers, as well as his shoes and the deck. Daisy was mortified.

"Oh, dear, I'm so sorr—" The rest of her breakfast took its leave.

Reed jumped back, barely escaping another spatter on his shoes.

"No worry! Missed me that time!" he exclaimed.

"I am terribly sorry," Daisy moaned. Her upbringing made her go through the motions of an apology, but she didn't really care. Her stomach refused to admit it was empty.

Tereza took her arm. "Come, Daisy. Come below and lie down."

Daisy didn't dare turn her head. The slightest movement made her guts clench. "No. I—" She swallowed again and again, warring with her innards. "I'd rather stay here a bit longer. You go. You shouldn't miss dinn—"

The very word made her retch bile. She wiped her mouth with her handkerchief.

Once more, she told herself. *Just once more and then you'll feel better. Go ahead, relax, let it all come out.*

She retched again on the next swoop, a dry heave that lasted throughout the plummet and lurch and well into another swoop. And she did feel better. A tiny bit. Perhaps.

"It'll be better if we move farther aft," Gilmore said. "You won't feel the motion so much amidships."

"Yes, come," Tereza insisted. "You'll feel better."

Daisy was sure she would never feel better again, but she let the three of them shepherd her along the rail till they were level with the funnel. One of the life boats loomed above them, jerking tightly in its falls each time the ship lifted and dipped. The motion was a little easier, Daisy admitted, but her gut didn't agree.

"Feeling better now?" Reed asked, looking worried as a hound.

Daisy nodded slightly. It was far better not to look at him, she discovered, or anyone else for that matter; just to stare at the distant horizon and move her head as little as possible. She gripped the rail with white hands. Tereza held her closely, and Daisy was grateful for the thin line of warmth on that side. "There must be something that will help," Reed whispered behind her back.

"Something warm to sip helps," Gilmore replied, adding faintly, "Sometimes."

"I'll fetch some tea," Reed said, and then repeated it more loudly to her.

Daisy tried to say no, don't bother, but he was already gone. She kept her eyes firmly fixed on the horizon, forcing them back into focus each time they threatened to notice the churning water.

This must be why they call it the Bounding Main, she thought miserably. She tried to think about something else, though she could hardly think at all through the fog of nausea, spray, and sunlight flashing on the confusion of whitecaps. She forced her thoughts to poor Mrs. Curmidge, who was surely feeling worse than this; but, no, nobody could be feeling worse than this.

Gilmore appeared beside her and draped a tartan

blanket over her shoulders. Tereza straightened it and made sure it was tight in Daisy's grip. Daisy nodded slightly, not daring to say even a thank-you. The weight of the wool was comforting, a little. She had purchased a heavy, waterproof Ulster topcoat for the trip, with a matching, flannel-lined cape to go with it, but the cape was down in her cabin. The Ulster should have been enough for such a sunny day. Who would have thought she could feel so cold? None of the travel books she'd read had warned that *le mal de mer* would freeze its sufferers from the inside out, not even Mrs. Ledoux's *Ocean Notes and Foreign Travel for Ladies*, where she had found the suggestion about the Ulster and cape. Nowhere had there been a mention of icy sweat! Daisy shivered violently.

"Are you ready to go below yet, Daisy?" Tereza asked.

Daisy shook her head once and the horizon swirled. "Maybe later," she managed.

"Everybody all right here?" It was a stranger's voice, a man.

Daisy made herself turn and smile, focusing carefully on the man so she wouldn't see any part of the swaying ship.

"Good morning, Mr. MacBreive," Gilmore was saying. "Just a touch of seasickness."

A touch? she thought. *I've been clubbed in the stomach!* Daisy kept smiling. She didn't dare open her mouth to speak. After an awkward moment, Gilmore jumped in.

"Miss MacLaren, Miss Skovajsová, this is Third Officer MacBreive."

MacBreive tipped his hat and gave Daisy a thin smile stretched wider by an equally thin, waxed mustache. "I'm sorry to see you under the weather, Miss. Hopefully, it'll pass quickly." His accent was American, clipped and a bit condescending. Daisy struggled to hold her smile. Her eyes kept trying to wander, and with them her mind.

"Some get over it in a day or less," he was saying. "If not, try a mustard plaster and oat cakes dipped in marmalade. The ship's doctor swears by them."

"I shall bear that in mind," she managed, almost gagging at the mention of food.

"Good. Make sure she has plenty at hand, Gilmore. Good day, ladies."

Another brisk tip of the hat and he was gone, shoes clicking on the deck. Daisy quickly turned back to the rail.

After a brief eon of misery, Reed reappeared, both hands filled with glasses and bowls.

"Well!" he exclaimed. "Any better yet? No? One of these should do it, I suppose. There was no lack of advice from the waiters and other passengers and all. I've brought up what seemed the most, well, promising."

"Usually, just a sip or two of warm water—" Gilmore tried to say, but Reed rushed on.

"This is flat beer. The fellow insisted no fizz at all; it pushes out too much, you see. And this is ginger water, guaranteed by a very nice lady on her third passage. And here are some dry biscuits to nibble on, with a bit of meat paste. And this is rosewater, from another lady; you're to sniff it. Oh, and here is a clean napkin, in case you need to wipe away . . . anything."

He pressed a bit of biscuit into her hand and urged her to try a tiny nibble.

Daisy loathed his friendly, cheerful, perfectly healthy face. She loathed them all, so concerned, so supportive, so smugly strong of stomach. It wasn't fair! But she let Reed give her the biscuit, let him convince her to take just a nibble, struggled to keep it down. And threw up on his shoes again.

&

Daisy stayed by the rail for over an hour. Then her father

appeared and tried to convince her to go below, out of the wind. She refused adamantly. The thought of being closed in, unable to see the horizon, brought her to the brink of another upheaval. Gilmore suggested she move back close to the funnel, which would not only shield her from the wind but was warmed by the smoke from the boilers.

"Yes," Tereza insisted. "It's also at the ship's center of balance, where the motion will be least."

Almost numb, Daisy gave in. Her father and Reed hurried below and returned with the two sea chairs Daisy had purchased for the trip, another good suggestion from Mrs. Ledoux's book. On the other hand, Mrs. Ledoux had stated clearly that seasickness was like a toothache: "hard to be borne but rarely fatal to life." Obviously, the woman had never suffered from it herself. Daisy was sure she was dying. She sank into a stupor in the lee of the warm funnel, huddled on her chair in the tartan blanket, peering blearily out at the broken horizon, which had the infuriating habit of disappearing, now up behind the lifeboat, now down below the rail. Her only consolation was the knowledge – confirmed by grim observation of others dashing to the rail – that she wasn't the only one laid low. Her mind conjured scenes of shipwreck, happy to sink the *Lewis* and maroon them all if she could only be rescued from this misery.

Her companions took turns keeping her company in the second chair while the others dined and warmed up in the saloon. As the sun sank toward the horizon behind the pitching stern, they all urged her again and again to go below and lie down. Suddenly, Mrs. Curmidge appeared, led by Tereza and Gilmore. She looked no different from the day before, except for a nearly invisible black ribbon pinned to the charcoal gray sleeve of her jacket. Grief had not softened her frown.

Daisy tried to rise but could only manage to sit up a

little straighter. She reached for Mrs. Curmidge's hand. "Oh, I am so sorry—" she began.

"You look sorry enough." Mrs. Curmidge sniffed. "Really, Miss MacLaren; suffering out in the cold and wind like a silly girl? Against all advice and your father's orders, I might add. *Hmph*! He spoils you, you know. I suppose it's to be expected, him trying to raise you . . . alone."

For just a moment, Mrs. Curmidge's grim resolve seemed to break, her eyes to glisten. She sniffed powerfully and the moment was gone. "A young lady needs a mother. Barring that, a proper chaperone." She glared at Tereza, Gilmore, and most particularly Derek Reed, who visibly shrank. "You're coming with me, down to your cabin, and no arguments. There's a chamber pot in the washstand if you need it, and plenty of stewards to haul out the mess. The Good Lord knows we paid enough for that service. Now, divest yourself of that woolen shroud and come along."

She held out her arm, and Daisy had no choice but to obey. Tereza rushed to help her up, while Gilmore and Reed hovered at the edges of her blurry vision, held at bay by Mrs. Curmidge's glower. Despite the renewed protests from her stomach, Daisy took comfort in the thought that Mrs. Curmidge had at least come out of her lonely cabin. It had taken Daisy to the Gates of Hell to do it, but she had found a way to help the poor widow back into the company of others. It was small comfort, but Daisy clung to it like a life ring.

Daisy was sure she would never be able to sleep, but she woke the next morning as if from a trance. The ship was still heaving, but she was not – until she stood up and a wave of nausea breached her defenses. Daisy cradled the chamber pot in her lap, taking deep breaths till the wave subsided. Then, very carefully, she scrubbed her face in hot water (*Bless these steam-heated ships!*) and dressed in her warmest clothing, including a front-laced bodice that she tied as loosely as propriety allowed.

Style to the Devil, she thought grimly. But she brushed her hair a full one hundred times to make up for it. It was an act of normalcy that help for a moment. With a final deep breath, she stepped resolutely to the cabin door and pulled it open.

Mrs. Curmidge was just outside, hand raised to knock. She looked Daisy up and down with a critical eye.

"It'll do," she said. "Better than I expected, to be honest. Certainly better than the other silly chits on board. Believe me, this will be *my* last voyage." She took Daisy's arm and led her to the saloon.

The smell of breakfast almost sent Daisy right back to her cabin, but Mrs. Curmidge's firm grip kept her moving toward her seat. Her father and the others were already there, even the count, who seemed sincerely chagrined by her state. But everyone of them had a half full plate in front of them, as though the world weren't turning topsy-turvy every other minute. The count rose, followed by her father and the other gentlemen.

"Sit down and leave her alone," Mrs. Curmidge growled. "She needs air, not useless chatter. Waiter! Dry toast, strong tea, and honey, and be quick about it!"

She sat Daisy beside her father and then shooed the professor down a seat and settled beside Daisy.

"You seem better, my dear," Father said.

"Yes, I'm sure you're looking much better, Miss MacLaren," Reed put in. "Why, yesterday, you looked like, well, death warmed over. There's more than a spot of color in your cheeks now. 'Be thou the rainbow in the storms of life. The evening beam that smiles the clouds away, and tints tomorrow with prophetic ray.' Byron, of course," he said, grinning widely.

"*Qui d'autre?*" the count murmured, a welcome note of humor.

Mrs. Curmidge humphed. "Stop blithering, you young fool, and let her eat. Go on, girl, swallow this honey and drink your tea." She spooned a blob of honey down Daisy's throat and pressed the teacup to her lips. "Build your strength. The battle isn't over yet."

The sweet honey didn't immediately try to claw its way back out. Daisy tried a sip of tea, which Mrs. Curmidge had sweetened to the point of syrup. It stayed down, too. She began to relax just a little. The problem was, the saloon was in the stern. Each rise rose farther; each dip lurched deeper. Mrs. Curmidge held out a piece of toast, and Daisy closed her eyes.

That turned out to be a very bad idea. She opened them quickly and tried to focus on the ceiling, but the large lamps hanging between the skylights swung alarmingly. She fixed her gaze on the piano.

Mr. King, sitting across the table, leaned forward to speak to her.

"I, too, have been seasick, Miss MacLaren" he said, "but I found there was a cure. Yes, despite the claims of doctors and seamen – skeptics all – I was able to be cured. What's more, I have learned the technique." He sat back and glanced at the others around them. "It's true; as you can see I am unaffected by the ship's motion."

"*En ce cas*, you must not keep us in such suspense, *Monsieur* King," the count said dryly. "What is this *merveilleux* cure, this secret the rest of the world denies?"

"Mesmerism, quite simply," King replied, "and it is no secret, it is only denied by those who scoff at that which they do not understand."

"Mesmerism! Surely you can't be serious, King!" Professor Skovajsa exclaimed. "You, who have studied the principles of engineering? Who have flown in an airship?"

"For those very reasons, my dear professor," King replied. "I value knowledge. I value the exploration of the unknown. I use the tools that modern science offers us."

The professor grew red in the face. "Science? Mesmerism is not science!"

"Call it hypnotism then, if you must, but do not discount it simply because its mechanism is not fully understood. Who understands completely what keeps an airship aloft and allows it to move across the wind? Does that prevent one from flying in it? What do you say, Mr. Count? Did you understand flight when you set out to catch this ship? Did you need to?"

"*Non*, I understood only that it worked, that is true enough."

"*Voilà!*" King replied, with a flourish of his hand. "So it is with mesmerism, which Mesmer himself likened to magnetism. Perhaps it modulates the ebb and flow of tidal forces in the brain – brain waves, as it were. Perhaps it stimulates the body's own powers of healing by bending the very aether, by which thoughts are conducted in the mind. We don't know. But we who have used it and benefited from it, we know it works!"

The professor had gone white. "The aether, sir?" he grated. "You know nothing about the aether. Mesmer knew nothing about the aether! He was mistaken, misguided, and . . . and . . . *hlupák!* An idiot!"

"Please, gentlemen," Daisy moaned. Her stomach was twitching with each word.

The professor drew up short, then gave her a quick bow. "Forgive me. I forget myself."

He strode out, fuming. Tereza sat frozen, stunned.

"Should we . . . ?" Gilmore began.

"No," Tereza whispered. "I'll go." And she, too, hurried out.

Gilmore stared after her.

"*Alors quo*, do not just sit there, young man," the count remarked. "Go to her aid."

Ewan nodded and left.

It was all too much for Daisy. "If you'll excuse me," she managed, then fled as fast as she could, out of her swiveling chair, out of the saloon, up the stairs, and across the deck to the rail, where she hung desperately, wondering how so little toast could cause so much agony.

Mrs. Curmidge appeared beside her soon after, herding Reed and her father along with the sea chairs, the blankets, and Daisy's encompassing Ulster and cape. She pried Daisy from the railing and established her once again in a wool cocoon in the lee of the funnel. A few other green-gilled sufferers were already gathered there, huddled beneath the tall air scoops that ventilated the boiler room directly beneath them. Mrs. Curmidge chivvied them to the other side of the ship. Daisy was happy not to have to share her misery. Each time one of the others lurched to the rail, her own stomach was all too eager to follow. Then she felt ashamed for her selfishness. And then the wind picked up again, the ship's lurching gavotte became cruelly deliberate, and she no longer cared.

Her father and Reed stayed with her for a while but eventually succumbed to the chill and went below. Mrs. Curmidge, wrapped in her own blanket in the other sea chair, stayed resolutely beside her. The count came by to express his condolences but had the sense not to burden Daisy with conversation. A few kinds words and he took his leave.

Moments or hours later, Mr. King arrived.

"Still under the weather, Miss MacLaren? Yes, clearly. No need to say a word; I can see that the sea still has you in its grip. I took the liberty of asking First Officer MacKay when he thought these heavy seas might abate, but his report was none too helpful. He did say he'd seen worse, so I suppose we can thank God for small favors, begging your pardon, Mrs. Curmidge. No disrespect of the good Lord intended."

She sniffed. "None taken, Mr. King. Thank you for your kind words, or did you have something more to say?"

King was not so easily brushed off. "As a matter of fact, I did. Miss MacLaren, I meant every word that I said this morning in the saloon. I used to suffer from seasickness as violent as that from which you suffer now. Mesmerism – hypnotism, call it what you will – was my tonic and my cure. Since then, I have provided relief to many other fellow sufferers. Your nausea – harsh, cruel, and wretched as it may be – is but a symptom of a disturbance in your mind brought on by a dis-balance, as it were, between the motion perceived by your internal magnetometer and that felt by your limbs, organs, and eyes. Your mental gimbals cannot adjust quickly enough to the mad heaving of the sea, which causes the ebb and flow of animal magnetism surrounding your own physical geology, as it were, to slosh and swirl like eddies in a tidal pool."

Daisy swallowed hard.

"Get to the point, man," Mrs. Curmidge growled, "or let the poor girl rest!"

"Or course. Forgive me." King bowed. "Let me treat you. Mesmerize you, that is. If nothing else, it will bring you an interlude of relief and calm. If your mind is open to the full power of the Mesmer technique, that interlude will be lifelong. I assure you, the process is completely harmless and painless and will not make you worse. I guarantee it."

"Good Heavens!" Mrs. Curmidge exclaimed. "You can't seriously expect—"

"Yes!" Daisy gasped, gripping Mrs. Curmidge's arm to silence her protest. "Yes, Mr. King. I will be happy to give it a try. At this point, the only other option would be be to fling myself into the sea."

"Now, dear girl, are you quite sure? You hardly know this . . . this mountebank." Mrs. Curmidge glowered at King with enough force to cow a bear. He regrouped and forged on.

Drawing himself up to his full height, which was not all that tall, he proclaimed, "My dear ladies, I will overlook the implied insult and merely say that I have treated governors and congressmen, actors and businessmen, rich and poor alike from New York to Berlin, Ontario to Oregon and the capitol cities of all thirty-eight states."

Mrs. Curmidge sniffed. "Well, so you say. But I will leave it up to Miss MacLaren. She is of age, and it is, after all, her stomach. But if something should go amiss, Mr. King, you will answer to me first."

He bowed. "It would only be just."

"Yes," Daisy said. "Please. As quickly as you can."

"Very well. Good." King drew out a large handkerchief and mopped his brow. Then, resettling his hat firmly against the wind, he produced from the same pocket a small wand, about the size of a soup spoon, though with a straight handle and a flat, round tip. A lavender starburst was printed on the tip. Bending over Daisy, he held the wand up a little ways before her face and gently tipped it right and left, right and left, studying her eyes.

"Good," he murmured again. "Excuse me, Mrs. Curmidge. If I may sit?" He indicated the empty space at the end of her sea chair. Her short legs left ample room for even King's well-padded rump.

She sniffed. "If you must."

"It will help, thank you." King sat and again held up the wand. "Now, Miss MacLaren, if you would be so kind as to watch the star?"

Daisy took a deep breath and focused on the lavender

starburst. King held it very still and began to speak in a low, soothing voice. He was a baritone, Daisy noted, with just a bit of a husky note. He probably sang well, she thought. Then she shooed away the distraction and tried to listen to his words, telling her to relax, to breathe evenly, to listen only to his voice—that was easy enough— to relax, be calm, feel the world grow steady around her, to be deeply relaxed, a heavy relaxation, peaceful in a way that settles all fears, nothing can harm her, nothing can upset the calm; droning on like that, encouraging her to relax, let go, feel calm and trust in the world, and so on, all one soft, droning, baritone flow of words while the starburst grew to fill her mind even after her eyes closed of their own accord and she sank into the warm, woolen cocoon of King's voice.

He told her she was a wonderful subject and had nothing to fear but everything to gain. He told her she felt wonderful and strong and healthy and was loving her voyage, so happy to be at sea, on the brisk and charming sea where everyone was so interesting and helpful like Mrs. Curmidge and he, King, who would bring her nothing but comfort and well being, she could trust them both completely and her stomach would stay easy and calm, free of any hint of unease or upset and she could rest comfortably with them. And Mrs. Curmidge, too, could trust him completely, he would serve her just as well as he would Daisy. Both of them could relax and rest in his presence and then when he said a special phrase they would feel so grateful they would do as he asked. Miss MacLaren, you first, Mrs. Curmidge, rest now. Miss MacLaren, when you hear me say Whippoorwill Station you will be sick again and fall to your knees. Do you understand? Whippoorwill Station will make you sick and you will fall to your knees. Nod twice if you understand.

Daisy nodded twice. Why not? He was such a helpful

man.

Thank you. Rest now. Rest. While I speak to Mrs. Curmidge. Yes, your turn now, Mrs. Curmidge. When you hear me say Rochester Falls you will hand me whatever you are holding. When I say Rochester Falls. Do you understand? Nod twice if you do. Thank you.

Now I will count to five. And when I reach four, you Daisy, and you Mrs. Curmidge, will forget everything you just heard until I say the words I just told each of you. Nod if you understand. Good. And when I say five, you will wake up, calm, relaxed, completely healthy and at peace with the sea.

One, you are feeling calm, relaxed, and trusting.

Two, your mind is balanced; your stomach is settled and soothed.

Three, you can't wait to enjoy the rest of the voyage.

Four—

Chapter 10

The Mal-de-Mer Device

Tereza hurried after her father. She hiked her skirts as high as she could in the narrow passageway, but he was almost running.

"Father, please!" she called. He ignored her and charged into the saloon, almost bowling over a startled waiter by the bar. She caught up to him only because he jerked to a stop, staring blankly at the almost empty tables.

The passengers still remaining looked up, startled from their card games, books, and quiet conversations. The waiters paused, trays and towels still. They all stared back.

And no wonder, she thought, embarrassed and angry. *He looks ridiculous!*

Instead of his usual top hat, her father was wearing an apparatus, a helmet-like frame ringed with spiraling wires on knobs of ceramic and brass. A heavy cord ran down from its crown to a bulky black box cradled in his arms. And if that weren't enough to draw stares, he had covered his jacket with his canvas work apron, its many pockets bulging with half-seen tools, calipers, voltmeters, and other objects Tereza was sure the other passengers couldn't even guess at. More than ridiculous; with that dazed glare on his face, he looked alarming.

He turned to her abruptly. "They must be on deck," he snapped. "Yes, Miss MacLaren would have gone up for the air."

Before she could react, he charged back out to the stairs.

Tereza stifled another cry and ran after him.

Mostly she was anxious. When she'd followed him back to their cabin, she'd found him hauling his portmanteau off the lower berth on his side. He yanked at it so angrily that he almost fell backward when the ship heeled into the next wave. The case slipped easily over the edge and thudded onto the floor.

"Are you all right?" she asked. "What are you doing?"

He muttered something unintelligible, stood the case on end, and began undoing the latches and buckles.

"Really, Father, what can you need so desperately?"

"You will see," he said curtly. "They all will. Mesmerism! Did you hear him? And the others? Not a one of them took him to task for his absurd claims."

He swung the halves of the portmanteau wide and bent to pull out the bottom drawer on the right. There, under a rag of toweling, was the apparatus. He lifted out the headpiece and held it up as high as the cord would allow.

"This," he announced, "this will show them."

Tereza recoiled as if it might explode at any moment. The reaction came without thought, in a rush of fear. Her heart raced. An image of the Bell Cannon, humming with unbridled energy, flashed before her. Her ears rang.

She squeezed her eyes shut and shook her head, forcing the vision away. She took a slow, deliberate breath. The ringing faded. Her heart calmed a little.

"Show them what?" she asked. "That you're the madman they think you are?"

Now he recoiled.

"You, too?" he demanded. "You think that, that *horská banka*, mountebank, charlatan can cure seasickness with some hocus-pocus like Mesmerism?"

"And that will?" she snapped.

"Yes! Because it is based on science, on physics and

anatomy, not on myth and magic." He began to lecture her. "Properly installed on the head, it induces a calming sine-wave-like flow in the aetheric wave patterns in the frontal lobes and the opposing regions in the cerebellum. It soothes the mind and thus the functioning of the upper and lower gut. I designed it specifically to treat sea-sickness."

He stopped. He stared at the headpiece, its quivering wires and shining knobs. Tears started in his eyes.

"I . . . Your mother," he said quietly. "She had a very hard time when we came to America. Seasick the entire crossing. The idea came to me then, fully formed. I knew it would work. I knew how to make it work. But I had no tools, no materials on that ship. I made a start as soon as we were settled, but the other work, the . . . Well, you know how it was, how busy I was, how the Army and the Senators kept after me."

He ran his hand across his eyes, wiping the tears aside. Tereza blinked hard to keep her own eyes clear. She did know.

"But you finished it," she said.

"Yes, I finished it. Last week." He looked right at her. "For you. In case you were like her, but you . . . You took after me in more ways than one, it appears." He shrugged. "Now there is Miss MacLaren. And why not? She is suffering." The words were kind, but there was a note of petulance in his voice.

"So this is for her? To help Daisy? Not to show up Mr. King?"

"Well." He tried to smile. "Two birds with one stone?"

Tereza could not smile back. She couldn't ignore the word he'd left out. "Have you tested it?" she asked. "When? And where was I? You should—"

"Of course I tested it!" he growled.

Her anxiety grew. "On what? On whom? After what

happened last time—"

"What happened last time? You dare lecture *me* about that? I'm the one who can't remember, and all anyone can tell me is that people died. Not how, not why. Do you realize how that eats at me?"

She did, but she didn't want to remember, a fact he refused to recognize.

"And that is why I made sure to test it!" he seethed, voice rising. "In the cellar, away from everyone else! While you were sleeping!" Finally he paused, breathing heavily. When he resumed, he seemed more in control. "I assure you, this apparatus, with this power supply, could not possibly affect anyone farther than a handspan away."

"How do you know that for sure?"

"Because nothing happened! Tereza, please. Look at it." He held it out to her. "It is not the Bell Cannon."

And it wasn't, but now she could clearly see the small resonators at the top of each knob. The tiny, knurled tuning bolts at the center of each cupped disk. Someone's brain would sit in the very center of its effect.

"When did you last tune it?" she asked quietly.

"When I tested it, of course."

Tereza remembered clearly the last time she tuned the Bell Cannon. "Could we tune it again now, please?" she asked.

"Fine!" He thrust the apparatus into her hands and pulled his work apron from among his clothes hanging in the other half of the portmanteau. "You are are making far too much of this," he complained, donning the apron. "Look at it. Heft it. You can see and feel how sturdy it is. And you can be sure I tuned it as carefully as I have ever tuned any device."

"Yes, but . . ." Her heart was racing again.

"But what?"

But he had finished the tuning of the Bell Cannon that

last time. Was it her half of the bell that had been out of tune? Or his?

"Oh, for Heaven's sake, I'll show you!"

He sat on the berth, took back the headpiece, and settled it in place carefully, so the criss-cross framing was centered directly above his nose. An extension of the central arch protruded downward between his eyes, making it look even more like an outlandish Viking helmet. Then he lifted the battery onto his lap and checked the connections at either end of the cable.

"So," he said. "All I need to do next is turn it on."

He put his hand on a switch on top of the battery.

Tereza slapped her hand down on his.

"Father!" She sat beside him, keeping a firm grip on his hand. She tried to sound calm, sure of herself, but she couldn't keep her voice from trembling. "Wait, please. I just want to be sure."

"*Sakra!*" He pried her hand off and stood, fumbling with the battery to keep it from falling. "This is not like last time! Whatever happened then! Did you not even listen? I tested it. On me. It is fine!"

Without another word, he turned on his heel and charged out the door, slamming it shut behind him.

Teresa sat still an instant, stunned. Then, echoing his curse, she bolted after him.

Ewan Gilmore had been standing outside, halfway between his cabin and theirs.

"What's happened?" he'd asked. "What's that thing he's wearing?"

Tereza had wasted a few moments trying to phrase an answer that would make any kind of sense, then just shook her head and ran after her father.

Ewan followed them as fast as he could without actually

running, dodging a steward laden with a chamber pot, then stuck behind a pair of dawdling passengers. He arrived at the saloon just as the professor came back out and turned up the companionway, taking the stairs two at a time. Tereza was right behind him. The look she gave him was just the same: a mix of anger, frustration, and fear. This time, she didn't even try to speak. She raced up the stairs after the professor. Ewan followed, with the colonel, the count, and a chattering knot of curious passengers right behind him. He could hear them wondering at the professor's odd appearance as they clattered up the steps. More than odd, Ewan had to admit. The wired headpiece was enough to make any sane person worry.

The professor slowed down when he stepped out onto the deck, marching forward like the engineer general of an untrained gentry army who had only signed up for the show. The wind rattled the wires on the helmet, but he didn't seem to notice. He strode to the shelter between the engine room ventilators and the funnel, where Daisy MacLaren and Mrs. Curmidge were stretched out on their sea chairs. King was just rising from a seat on the end of Mrs. Curmidge's chair. Ewan studied Miss MacLaren's face, wondering how her wave-tossed stomach would handle this new excitement. She stretched and rubbed her eyes, as if she had just woken up. Mrs. Curmidge was doing the same, and to Ewan's complete surprise, both were smiling. On Daisy MacLaren, the expression was lovely, but Mrs. Curmidge looked like a shark closing in for the kill.

Tereza had gone straight to her father first, but now she went to Miss MacLaren's side and knelt. "Oh, Daisy. Are you feeling better? You look it." The passengers from the saloon moved closer, an intent half moon of curious faces loving every minute of the show.

"Why, yes," she replied, sounding as if she had only just realized it. "I feel much better!"

"That's wonderful!" Tereza exclaimed. She looked back at her father, smiling with obvious relief. "Did you hear that? She's better!"

"You say better?" the professor asked. "How is that?" Tereza's smile faded back into worry.

"Well, I . . ." Miss MacLaren glanced up at her father, who had moved to her other side, gave him a bright smile, and took a deep breath. "I can't say I feel perfect, but my stomach seems to have come to its senses and relearned its proper place in my anatomy." She laughed. "You see: I can even joke about it! I do feel a bit dizzy still, but even that is greatly lessened." She turned her smile on King. "Thank you, sir! I don't remember exactly what you did, but it seems to have worked. Do you see, Mrs. Curmidge? I can carry on a real conversation. You must tell me what Mr. King did and said to bring about this miracle!"

Mrs. Curmidge shed her sharky smile and regained her frown. "I am not sure exactly what transpired," she said, eying King suspiciously. "I must admit to feeling a bit . . . different myself."

"Why, you must have been mesmerized, too!" Miss MacLaren exclaimed.

"Mesmerized?" the professor echoed. "You let this humbug attempt to mesmerize you?"

"Not 'attempt,' Professor Skovajsa," Miss MacLaren said. "He did mesmerize me, and Mrs. Curmidge, too, it would seem."

"And you feel better?" The professor was dumbstruck.

"At the moment, yes," Miss MacLaren replied, "much better."

"But that's— You're sure?"

"Father," Tereza warned, still kneeling at Miss MacLaren's side.

"Yes, I'm sure," Miss MacLaren replied. "Mr. King's actions have worked. He is no humbug."

King raised his hands in a gesture of humility, though he looked as smug as a cat with cream. "You are too kind, Miss MacLaren," he said, "and I must warn you that the first treatment is sometimes only temporary."

"If so, it will have been worth the respite, and I shall know who to come to for a second treatment, and a third and fourth, if need be. I cannot tell you how grateful I am!"

"Oh, well." King shrugged with false modesty.

Mrs. Curmidge sniffed. "Yes, all well and good, sir, but Professor Skovajsa, whatever is that outlandish contrivance on your head?"

The professor glanced upward, frowning. "This, yes. It looks rather awkward, I admit, but I assure you it is quite comfortable. Even the power supply is not nearly as heavy as it might appear." He hefted the black box in his arms, which only made it seem heavier.

"But what *is* it, man? Some sort of hair curler? A cure for baldness?"

"Nothing so foolish!" he snapped. "This apparatus, my dear lady, could be a boon to every traveler at sea. It is a cure for seasickness."

Everyone gawped. Ewan saw his own skepticism reflected in the faces surrounding them. Only Miss MacLaren seemed pleased.

"My dear Professor Skovajsa," she exclaimed. "You made this . . . apparatus for me?"

"Well, I began the work for Tereza, actually," he admitted. "Her mother, you see . . ." He stumbled to halt, swallowed hard, and started over. "I worried that Tereza would develop the condition, yes. Happily, it has turned out otherwise. You, however, have not been so lucky. Nor have many others here on board. I thought to keep it a secret. I am aware that many people do not welcome new discoveries; that I travel under something of a cloud. Nonetheless, I could not sit still and watch you suffer."

"*Hmph.* Nor could you let Mr. King's challenge go unanswered, I warrant." Mrs. Curmidge fixed him with her beady glare. "Well, you lost that race. What do you plan to do with your *mal-de-mer* cap now? Find another poor soul for your experiment?"

The professor met her glare with his. "Madam, your implication is insulting."

Mrs. Curmidge waved a hand. "Oh, keep your hat on, Professor, or whatever it is. You misunderstand me, as usual. I would volunteer myself, were I so unlucky as Miss MacLaren here. The fact is, you need a poor *seasick* soul to determine if this ridiculous-looking apparatus of yours works. You can wear it all you like, but you weren't stricken to begin with. You need a sick subject, am I not right?"

The professor sketched a small bow, rattling the wires on his helmet. "Forgive me, madam. You are correct." He turned to the other passengers, quickly spotting the seasick ones who had crept around the funnel to see what was going on. Some began to creep back the other way.

"I am not fully recovered," Miss MacLaren declared. "Better, yes, but my head still swirls a little with each wave and my legs remain quite shaky." She swept the blankets aside and sat upright on the edge of her sea chair. "Please, let me be your subject, professor."

"Daisy, I don't think that would be wise," Colonel MacLaren said quickly.

"But I do, Father," Miss MacLaren replied firmly. "Professor Skovajsa needs a subject who suffers from seasickness, and I'm sure his apparatus is completely safe."

"Exactly. That's what I meant," the colonel said, flushing. "But you are no longer a proper subject. The professor needs someone who has *never* been treated by Mr. King. Otherwise, he couldn't prove which treatment did the trick."

"I'm afraid the colonel is correct," the professor said. "Whatever the true cause of your daughter's current symptomatic reprise, we cannot let it compromise the action of my apparatus."

The colonel looked very relieved; Miss MacLaren looked miffed.

"Who will volunteer, then?" she asked. She stood, supporting herself with both hands on the raised back of her sea chair, and scanned the circle of faces, smiling. "Who needs relief from the terrible, uncontrollable misery that I know some of you are suffering?"

No one replied.

"Actually, I'm feeling a little loose, uh, shaky myself," Derek offered.

"No, no," Miss MacLaren said. "It must be someone truly ill. They will prove unconditionally that the professor's apparatus works. And they deserve the relief, believe me!"

"Seems to me they want Mr. King's treatment," one of the gentlemen muttered, "not a shot at boiling their brains."

Ewan thought it might be the same man who had muttered *get rid of him* at supper on the first night.

The professor's jaw clenched. "It does not create heat. It uses tuned aetheric resonance to modulate the brain's own waves, thereby settling the body's humors, which calms the centers of balance and vertiginous proprioception, which in turn calms the stomach."

"Well, that's certainly clear," someone else muttered.

The professor's face reddened. "I will show you," he declared. "I am not ill; thus, it will have no effect on me whatsoever. You will see it is perfectly safe!"

He reached for a switch on top of the black box. Everyone stepped back. The people at the rear ducked around the funnel. Ewan stepped between the professor and Tereza.

She pushed him aside. "Father, wait!" she cried. "Let me check the tuning. Please."

The professor's hand paused on the switch.

"I've already tuned it, my dear," he said. "I've told you that."

"Let me check it again," she begged, voice rising. "Please. *Please!*"

"Tereza, please, stop acting like—"

"Father, I am not a child!" Her face flashed from anguished to angry and back. "Listen to me – please. You must let me check the tuning. This time you must!"

The professor's face went blank. Eyes fixed on Tereza, he drew a long breath. "Very well. If it will calm you down. Excuse me, gentlemen, ladies. We will return shortly."

He turned and strode up the deck, pausing only a moment to be sure that she was going with him. The circle of passengers parted quickly to let them through.

"Well, that was a close shave," the sarcastic gentlemen remarked.

"You don't really believe . . . ?" someone else began, but Ewan didn't wait to hear the rest of their snide chatter. He hurried after Tereza.

Aunt Nellie stepped from the shadow of the deckhouse and stopped him. "Could I speak to you for a moment, Mr. Gilmore?" she asked, nodding politely to one of the passengers who happened to be standing nearby.

Ewan watched Tereza's back disappear into the companionway. "Yes, Aun— Purser," he replied.

"Come along to my office, out of the weather. I have some documents to show you."

Aunt Nellie led him to her office, closed and latched the door behind them, and sat behind her small desk, motioning him to the hard chair against the opposite bulkhead.

"Now, what was that all about?"

He told her as much as he knew.

"He was ready to try that *doolally* thing on one of our passengers," she remarked. "Would you have let him?"

"I . . . Well, I don't know," Ewan admitted. "Tere—Miss Skovajsová sure didn't like the idea."

"No, the lass didn't, did she." Aunt Nellie leaned her chin on the tips of her steepled fingers. "That worries me, too, but I'm more worried now that you might have let one of our passengers put on that witch's hat and try it out."

"Even the professor? On himself?" he countered.

"What happened the last time he tried out one of his fancies?"

"That was a weapon of some kind," Ewan protested.

Aunt Nellie sighed. "True enough. We're adrift twixt a rock and a hard place, Ewan. The man meant no harm and was certain enough about it to be willing to test the thing on himself. But he's not acting normal, either. And you heard the lass as well as I did; better, more like. '*This time* you must.' Remember, no one knows what happened when things went wrong the last time, not even him. A lot of people died then, but he can't remember how or why. I think maybe the lassie can. Do you think you can find out?"

Ewan hesitated, remembering Tereza's changing moods whenever her mother came up or a bell caught her off guard. He didn't want to be the one to make her look that way. But this was for the ship. "I'll try," he said.

"Good. It would make me feel a lot better to know. Go then."

"Wait," Ewan said. "About the reverend, do you think the doctor's right? That he just fell and hit his head?"

"What do you think?" Aunt Nellie asked.

"I don't buy it," Ewan replied, and told her why.

Aunt Nellie heard him out, then studied his face for a minute. "You truly think someone on board was trying to kill the professor?"

"I do," he said.

"Who?"

Ewan shrugged. "I'm not sure, but there's one fellow who keeps making comments."

Aunt Nellie nodded. "George Baskins. I heard him at supper the first night and again just now." She shook her head. "He's a regular, goes east every fall with a sewing machine or two, comes back with orders, ships them with us, too. He booked his ticket in June, long before anyone knew the professor would even wake up."

"That's just it," Ewan said. "He's found himself on board and he's afraid. Or maybe he knew someone who died in the accident."

"Could be," Aunt Nellie replied, "but Baskins has always shown a sharp tongue and little action. We'll keep on eye on him, but don't let him distract you from everyone else. And don't let Miss Skovajsa distract you either."

"Skovajsová," Ewan corrected. "It's how they say it for wives and daughters."

"Just what I mean," Aunt Nellie warned. "A distraction. You're to watch over the professor. Don't keep your eyes glued so tightly to the daughter. It's not likely you'll ever see her again after we dock."

All the more reason to look as much as I can now, Ewan thought, but he kept mum.

"I got you this job to keep the professor safe," Aunt Nellie reminded him. "Stick by him, not by his lass. Keep your eyes open, and while you're at it, be ready to stop him just as quickly as you'd stop someone coming after him. D'you ken what I say?"

"Yes, Ma'am."

Ewan hurried below to wait outside the Skovajsa's cabin. Angry voices, hushed but obvious, carried through the cabin door as he arrived. It swung open and out came Tereza, wearing the helmet, battery clutched in her thin hands.

"I will not permit it!" the professor exclaimed from within. He hurried out on her heels and grabbed her arm.

"I tuned it and *I* will test it!" Tereza snapped. And before he could stop her, she flipped the switch.

Ewan jumped toward her, reaching for her hand, but it was too late. The wires on the helmet bounced and vibrated, humming like a chorus of harmonious bees.

That was it. Ewan watched, frozen, as Tereza's eyes looked up and sideways, right and left, as though she were trying to peer inside her own skull to see if her brain was starting to boil. Apparently it wasn't. She let out a sigh of relief. So did he.

"I feel nothing," she said.

"Nothing?" her father demanded. His face was as worried as hers had been on deck.

"Vibration. A faint . . . rather pleasant . . . singing, in a way. But . . ." She shook her head slowly. Then, suddenly, she seemed to notice Ewan. Her eyes went down to his hand, on hers, on the switch. She blushed. "No, nothing."

Ewan jerked his hand away, blushing himself.

Her eyes rose to meet his, sparkling. "You see, there was no need to worry once I had checked the tuning," she said.

"Yes, of course," her father replied, "but now I insist you give me the headpiece so I can take it up on deck and find a seasick subject."

She did, and the three of them went back up together. But there was no one on deck except a few perfectly well stalwarts striding briskly back and forth, taking the air. Puzzled, the professor led them down to the saloon, where they found the entire complement, including both MacLarens, crowded around the stern settees, watching avidly as King hypnotized a trio of seasick passengers. The others, still pale as death, with chamber pots ready before them but hope brimming in their eyes, waited stoically at tables three and four for their turns.

A few people noticed the professor and nudged their companions, sending a ripple of glances their way. There were whispers, instantly shushed. King's performance was too entrancing. The professor and his apparatus had been reduced to an oddity.

He turned stiffly and left.

Ewan started to follow.

"Don't," Tereza said. "He'll want to be alone."

"He won't try something else, will he?" Ewan asked.

"He'll just sulk." She sounded relieved. "Really, it's better this way."

Mrs. Curmidge shushed them, frowning.

"I'll just see him safely back to your cabin," Ewan whispered, and left her to stick to his duty.

Chapter 11

Suspects & Stowaways

Early the next morning, a sharp knock on the cabin door brought Ewan struggling out of a deep sleep. It was Ranald Morrison, sneering down his long nose.

"Look quick, Gilmore. Your charge just pulled a polka up the companionway with his skinny lassie." He turned and stalked away before Ewan could dredge up a suitable retort.

That's twice, you bampot, Ewan fumed.

A dozen replies popped into his mind as he struggled into his clothes, trying not to wake Derek and King, both still snoring in their berths. Still irked, he made a quick dash to the head, then hurried on deck, face damp, trying to scrub his hair down into a part. At the top of the companionway, he gave up and jammed the derby down to hold it in place.

He found Tereza and the professor at the starboard rail, as far forward as the mate would allow, watching the sun peel itself free of the horizon. As Ewan walked up, Tereza turned slightly, gave him a rapt smile, then returned her gaze to the dawn.

"Beautiful, isn't it?" the professor remarked.

"Yes, sir," Ewan replied, staring at Tereza's profile.

"The simple mechanics of dawn put mankind's most celebrated art to shame," the professor went on, his nose apparently back in joint.

Ewan squinted against the glare and realized the professor was right: The sunrise was truly beautiful, and he'd seen more than a few good ones standing the morning watch as a deckhand. The sky was remarkably clear, with just a single line of cloud etched across the face of the sun. From a burnished gold glare directly ahead on the horizon, the sky melded through deepening shades across the arc of the sky, from tarnished gray above to pure black astern, where fading stars still showed.

Up in the eyes of the bow, Frasier's bagpipes began to skirl the morning's tune, an old, slow march. The wind picked up a little, as if to join in, and Ewan realized how much the seas had abated during the night. The *Isle of Lewis* rose smoothly on the swells, sliced through the peaks, dipped gently into the troughs, as though dancing. Tereza shivered, and the professor put his arm around her shoulders. Ewan, standing a polite two steps away on her other side, envied him.

She's not that skinny, he thought. *Ranald Morrison's just an erse!* Then he remembered Aunt Nellie's warning and tried not to be distracted.

The tune ended, the pipes droned away to silence. The wind and the wake resumed their own gentle song, with the constant thrum of the engine setting the pace.

Six more days, Ewan thought, and he hoped they'd all be as quiet as this.

They went down to join the gathering at breakfast and found the MacLarens already there, with Mrs. Curmidge. Derek was absent, probably still asleep. King was missing, too, and Ewan hoped he'd sleep right through the meal. Dinner the night before had been strained, and the professor had left before dessert, taking Tereza with him. King, on the other hand, had expounded happily on any and every topic. He'd bustled into the cabin well on toward morning, reeking of cigars and whiskey, and had hummed the entire time he got ready for bed, pausing only to chuckle now and then. Best to let him sleep it off so the professor could enjoy breakfast.

It was becoming Ewan's favorite meal: platters of eggs, kippers, bacon, potatoes, beets, fruit, and duff. Ewan had two helpings of everything and three of the duff.

Mrs. Curmidge sniffed as he filled his plate the third time. "The way this young man eats we'll run out of plums before dinner." Then she sighed. "The reverend did love his plum duff."

"It is the little memories that catch us by surprise," the professor said. He gestured toward the platter of fruit. "Eliška, my wife, was very fond of peaches at breakfast. Do you remember, Tereza?" She nodded. "Now I can't smell one without being reminded."

The professor's eyes gleamed with tears. He quickly dabbed the corners with his napkin under the pretense of wiping his mouth. There was a moment of awkward silence.

"My mother loved chocolate at breakfast," Miss MacLaren said.

"I'm surprised you remember, dear," her father said. "You were so young when she passed away."

"I do remember that, Father. With cream, whipped into a froth." Miss MacLaren smiled. "Every cup of chocolate gives me greater pleasure for it. I'm sure peaches will come to do the same for you, Professor. And you, Mrs. Curmidge; plum duff will always make you smile."

Ewan doubted that. In fact, he wondered just how broken up Mrs. Curmidge actually was. The professor's tears had been genuine, and Tereza's face had gone pale at her father's words. Even the colonel's eyes had softened when Miss MacLaren mentioned chocolate. Mrs. Curmidge merely eased up a little on her frown. And when Miss MacLaren suggested they all go on deck to take advantage of the sunny day, Mrs. Curmidge's frown returned in full force. She complained that it was too bright and, besides, she had a sour stomach from all the raw fruit, but if everyone insisted she supposed she would stick her nose out into the elements for a moment or two.

Miss MacLaren laughed, as if she'd never been seasick a day in her life, and marshaled them all up the stairs and out on deck, where she settled Mrs. Curmidge into one of the sea chairs. Then she led the others around the deck twice, before Derek suddenly appeared before them, eyes still a bit red but smiling broadly.

"Shovelboard!" he exclaimed, pointing at the deck beneath his feet. Painted on the varnished planks alongside the smoking cabin was a scoring block for shovelboard. "All we need are the tangs and biscuits!"

"What fun!" Miss MacLaren said. "Where do we find them?"

"The purser has them," Ewan replied. "I'll get them."

"Please do. We'll lay claim to the court."

"We'll help carry them," Tereza said. "Come, Father."

Ewan had hoped to speak to Aunt Nellie alone again – he'd had an idea as he was falling asleep – but he was just as pleased to have Tereza's company, even with her father along. They brought back four of the shovel-like tangs and a box of eight colored wooden disks, and the group spent the rest of the morning playing doubles. The count appeared just as the captain and officers came out on the bridge to take their noon sightings. Tereza was partnered with her father against the MacLarens, but she immediately relinquished her tang to the count and begged Ewan to take her up to the bridge to observe. The professor handed his own tang to Derek and joined in her plea.

Ewan was happy to oblige. Mounting the stairs to the starboard bridge wing reminded him just how much he missed his watches at the wheel.

Captain Morrison stood off to port, but First Officer

MacKay was happy to show how the sextant was used and explain the calculations and tables. Tereza understood it all easily and took her own sighting, which turned out to match MacKay's closely enough to earn an honest compliment. The professor beamed. She also flew through the calculation of longitude, leaving all the officers behind.

"Perhaps you should apply to work for the line," MacKay joked.

Everyone chuckled except Tereza. "Maybe some day I will," she replied.

The strained smiles on their faces had Ewan biting his lip to hide a grin.

They returned to the shovelboard game to find Miss MacLaren and the count matched against the colonel and Derek. Chatting gaily in French with Miss MacLaren, the count was sweeping the board. Derek glowered, gripping his tang like a trident. He looked every bit as sour as Mrs. Curmidge. The count's valet was there, too, so still he almost blended into the side of the smoking cabin. Jean-something. Ewan had completely forgotten about him. Servants ate down in steerage, even those who shared a cabin with their employers.

Daisy made the last shot to finish the match, soundly trouncing her father and Derek.

"*Bien joué!*" the count remarked, clapping lightly. "You are a natural, *Mademoiselle* MacLaren."

"And you, *Monsieur*, are a flatterer," she replied. "The match was entirely yours to win."

"*Mais non!*" he protested. "*Cette victoire vous rev—*"

"I suppose we should get ready for dinner," Derek said, taking the colonel's tang and reaching for Miss MacLaren's. "Ewan, could you gather up the biscuits, please?"

"Is it that late?" the colonel asked, pulling out a gold

pocket watch.

Mrs. Curmidge sniffed. "I, for one, would enjoy a rest from this relentless glare," she announced, heaving herself into a sitting position. The count's valet stepped forward to offer his hand, but she glared him back against the wall.

"I can manage perfectly well on my own, if you don't mind," she growled, then struggled with the blanket, gravity, and the roll of the ship, nearly tumbling onto her face. Miss MacLaren rushed over just in time.

"Yes, a little rest would be a good idea," she said, holding Mrs. Curmidge's hand. "In the excitement of the game, we missed the eleven o'clock tea."

The count sent his valet to return the tangs and biscuits to the purser while the rest made their way down to the cabins. As soon as Tereza and the professor had closed the door behind them, Ewan made an excuse to Derek and hurried back up to Aunt Nellie's cabin. He waited impatiently for one of the other passengers to finish some business with her, then closed the door and asked if he could get a copy of the passenger manifest.

"Cabin only, or do you want to see steerage, too?" she asked.

"Better be both, I guess," Ewan replied. "Do they show the date when everyone booked?"

"You want to see who booked after the Skovajsas, don't you."

"I do. Does the manifest show that?"

"No, but your mother's final list does, even the *puir de'ils* sent back by immigration." Nellie pulled a folded sheet from one of the pigeonholes above her desk, opened it, and laid it out on the counter. "The manifest is alphabetical. Your mother's list here is in booking order, with the cabin numbers beside the names. 'S' for steerage. The count and his man aren't on it, by the way. I added them to the manifest, but not here." She pulled out a pen, made a quick note on the end of the list, and handed it to him.

Ewan scanned it. "Aren't the cabins assigned in booking order?"

"Not always. It depends on how many want a private cabin, how many in their party, things like that." She studied the list with him. "This passage is a light one so they're mostly in order."

"Can I have this?"

"For now. But don't lose it."

He promised he wouldn't, folded it, and tucked it into his inside coat pocket. He wasn't sure he'd learn much from it, but one thing had jumped out right away: the Reverend Harold Curmidge, party of two, was right below the name of Professor Jakub Skovajsa.

His mind leaped to the obvious conclusion: The Curmidges were tracking the professor. But that made no sense, unless the reverend was traveling under a false identity. Ewan knew there were card-sharpers who booked round-trip passage several times a year under different names just to fleece their fellow passengers. There was probably one on board right now, given the lively card games going on every night. But King was a far more likely candidate for that role. The reverend hadn't shown the slightest interest in cards. If he had, Mrs. Curmidge probably would have frowned him over the rail and into the sea. And he was dead now anyway.

Ewan jumped to another, more awful conclusion: The professor had killed Reverend Curmidge!

Maybe he really had been following the professor, who was going to a rendezvous with the reverend. Or the other way around, with the professor lying in wait for the reverend in the dark of the ladies' cabin, ready to club him.

But why? he demanded. *Why would Professor Skovajsa*

kill Curmidge? Why would the reverend be tracking the professor?

It came down to what the professor had done, and no one knew for sure what that was. It involved the Army, had killed some Senators and soldiers and the professor's own wife, and left the whole country wondering and afraid. That was the problem, not knowing for sure. The reverend could have been acting on some fearful impulse to get rid of a threat. The professor could have been afraid of the reverend.

But Ewan couldn't believe it – of the reverend, yes, as unlikely as it seemed, but not of the professor, not in the dark with a club. Not cold-blooded murder. Someone else must have done it, for some reason that he couldn't guess. Not yet at least.

Ewan pulled the passenger list out of his pocket and unfolded it for another look. He had wandered to the very stern, lost in his thoughts, and now he jammed his derby down tight and ducked into the lee of the stern cabin to keep the wind from wrestling with the corners of the sheet. The Stars and Stripes flapped overhead. The engine throbbed. Each wave sent the stern lifting and dropping into its own wake. He ignored all that and went down the names at the end of the list: the Skovajsas, the Curmidges, King, Ewan himself, the Count du Beausoleil and his valet, Jean-Martin Larousse. And the *"puir de'ils"* being shipped back to Europe.

"There you are!"

Ewan jerked upright, almost losing the sheet to the wind. Tereza was smiling at him from the corner of the stern cabin.

She came over. "I've come to remind you."

He held the sheet close to his chest. "About what?"

She shook her head, though her smile stayed. "I knew you'd forget. The engine room. You said you'd arrange a visit."

"Oh, I haven't forgotten. It's just . . ." He shrugged. ". . . busy."

"Uh-huh. What are you reading that keeps you so busy?"

"Oh, it's— How did you find me?"

She smiled again. "I went looking." She leaned close and peered at the back side of the sheet. "That's the passenger list. Who are *you* looking for?"

"No one," he said quickly. "No one in particular."

"Oh. Do you always get so lost in idle reading?"

He struggled to think of a good answer, and her smile disappeared.

"I'm sorry," she said, turning away. "It's none of my business."

"Wait!" he called, reaching out and almost losing the paper again. "I'm . . . I'm trying to figure out who killed Reverend Curmidge, and why."

She turned back, eyes gleaming. "You don't believe the accident story either!"

"No. No, I don't."

She pointed at the list. "Who do you think did it? And why?"

He held it out so they both could look at it. "I don't know yet. I was checking who booked after you and – and after the reverend and Mrs. Curmidge. In case one of—"

"After us," she said. "Father and me. You think it has something to do with us."

He met her wide gaze. "I do. I think the murderer mistook the reverend for your father."

She paled but nodded. "I do, too," she whispered.

"Your father—"

"Was making a weapon," she said. "It . . . misfired. I don't know exactly what happened, but I think . . . I'm afraid—"

The ship's bell rang sharply, four peals blown aft by the wind. Tereza stiffened, then clapped her hands over her ears as the lookout repeated the bells. She was breathing rapidly, staring at someplace else, eyes hollow.

Ewan stuffed the list back into his pocket and took her hands in both of his. "It's all right," he said. "It's done and over. Look at me. Tereza, look at me!" He shook her hands, and her eyes refocussed on his. "The engine room. Think of the engine room! I'll get you a visit, I promise!"

She blinked. Took a deep, shuddering breath. Then another. Her lips began to move, as if she were silently counting sheep.

"Are you all right?" he asked, searching her eyes for any hint that she might faint.

She nodded and freed one hand to wipe her eyes. "I'm sorry," she said. "Five, six times in a row it won't bother me, and I think I'm finally past it. But the next time, it overwhelms me. I can't—" She clenched her lips, suddenly angry. "I can't stop it! It's like a curse! A ghost that pops out whenever it feels like it!" She took another breath, blew it out. Stiffened her back. "It's gone now. I'm all right. Let's look at that list!"

He pulled it out and passed it to her but let go too soon. The wind gusted again, and the sheet swirled from her hand, swooping and flapping like a maddened bird. They watched in stunned silence as it made a final fillip and dropped into the foaming wake a dozen yards behind them.

Aunt Nellie's going to damn well kill me, Ewan thought.

"Oh, no," Tereza moaned. "I've lost it!"

"Not your fault," Ewan replied. "I should've . . . . I shouldn't have been . . . Anyway, it's gone and that's that."

"But the names!"

"Don't worry, I remember the ones after you and the Curmidges. It's not many: King, the count and his man, me, and—"

She stared at him, puzzled. Waiting. "And?"

"Derek," Ewan muttered. "He's not on the list."

"Mr. Reed?"

"He's not on the list," Ewan repeated. "Not anywhere. He's not a passenger, he's a stowaway."

Chapter 12

Another Walk in the Dark

Ewan's first thought was to go tell Aunt Nellie. Tereza stopped him.

"It can't possibly be him," she said. "You've seen what he's like around Daisy."

"I know," Ewan said. "Too mawkish by half, I'd say. What if it's all an act? All that poetry? He sticks out like wart on a crone's nose."

"I suppose he could be acting," she said, "but if we have him locked up now for a stowaway, we'll never know for sure. And he could have confederates on board." Her eyes narrowed; Ewan could see her working out the angles. "If we catch him out in his act, we can catch them, too." Ewan didn't doubt she would.

"So we'll have to keep watch on all the others," he said. "Look at them: King, the count, the valet. Anyone of them could be someone else in disguise."

"Hiding in plain sight, yes. Any one of them."

She began to grin, then stifled it. "Excuse me. I couldn't help thinking of Mrs. Curmidge. She's not really a crone, just . . ." She shivered. "Never mind. We'll watch them all and discover how to draw them out." She sobered suddenly. "The ship's bell – it rang four times. That's 2:00 p.m. We're late for dinner. Father will be worried sick."

They hurried forward and down to the cabins, where they found the professor staring out the porthole at the tiny circle of sky and sea. He turned quickly as they came in, his expression shifting between relief and irritation

"Well, finally, there you are!" he snapped. "I've been

wondering—"

"I'm sorry, Father," Tereza said quickly. "Mr. Gilmore and I got caught up in a discussion of the ash cycle."

The ash cycle? Ewan tried to look like he knew what she meant.

"And," she added, "he has arranged for us to visit the engine room after dinner!"

The professor brightened immediately. "Has he? That forgives a great deal! Thank you, young man. And please forgive my vile temper. As Tereza I'm sure has told you, I'm inclined to dark moods since . . ." He forced himself to continue. ". . . since her mother died. This distraction will do me good. Shall we go to dinner? We will undoubtedly provide the primary topic of gossip and rumor until we arrive."

King was not in his usual chair in the saloon, or at any of the other tables, which Ewan took as a blessing. Not that he held anything against King; he just didn't want another argument to spoil the professor's fragile mood and upset Tereza. Though, on second thought, any distraction from the upcoming trip to the engine room would have been a bigger blessing. The professor mentioned it to the others of course, and they all asked to join in. It seemed that, while he and Tereza had been studying the passenger manifest, the others had become best of friends. Daisy and Derek were even on a first-name basis, to his obvious delight.

"You must include us," Daisy explained with a grin. "We are all members of the same club."

"Club?" Ewan echoed, lost again.

"The Scots-American Trans-Atlantic Late Season Shovelboard League!" Derek exclaimed, sounding so unlike a murderer that Ewan was sure he couldn't be acting – or was the best thespian ever to mount the stage.

"We'll play every morning, tally the total on the last day, and crown the winning duo at the final supper."

Mrs. Curmidge sniffed. "Assuming the weather holds, which it won't."

Third Officer MacBreive was at the head of the table for this meal. Now he leaned back, dabbed his mouth with his napkin, and remarked, "I daresay you'll have better luck with the fall weather than you will with the chief engineer." He raised an eyebrow at Ewan. "You say he's expecting you and your 'club'?"

MacBreive was a prickly, persnickety man, older than both the first and second officers and never likely to attain their rank. Ewan returned his gaze with a tight smile, very aware that the professor could hear every word.

"It's all arranged," he lied. "I just need to give him a few minutes warning beforehand." To show just how certain he was, Ewan took a long sip of his water, then realized he had picked up the wrong glass. He nearly choked on the professor's wine.

"I pray you all, do not hit his back," the count warned, and the tension dissolved in general laughter.

As the meal was ending, Ewan excused himself to go plead with Chief Engineer MacLeod. Aunt Nellie caught up to him just as he reached the landing outside the ladies' cabin.

"Gather up your club, and get right down to the engine room," Aunt Nellie said. "I'll go ahead of you now and prepare the MacLion for your arrival."

"He doesn't even know we're coming yet," Ewan admitted.

"That was plain as the nose on your face. Be there in ten minutes, no more!"

"Yes, Ma'am!" Ewan replied, swamped with relief. *MacLion* was hardly an exaggeration of MacLeod's temper.

He went back down to report the new schedule.

"Splendid," MacBreive drawled. He gave Ewan a knowing look. "Perhaps I should join you? Given the chief engineer's, shall we say rude, manner, it might help smooth the way."

The friendly offer was a surprise. Ewan would have welcomed it from Sorely MacKay – the first officer and the chief engineer were at least of equal rank – but MacLeod had no patience for deck officers in general. It was his opinion that the engineers did all the work, while the deck officers took all the credit. MacBreive's presence would probably make matters worse.

"Well, thank you, sir," he began, "but—"

"It's nothing really," MacBreive answered. "We wouldn't want the ladies to be disappointed, would we? Shall we go?"

"Not I, certainly," Mrs. Curmidge announced. "I shall return to my cabin."

"Are you sure?" Daisy asked. "It should be most interesting."

Mrs. Curmidge sniffed. "I've seen those sweaty, soot-stained ruffians come out on deck at the change of the watch. I assure you, their hot hole is no place for a lady."

"We'll escort you to your cabin, then," Daisy said. "We do have time, don't we, Mr. Gilmore?"

"Oh, no, you all run along," Mrs. Curmidge said. "It's obvious such things fascinate you, for what reason I can't understand. Officer MacBreive, perhaps you could escort me. I'm sure you've seen the engine room more times than you can count."

"I have, ma'am," MacBreive agreed. "And, since no other gentleman is available, I will be happy to see you safely to your cabin." He took her arm, then glanced back at the others with a look of long suffering. "I'm afraid you're on your own, Mr. Gilmore," he said. "Your best course would be to keep your head down and agree with everything the chief engineer says."

&

The engine-room companionway sat amidships, aft of the funnel and the four tall ventilator scoops. To Tereza, the first step inside was a step between worlds: from chill winds, wide open skies, and the sweeping expanse of the sea to a dim, close, reeking, ringing cauldron. The deck here was an iron grating that caught at heel and toe. The railings were iron pipe, slick with oil and soot. The ladder went down steeply, canting this way and that as the ship rolled. She had grown accustomed to it in the companionways, but those were wood paneled, wide, and well lit, their steps painted with a gritty lacquer. Not nearly so steep. And not open to the view below.

Tereza was enthralled.

The boilers were directly beneath her – three of them, huge steel cylinders running in parallel across the entire beam at the widest frame in the hull. At the very bottom, a good thirty feet below, she counted eighteen iron doors opening onto eighteen furnaces, six per boiler, three on each end. Doors into the fires of a man-made, sea-borne volcano. Each time a door swung open, a blast of red-orange light and roasting heat rolled into the engine room and up the tall chamber beside the funnel, to engulf her and the others where they clung to the slick railing of the ladder. A few of the doors were always open. The burly stokers, chests clothed only in sweat-streaked soot, speared slice bars through the seething mounds of fire to settle the ash, then banged their shovels against the door frames to call for more coal. The trimmers were kept in constant motion, filling and hauling carts of coal to feed the ever-hungry fires.

The ringing was constant, too, counterpoint to the squeal and grind of the coal carts, the rattle of the coal, the roar of the flames. The shouts of the engineers were barely audible above the rest the din. Caged electric lights showed the way down, a receding line of yellow, fitful accents in the fire-stained murk.

Ewan led the way, moving slowly, with constant warnings to watch her step. Tereza pressed forward behind him, ignoring her father's offer of a helping hand. She tried to look up, down, right, and left all at once, taking in every detail in darting glances. Behind them, Daisy and the colonel descended much more carefully, with Derek hovering just a step above. The count, joined now by his valet, lingered at the top for a little while, then came down easily, as though it were a jaunt down a city street.

The descent took them past the cabin level and steerage, then opened out into the hold, revealing the coal bins running along the sides of the hull. Farther aft, they could glimpse the engine itself. The ladder ended at the engineer's station, a grate-floored balcony hanging above the hellish domain of the black gang. The grating did nothing to keep out the heat, noise, and soot, but the height and the view made demons of the engineers, overseers to the sooty souls laboring below them.

And there was Chief Engineer MacLeod, Lucifer in a sharp uniform, glaring at them from the control panel, a crowded rack of gauges and valves. Tereza fixed on it, fascinated, smiling. An oiler standing beside it watched her with grim interest.

"What the Devil is this crowd you've brought me, Gilmore?" MacLeod demanded. His voice bellowed clearly above the din.

"Now, sir, there are ladies present," Derek admonished, taking a protective stance beside Daisy. She flashed him an irked frown, then turned back to MacLeod with a pleasant smile, a greeting on her lips.

He cut her off with another bellow. "And who invited them to come? Not me! This is no place for frilly skirts and soft ears! So let me invite you to haul your—"

He reminded Tereza of one of the blustering generals her father had worked with. She walked past him, staring aft at the engine. "Excuse me, Mr. MacLeod. This is a double compound engine, I see. What are the two bores? And the stroke; it looks to be about four feet. Is that right? Mr. MacKay said the engine could achieve 3200 horsepower. Let's see. I would guess a fifty-five-inch bore for the high-pressure cylinder and – what do you think, Father? – About ninety for the low-pressure?"

"That would be about right, yes," Father replied, joining her. "And the pressure entering the first cylinder would be?"

"About sixty pounds," Tereza replied.

"Sixty-three," MacLeod snapped. "The bore is fifty-seven inches. You were right about the ninety," he added begrudgingly. "And the stroke. Now I have to ask you, please—"

Tereza was not about to let him chase her away. "And Mr. MacKay was correct? About the horsepower?" she asked. "Surely it should be more like 3500. An engineer with your experience should have no trouble—"

"Don't try to flatter me, miss." MacLeod grimaced, as though struggling to stay out of the conversation. He failed. "We've managed 3600 on a short run," he admitted. "Don't tell the owners that. They're not interested in blue ribbands, just the schedule."

"And the captain?" Father asked. "I can't image he enjoys being bested by his rivals."

MacLeod frowned. "Morrison cut his teeth on canvas. He'd be keen enough to race under sail, but with steam . . . Well, he's afraid of it, truth be told. Doesn't trust it. Not that he doesn't like to beat his own time, but give him but an hour or two ahead of schedule and he's content."

"He's not an engineer," Tereza replied, not even trying to hide the scorn in her voice.

Father was more lenient. "The captain simply doesn't realize you'd never endanger the engine."

"I'm sure he's happy to take the credit for every safe and timely passage," Tereza protested, "while Mr. MacLeod and his crew do all the work! And that's not flattery, sir, it's simply fact."

"Aye, that," MacLeod agreed. "Would you like a closer look at the engine?"

"Oh, yes!" she replied. "Please, show us everything." A hundred more questions filled her mind.

He led them aft along a narrow catwalk to the engine well, answering almost as quickly as she could ask. Pounds per foot, tons per hour, temperature gradients, average knots, the caloric output of anthracite, and more.

Ewan watched with something approaching awe. Her enthusiasm was infectious. Her eyes shone. And MacLeod was as happy as she was. Ewan felt a twinge of envy.

"She hath bearded the lion in his den," Daisy remarked.

"'And singed the original cricket upon his own hearth,'" Derek intoned. He grinned at their confusion and added, "Byron, of course. Amazing how it suits, eh?"

Tereza and the professor spent almost three hours in the engine room, and Ewan stayed with them. By the time they finally clambered up the ladder and back into the chilly evening, he felt as sweaty and sooty as the stokers and trimmers looked. He blessed the gray skies and cold wind and vowed never to become an engineer. Tereza, on the other hand, was still glowing through the soot that dusted her face, hands, hat, and clothes. She thanked him again and again for arranging the visit. He felt no guilt at all at accepting her gratitude; in the past three hours he had sweated enough to earn it.

The others, led by the count, had left after a brief glimpse at the engine. Ewan and the Skovajsas had missed tea time and the afternoon shovelboard match, and, needing more time than usual to clean up and change, were almost late for supper. Still energized from the visit, the professor and Tereza stayed up later than usual, chatting in a corner of the saloon with Daisy, the colonel, and Derek, then taking a final walk around the deck after the MacLarens decided to retire. As much as he welcomed every minute in Tereza's company, Ewan was exhausted when he could finally bid them goodnight and see them into their cabin.

He wasn't at all surprised to find Derek already sound asleep in his berth. King was absent, as usual, probably still in the smoking cabin. Alone with Derek for once, Ewan studied his boyish face. If he was plotting something against the professor, it certainly didn't show in his sleep. His valise, on the other hand, might yield more. It was tucked right under his berth.

Shaking off fatigue, Ewan knelt and carefully slid out the valise. Derek had left the buckles undone and the latch unlocked. It opened with a snap when Ewan pressed the catch. He froze, but Derek didn't move. Ewan slowly lifted the lid. Two poetry books lay on top of the clothes, next to a shaving kit and a small flannel bag that turned out to hold a second pair of shoes. A pocket inside the lid held a writing set, papers covered with scribbled poems, and a thin leather wallet with a few small bills and a draft on a Kentucky bank for another fifty dollars – hardly enough to tour the Continent. Ewan smiled grimly. Ranald Morrison wouldn't see much of a tip from Derek when they docked in Glasgow.

Unless Derek had means to get more. Someone to wire him cash when he needed it. An accomplice. A master. But then why would he need to stow away?

Irked that he couldn't say for sure, Ewan dug through the clothing – shirts, handkerchiefs, trousers, underthings, socks, and finally, beneath it all, the rasp of very coarse cloth. A burlap sack. Hiding a rough jacket, with trousers to match. And squashed between the sack and the bottom of the valise was a battered, wide-brimmed hat.

The memory clicked on like an electric light: Coming up from steerage. The man at the saloon hatchway. The thick accent. The glimpse of blond hair beneath this very hat.

Ewan sat back on his heels. If he'd needed more proof that Derek was a stowaway, he had it now. But it didn't prove that Derek was stalking the professor. Or had murdered Reverend Curmidge. If anything it made it less likely. Ewan finished ransacking the valise but found nothing more that could be called evidence. No club or any other weapon. He stood and checked Derek's jacket and overcoat, draped atop the spare upper berth. They held nothing more than a handkerchief and a thin pair of gloves. That left the trousers, but Derek was wearing them.

Ewan carefully tidied the contents of the valise, shut the lid, and slid it back under the berth. He studied Derek's sleeping form one last time. Finally, he leaned over and slowly, carefully, slid his hand under Derek's pillow.

Nothing there.

Derek's eyes fluttered. He drew in a deep, wet breath and rolled onto his side. Ewan slipped his hand out, stepped back, and turned around, quickly doffing his tie and shrugging off his coat. Derek sighed and went quiet.

Ewan let out his own slow sigh of relief and tiptoed over to next berth, where King's much labeled valise was lying right on top, unlatched, with the end of a necktie hanging from under the lid. Ewan opened it and began searching inside. Clothes, colored scarves, packets of playing cards, a slender wand, a pair of phony roses, a papier-mâché thumb, a Chinese puzzle box. Ewan shook the box and tried to figure out the trick, but it wouldn't open. He muttered a curse and tucked it back in with the rest of the gear, trying to arrange it the way he'd found it, making sure to leave the end of the necktie hanging out.

When he turned away, Derek was watching him with bleary, puzzled eyes.

Ewan smiled. "Woke up, did you? You were thrashing about there so much I was sure a bad dream had swallowed you whole. Sorry if I disturbed you. Just getting into bed here. Don't mind me, I'll be quiet as a mouse." He forced himself to stop babbling and continued getting undressed.

Derek grunted and rolled onto his side, still facing Ewan. He closed his eyes, but Ewan could tell he didn't fall right back to sleep. Ewan turned off the light, crawled into his berth, and lay still, listening. After a minute, he shifted and tried to breathe more slowly, feigning sleep. Tired as he was, he almost did fall asleep, but Derek's next movement brought him back from the edge of the abyss. Derek slid out from between his sheets.

Ewan forced himself to lie still, to keep his breathing slow and steady. He kept his eyes closed, trying to see with his ears. Derek's feet landed softly on the deck. His valise whispered out from under the berth. Clicked open. Clothes shifted. The lid clicked shut. Then more stealthy movements. Derek was getting dressed. Ewan stiffened and Derek froze.

Ewan snorted, swallowed, and went still again. After a few long minutes, Derek finished dressing. The door clicked open, admitting a brief gleam of light, then shut again. Ewan counted to fifteen, threw off the covers, and hurried to listen at the door. Nothing. Maybe Derek had just gone to the head, but maybe not. Ewan wasn't going to wait to find out. He pulled on his clothes, grabbed his hat, and slipped out into the companionway. It was empty. So were the heads and the baths. Ewan hurried aft, listening for voices behind the cabin doors. He paused a second at the stairs, listening for anything more than the throb of the engines, then decided to check the saloon first. It was empty now, too. If Derek had slipped out to meet someone, it would have to be on deck or in the smoking cabin.

Ewan hurried up the companionway stairs and paused to check the ladies cabin first. A chill went down his neck as he shuffled into the dark room, half expecting to trip over another body. But the cabin was empty. With a foolish surge of relief, Ewan went out on deck.

He found the ship mantled in fog. The horn sounded just as he stepped out, and he realized he'd been hearing it belowdecks the whole time. He'd been so focused on Derek's movements that he hadn't even noticed the deep-throated moan. The sounds of the sea and the wake were muffled, too. There was part of a moon somewhere up in the sky, but the drifting fog hoarded light. The companionway light flowed no farther than a few feet from the dark gray deckhouse. The lifeboats hovered like distant clouds. The rail was all but invisible.

Ewan stood a moment to let his eyes and ears adjust. He started aft, toward the smoking cabin, then heard something the other way, footsteps maybe. He turned back, peering into the gloom. Far forward, the ship's port running light was a dim orb of hazy red. He went forward, trying to mute his own footsteps on the damp planks. The horn sounded again as Ewan passed the end of the deckhouse. He could just make out the engine room skylights, the ventilators, and the bulk of the funnel, looming overhead. He took one more step and an arm looped around his neck, jerking him backward, choking off his startled cry.

Chapter 18

The Fight in the Fog

Ewan grabbed at the arm with both hands. It loosened a moment, but only to yank a thin strip of twisted cloth around his neck. And tighten it. Ewan thrashed, fighting for breath, but the man behind him was strong and the cloth tightened more, a line of pain encircling his throat. Ewan's shoes slipped on the deck and slid out from under him, throwing them both sideways. The makeshift garrote dragged up over his chin, and Ewan managed a breath, but no more than a tiny bleat before the attacker regained his balance and jerked the strip down again.

It was the damned derby that saved him. It had jostled loose and slipped down under the attacker's left hand and the end of the garrote. Ewan clawed three fingers beneath the derby, into the gap between the twisted cloth and the corded veins of his neck. He pulled desperately. Jerked his head backward. Punched back with his other elbow. Reached over his head, groping at his assailant. The man held against him, forcing him down to his knees, to the deck, pressing his face into the hard, seamed planking. Ewan's vision started to cloud. He redoubled his efforts, but he could feel himself weakening, feel his heart skipping, feel his lungs aching, knotting. His left fingers went numb under the cutting cloth; he clawed at the deck with the others. The fog thickened, darkened. The ship's horn moaned faintly, at some great distance beyond him.

Suddenly the weight on his back was gone. The cord went with it, a painful jerk that brought Ewan halfway back to his senses. He dragged in half a breath, his throat cramping at the effort to break the knot in his starved lungs. He drew in another and found the strength to lift himself onto his elbows. His vision spun, his ears whined. The pain in his neck flared as soon as he tried to lift his head. He forced it up despite the pain, drawn by a shout from some great distance.

There, blurred by fog and pain, not more than ten feet away, two figures struggled. Under the dark bulk of a lifeboat. Pressed against the rail. One tall, one short, writhing shadows, grappling, punching. An arm drew backed, stabbed in. Again. The tall figure jerked, cried out. The shorter heaved him across the rail, then tore loose, flew aft, out of Ewan's tight circle of vision. Ewan was up on his knees now, crawling, now on his feet, stumbling forward. The tall figure lurched, half over the rail. His coat was blue, braid at the cuffs. Head bare, face bleeding. MacKay. Ewan reached for him, grabbed at his arm, tried to get an arm around him.

His hand hit something hard, closed on it. A handle. A hilt. A knife, wedged in deep under MacKay's left arm. The boat heeled, dipping its bow to a wave. MacKay's tall weight shifted too far. Ewan groped at him, pulling. Tried to cry out, but his voice was no more than a painful croak. The knife slid out in his hand. MacKay began sliding across the rail. Ewan dropped the knife and fought for a better grip.

Then someone else was there, reaching past Ewan, grabbing at the heavy wool coat. Together they held MacKay a moment, but the roll of the ship and the weight of the man were too much – MacKay wrenched free and fell.

"Man overboard!" the other yelled. "Man overboard!"

It was MacBreive. And now others arrived, deck crew on watch. MacBreive ran to the ladder, up to the bridge, calling to the quartermasters. Leaving Ewan in the circle of men, the bloody knife at his feet.

Ewan sat stiffly on a hard chair in the wardroom, struggling not to slump. His mind felt numb, but his body ached in a dozen places. He could hardly turn his head and barely whiper; speech was a stab in the throat. A stinging weal circled his neck. That was all that kept him out of the brig – it was obvious someone had tried to choke him to death. MacKay would never have done that, the whole crew knew it.

But they'd been ready to believe that Ewan would knife MacKay. That fact burned hotter than the weal.

The knife lay on the wardroom table in front of Captain Morrison.

"Not one look at his face," the captain repeated.

"No, Sir," Ewan whispered. But he was sure it wasn't Derek; he and MacKay were of a height. The attacker had been shorter. "Sorry, Sir."

"Third?"

MacBreive was standing to the side. "I didn't see anyone else at all, Sir."

Aunt Nellie spoke up unasked. "Whoever it was took good advantage of the fog." Like all the others, her face was set, but her voice revealed her grief. Ewan remembered how much she'd liked MacKay.

"Do you take that to mean something, Purser?" the Captain asked.

"I don't think the *murtherer* meant to spill blood. It was a garrote he used on Ewan; not so quick but quiet, if you know what to do. And plenty of ocean to hide a body. It would have worked, too, except for MacKay. That's when the knife came out, when it was two to one. Who knows what else the *blackgaird* had tucked away in his pockets?"

The captain laid his hand on the table beside the knife

and tapped his fingers in slow rhythm.

"Do we have anyone Russian among the passengers?" he asked.

"No, Sir," Aunt Nellie replied. "Not by name, at least. Steerage neither."

"British Army or Navy?"

"That I can't say, Sir."

"Check on it, Purser. The gentleman might be around my age."

"May I ask why, Sir?"

The captain raised an eyebrow.

"It would help to know what questions to ask." Aunt Nellie explained.

The captain tapped his fingers again. "I saw knives like this in the Crimea," he said. "The Rusky sailors carried them."

Ewan took another look at the knife. The blade was blued steel, unpolished, eight inches long at most, still streaked with drying blood. It had a small, gray guard, and hard, black twine wrapped the hilt. The pommel, gray like the guard, was engraved with a double-headed eagle ringed by Russian letters.

"What does it say on the end there?" MacBreive asked.

The captain grunted. "Nothing that names the owner, we can be sure. Lock it up, Purser, if you please." He turned his gaze on Ewan. "You were assigned to keep watch on Skovajsa, Gilmore. Next time you think he's out and about, don't let him get away."

"It wasn't Professor Skovajsa, Sir," Ewan protested.

"So you said: too short, too strong. But Skovajsa's likely the one who was supposed to die. I don't want him or you wandering the decks in the middle of the night again. Understood?"

"Yes, Sir."

"And have the doctor look at your neck, Gilmore.

That's an order," he added. "He's drunk at times, but he'll have a salve for the weal and a tea for your *thrapple*. Go."

Ewan stood, saluted, and went, trying to hide the pain each movement cost him.

Aunt Nellie followed him out, cradling the knife in her hands like it might try to bite her. She led him to her office and made him sit while she wrapped the knife in a hand towel and put it in one of the drawers in her safe. Then she took something from another drawer and held it out.

It was a Derringer pistol, small, double-barreled, pearl-handled. Ewan stared at it numbly.

"Take it, Ewan. Keep it close. Don't show it unless it's clear you need to."

It was heavier than it looked, a solid weight for all its small size. The grip seemed tiny, not quite made for a grown hand. He clutched it awkwardly.

"It's loaded," Aunt Nellie said, "but you have to cock it before you pull the trigger. Cock it again and it fires the lower barrel. And here's two more rounds." She dropped two squat cartridges into his other palm, then spent a couple of minutes showing him how to load the little gun.

"Don't try to shoot anything more than a few feet from you," she said. "You'll likely miss. This is for the next one who tries to kill you up close."

A painful lump swelled in Ewan's throat. "I'm sorry about MacKay," he croaked. *He died because of me.*

"Don't blame yourself!" Nellie snapped. Then she pulled him into her arms for a moment before setting him back up straight. "And don't blame MacKay; blame the *murtherin' snaik* who did it. I'm sure I don't have to remind you he's still on board."

"What about you?" Ewan asked. "You sleep alone here."

"I sleep with the door locked, don't worry.

Besides . . ." She patted the side of her jacket. ". . . that one's got a twin. Now you keep watch on Skovajsa and the lass, and yourself, too. Don't make me have to tell your mother any worse news."

Ewan gingerly slipped the Derringer into his coat pocket, mumbled a thank-you and left. The high sill at the cabin doorway almost tripped him, but he caught himself on the bulkhead and carefully made his way down the companionway to the cabin deck. He had a hard time focusing on the steps; his mind kept jumping from one blurred scene to the next, but always returned to the moment when he was pressed face-down on the deck and realized he couldn't break the murderer's grip, couldn't loosen the garrote. Couldn't breathe, and his eyes were going dark.

He shook his head, and the pain in his neck jerked him back to the present. He was standing still at the bottom of the ladder, staring at nothing. Two of the stewards, perched on stools, with shoes and brushes hanging in their hands, watched him warily. He tucked his chin and hurried past them and though the narrow side passage, where he found Ranald Morrison perched on his own stool by the count's cabin door, shoes and kit beside him.

He sneered at Ewan. "Look at the sport. Not so fancied up now, eh? Lost your silly dome. Almost lost your life, they say. Well, the wrong man went overboard, that's sure enough."

Ewan's throat hurt too much to make reply. He clenched his fists and fumbled his way into his cabin.

King was there now, snoring. Derek was there, too, silent as a sleeping babe. Ewan stared at his unlined face, wondering where he had gone, and why. Derek wasn't the murderer, he was both too tall and too skinny. Too much of a cake. Ewan couldn't believe it was an act, but maybe

Derek and the murderer were working together. If so, they must have some way to communicate. That might even be why both of them had gone out on deck tonight. And if they tried it again, Ewan was determined to catch them both. That's why he hadn't squealed on Derek, to make him think no one suspected him. Ewan wasn't sure if it'd been smart, but it was too late now. He was committed.

He dragged off his coat, pried off his shoes, and started to pull down the covers on his berth when a dark lump on the pillow startled him into a painful gasp. It was his derby, mashed almost beyond recognition. Smeared with tar from the deck seams. Creased where the garrote had caught it. Stained there with Ewan's blood. His hands shook as he held it, gasping for breath.

Clenching the hat in his fist, he charged back out the door and across the well to Ranald Morrison. He shoved the mangled hat under Ranald's nose.

"You stay out of my cabin!" he croaked, and when Ranald tried to speak, Ewan jammed the derby against his chest "Shut up!" he growled. "I don't want to hear another word from you this passage! Or I'll make you eat this damned thing! Understand?"

He dropped the derby into Ranald's lap and stumbled back to his cabin.

Chapter 14

Tereza's Tale

The news that First Officer MacKay had been lost overboard whispered through the ship as soon as the early risers stepped out of their cabins. Daisy prayed it was only a cruel rumor, but Captain Morrison made a formal announcement in the saloon at breakfast. It was an even crueler truth, a tragic accident, he called it, but every one of the passengers had already decided that foul play was involved. The captain's grim face, more dour than ever, merely confirmed their joint opinion. The night had been relatively calm, despite the occasionally confused sea. The wind had been light; MacKay was an experienced seaman; he had served on the *Lewis* for seven years and knew every inch of her deck better than his own rooms ashore. No one had seen him take a single sip of wine or whiskey during meals. What possible accident could have caused him to fall over the rail?

One look at Ewan was all Daisy needed to be absolutely sure it was no accident. Ewan arrived in company with the professor and Tereza. She looked absolutely stricken: pale and drawn, very much as she had looked when she'd first come on board. But Ewan looked even worse. His face was splotched with awful bruises, and a wide plaster encircled his neck just above his collar, which was noticeably soiled. His voice was hoarse, and he winced whenever he tried to swallow. Every movement seemed to cause him pain. But he tried to brush away all attention – tried too hard, in her opinion.

"I got tangled in the fall on the forward davit for the

number three lifeboat," he told them. "Jerked me right off my feet and swung me against the davit, then came loose all of a sudden and dropped me flat on my face on the deck. I hit every bar in the railing on the way down." He was a terrible liar.

"It's a lucky thing you fell within the railing," Mrs. Curmidge remarked dryly, "or you'd have joined poor Mr. MacKay in the sea. I suppose that's where your hat must have gone?" she added. "It is rather . . . unfortunate to see you without it."

Ewan blushed and lifted a hand—painfully—in a failed attempt to smooth down his hair. "Must have done," he croaked. "I couldn't find it anywhere. Sorry, I hope it's not —"

"Please, Mr. Gilmore, don't apologize," Daisy said, swallowing hard to force down a lump of tears. "Losing a hat is a very minor trick of fate compared to what else occurred last night." Everyone else murmured an agreement. "I understand it was very foggy," she continued, choosing her words with care. "It must have been quite chilly on deck."

He tried to nod, quickly reconsidered, and mumbled a hoarse, "Yes."

"Did you see Lieutenant MacKay?" she asked. "It's a solemn thought, isn't it? You may have been the last to speak to him."

Mrs. Curmidge sniffed. "If so, I hope it was a kind word."

"I didn't see him," Ewan replied, but his face told a much more complicated tale. First sadness, so deep that his eyes glistened. Then his jaw clenched, and anger dried the unshed tears. Daisy felt tears well again in her own eyes.

"She is a cruel fate who takes away a man in the prime of his life," the count said quietly, "particularly one so blessed with health and good future as *le lieutenant* MacKay. The loss of your dear husband was great, *Madame* Curmidge. This new loss doubles our grief."

"Well said," Father replied.

"'Men are the sport of circumstances when it seems circumstances are the sport of men,'" Derek said, to no one in particular. He had been uncharacteristically somber all through breakfast. In fact, this was the first thing he'd said all morning.

"Byron, one assumes," the count remarked.

Derek nodded. "And it's true, isn't it? MacKay seemed to have it all going for him: good looks, good voice, solid career, respect. Knew what he was doing. Then, from one moment to the next, he's fallen overboard and been lost in the fog. It could've happened to any of us out on deck last night. Leaning over the rail, looking down to watch the foam wash against the hull, wondering . . . about tomorrow or the distant future or, um, some special person perhaps. Then, unexpected, a confused sea, a stumble, into a fall of rope perhaps, a lurch against the rail at just the wrong moment and he's over. Into the very foam he'd been watching the moment before." Derek shuddered. "It must have been terrifying to see the ship's lights disappear into the dark."

"Why didn't they stop?" Tereza asked, voice thin. "Why didn't they go back to find him?"

"They didn't know immediately, my dear," the professor said, taking her hand.

"Stopping doesn't help," Ewan rasped. "Takes too long. Steer a circle instead, back past where he fell, so's to come up on the same course. Very hard to do right; wind, current, speed, time. Officer MacBreive tried, but . . ." He shrugged. "Captain got to the bridge too late."

Mrs. Curmidge sniffed. "It sounds to me like the third officer needs a bit more training."

"He's been third long enough, five years at least," Ewan replied.

"And yet older than MacKay," the Count remarked.

"Only a few make it to first," Ewan said. "Only so many places available."

"There's a place open now," Derek said. "I suppose the second officer will move up, which would give Mr. MacBreive a chance— Not that I mean . . . Well, one man's misfortune is another man's gain and all that. Sad how it works out."

Yes, Daisy thought, *sad. And criminally so.*

After breakfast, Daisy went on deck with Tereza and Mrs. Curmidge. It was a pleasant change to be away from the men. Her father had gone to the smoking cabin, while the count and his shadow valet had gone to their cabin. King, now famous, had been invited to the ladies cabin to hypnotize several "relapsed" sufferers of seasickness. The professor, obviously relieved to see King gone, if not happy about the reason, had elected to peruse the library at the back of the saloon, with poor, bedraggled Ewan for company. Even the ever-solicitous Derek had made an excuse and disappeared.

Daisy strolled forward on the starboard side with Mrs. Curmidge and Tereza until they reached the number three lifeboat, which hung near the smokestack. The fog had dissipated, and the seas, if not calm, were at least regular. The ship rose and fell in a slow, steady rhythm that soothed the constant vibration of the propeller beneath them. In normal circumstances, the view out over the water would not have inspired thoughts of death, and definitely not of murder; but a single look at the neatly tied and coiled arrangement of the ropes holding the lifeboat gave the lie to Ewan's story.

Daisy continued forward, around the deckhouse, then back aft to the seclusion behind the stern cabin. "I don't believe it," she said.

"It's not a matter of belief," Mrs. Curmidge stated. "The man's gone; simple fact."

"Oh, that I believe far too well. I don't believe it was an accident."

Mrs. Curmidge sniffed, and Daisy began to wish the woman would stop doing it.

"You are welcome to doubt me, Mrs. Curmidge," she said, "but I do think Mr. MacKay was too careful an officer to make the sort of mistake that would pitch him over this rail." She slapped the rounded wood surface. It was chest high on her, and would have come to MacKay's midriff at least.

"So you think someone pushed him." Mrs. Curmidge's tone was as irritating as her sniff.

"I do, and I don't doubt that Tereza agrees."

Tereza blushed under their double gaze. Her eyes looked even more hollow. "I . . . I'm not sure what to think," she said. "No, I take that back. I agree with Daisy. And I fear I know who could have done it."

"You do? Tell us! Who was it?" Daisy exclaimed.

"Not a specific name," Tereza admitted. "A reason. A reason why some people on board might want to . . . harm someone else." She gripped her parasol with hands gone white. "It's because of us," she murmured, glancing away, "my father and me."

That was Daisy's thought exactly, but she hadn't wanted to say it out loud. And she'd been right not to; Tereza looked absolutely guilt-stricken.

Daisy laid a hand on her shoulder. "No, Tereza. You can't blame yourself or your father, not for this. Whatever happened back in the States had nothing to do with Mr. MacKay."

"Didn't it?" Tereza replied. "His ship agreed to carry us when no other would. Several people on board have already made comments."

"Insults from despicable boors!" Daisy protested.

"They still meant them. I see their glances whenever we go into the saloon or pass by on deck." She shivered, but not from cold. Her soft voice rose and took on an edge Daisy had never heard before. "They are worse than despicable!"

"Ignorant, more like," Mrs. Curmidge said.

"Yes, ignorant! They have no idea what happened, how horrible it was. They just keep hounding us. I thought we would leave that behind." She stared back along the wake.

Daisy moved closer. "It must have been horrible indeed. It is said that ignorant people live in fear, and fear begets unreasonable anger. Perhaps if we all knew . . ."

Tereza shook her head.

"Brooding can only make the horror worse, young lady," Mrs. Curmidge said. "It might do you good to get it off your chest."

"Mrs. Curmidge is right," Daisy said. "When my mother died, I was inconsolable for months, bottled up, sad and angry. I wouldn't say a word to anyone. I actually hit the poor maid assigned to be my first governess; more than once, and I refused to apologize or say even a single word to anyone, not even to Father. But, finally, I was able to speak of it, and it made a huge difference. I could finally grieve properly. When you are ready to speak, Tereza, we will be ready to listen."

Daisy braced herself for another sniff. Instead, Mrs. Curmidge patted Tereza's shoulder. "Yes, whenever you are ready, my dear. Sooner will be better than later, I'm sure, but the choice is yours."

Daisy held her breath in hopes that this surprising

glimpse of a more gentle Curmidge would loosen Tereza's tongue, but she was disappointed. Tereza appeared to ignore them both.

"That's smoke," she said, suddenly bright.

"I beg your pardon?" Mrs. Curmidge said, taken aback for once.

Tereza pointed. "That dark streak behind us, it's smoke. A ship. It's catching up."

Daisy stared at the horizon, where a thin, dark line rose into a flattened cap of cloud.

"Where?" Mrs. Curmidge demanded. "Oh, there. Yes. You have sharp eyes, young lady. I wonder what it is."

"Another liner," Tereza said. "They follow the same shipping lanes." Her relief at the change of topic was plain on her face.

"So do the freighters," Mrs. Curmidge rejoined, back to her usual bristling self.

Daisy pulled the small spyglass from the deep inner pocket of her Ulster. The trailing ship was much too distant, nothing more than a tiny silhouette coming head on. She handed the spyglass to Tereza, gave her a moment or two to peer at the oncoming ship, then returned to the mystery.

"I have to say, I don't believe a word of Mr. Gilmore's story about his bruises. It would take a tempest to loosen one of those lifeboat ropes, and a much longer drop to bang him up so badly."

"More likely drank too much and got in a brawl with some sailor," Mrs. Curmidge said.

Tereza stiffened, chin lifting, but didn't lower the telescope.

"A fight, yes," Daisy said quickly, "but surely not one he started. Don't you think he might have been involved somehow in Officer MacKay's so-called accident? Perhaps he tried to stop it and was beaten for his efforts. He is probably lucky to be alive."

Tereza lowered the telescope, her face turned pale and hollow again. "I . . . I hadn't thought of that," she murmured. "Oh, *zatracenĕ!* It's all because of us!"

Daisy and Mrs. Curmidge both tried to assure her it wasn't, but she cut them off.

"Don't you see, Mrs. Curmidge? Even your husband's death is suspicious. Ewan thinks so, too. We think the killer mistook Reverend Curmidge for my father."

Mrs. Curmidge opened and closed her mouth like a gasping fish. "He does?" she finally managed. "That's . . . that's ridiculous! They look . . . looked nothing alike."

"Not from the front," Daisy agreed, "but they had a similar height and build. From the back, in the dark, they might be mistaken." She turned back to Tereza, very intrigued. "Did Mr. Gilmore say anything more about his suspicions?"

Tereza hesitated a moment. "No. Only that it was supposed to have been my father."

"Well, if he's right," Daisy said, "I suppose it would have to have something to do with your father's accident."

Tereza's face closed up again.

"But only Mr. Gilmore can tell us why he thinks that," Daisy went on, "and only he can tell us how he received his beating. And I do wonder why he was wandering around the deck last night. What do you think, Tereza? You seem to have gotten close to him – in a friendly way, of course," Daisy added quickly when she saw the blush flooding Tereza's pale face. "What do you think, Mrs. Curmidge? Should we go find him and have a little chat?"

They found Ewan in the saloon, but still keeping company with Professor Skovajsa. Tereza would not think of discussing their suspicions in her father's presence. Irked, Daisy resolved to wait them out, but then she remembered the ship in their wake. She went right to one of the waiters and asked loudly if he might know what ship it was that was catching up to them.

She didn't expect the waiter to know, but her question emptied the saloon in a moment, and the rush to the stern rail drew everyone out of the ladies cabin and smoking cabin, too. There was a great deal of chatter about what ship she might be and how long it would take her to catch up and pass the *Lewis*. An active round of betting arose on both points. The purser brought word that it was most likely the *City of Richmond*, of the Inman Line, which had been scheduled to leave New York two days after them, and the odds in the betting pools began to change frantically. It was very difficult not to get caught up in the diversion; everyone seemed so desperate to forget the two deaths that had laid such a pall of gloom on the voyage.

Unfortunately, Ewan stayed close by the professor's side through the rest of the morning till dinner time. By then the pursuing ship was almost upon them, and few passengers wanted to go in to eat. Since dinner was the hour when the steerage passengers were allowed out on deck and the trimmers of the black gang came up to dump the ash from the furnaces, it made for a very crowded deck: steerage forward, cabin class aft, and a chain-gang of soot-blackened trimmers stretched between them on both side decks like human fences.

Daisy's spyglass made the rounds of their little club. It revealed that the ocean greyhound chasing them was indeed the *City of Richmond*, a lean, three-masted ship, over a hundred feet longer than the *Lewis* but just as narrow, with a pair of raked funnels and a swooping clipper bow. The band in steerage fetched their instruments and struck up a rousing rendition of *Hail, Columbia* as the *Richmond* drew near. Signal flags bloomed on the shrouds of both ships, and semaphore flags waved from each bridge as she passed.

"They know about the deaths now," Ewan translated. "The proper authorities will be waiting to meet us at the pier."

"If only we could transfer you to the *Richmond*, Mrs. Curmidge," Daisy said, "this wretched voyage would be over for you two days sooner at least."

Mrs. Curmidge sniffed. "I'm sure many others here have that same wish. I daresay you must be wishing you had waited for the *Richmond* to depart, Mr. Count, rather than rushing off so frantically in an air ferry, of all things."

"Not at all, *madame*," the count replied. "I was rushing to leave, not to arrive."

"Whatever for? Not a slew of creditors, I hope."

Daisy was shocked by the implied insult, but also intrigued. The count's exciting arrival on board now seemed suspicious.

The count merely chuckled. "My finances are well founded, *madame*, for which I daily bless my frugal ancestors. No, it was not a lack of funds that put me in such a flight, it was a surfeit of attentions. A certain person had become embarrassingly *importune*. It was best for me to be elsewhere."

Daisy was doubly shocked and even more intrigued. She wondered who that certain person might be. It was not something one could ask, of course.

Mrs. Curmidge didn't seem to care so much about *who* as about *what* had happened. "Whoever she was, I suggest you pay more care to your own attentions on this passage. There is no way to rush off from here until we reach Britain."

"*C'est vrai*," the count agreed. "But there is also no way here to make advances, *n'est-ce pas*? Here, one is protected by proximity of the crowd. There is nowhere to be alone *en tête-a-tête*."

Except on deck at night in the fog, Daisy thought.

&

By the time the steerage passengers were shepherded back down to their deck, the *City of Richmond* was well in the lead. Among cabin class, the losing bettors paid off, and a new round of betting arose over when she would pass out of sight. That gathered far less interest, and most of the cabin passengers headed for the saloon. Daisy waited until her father, the professor, and Ewan were just about to step into the companionway, then moved in quickly.

"Mr. Gilmore?" she said, touching his sleeve. "Could I ask you a question, please? About the rigging?" She gestured aft and upward vaguely.

Her father gave her a curious glance, but Daisy knew he'd consider Mrs. Curmidge to be a more than sufficient chaperone. As she expected, he gave her an acquiescent nod and continued inside with the professor. Ewan watched them go, obviously torn, but a faint smile from Tereza appeared to tip the balance.

"OK," he croaked. "What do you want to know?"

She led him toward the stern, Tereza and Mrs. Curmidge following. "It's not actually the rigging," she said, once they were well out of earshot of the few passengers still on deck. "It's about your suspicions regarding Reverend Curmidge's 'accident.'"

As Daisy explained her suspicions about MacKay's death, Tereza and Mrs. Curmidge stepped up on either side. Ewan looked around at the three of them with something akin to panic on his battered face.

"Please tell us," Tereza asked, sounding more resolute. "The reverend is already dead. My father is in danger. We should know."

His face was gaunt, almost gray beneath the bruises, as he described in a few hoarse words what had happened to

Officer MacKay. It was the barest description, Daisy guessed, severely censored in an attempt to shield them from the violence so starkly evident on his face. She could not hold back her tears or anger.

"How awful!" She scrubbed at her rebellious eyes with her hanky. "Poor Mr. MacKay. That he should run afoul of such a monster on his own ship!"

Tereza was clutching her parasol to her chest again, staring through tears at Ewan. "He barely saved your life," she said, her voice thick.

"We must do something!" Daisy declared.

"We must not rush off half-cocked," Mrs. Curmidge chided, resolutely dry-eyed.

"Yes, thank you, Mrs. Curmidge, but it is so hard to sit idle. Tereza, you said yourself that all this tragedy must stem inadvertently from your father's activities. Now is not the time to keep secrets. Please tell us what happened."

Tereza stood stiff as a rod, a study in misery. "I can't tell you. I promised."

"Promised whom?" Daisy exclaimed. "And why?"

"I can't tell you," Tereza replied.

Mrs. Curmidge sniffed.

Daisy ignored both responses. "Was it your father?"

"How could it be?" Mrs. Curmidge countered. "The poor man himself doesn't remember, does he, my dear? You said so not two days ago. It was some general, wasn't it. Or a politician, perhaps; one of their so-called Senators. Or the judge?" She waved every possibility aside. "Surely you see it doesn't matter; neither who nor what they are. They are back there, at the other end of that wake. After booting you and your poor father out of their uncouth, upstart country."

"Whoever it was, they had no right to ask you to promise any such thing," Daisy said, "and you certainly are not bound by such an improper imposition now. If you need to speak of it, then you should, without doubt or guilt."

Tereza stared at them, looking even more rigid, if such a thing were possible; so uncertain, so lost that Daisy was almost ready to apologize and drop the whole thing. But Tereza turned toward Ewan, an unspoken question in her eyes.

He nodded. "They're right, we have to know. Before someone else gets hurt. It'll be OK. We'll keep your secret."

Relief freed Tereza from her own strangling grip and let loose the tears she had been trying to dam.

Mrs. Curmidge offered her a handkerchief. "Take this, dear. You should always carry several."

Tereza took it, grateful for the first time that Mrs. Curmidge was on board. She dried her eyes and, after a few deep breaths, managed to keep them dry. Then, in a voice hardly more than a whisper, she told them about the Bell Cannon and everything that had happened on the day of the test. As much as she knew, at least. Each word spoken was another weight off her heart.

"Thank God you weren't there when it exploded," Daisy said.

"Sometimes I wish I had been," Tereza replied, and that admission was the greatest relief of all.

"Tereza, no, you can't mean it!"

"I do."

"But why?"

"It was my fault. I didn't tune the resonators properly. That's the only possible cause for the explosion."

"Now, now, child," Mrs. Curmidge protested, "you are remarkably knowledgeable in your father's profession, but you are hardly a trained engineer. There was more to this cannon thing than resonators, whatever they are. There could easily have been a fault in some other bits."

"If only your father could remember," Daisy said. "He would tell you you weren't to blame."

"After all," Mrs. Curmidge added, "it was he who sent you away and then finished the preparations himself, he and that assistant fellow with the German name." She sniffed. "If you wish to find error and place blame, I suggest you seek no further than the German."

Tereza refused to hear it. There was more to admit. "My mother, too . . . I . . . When we reached the house, I was so angry I ran upstairs, then immediately snuck down the back way and out the kitchen door and through the woods to the road. To return to the test. I was determined to finish the job I had started, to show Father he was wrong, that I did belong there." Tears flooded her eyes again. "What an idiot I was!" She swallowed more tears, then managed to draw another deep breath and continue.

"It was five miles," she whispered. "I expected to walk – no, run! – all five miles back in five minutes so I could charge in and . . . and do what? Argue with my father until the Secretary of War arrived? Stupid! I was so stupid!" She looked round at them all, begging them to agree.

"You were afraid for your father," Daisy said. "That's a very good reason."

Tereza shook her head. "Five miles. I hadn't gone two when I heard the buggy behind me. I hid in the woods and watched Mother drive by. I knew she was after me, but I didn't call out to her. Didn't try to stop her. I followed her. So stubborn! I killed her, don't you see?" Her voice broke and she struggled to control it. "She went back looking for *me*. She was in range of the cannon. Because of me."

She couldn't hold back the sobs. Daisy stepped close and gently rubbed her back. Mrs. Curmidge produced another handkerchief and pressed it into her hand.

"Take hope, dear," she said. "Surely it was a quick and painless end."

Tereza, still sobbing, shook her head. "No!" she cried, "It was terrible!"

"Now, now. How can you possibly know that?"

"I heard her screams. I was close enough. I—" The humming started. She dropped the parasol and clenched her hands over her ears, certain the bells would sound next. "I felt . . . awful things. Crawling. Touching. In my . . . gut. My heart. Every part of me. Humming. I heard it, the aether. It rang. Howled. Inside me. All through me. It screamed. Here!" She pounded her palms against her temples. "It was here! Screaming! It was me!"

Ewan grabbed her hands. "Tereza, no! It wasn't you. It was the cannon."

"It was the aether, vibrating my brain. It should have stopped my mind. Killed me." She tore her hands free and slapped them down hard on the rail. "Like that! But it didn't. It stirred my brain, like the peal of a great bronze bell stirs the heart, pealing again and again, vibrating, exciting the aetheric waves in my brain. *My* brain. *Me*."

"It stirred up your emotions into something that was *not* you," Daisy insisted.

"That is right, young lady," Mrs. Curmidge said. "Even the saints had to fight with the Devil inside them."

"I didn't fight them. I ran. I heard her screaming and I ran." It was the hardest thing to reveal. "I left her," she whispered.

"There was nothing else you could do," Ewan said. "If you'd run toward her, you'd've died."

"Something in you knew that and simply would not let you go closer," Daisy said.

Mrs. Curmidge sniffed. "You were lucky you still had the will to run. Everyone closer died. Except your father, of course, and by what miracle he lived, I'm sure we will never know."

"A piece of the apparatus hit his head and knocked him senseless," Tereza said. "For months." Focusing on stark details helped dim the humming." The doctors said the blow should have killed him." She drew in a trembling breath.

"But it didn't," Mrs. Curmidge stated. "There, you see: It was a miracle, obviously. You and your father were meant to survive. I would not presume to second-guess our Lord's intent, but I have no doubt that He has some purpose for you both. In due course, it will be revealed."

Then Father stalked from behind the stern cabin. "Too much has been revealed already!"

Chapter 15

A Note from a Spy

Jakub glared at Tereza, barely able to keep from grabbing and shaking her. She drew back.

"Father, you weren't supposed ... The doctors said you shouldn't be tol—"

Jakub's rage soared. "Doctors be damned! What do they know about aether? About my work? What do these three know!" He turned his anger at her companions. "How could you tell *them* such things and not tell *me*?"

"Professor, please," Miss MacLaren said, "you're both under a great strain."

Jakub tried to control his temper. He was being irrational, he knew it, he hated it, but the thought that this young woman should have wormed her way so deeply into his daughter's private memories – memories that she should have kept secret—

But not to me! The thought rang in his mind. Like a bell.

"Three months of my life, gone! Wiped out! All memory of it: the final construction, the tuning, the preparation, even the trial. Even the failure! All of it, gone! Everything I need to know to understand what went wrong." He turned back to Tereza. "How could you not tell me?"

Jakub felt himself start to shake, his thoughts to scatter like wind on water. As they had whenever he tried to remember the accident. He fought it with all his might, and this time, panting, he held it back.

"Heavenly days, Professor," the Curmidge woman

brayed, "you'll burst a vein. By all means, control yourself."

Jakub gritted his teeth. "You have no idea, madam."

"I have some idea," she retorted. "Your memory has been addled by the action of your own invention. Do not blame your daughter for that, or for listening to trained medical practitioners who undoubtedly warned her against just the sort of outburst we are seeing right now! Your brain has forgotten for a reason: to protect itself from the shock of knowing how so many died."

"Mrs. Curmidge!" Miss MacLaren exclaimed. "Gently, please!"

"The time for gentleness has passed, as the Professor himself seems to have realized." She peered at him through her toad-like eyes. "People are dying again, sir, aren't they? And you and your cannon thing are the most likely reason. Why? What happened? If those answers were made known, the murderer would have no reason to stalk you."

Jakub stared at her. Was the woman insane? "What are you babbling about?"

She gestured at Gilmore and outlined his suspicions. "You see, the first officer and my—" Her voice caught. "—my husband are only the latest to die. I have a right know the reason!"

"Please," Miss MacLaren repeated. "There is no need for both of you to shout. Professor, you see the predicament we're in, don't you? Since you have forgotten what happened, Tereza's memories are all we have to go on, unless, of course, we could somehow retrieve your memories."

Jakub stared at her, head spinning at the sudden change in tack.

"I know that lost memories sometimes do return as shock and grief wane," she said, but I fear we don't have the luxury of time. Yet, there is a way to extract forgotten memories from the shocked mind."

Jakub realized what she meant. "No," he growled.

"Hypnotism," she said, charging on. "It is a proven practice. And we have on board a practitioner of the first ord—"

"No!" Jakub's rage returned in force. "If you think that I would submit myself to the chicanery of that mountebank, that posturing fake and his counterfeit 'science' of the mind, you are even more demented than you sound!"

"Professor! There's no need for such insults!" Mrs. Curmidge scolded.

"Don't presume to lecture me, madam! God help me, is there not a single rational person on this floating asylum?"

"Father!" Tereza cried. "You're being—"

"What? I'm being what? If your mother were here now, she would—"

"She's not here! She's dead! Have you forgotten that already, too?"

Tereza covered her mouth and rushed away.

"Tereza!" Miss MacLaren called. "Wait!"

"I'll go after her," Gilmore said.

"No!" Jakub barked. "Let her go. She . . . she has done this before. In time, she'll . . ." *God help me*, he thought. *I need you more than ever, Eliška.* "She will come to her senses soon enough."

Mrs. Curmidge sniffed. "I wonder when you will come to yours, Professor. This infernal cannon or bomb or whatever it is has torn your family apart."

"Can no one understand? It is neither a cannon nor a bomb, it is a resonator!"

"But it is a weapon," Miss MacLaren stated, "or was intended to be, was it not?"

"It was a defense, young lady, not a weapon."

"And yet it killed many people."

Jakub felt almost overwhelmed by this obdurate failure to understand even a word of what he was saying. "You make the same small-minded mistake as every general and politician, every soldier and civilian who ever encountered the concept. It is not a weapon; it is a wall, a moat, if you will. Yes, a moat of unseen matter, resonating on the wavelength of the human brain. Yes, attackers will die if they try to cross it, but only so that many more people will live. It will be obvious to anyone who dares attempt war that every attack is doomed. Attack will be fruitless. War itself will be doomed!"

She stared at him a moment, as if his words were finally sinking in. Then: "But it didn't work, did it."

Jakub drew in a deep breath and let it out slowly.

"Not this time. And the problem was not the fault of the apparatus. The design is sound. The prototype worked perfectly. The failure could lie in the scaling up, or in the power supply, or – most likely – in the tuning. But whatever fatal fault was at its root, it is entirely mine."

"Tereza is certain it is hers," Miss MacLaren said.

"She is wrong!"

"You'd best tell *her* that, Professor, not me."

"Which I will, as soon as you stop hounding me."

She at least had the courtesy to apologize.

"I'm sorry if it seems that way, sir. Please believe me that our concern was merely to prevent any further harm to you and Tereza and everyone else on board. Your loss of memory—"

"Is temporary." Jakub heard his own voice waver with doubt, and a ripple of panic chimed in his heart. "It has to be. And when I remember, I will be able to reconstruct the problem – in my mind of course. In my calculations. Which I will test again with the prototype. And when I do

—"

"Excuse me, Professor," Gilmore said. "You still have the prototype?"

"Yes, of course I do," Jakub replied. "It wasn't there at the final test of the full-sized apparatus, thank God. It was safe at home."

"Where is it now?" Gilmore asked, his bruised face showing some alarm.

"Don't worry," Jakub assured him, "It is not connected to the power supply; I would never leave them connected. It is quite harmless without power."

"But where is it?" Gilmore insisted.

"With our hold luggage, of course," Jakub replied, irritated by all this fuss over such a minor detail. "It's quite safe. And I assure you no one knows it's there. And of course I have no intention of doing anything with it here at sea. But I will need it, you see, to test for the failure. When I remember; that's when I'll need it."

Mrs. Curmidge threw up her hands. "And yet you won't take the simple step that would enable you to remember now."

Jakub inhaled very slowly, counting backwards by sevens from ninety-one.

. . . dvacet jedna, čtrnáct, sedm, nic.

"Madam," he answered coldly. "You are wasting your breath. Now that I know what Tereza knows, I'm sure I'll be able to recall everything, without any recourse to King's useless mumbo-jumbo. Tereza will be my memory."

"But she was not there where it happened," Miss MacLaren said.

"Enough!" Jakub snapped. These women were insufferable! "She will do for me. Already, at her description of her mental state at the time, I have had flashes of insight, hints of recollection."

Miss MacLaren's gaze sharpened. "What are th—?"

Jakub waved her off. "Mere glimpses now, but I'm certain they will grow in length and detail. I'm afraid they can't help you in your investigations. It is alarming, I admit, to think that others should die on my . . . our account. There I cannot help you. If— When something germane occurs to me, I assure you, I shall come to you immediately."

"Thank you, professor," Miss MacLaren said. "And I apologize again for our importunate manner. We will leave you to see to Tereza. Would you, perhaps, like some company?"

Jakub felt much calmer now that he had managed to make them see his point of view, but he needed to be free of their *zatracené* presence before either of them opened her mouth one more time.

"Thank you, but no. It will be better if I speak to her privately. Good day."

He nodded and turned away but hadn't gone two steps before the count rounded the stern cabin, followed by his valet.

"*Tiens!* This is where you are hiding, eh?" He nodded to each in turn. "*Professeur, madame, mademoiselle.* And you, *monsieur* Gilmore. I have been looking for you since dinner." He turned to his valet. Larousse, *le chapeau, s'il vous plaît.*"

The valet handed him a hat. Turning back to Gilmore, the count held it out.

"I would like you to have this, if it fits you. I have learned from Officer MacBreive that your own was ruined in your fall last night. *Quelle dommage.* One must not be without a proper hat on ship, *n'est-ce pas*? The ladies would shun you!"

"Some might, but they would be fools," Miss MacLaren said.

Mrs. Curmidge sniffed in obvious disagreement. Jakub

decided he'd had enough.

"If you will excuse me," he said, nodding again in the general direction of everyone. As he turned the corner of the deckhouse, the count was forcing the bowler on a protesting Gilmore. Jakub hoped the young man would simply take it and get the embarrassment over with. In the end, he would have to give in. MacLaren would join forces with the count, Curmidge would stick her sniffing stump of a nose into it, and the scene would quickly degenerate into a maudlin duel of "Oh, I couldn't" and "Please, I insist."

Jakub shook himself, wondering why every interaction felt so dour, so difficult, so . . . so *otravný*. Aggravating. He was a man of science, of reason. Petty human foibles should not weigh so heavily on his spirits. God knew he had flaws enough of his own, but since losing his memory – and his sponsor and his career and his adopted country . . . and Eliška . . .

A bell rang. And again. And again. Bright, metallic notes, bronze on bronze, rings of bright sound rolling out from a dropped stone in the center of his mind, rebounding at the edges, overlapping till all there was was sound and bright colorless light and the name *Eliška* echoing among the peals.

"Are you all right, sir? Sir?"

Jakub blinked several times before he could see beyond the fading aura of sound. He was standing stock still on the gently rolling deck of the ship, a few steps away from the ladder to the bridge. A man in a uniform – a steward, he realized – was staring at him worriedly.

Jakub cleared his throat, which was strangely stiff. He blinked again, and discovered his eyes had somehow filled with tears. His face and beard were wet. He fumbled for his handkerchief.

"Yes," he managed. "Yes, I am fine. I . . . distracted by

a . . . a thought. It's over now. I'm fine. Yes."

He was babbling, and the steward looked more worried than before. Jakub blew his nose and took a deep breath. "Really, I am fine now. Thank you."

He brushed past the steward and hurried to the companionway, trying to at least appear steady. The constantly moving deck mocked his effort. He paused at the top of the steps and blew his nose again, then took several deep breaths until his heart had stilled and his eyes were clear enough to brave the descent. He sagged against the stair rail, feeling old and tired and stupid. The spells had been less frequent and less pronounced in the past three days, despite the awful events. He had been able to pretend they were no longer a problem, the deaths not his concern. All the deaths, even the ones he could not remember. Particularly those.

This past conversation had proved him wrong; this last spell underscored his folly. He'd been deceiving himself. He had let the ship's seemingly unchanging position at the center of an infinite horizon remove him from any concern but eating, sleeping, and watching the antics of those around him. He'd behaved as though he were merely a spectator to his own life, no longer an actor in that tiresome play. Not at all confused and powerless, because it didn't matter. It was not his problem. It was, after all, forgotten.

And remained so. Try as he might, he could not recall the few weeks before he awoke in the hospital, to find Tereza reading beside his bed. To see her gaunt face and stricken eyes, and the tears that came when she realized he was awake and she had to tell him they were alone, a family of but two. Try as he might, he could not recall. Even the shreds that had come to him on hearing Tereza's story were fading. The confusion of that loss, and all the losses contained within it, still clouded his days.

He clung to the shreds. Tereza did remember, and far more than he'd realized. He needed to speak to her.

Jakub stuffed the handkerchief into his pocket and made his way down the stairs to the cabin deck. He heard King's voice behind him, echoing from the passageway that led to the saloon. He hurried forward to cabin 12. He couldn't bear to face the man, or even hear his voice. He fumbled with the latch, slipped inside, and leaned back against the door, grateful for its thin protection. Not a sound came from outside, only the constant vibration of the ship's huge engine. The cabin was quiet, calm.

Empty.

"Tereza?"

Jakub peered against the glare of the porthole. Had someone pulled aside the curtain?

"Tereza?" He repeated.

She was not in her berth.

Where has she got to? he wondered.

He turned back to the door, thinking to go search for her, but was stopped by a small square of white at eye level on the mahogany panel. It was a note, attached with a bit of sticking plaster. Jakub peeled it off and carried it to the light of the porthole.

It was written in Bohemian. Poorly written. Jakub scanned it hurriedly, stumbling over the misspellings and botched grammar. Heart pounding, he reread it. And again.

> *professor Skovajsa, worry not, unharmed daughter is*
> *sleeping. but how easy to disappear, yes? Like seasick helmet.*
> *Which is valuable more? be considering when offers english*
> *spy for weapon plan. go home. secret be until new message.*
> *daughter return soon. Denisovitch*

Chapter 16

Seeking Tereza

Ewan paused outside the Skovajas' cabin, hand raised to knock. He heard hurried thuds and clunks behind the mahogany door, as though the cabin inside were being ransacked. There was a muffled cry, something coarse in a foreign language, angry or afraid, he couldn't tell which. His heart began to race. He pounded on the door but didn't wait for an answer. He threw his shoulder against it.

It wasn't locked. He tumbled inside with a crash, almost tearing the door off its hinges. Professor Skovajsa jerked upright, an empty suitcase dangling open in his hands. His hair was a tangled cloud, his tie undone, collar askew. They stared at each other, wild eyed.

"What—?" Ewan began.

"It's gone!" The professor cried.

"What's gone?" Ewan demanded. A sudden dip of the bow sent him back against the door, slamming it shut.

The professor gave no notice. "The apparatus! It's gone! They've taken it!"

Ewan's alarm soared. "The apparatus? You mean the prototype? The weapon?"

"What?" The professor glared. "No! Are you thick? I told you, it's safe in the hold. I mean the aetheric helmet. For seasickness. It was here. You saw it." He threw the suitcase onto a berth. "Now it's gone, just as he said."

"Who said?"

"I don't know! Denisovitch!" The professor sank to the berth beside the empty suitcase and buried his face in his hands. "They've taken the helmet, too."

"Denisovitch?" Ewan felt like he *was* thick. Then it sank in. "Too? He took something else? Wha—?" The final detail clicked home. He scanned the small cabin frantically. "Where's Tereza? He took Tereza?"

The professor nodded, muttering through his hands. "She's gone. Everything is gone."

Ewan tried to pull himself together and think clearly. "I'm here now," he said, as calmly as he could. He went to the professor and laid a hand on his shoulder. It shook uncontrollably; the professor was sobbing. "Don't worry, sir. They can't have taken her far, not on board ship. We'll find her, and this Denisovitch fellow." Ewan felt rage threatening his hard-won calm. *And when we do, he'll wish he had never come aboard.* "I'll tell the captain."

"No!" the professor gasped, looking up. "We can't tell anyone. She'll come back as long as we keep secret, the note promised."

"What note? Show me!"

The professor hesitated, then pulled a wrinkled square of paper from his coat pocket. "It's in Bohemian," he said, and read it in English. "The writer, this Denisovitch, he is Russian."

Ewan stared at the signature. "How do you know?"

"It's a Russian name. His Bohemian is terrible also."

"If it's even his real name," Ewan muttered. "But his meaning's clear enough: He's trying to scare you into giving him your cannon. But why this way? Why not just come out and offer you a job?"

"I received several offers after the inquest," the professor admitted. "Germany, France, the Ottomans; even a Raj in India. And, yes, Russia, from a man claiming to be Denisovitch. He wanted to arrange a meeting. I ignored him. I ignored them all."

"Why?"

"I don't trust any of them," the professor said. "Any

more than I would trust the Americans now. Of them all, only General Burton seemed to understand. But he is dead, along with Senator Clemens, the major, the Secretary – every person who had any inkling of what I was doing. I'm glad now the judges gave into the mob and made us leave. As for the others, they are just the same, from the Russians on down, interested only in conquest and empire. In starting wars. My apparatus has a higher purpose."

"So you said," Ewan replied, "but that's not helping Tereza any. What about the English the note talks about? Half the people on board are English. Has any one of them made an offer?"

The professor shook his head. "Everyone has stayed very far away from us. Except for you and the MacLarens, Mrs. Curmidge, Mr. Reed, the count – our table."

"And King," Ewan noted.

"Yes, that one." The professor's tone went cold. "But he is American, and a charlatan of the first order. Hardly the type the English would trust to spy for them."

"I suppose," Ewan said. "And maybe it's no one at all. Maybe this Denisovitch is just trying to set you up. Either way, the captain needs to know."

"No!"

"We can't just sit here like a pair of geese, waiting for the ax to fall!" Ewan remembered the garrote, steadily tightening, closing his windpipe no matter how hard he struggled. He turned to go.

The professor grabbed his shoulder, awakening the pain in his bruises. "No! The note says be secret! She will return!"

There was a knock on the cabin door. They both froze for an instant, then Ewan pulled free and threw the door open.

Daisy MacLaren stood outside, a startled look on her

face.

"Excuse me, Mr. Gilmore," she said. "I didn't mean to interrupt you." She looked past him, taking in the mess the professor had made of the room. "Where is Tereza?"

They both answered in the same breath:

"Gone to the powder room," Ewan said.

"Gone for a walk," the professor said.

They looked at each other, crestfallen.

"Gone, at the least," Daisy said. She fixed them with a stern look. "What's happened? The truth, please."

"She's been kidnapped," Ewan said.

"No," the professor moaned.

"Supposedly by Russians." Ewan pulled the note from Professor Skovajsa's trembling hand and showed it to Daisy. "We need to tell the captain."

"No!" the professor snapped. "Then we will never see her again! Like Officer MacKay!"

"It's broad daylight," Ewan argued. "They won't have the chance. We'll find her befo—"

Daisy raised a hand. "Softer, please, Mr. Gilmore. You're upsetting Professor Skovajsa, and these walls are thin. Mrs. Curmidge is next door, and those three bankers on the other side. There's no need to involve them."

"But we can't let him get away with it!" Ewan hissed.

"We shan't," Daisy said briskly. "We will search for her, but quietly. You know the ship and the crew and can enter places we normal passengers are not allowed. I'll enlist Mr. Reed and make the rounds of the deck, the saloon – all the places she might reappear if she slips free of her captors on her own."

A glimmer of hope showed in the professor's eyes. "Do you think she could?"

"She is intelligent and strong willed, sir. I don't doubt she is capable of many things you don't give her credit for."

"I will come with you!"

"No. You need to stay here, in case she returns while we're searching. You must be on the alert and hope for a glimpse of her captor."

"She'll be able to tell us," Ewan said. "At least to describe him."

Daisy looked dubious. "Perhaps, but this kidnapper, Russian or not, has shown himself to be clever and ruthless. The note says she is sleeping, so he may have used a sedative. Certainly, he will have bound her and quite likely used a gag, perhaps even a blindfold, so we cannot assume she will have seen him, nor that she will escape." She clapped her hands. "Now, no more talk. Mr. Gilmore, search everywhere. I'll find Mr. Reed, and don't worry, Professor, I shan't tell him why I want to wander the decks." She lifted her eyes to the heavens. "Not that he will wonder."

A sudden suspicion niggled at Ewan's thoughts. "Where is he, anyway? I haven't seen him for hours."

"Since breakfast," Daisy agreed. "He seemed quite shaken by the news of Mr. MacKay." Her face fell for a moment, but she quickly revived. "Enough gloomy talk. I'll find him, never fear. Professor, I'll check back regularly."

She slipped out the door quickly, jaw set, eyes gleaming.

"Amazing," the professor murmured. "She reminds me very much of . . ."

"Will you be all right alone, Professor?" Ewan asked.

"Yes." He waved a hand. "Go. Go carefully. Try not to . . ." He choked back a sob, swallowed, and straightened his shoulders. "Just go."

"I'll find her, sir," Ewan promised.

He went to his cabin first, but Derek wasn't there. Nor

was King. He looked up and down the passageway, wondering where to look next; where someone could hide a captive for a few hours and not be noticed. The closest places were right beside him: the latrines and bathroom. They were very public, but Ewan checked anyway. As he expected, the stalls were empty and the three deep tubs, too.

The next most likely place was a cabin. All the doors were shut, and he longed again for his uniform. A steward had excuses to check the cabins. Still, he had to give it a try.

He went down the passageway and back up the other side, trying the doors one by one. A good half of the cabins were locked and some of the rest were empty, but he surprised more than one passenger dozing, a few dressing for dinner, an intent game of dice (which wasn't allowed on board), and a couple wriggling under the tartan blanket on a narrow berth. He said, "Excuse me, wrong cabin" each time and ducked back out in a medley of gasps and curses and a mix of startled expressions that would have been funny in any other circumstance. He ended up back where he'd started with nothing more to show for it than a few blushes.

Where else? He envisioned the ship from keel to wheelhouse and stem to stern. It had to be someplace private. Assuming it wasn't one of the locked cabins, that left only the hold. It also had to be somewhere a passenger could get to in the middle of the day without being noticed. That ruled out the hold . . . unless. There were three ways into the hold when the hatches were closed and sealed. The first one was through a trap door in the forward hatch and down a vertical ladder – not likely in broad daylight and carrying a captive girl. The second was through the engine room – crowded every minute with the black gang, watched over by MacLeod and his engineers. The third was through the fo'c'sle, where the deck crew ate and slept. But it was often empty during the dog watches at the end of the afternoon. Any crew there at that time of day were usually asleep. The fo'c'sle companionway ran all the way down to the hold. There was a hatchway at each deck but, with care and luck, it could be done, even burdened with a hostage.

Ewan went forward past the the bathrooms to the bulkhead between the cabin deck and the fo'c'sle. The hatch was steel, with a veneer of walnut, heavy bronze hinges, and a large bronze lever to clamp it shut. The lever gave slowly to a firm twist. Ewan glanced back to make sure no passengers were in sight, then pushed the lever all the way down, eased the hatch open just wide enough, and slipped through.

He was on the landing opposite the deck crew's mess. Its door was closed, but he could hear dim voices inside and the clink of a spoon in a cup. Ladders led up to the main deck and down toward steerage. Ewan went down, treading softly on the iron steps. Electric bulbs cast a dim amber light barred with the hard shadows of stairs and railings. There were more faint voices below. Ewan slowed.

The next landing opened onto the seamen's berth, a large room lined with bunks in stacks of five. A closed hatch opposite, identical to the one he'd just slipped through, led into steerage – the source of the voices. The seamen's berth was quiet. Ewan took a deep breath, padded quickly across the landing, and continued down the final ladder toward the hold.

The ladder ended in a dimly lit, narrow space just above the bilge. The sides of the hull closed in sharply, both down toward the keel and forward toward the stem. The plunge and lift of the bow was at its worst. There was no fine paneling down here. To his left was a bare steel bulkhead, with a single hatchway to the hold in its center. The hatchway was sealed by a heavy iron door with a very stiff latch, operated by a long bar. Ewan laid all his weight onto the bar, grunting as it inched around just far enough to free the latch. The hinges were stiff, too, on purpose; the heave of the ship would have thrown the hatch open and shut with dangerous force. He slid through the narrow gap, squinting into the gloom.

The hold here was fourteen feet high. Two lights mounted on the ceiling glowed feebly on racks of shelves to port and stacks of crates to starboard of a center aisle. In the dim light, Ewan could just make out the sealed hatchway to the engine room, halfway down the length of the hull. There were other lights, and he felt on the bulkhead for the switch.

Someone groaned behind him.

Ewan froze, slowly slipped his hand into his pocket, and gripped the derringer firmly. He turned and peered back out the hatchway. There was no one on the landing, and he wondered if the ship itself had been groaning under the strain of the seas at her bow. The groan sounded again. It was coming from the other side of the landing, behind the ladder. There was a narrow hatchway there, also sealed with an iron door, this one pierced by a small, barred window at eye level. The brig. Someone was locked up inside.

Ewan slipped out, eased the hatch shut, and heaved on the bar to seal it. The latch squeaked. Ewan froze again. His hand went back to his pocket.

When the brig stayed silent, he tiptoed to the ladder. He'd crept up two steps when the groan came again, along with a rustle of cloth as someone moved. A lot of cloth. Another, louder groan came, light and high pitched.

Tereza! Ewan thought. *Of course, you bampot! Where else?*

He hurried back down and stared through the little

window. The brig was darker than the hold, lit only by the dull beam through the window, now three-quarters blocked by his head.

"Tereza?" he whispered.

She lay still, but he could make her out now, a pale heap on a low berth along one side of the narrow, triangular cell. The latch was unlocked – it could only be opened from the outside anyway. Ewan pushed the hatch wide and was bending over Tereza in a moment. She was half on her side, hat missing, hair gone loose and all astray across the blue-ticked pillow. Her bag and parasol lay beside her, half hidden by her skirts. Her eyes were closed, but her head moved slightly, as though she sensed someone was there.

"Tereza!" he hissed, shaking her shoulder gently.

She cried out and flailed her arms, eyes barely open. She said something, but her voice was so slurred, he couldn't understand it.

"Tereza! Wake up!" He shook her shoulder again.

"No!" she cried, and her hand found the grip on the parasol. She swung it wildly toward his head. He tried to duck but—

Everything went white.

Chapter 17

Rising Passions

When Ewan's vision cleared, he was lying on his back on the cold metal deck with a taste of bile in his throat. His head felt ready to burst. His joints ached, even his fingers. Even blinking hurt. Tereza's face floated into his field of view, wavering like oil on water. She blinked back at him, eyes groggy, and almost fell off the bunk. He reached up and caught her by the shoulders. Every bruise on his body throbbed.

They groaned in harmony.

"I'm sorry," she said. "So sorry." Her voice was as groggy as her eyes.

"Me, too," he replied. "I shouldn't have startled you." He tried to smile. "Should have known better."

"Poor Ewan." She reached down to touch his face.

He couldn't support her any longer. His arms collapsed, and she slid the rest of the way off the bunk.

He groaned again as the various angles of her body settled against all the bruises on his.

"Oh, I'm hurting you," she whispered.

"No, not you," he said. "I was already sore."

"This can't be helping," she said, settling closer.

"It's fine." And it really was, he realized. "I'm just glad I found you." And glad for this chance to hold her.

"Me, too." Her head lay on his shoulder, her lips brushed his neck. He wondered if she realized and decided it didn't matter. Despite the pain he felt a thrill.

They lay that way for a couple of minutes.

"We'd better go," Ewan said finally, though both his

heart and his aching muscles argued against the notion. "Before he comes back."

"Oh!" Tereza pushed herself half up, staring toward the open hatchway. "Where are we? How did I get here?"

"The brig," Ewan replied, untangling himself enough to sit up. "And I was hoping you could tell us. Come on. We'll talk once we've got you someplace safer."

"Can we get out?" she asked.

He glanced at the door to be sure. Yes, he'd left it open. But actually getting to it wasn't as easy as glancing, and getting out and away was worse. Neither of them could stand up without swaying or walk without weaving. The motion of the ship sent them stumbling against the bulkheads, tripping against the hard edges of the steps. They clung together, supporting each other over the lip of the hatchway, to the ladder, then up the ladder, struggling to swallow their gasps and moans. Tereza muttered Bohemian words that could only be curses. Ewan felt seasick for the first time in his life. But they made it without falling, retching, or being seen. They tumbled into the Skovajsa's cabin, still gripping each other by the waist.

The professor sprang to his feet with a cry.

"Tereza! *Zaplať pánbůh!*" He threw his arms around them both, almost sobbing with relief. Questions tumbled out as he held them. "Thank God. Thank God. Are you hurt? Where were you? Did he— Were you . . ." He struggled for words.

"I'm fine, Father," she said. "No one harmed me. Please, let us breathe. Ewan is . . . bruised, remember."

"Yes, forgive me." He let them go, then took her hand and led her to a bunk, making her sit. "What happened? How did he capture you? Ewan – Mister Gilmore, excuse me – did you see him?"

"No, sir. She was alone. In the brig. Up in the bow, hold level." Ewan leaned against the upper bunk. The pain was less, his stomach easing, but now he felt weak in the legs.

Professor Skovajsa sat beside Tereza and took her hand. "How did he manage to drag you there? You had your mother's parasol, yes?"

Tereza nodded, and Ewan held it up. He'd made sure to bring it, and to be the one to carry it. Just in case.

"I had no chance to use it, Father," Tereza said. She rubbed her eyes with her free hand. "I had come into the cabin. Someone . . ." She shuddered, then took a deep breath and settled herself. "Someone grabbed me from behind and pressed a cloth over my mouth. It must have been some type of sedative. I tried to hold my breath, to break loose. The parasol . . . The strap was around my wrist, but I couldn't lift it. He was too strong. He hit my ribs and I gasped and . . ." She shook her head. "I remember everything getting dim, fading. Then nothing, until Ewan . . . woke me in the brig."

"He probably carried her down over his shoulder," Ewan said. "It'd be easy enough for a strong man to do. Just a matter of not getting spotted."

The professor looked from her to him and back. "And you're sure . . . ? You're all right?"

Tereza blushed. "I'm sure, Father. My head still feels thick but that's all." She stood briskly. "It's poor Ewan who's been hurt. First last night, and then now." She took his hand openly. "I hit him with the parasol."

Now Ewan blushed, but she gave a quick squeeze and let go.

"It was my fault, sir," he said. "I startled her when she was just coming awake." He shrugged. "You'll be glad to know it works."

The professor cleared his throat. "Yes, well, that's good, I suppose. I'm sorry you had to be the subject of this unplanned test. But now we are all back together and things are more normal. So . . ."

"Yes, what now?" Teresa said. "What do we do about this monster? If only I had seen him, we—"

"All we know is his name may be Denisovitch and he may be Russian," Ewan said. "I think you should read her the note, sir."

The professor hesitated, but Tereza took it from him and read it easily, her face deepening into a scowl that rivaled Mrs. Curmidge at her worst. She shed the last semblance of grogginess as she peppered her father with questions about the Russian offers.

"You should have told me!" she fumed.

"You had enough to worry about," he protested. "Besides which, I was not about to accept the offers. I had no idea it would come to this."

"The point is," Ewan said quickly, before the storm on Tereza's face could rise to a full gale, "it *has* come to this. I don't think he wanted to harm you, Tereza. The note makes it pretty clear: This was just a threat. He wanted to show how easy it would be for him to . . . get to you. Now we know you're in danger, both of you. We need to tell the captain."

"No!" the professor snapped. "The note says clearly—"

"I've heard it!" Ewan snapped back. "What's clear is that there are spies on board, Russian and British, from the sound of it. One of them, maybe named Denisovitch, murdered Officer MacKay. And almost killed me first." He swallowed hard, fighting the vivid memory. "I can't protect you by myself." He looked Tereza in the eye. "I won't risk your life."

She met his look head on. "If we tell the captain, he'll set a guard, and everyone on board will know in an instant, including the British. We'll have no chance to catch them. They'll just lay low until we reach Glasgow. And once we're there, we won't be able to trust anyone!"

"You'll be in Scotland," Ewan protested. "It's the English you have to worry about."

"There are Scotchmen working for the English, I'm sure," the professor said glumly. "You're naive to think otherwise."

"Only in the Borders," Ewan muttered. "Even so, I can't just troll you out on deck like bait for a school of sharks!"

"Not alone," Tereza agreed. "But there's Daisy and Mr. Reed."

"Not enough," Ewan said.

"The count."

"We can't trust the count," Ewan said. "Not the way he arrived. He could have been following you."

"So now there are French spies, too, I suppose?" Tereza remarked.

Ewan threw up his hands. "Maybe there are. We can't be sure of anyone who boarded after you did. I showed you the list. We can't even trust Derek."

"Then who can we trust?" she cried.

There was a tap on the door, and Daisy spoke outside. "Tereza?"

Tereza went to the door, then paused with her hand on the latch. "Oh, my," she said in a stage whisper. "It could be an American spy!" Then she opened the door. It was Daisy and Derek both.

"Thank Heavens!" Daisy exclaimed, throwing her arms around Tereza.

Derek caught Ewan's eye and winked. "Well done, Gilmore. Well done, indeed!"

Tereza pulled them inside and shut the door.

Daisy took her hand. "You're not harmed? Tell us!"

Tereza told her brief story, then Ewan's part, and finally read the note for Derek's sake. Ewan watched closely, but neither of them seemed to feign their surprise.

"No one but us can know," Tereza explained. "We must catch them out before the ship reaches Glasgow."

"That's just a few more days," Daisy said. "We will not leave you alone for a moment! We can recruit Mrs. Curmidge, too."

"No," Professor Skovajsa protested. "We are too many who know already."

"Very well, then, just us." Daisy smiled. "It will be easy enough to have her about without her even knowing, and she will certainly create a furor if someone tries anything odd."

"We can't be sure they'll try anything else, can we?" Derek wondered. "I mean, if it were me—"

"Not Denisovich, perhaps," Tereza said, "but I think the British will, if they think Father might make a deal with Russia."

"Will they think that?" Derek asked. "How will they even know he's been approached?"

"They'll have been watching," Daisy said. "They may very well have noticed all this upset, but even if they haven't, we can leave clues."

"They'll be watching Father, not me." Tereza said. "Ewan's presence might keep them at a distance, but Ewan can pretend to be distracted." She flashed him a quick smile. "And Father could ask around about Denisovitch."

"Of course!" Daisy agreed. "Professor, you could ask the purser if anyone of that name is aboard. Or anyone with a Russian name or passport or accent."

"There isn't," Ewan said. "The crew is already on the lookout for Russians."

"We know that," Daisy said, "but the passengers don't, and the Professor can pretend he doesn't and make an apparently idle inquiry. In the saloon this evening, in fact. You can ask Mr. King, first."

"King? Why him?" the Professor demanded. "What's

he got to do with this—?"

"Nothing, I hope," Daisy assured him, "but everyone is suspect, and King booked his cabin right after you did. He has also met everyone on board through his seasickness cure and would be a logical person to ask. He might even spread the word."

"And, when you ask King, Ewan can suggest you also ask the purser," Tereza said, "which you can then do loudly, Father, right after the meal, before too many people have left the saloon."

And so Tereza and Daisy plotted their plan of attack.

"I'd best keep watch through the night," Derek volunteered. "Our cabin is right across the way." He squared his jaw. "They won't get past us, you can be sure."

"Good," Daisy said. "Now, it's almost time for supper; we'd best get ready. Tereza, I'll wait here while you tidy up, then you can join me. Gentlemen?"

Derek and Ewan quickly excused themselves, and the professor followed them out.

"Mr. Gilmore, a word, please?" He waited, with a pointed glance at Derek.

"Yes," Derek said, suddenly realizing the Professor wanted privacy. "I'll get cleaned up and hurry back to relieve you, Gilmore. Constant watch it is."

The professor waited till he disappeared into their cabin.

"I want to apologize again for your mishap with the parasol," the professor said. "And also to thank you. If there is anything I can do to repay you, you must let me know immediately."

Ewan was embarrassed. "It was nothing, Professor. I'm glad it turned out as well as it did. I just . . ." He hesitated at bringing another worry to the professor's attention. "I just worry that the sedative has done something to Tereza," he went on. "She's all abuzz, if you see what I mean, sir. Like she's drunk, only her mind's clear as a bell. I'm sorry, I mean—"

"That's quite all right," the professor said. "But no, the sedative hasn't changed her at all. It has brought her back to us. What a relief! Finally, she's acting like her old self."

&

The evening went as planned, though not as hoped. King was delighted when the professor approached him to ask about Denisovitch, but was sorry to say that none of the passengers went by that name.

"Denisovitch?" Derek asked loudly. "Isn't that a Russian name? I thought you were Bohemian, professor. Is this a colleague of yours, a fellow scientist?"

Ewan scanned the faces at the other tables as the professor mumbled a reply. Not a single eyebrow raised, not surprising if Denisovich was as professional as he seemed.

After the meal, everyone scattered to their usual pursuits: cards, books, and music in the saloon; cards and cigars in the smoking cabin; cards, needlepoint, and gossip in the ladies. A few people braved the wind and went out on deck, including the professor, with Ewan and Derek in tow. The two if them made a point of letting him go on ahead while they stopped for an imaginary discussion by one of the lifeboats. Derek asked Ewan how he had managed to get caught up in the fall and choked so badly. Ewan fumbled for a reply that wouldn't sound like nonsense, then remembered Aunt Nellie's advice and changed the subject to Derek.

"And where did you go in the middle of the night last night?" he asked. "I noticed you'd left the room."

"You did?" Derek cleared his throat. "Yes. Well, I did go out. I had to visit the, what do you call it, the head. That's the nautical term, isn't it?"

"You didn't go straight to the head," Ewan said. "I saw you go up on deck."

"What? Did you follow me?"

"Yes, I did. But I lost you in the fog and then— Never mind. Where did *you* go? That's what we're talking about."

"We are, aren't we. Yes. Right." Derek squirmed. "If you must know, I went, was trying . . . You see, I have been trying to become more acquainted with Miss MacLaren. She is rather . . . appealing, don't you think?" He paused, but Ewan waited in silence. Derek sighed. "I'm afraid she finds me rather ordinary. So I thought if, perhaps, I could present her with a, uh, a little . . . token, as it were, of my . . ." He jammed his hands into his pockets. "Dash it, Gilmore, you do make it awkward! I wrote her a poem, if you must know. It's not Byron, of course, but I thought I could better express my regard for her, and demonstrate some of my, uh, un-ordinary qualities, such as they are, in words. In a poem."

Ewan stared at him, agog, wondering if any spy – any professional actor, for that matter – could play a role so well.

"I don't suppose you'd read it for me?" Derek mumbled "Just as a favor, of course. To see how it sounds to another's ears. To see if it's ready. For her." Hope hung on every word.

It was the last thing Ewan wanted to do. "Sure, why not," he lied.

Derek's smile shone through the gloom. "That's awfully swell of you! I have it in my notebook, in the cabin. I'll just—"

"Later," Ewan said. "He's getting away from us." The professor had just passed under the bridge and was disappearing around the forward deckhouse.

"Oh! Right!" Derek exclaimed, and dashed up the deck.

Ewan hurried in his wake. They turned around the deckhouse and found the professor speaking with King and Mrs. Curmidge.

". . . had hoped to visit Russia this trip," King was saying, "but my agent in Berlin said it would be best to wait till the whole Ottoman affair had died down completely. Oh, good evening, Gilmore, Reed. Lovely night, isn't it?"

Mrs. Curmidge sniffed. "If you don't mind cold cockles. I imagine Russia must be like this. I can't imagine wanting to visit there or anyplace so far north at this time of year."

"What do you say, Professor?" King asked. "Have you been to Russia?"

"I was in Saint Petersburg once, to visit the university. It was a pleasant enough place."

"Was it?" Derek asked brightly. "Will you be visiting again this trip?"

The conversation snagged for a moment on the foolishness of the question, but the professor finally took the cue.

"I hadn't been planning on it, but circumstances—" He let the pause hang, then changed course. "No, I wouldn't think so. Not unless—" Another pause. "No. I'm sure not."

"Who knows, my good professor; something might come up to change your mind," King remarked. "One can never be sure which way the winds of fate will blow."

The professor pretended to consider the thought. "One should never discount random chance, I suppose."

"One should certainly try not to," Mrs. Curmidge stated. "This chill breeze, on the other hand, is blowing me toward a warm blanket and rest. Is it too much to presume that one of you young gentlemen would deign to escort me? I don't fancy navigating the distance alone, particularly not after last night's grim events."

Ewan sagged. Only last night, yet so much had happened since. The combined bruises renewed their aches and pains. He needed a long rest.

Derek saved him from Curmidge at least. "I would be happy to be your escort, ma'am. I'm sure Mr. Gilmore would rather stay with the others."

Not that Ewan had any choice. The only consolation was not having to read Derek's poem with such a headache. And the professor didn't linger long in the smoking cabin. They left King in conversation with a silk buyer and a Philadelphia oil man and, joined by Colonel MacLaren, fetched Tereza and Daisy from the ladies cabin, and made their way down to their berths.

Derek was waiting for Ewan in their cabin, poem at the ready. Ewan begged off with a mention of his bruises and a promise to read it first thing in the morning. Derek's face fell.

"You should grab some sleep now anyway," Ewan told him. "You're on watch come midnight. I'll wake you then."

Derek protested that he didn't feel the least bit sleepy, but was snoring almost the moment his head hit the pillow. Ewan, to his own surprise, didn't feel sleepy at all. He felt dazed enough, but his body hurt and his thoughts wouldn't settle down, lurching between memories of the fight on deck to the feel of Tereza's lips on his neck. He went out and walked up and down the passageway, but it didn't help. He paused to listen at the door to the Skovajsa's cabin and made out a gentle snore. A louder one came from Mrs. Curmidge's cabin; he didn't even have to stand close to hear it.

Ewan turned toward his own cabin, and his foot bumped a pair of the Professor's shoes, set out to be shined by the steward. Ewan studied them, amazed at how different this crossing had turned out to be: neither deck crew nor steward, and not really a passenger either. On a whim, he went to the locker beside the bathrooms and fetched back one of the shoeshine boxes. He sat on it, pulled out the shoeblack and rag from the top drawer, picked up the professor's right shoe, and began to rub on the polish. He felt his body and mind relax and almost smiled.

Two minutes later, a harsh voice jerked him out of his reverie.

"What the bloody hell do you think you're doing?"

It was Ranald Morrison, glaring down at him, arms akimbo.

Ewan, still half dazed, stared at him. "Polishing a shoe. What's it to you?"

"That's my passenger and my tip," Ranald snapped. "I'll thank you to keep your clumsy hands off his shoes."

"Bugger off, Ranald," Ewan growled. "I'm doing you a favor here."

"Favor? You're making me look bad, is what you're doing." He snatched the shoe out of Ewan's hand. "You want to mess up somebody's shoes, do it to your own passenger. But wait, you don't have a passenger, do you?" He reached out and flipped Ewan's new bowler to the back of his head. "Just a fancy hat and a sharper's suit, so you can run around like a wee laird and trade winks with the gentleman's daughter."

Ewan flushed. "I'm not winking at anyone, bampot, and you know it! I was ordered to play passenger, to keep them safe!"

"Oh, good one, Gilmore," Ranald sneered. "Keep them safe, you say? Did MacKay know that?"

Ewan lunged off the box and smashed the opened can of shoeblack into Ranald's face.

Chapter 18

Imprisoned

Ewan paced the width of the brig and back, five short steps each way. Then three steps and a long stumble as the *Lewis* dipped, bow first, into the next wave. The brig, in the very pinch of the bow, dipped and soared more than any other part of the ship. After pitching twice against the hard iron plates of the riveted hull, Ewan found the rhythm, but still had to keep a hand sliding on the rail of the upper berth to steady himself. He'd tried lying down, but that gave too much lee to his thoughts. He had flown off the handle as quick as an ugly drunk at the bottom of the bottle. And what good had it done him? Landed him here, that's what, an inch above the bilge, with no way out and no way of knowing how Tereza was faring. Or what she thought of him now, and that was the worst of it. He would rather have traded a few more punches with Ranald Morrison than suffer the blows he gave himself.

Ewan had taken the captain's reprimand for just what it was. He deserved it – he had struck the first blow. So he hadn't tried to argue it was Ranald's fault, hadn't even complained when the captain merely confined Ranald to his berth in the glory hole instead of the brig. Better to be locked up alone than with that jeering snot. No, Ewan had no one to blame but himself. And now he had to deal with it. Which he could only do by pacing – one, two, three, stumble-catch, turn, one, two – and all the while kicking himself for losing his temper. And worrying about what was happening to Tereza.

"*Hsst!* Ewan!" It was Derek, peering through the tiny,

barred window. He held his fingers up to his lips and whispered, "How are you doing, sport?"

Ewan took three short steps to the door. "How's Tereza? And the professor? What's happening up there? Why aren't you with them?"

"They're fine, just fine. Everyone's fine, really. Miss MacLaren and the colonel are standing duty, as it were, with Queen Curmidge in tow. No sign of any Ruskies or Redcoats or spies of any other ilk. Rest easy. But, look, I daren't stay long; wouldn't do to get caught fraternizing with the prisoner. Sorry, that was rather rude, wasn't it?"

"It's all right," Ewan said. "I *am* a prisoner, by my own damn fault. Are you sure—?"

"Not your fault at all, if you ask me," Derek protested. "That steward should be in here, not you. You're the passenger, after all. If he can't control his cheeky—"

"It's all right," Ewan insisted. "What did Tereza say when she found out? Was she angry?"

"Oh, she was angry, you can be sure of that."

Ewan sagged against the bulkhead.

"What?" Derek said. "Oh. Fear not, she wasn't angry at you, not at all. You should have heard her go on about that steward. And the captain! Why, she was all set to storm the bridge, cheeks blazing like banners unfurled in a storm, the dart from her eye a spear of vengeance ready to launch at the man who would dare lock you up in the hole from which you had just so recently rescued her own fair soul."

Derek paused for a deep breath. "Right. That was downright stirring, wasn't it? Which reminds me, I've brought you something to read." He pulled a folded sheet of paper from his inner pocket and passed it through the bars. "And Miss MacLaren sent this, from breakfast." He pulled a folded napkin from a side pocket, tried to pass it through and, when it wouldn't fit, squished it gently until it did. "And now I must be going. When you've read . . . Well, when you're out, we can talk about that." He gestured toward the sheet of paper. "The poem. Or I'll come down again if you're not out by dinner. Right? Be at ease. Don't worry, Daisy and I— Miss MacLaren and I will keep close watch. Don't lose heart; a battle was lost, but the war shall be ours!" He tiptoed away.

Ewan felt a little dazed. He remembered only one fact from Derek's patter: Tereza wasn't angry with him. A huge grin spread across his face. He sat on the lower berth, suddenly very tired but also much more at ease. He unfolded the napkin on his lap, revealing a pair of large, fragrant scones, a bit mashed together but still with a touch of warmth. Daisy had smeared thick layers of butter and jam between them, and it oozed from the crumbling seam. He licked it up.

It was delicious. Ewan leaned back against the pillow and devoured the rest, then fell asleep to a vision of Tereza charging down on Captain Morrison, cheeks blazing, jabbing a spear at his broad, brass-buttoned chest.

When he woke, his neck was stiff, his hands cold, and the crumbs from the scones were scattered across the bed. He was also lying on top of Derek's folded sheet of paper. He stretched, brushed off the crumbs, then used the chamber pot before going to the window to read the poem. It scrawled down most of the page.

Epistle to a Shipboard Friend was the title.

"She walks the deck a swan among gulls,
Or yet more my albatross,
But gladly borne about my neck,
Symbol of my silent troth . . ."

Ewan groaned but doggedly read on.

Halfway through, he heard soft, slow footsteps on the ladder. He slipped back to the bunk, tucked the poem under the pillow, then quickly remembered the napkin and shoved it under, too. But it was Daisy herself who stood on tiptoe to peer through the square of bars.

"I must say, you look comfortable enough, Mr. Gilmore," she whispered. "Derek described a battered soul racked by remorse and anguish, pining for the company of his one true love."

"Daisy! Hush!" It was Tereza's voice, off to the side. Ewan felt the blood rush to his face.

Daisy chuckled. "There, you're both blushing, so I guess it must be true."

Tereza huffed almost like Mrs. Curmidge. "You're terrible! Let me see him."

She appeared in the window, cheek to cheek with Daisy. "Are you all right?"

Ewan got over his fluster and hurried to the door. "Well enough, but for being in here. What about you? Are you keeping safe?"

"Don't worry, sir," Daisy replied. "We've been guarding her as closely as the Queen. And not a soul has shown more than the slightest interest in her or the professor, though I've noticed a few arch glances and whispered asides when we stroll past."

"What do you mean?"

"That *your* absence has not gone unnoticed. You and Tereza, I'm afraid, are the objects of shipboard gossip. Mr. King reports that a betting pool has started over the reason for your fight with that vile steward. Not that anyone will ever learn the truth of it, I'm sure, but it does provide a reason to bet, which seems to be the only thing most of the passengers find the least bit exciting. You'd think we were becalmed in the doldrums."

Ewan tore his eyes from Tereza's face. "What a minute. King reported that? You haven't told King anything have you?"

"Of course not. The professor has simply renewed the

friendship, as we suggested, and King has been serving well as our ear to many other conversations. Not that I doubt he placed the first bet. He keeps prying to see what we know about the fight."

"It wasn't really over me, was it?" Tereza demanded. "I hope you weren't that foolish."

"No," Ewan replied quickly. "Not at all. No."

"Methinks the laddie doth protest too much," Daisy said, smiling again.

"Well, he did insult you, in a way, and I could hardly . . . but it was also about Mr. Mack—" His throat closed on the name MacKay.

"Please stop." Tereza slipped her hand through the bars as far as she could. "I know you didn't start it, and that's all I need to know. You wouldn't have struck him without good reason."

He took her fingers, grateful, wishing he could forgive himself that easily.

Daisy interrupted the silence after a moment or two. "We can't stay long, lest we be caught. We just needed to see for ourselves that you were not suffering unduly."

"And to bring you this," Tereza added. She produced another wrapped napkin, this one enfolding a meat pie from dinner. She had to break it in half to fit between the bars. Then, with more assurances that all were safe, and a promise from Tereza that she wouldn't leave her cabin without the parasol, they tiptoed out of sight.

Ewan returned to the bunk, not the least bit hungry. The visit had been a relief, but much too brief. He brought out Derek's poem again then put it back down. Daisy's assurances weren't enough to stop the unease swelling in his chest. The killer was still on board, still watching, waiting for the English spies to make a move. Or the professor. All it would take was a single misheard word or misunderstood nod to a passing gentleman; just one false move and anything could happen. Now nothing stood between Tereza and Denisovitch but Daisy and Derek. Ewan stared at the poem in his lap. Derek's words were hardly reassuring. He folded the paper roughly and crammed it back under the pillow. Derek was mooning about up there while he was caged down here, with no idea of what was happening. He didn't even know what time it was.

After what seemed like hours, Ewan heard steps on the ladder again, loud and certain this time. The foc's'le messboy appeared in the window.

"Got your supper here," he announced. "Is the bampot full? Smells like it. Set it down by the door and get back on the berth."

Ewan followed the orders, and the messboy opened the door just wide enough to set a tray inside and take out the chamber pot.

"Back with a clean one and a pitcher when I get the tray," the messboy said, latching the door. His footsteps clattered more carefully back up the ladder.

Ewan fetched the tray and picked at the meal. It was what the crew had for supper, better than bread and water but it tasted like soot. He set it down by the door, half eaten.

Ages later, the messboy clattered down again, bearing the promised pitcher of water and clean chamber pot.

"Need anything else?" he asked, then laughed. "Say no, because this is all you get."

"What time is it?" Ewan asked.

"That you can have, but you can't keep it." The messboy laughed again.

"The time?" Ewan repeated.

"Just gone two bells in the evening watch. Cheer up, sport; they won't keep you in here forever. We're only four days out, right?" He clattered back up the stairs, chuckling.

Two bells. Nine p.m. Tereza would still be in the saloon, eating supper. Then she'd go to the ladies cabin or maybe for a walk on deck. Then to her cabin to sleep. He didn't think she'd attempt to sneak down here again, not at night. Too risky; even Daisy would have to agree. So another day gone and three more to go. Ewan began to pace – one, two, three, stumble-catch, turn, pace back, hand on the rail, all the while hoping to hear soft footsteps on the ladder.

Chapter 19

The Outrage

Tereza stared through Daisy's little telescope at the fast-approaching ship and the low, dark smudge of land beyond it – the northwest coast of Ireland.

Not green from this distance, she thought, strangely disappointed. In the shock of the ... accident and the travesty of Father's trial and the unreality of this deportation, she had given little thought to where they were going. Anywhere else had seemed a welcome refuge. What faced her now through the narrow aperture of the telescope seemed very gray and uncertain.

"Can you tell what ship it is yet?" Daisy asked.

"Not yet." Tereza forced her attention back to the oncoming ship. A thick plume of black smoke swelled behind it like a miniature thunderhead. She reported as much as she could. "It has two funnels and three masts. No sails set. I can't distinguish any colors, but it appears to have a black hull, with white cabins. There are flags, but I can't make them out."

"Perhaps this will help, ladies." Third Officer MacBreive appeared between them and offered Daisy his marine telescope.

"Thank you, Mr. MacBreive," she replied, "I fear I'm quite dazzled by peering into the sunlight. Perhaps Tereza ... ?"

MacBreive's smile thinned, but he maintained his stiff gallantry. "Certainly."

"Thank you very much, sir," Tereza said, passing the small telescope along to her father.

"You're quite welcome." MacBreive clasped his hands behind his back and cocked an eyebrow at the oncoming steamer. Tereza sighted through the big telescope and made out some sailors on deck. She could clearly make out the little signal flags now but was disappointed again. She needed Ewan here to translate them.

"I believe you'll find her to be a British dreadnought," MacBreive was saying, "most likely *HMS Alexandra,* by her speed and her topsides. Central battery ship. Top-notch design, of course, but already somewhat out of favor among the high command."

"Did you serve in the Navy, Mr. MacBreive?" Colonel MacLaren asked.

"No. I decided the future at sea lay with trade and travel. There will always be wars, of course, but with them comes a surfeit of lieutenants, all looking to be captains."

Father lowered the little telescope and turned from the rail. "There will not always be wars," he protested. "The time will come, and soon, when the cost in lives will simply be too great to pay."

"Father, please," Tereza said. "No one wants to talk about—"

"That is the problem!" he exclaimed. "No one will talk about it, neither the generals nor admirals nor senators, not the ministers, not even the newspapermen – no one is willing to admit the truth." He gestured toward the warship, the white bone of its bow wave now visible against the dark gray sea. "There lies a floating battery of cannon, built for the sole purpose of destruction and domination."

"And defense," Colonel MacLaren put in.

"Hah! Pure rationalization! An excuse to build more and ever larger ships, with larger cannons, with longer ranges, to intimidate and overpower. They are built to win wars, not stop them; not merely to kill, but to keep killing."

"I'm startled by your disdain, sir," MacBreive said coldly. "I believe you were yourself recently involved in the design of weaponry. Is that not so?"

"Yes."

Please, not again! Tereza thought. "Father! We aren't supposed to—"

"Oh, let me be, Tereza! Everyone knows it!" He turned back to the others, brandishing the telescope as though it were a pointer. "There is a world of difference between that dreadnought and what I designed. My cannon, to call it by the name that people think they understand, would stop that ship dead in its wake."

"And how would that stop wars?" MacBreive demanded.

"The cost, sir. One of my aetheric cannons, properly designed and situated, would render a fleet of such ships useless. It would level entire armies from five miles away, even farther." His eyes shone with a fervor Tereza hadn't seen since the failed test. In his gaunt face it was startling, almost frightening. "What government," he went on, "could afford to build and maintain such a useless force of men and matériel, only to have it destroyed in a moment? What citizen would choose to enlist, knowing that any attack was doomed to complete destruction? None! Instead, they would arise and remove the government that would attempt such a thing."

Tereza prayed the others would let him have this last word, but Daisy took up the argument.

"You speak of cost, Professor," she said gently, "and in the next breath, you speak of destruction, and then of men. It seems you mean to end war by killing all the warriors."

Father shook his head briskly. "No, no. The mere threat will be enough."

"I fear it would take at least one demonstration," Daisy replied.

"Yes, I'm afraid so," Father agreed, "but don't you see? That one demonstration would prevent an entire future of deaths."

"I can't say your initial demonstration achieved a sufficient level of threat," MacBreive remarked.

Every bit of relief Tereza had felt since telling her story melted away. A sudden memory of the tertiary bell filled her mind. The knurled head of the tuning bolt on the twelfth resonator hung before her. The discordant hum of the tuning fork swelled inside her ears. Her heart began to stutter. Then Father's voice broke in. She clung to it, trying to push the memory aside.

"That was an accident!" His face reddened, but he made an effort and calmed himself. Tereza's heart steadied. "The resonators were mistuned," he said. "I let myself be rushed by politicians and made an error, something I don't intend to let happen again."

"Again?" MacBreive cocked his eyebrow. "Do you mean to say you intend to continue work on this cannon, or whatever it is?"

"Of course I do," father replied. "The reason is honorable." He pointed again at the dreadnought. "And more necessary than ever. My design is sound. The model worked perfectly. It still does; I tested it again before crating it."

Tereza's grip on calm began to slip again. *How could you!* she screamed. Or would have. She couldn't get out the words. She began to count by primes, trying to clear her mind. *Three, five, seven, eleven, thirteen . . .* The debate went on around her, distant, faint, but impossible to ignore.

"Come, sir," Colonel MacLaren said, "after what happened to your wife, I would think—"

"What? That *I* would stop thinking? That I would

forget everything that I had been working for? She believed in this, too, you know; believed in it as much as I still do. Her death will haunt me till the end of my days, but her spirit would haunt me more if I did not finish what I have started. If I let her death be in vain!"

Tears were poised in his eyes. He turned abruptly and wiped them away, as if studying the dreadnought. Tereza turned, too, unable to maintain her count. She jerked the big telescope to her eye as if, by not seeing it, she could erase the scene taking place around her. Her view was completely blurred, and she realized she had tears in her own eyes. She blinked furiously. No one else said a word. The silence was as bad as the argument.

Tereza made herself look at the ship. She could easily see the bulge of its central battery, the recessed sides of the upper decks fore and aft. She could even see that the forward gun ports were open. And make out the lettering along her bows. She drew a breath and forced herself to break the silence.

"*HMS Alexandra*" she called out loudly. "You were correct, Mr. MacBreive." She turned and offered him the telescope. "Could you read the flags, please?"

MacBreive took it with a nod and a smug smile. Tereza stifled the urge to walk away. She wished so much that Ewan were here to translate, and made up her mind to sneak down as soon as possible to tell him what was happening. He had been in that tiny cell for two whole days and seemed ready to burst. Like her.

"The devil!" MacBreive exclaimed. "She's ordered us to stop."

"Stop? Whatever for?" Daisy exclaimed.

"To take on a pilot."

"This far out?" Colonel MacLaren asked. "Surely that's not normal practice."

"Not normal at all," MacBreive replied curtly. He

snapped the telescope shut. "Excuse me, I must go to the bridge." He hurried off, heels clicking sharply on the deck.

The *Isle of Lewis* was already slowing. Flags snapped up and down the signal halyards as Captain Morrison brought the ship to a long, gliding stop. The plume of smoke shrank to a trickle; the constant vibration settled to a slow pulse. The motion of the sea became annoying, then uncomfortable, as wind and wave set the hull to wallowing. Passengers crowded the starboard rail, watching as the *Alexandra* slowed to a crawl and began a creeping circle around them about a hundred yards away. Her sailors lowered a small boat, which pulled smartly through the swells and chop to their leeward side, where the *Lewis*'s crew had hung a ladder. An officer and two red-jacketed marines climbed on board, to be met by a glowering Captain Morrison.

The exchange was brief, and the officers disappeared into the deckhouse, only to reappear a few minutes later on the bridge. One of the marines returned down the ladder to the boat, which pulled back to the *Alexandra*. The other marine took station by his commander on the bridge. Black smoke poured again from the funnels of both ships. The *Alexandra* turned northeast, curving away from Ireland. The *Lewis* followed, picking up speed, settling back into her steady dip and rise to the vibration of her huge engine and screw.

All the while, rumor and conjecture swept in waves across the clustered passengers. Mrs. Curmidge and King had joined them right after MacBreive left. Derek appeared soon after, wondering at the slowing engines.

"Was down for a visit," he murmured to Tereza and Daisy while all eyes were on the approaching boat. "A bit tense over all this, our friend."

"He must know as quickly as we do," Daisy murmured back.

Tereza swore to herself he would. But sneaking away then was impossible without making another scene, and knowledge turned out to be a hard item to come by. King went snooping and came back accompanied by the count. They reported that the odds favored the murder.

"*Baliverne*," the count remarked. "It is nonsense, of course. True, any murderer must still be on board, but no ship has passed us since the lieutenant was killed. How would the *Alexandra* know?"

"What of poor Reverend Curmidge?" King countered. "That news would have arrived at least a day ago."

"The doctor pronounced it an unhappy fall, occasioned by failure of the heart," the count replied. "And, with all due respect, *Madame* Curmidge, the reverend was not so celebrated as to bring on such a response, not so?"

"Now, now," King objected.

"You may curb your chivalry, Mr. King," Mrs. Curmidge said. "I am quite capable of being insulted without any help. But I daresay Mr. Bo-solay is correct for once. The reverend was an ordinary person, hardly worthy of a military escort, even had it been murder."

"If not these deaths," Colonel MacLaren said, "what cause do you give for our escort, Count? What would bring the Royal Navy's newest dreadnought out to escort us in at such a careful distance from land, and still two days steaming from our destination?"

The count nodded to Father. "With hope you will pardon the suggestion, *Monsieur*, I suspect the knowledge of your presence on board has caused alarm in Britain. Perhaps they only wish to protect you from the public, but, more likely alas, they want to be sure that a similar accident does not occur on their shores."

Tereza dearly wished the count was wrong – she had prayed they would leave all that behind – but she was very afraid he was right. The argument with MacBreive and the colonel made it clear Father had no intention of giving up his research. Even if no one outside their circle knew that he had brought the prototype on board, the British authorities couldn't ignore the possibility.

Daisy seemed to agree. "But even so," she exclaimed, "To respond with such a heavy-handed show of military force is outrageous, an unconscionable breach of etiquette! You and Tereza are innocent civilians, Professor, not subject to military law. We shouldn't stand for it, Father. You must voice a protest at once!"

"I can hardly protest what we don't yet know, my dear," her father replied. "Patience."

&

It took a full day's worth of patience before the whole truth was known, and by then they were flanked by two more British warships: *Téméraire* and *Inflexible*.

"Certainly they are trying to make a point," the count remarked, "but still no one says why."

"We all know why!" Daisy snapped. "They just won't come out and say it!"

It was late afternoon, and the passengers had gathered on deck again, this time ostensibly to celebrate one of the milestones of every voyage. The ship was approaching the Inishtrahull light, unofficial boundary between the North Atlantic and the Irish Sea. Daisy couldn't help but remember it was also the spot where the *Isle of Lewis*'s sister ship had run aground so recently. Despite that unhappy fact, tradition ruled that this was the place where the winner of the Pool would be determined. The gentlemen had their watches out, but all eyes were on the bridge, waiting for the signal that they were abreast the lighthouse. Purser Gilmore came on deck, along with the chief steward and the boatswain, bearing the board showing the names of the members of the Pool and the arrival times each had bet on.

The signal came – a gesture from the captain, followed by a long blast of the ship's horn. The gentlemen looked at their watches, and a hum of speculation arose. The purser wrote the hour and minute on the board, two or three voices grumbled that her watch was off, others stifled expressions of dismay, but the majority of the passengers were merely spectators and gave the winner a round of applause.

It was the count.

"*Ça alors*," he remarked. "Here is a first. I have never before won the Pool."

Mrs. Curmidge sniffed. "I daresay you haven't suffered for the loss."

He winked at Daisy. "You would be surprised, *ma chère* Curmidge. Poor Larousse nearly starved to death the last time I lost a bet. Servants, you know . . ."

He shrugged eloquently, then went forward to meet with the chief steward and the boatswain, who offered him an envelope with his winnings. Half of the sum in the Pool went to the winner; the other half went into a fund for the crew. The count bowed to each of the men, thanked them, and gave the envelope back, to be added to their fund. Daisy started another round of applause. Mrs. Curmidge sniffed.

As the crowd began to disperse, the purser rang a bell and asked everyone to please retire to the saloon in fifteen minutes for an important announcement.

"Finally!" Daisy exclaimed, patience at an end. She began easing her father and the others toward the companionway, when the purser quietly joined them.

"Professor Skovajsa?" Mrs. Gilmore said. "I wonder if you and your daughter would join me for minute in my cabin?"

The professor stiffened. "About the announcement, I presume?"

"Yes. I'm afraid you're directly concerned. Please excuse us, everyone. We will see you in the saloon in fifteen minutes."

And with that, she led the Skovajsas away. Daisy caught Tereza's eye and tried to give her an encouraging smile, but Tereza's face was set, her fist white on the handle of her parasol.

Fifteen minutes later, Purser Gilmore appeared in the saloon with the second officer and the British Navy officer. The Skovajsas did not appear.

"Ladies and gentlemen, this is First Lieutenant Clarke of *HMS Alexandra*, flagship of the British Home Fleet." Purser Gilmore's voice carried clearly across the long room. "We are now steaming under the Flag Commander's orders. Under his direction, we will not be proceeding directly to the pier at Greenock. Instead, we will be forced to anchor outside the mouth of the Firth of Clyde, where you will be taken off to the pier on ferries. Fortunately, we're a day ahead of schedule, so you'll all arrive at the pier in good time to make whatever connections you've arranged." She paused, squared her shoulders, gave a hard look at Lieutenant Clarke, and continued. "I am not authorized to say more, but I will add that the Scots-American Line will be protesting this action to the Admiralty, the Board of Shipping, the Prime Minister's office, and Buckingham Palace, if need be. The Queen has friends in Scotland. Now, if you have any questions or complaints, you may direct them at Lieutenant Clarke."

She nodded brusquely to him and stepped back to stand grimly beside the second officer.

Out of the line of fire, Daisy thought, silently applauding the purser's last words.

To his credit, Clarke didn't flinch at the barrage of outraged cries that came from the gathered gentlemen and even a few of the ladies. The first question, of course, was a resounding *why?*

"It's for your own safety, I assure you," Clarke replied. "I am not at leave to provide details, but the Admiralty has reason to believe that this ship represents a potential threat to the people of Great Britain. We are here to prevent—"

"It's Skovajsa, isn't it?"

Daisy wasn't at all surprised that the accusation came from Mr. Baskins. The man had never stopped muttering about the professor.

"I am not at liberty—" Clarke began.

"Oh, give us credit for a few brains, Lieutenant," Baskins said. "We've been on board with that loony for nine days. We know what he did back in the States."

"Where is he now?" another man asked. "Have you arrested him?"

"Not at all," Clarke replied. "He and his daughter are being kept separate for their own safety."

"Their safety? What about ours?" Baskins exclaimed. "Have you taken away his gadgets?"

"His cabin has been searched, yes."

"What about his tools?"

"And his daughter's bags – have you searched them, too?"

So it went, and Clarke managed to respond to every question with very little in the way of an answer.

Finally Daisy spoke up. "Lieutenant, I'm sure we all appreciate the concern you have for our well-being and that of the British people. I'm just as concerned about the well-being of Professor Skovajsa and his daughter. Will they be ferried ashore with the rest of us and allowed to continue their journey?"

"I certainly hope not!" Baskins said. "The man should be locked up."

"The professor was granted United States' citizenship, last I heard," Daisy stated, "and his daughter is most certainly a citizen. He was tried in an American court and found not guilty, while she has never even been accused. They are innocent of any imaginable crime."

"This is not the United States, Miss," Clarke replied. "Nevertheless, neither of the Skovajsas is under arrest. As I said before, they are being kept separate for their own safety. You, sir," he said to Baskins, "are not the only person who harbors ill will toward them. There have been crowds in the streets demanding that he not be allowed to land here. If the rabble had had their way, this ship would have been turned back to New York long before you sighted Ireland. The fact that you are this close, and will be allowed even closer to be ferried ashore, is due to our concern for your safety. You should be grateful. Now, please go to your cabins and prepare your luggage for departure at first light tomorrow. Unfortunately, we're still a few hours out from a safe anchorage, or we would take you all off this evening. That will be all, thank you."

As he left the saloon, the passengers erupted in angry conversation. Daisy grabbed her father by the arm and pulled him toward the exit.

"What are you up to now, Margaret?" he asked.

"Lieutenant Clarke did not answer my question. We need to find out just what these people are planning to do with Tereza and the professor."

She hurried him to the purser's office, where they found Mrs. Gilmore alone.

"Excuse us," Daisy said, "but we have another question for Lieutenant Clarke."

"He's on the bridge, where you're not welcome to go right now," Mrs. Gilmore replied, "but I can guess your question, and the answer is no."

"No?" Daisy echoed.

"No, the Skovajsas will not be ferried ashore and allowed to continue their journey. And the *Lewis* won't be landing here, either. They're to be kept on board while the ship is escorted to a so-called safe harbor, where she will be completely emptied and searched from masthead to keel truck and stem to stern. Just to be sure we're not a floating bomb, you see."

"And then?" Colonel MacLaren asked.

Mrs. Gilmore's frown deepened. "They won't say."

"Where is this safe harbor?"

"They haven't said that, either, but I suspect it'll be somewhere at the west end of Ireland, or the top of the Highlands, where the people aren't quite so British and their well-being not much of a concern at Downing Street."

"But what of the professor and Tereza?" Daisy demanded.

"They'll be kept safe, I imagine. The public may be panicked, but I'm sure the parcel o' rogues at the Admiralty is very interested in just how that weapon of his works. They're not afraid of a big explosion; they're afraid someone else will get their hands on the man behind it before they do."

"They've good cause to be worried," Daisy muttered. "He is under arrest, then?"

"As good as."

"Father, we must do something," Daisy said. "They're our friends."

"That won't get us far," he answered, "but they are citizens of the United States, as you said. I'll wire the ambassador in London and lodge a protest as soon as we're ashore."

"I am not going ashore," Daisy said. "I'm staying on

board with the Skovajsas."

"They'll hardly allow that," the purser said.

"I'll make such a stink they won't be able to refuse me," Daisy replied. "After all, I can hardly let Tereza sail off alone, the only woman on board and not yet of age. I shall be her chaperone."

"You're hardly of age yourself, young lady," Mrs. Gilmore said, "and let me remind you that I will be on board. Despite the uniform, I am a woman."

"Certainly, but you have your own duties to the ship," Daisy replied. "Besides which, Scottish though you are, you're also a British citizen and hardly objective in the matter. I am the daughter of the United States Consul to Scotland, whom you have just heard express outrage and his intention to take this matter to the highest levels."

The purser grudged her a small smile. "You'll never convince the captain, lass."

"Then I will let him consider the fate of the Scots-American Line and his good name if any harm should befall Tereza while she is under his care. If I am her chaperone, all blame will fall on me, my father, and the United States government."

The purser shook her head. "You can try it, lass, but I have to tell you the *Sassenachs* will never fall for it."

Chapter 20

Pariah Ship

Ewan stared in disbelief at the sheet of paper Derek had thrust into his hands. British warships had surrounded the *Lewis*, she would not be allowed to enter the Clyde, Tereza and her father were being held in their cabin with an armed marine at the door – Derek had just told him all of this, then handed him a new poem to read.

"I, uh, I could tell you didn't really like the first one," Derek was saying, "so I made some changes, you see. To freshen it up. In a way."

"I never said I didn't like it," Ewan protested. "It just wasn't my . . . my—"

"Your sort of thing. I understand. But, you see, the more I thought about it—"

Steps sounded on the ladder. Ewan and Derek froze. The steps kept coming.

"Into the hold! Quick!" Ewan hissed.

Derek rushed out of the cell and across to the heavy hatch. He fumbled at the lever, heaved. It squealed in protest. Derek froze again. The steps came closer. He looked around, desperate, then scooted into the shadows behind the ladder.

"No, no!" Ewan whispered, gesturing wildly. "Come back! Under the berth!"

Derek shook his head, crouched into the corner where the hull met the bulkhead, and tucked his head under the lapel of his coat. The top of his blonde hair seemed to glow like a lantern.

Ewan muttered a curse, eased the door shut till the

lock clicked, and threw himself onto the berth. There were two people at least, in a hurry. He lay back against the pillow and pretended to be asleep as they came down the final flight.

"Ewan, wake up!" It was Aunt Nellie. "It's time you were out of there."

Ewan was back at the door in a nick. Aunt Nellie was at the window, with James Gilmore behind her. She opened the door, but stopped him from rushing out.

"Not so fast. You need to change first. Here." She handed him a folded set of clothes.

Ewan stared at the tartan vest that lay on top of the stack. It was his steward's uniform. He was surprised to feel disappointed.

"Why . . . Aren't I going to . . . What about the Skovajsas?"

"Don't worry, you'll still to be watching them. Now put these on," she ordered. "We don't have all day."

She turned her back and told him all that had been happening since *HMS Alexandra* appeared, everything that Derek had already described. Then she told him of Daisy's visit and turned to face him.

"Now I want to know why in Hell you didn't tell me young Tereza had been attacked. Nor that someone had stolen the professor's seasick hat. Nor about the note from the Russian."

Ewan was buttoning his trousers but he felt caught naked. "I— The note said—"

"*Haud yer wheesht*! I know what the note said. I know you thought her life was in danger. But damn it all, lad, did you really think you and Miss MacLaren and that *bletherskite* Reed were enough to ward off a trained killer? The man's already murdered MacKay and most likely Reverend Curmidge, and he fair near choked the life out of you, didn't he."

"He caught us all by surprise!" Ewan protested.

Aunt Nellie glared him down. "Not MacKay, he didn't. And you can bet the Pool he's got more than one knife still. You had a ship full of crew ready to help, and you should have known to make use of it. That's what *shipmates* are here for."

"Like Ranald Morrison?" Ewan replied.

"One bad apple, a sharp-tongued stuffed *sark* you should have known to ignore. You can't let a bampot like that smear your opinion of the captain or MacLeod or the rest." She threw up her hands. "*Och aye*, I should send you ashore with the passengers."

"Well, why don't you?" Ewan demanded. "It seems clear I've done nothing but harm."

Aunt Nellie took a deep breath. "Because there's no one else the captain cares to risk," she said. "When the passengers go, he's sending off all but a skeleton crew with 'em. That leaves you to stand watch on the Skovajsas and Miss MacLaren."

"Why a skeleton crew?" Ewan asked.

"Because Captain Morrison doesn't trust the English," James said. "He wants the crew out of harm's way, everyone but the minimum needed to run the engines and man the sails. All the rest – stewards, waiters, cooks, barber, even the doctor – they're all going ashore. I think MacDonald and MacBreive would be, too, if MacKay was still with us. The chief cook is staying aboard, at least, with an assistant, and Frasier as mess steward." He grinned. "We won't starve."

"You'll be the steward for the Skovajsas and Miss MacLaren, and their waiter, too," Aunt Nellie said. She relented enough for a thin smile. "Maybe it'll teach you some humility."

"Will you be staying?"

Her smile disappeared. "Yes, but only because I

convinced the captain he'll need a witness of my rank to whatever happens. I tell you, Ewan, this is no easy game you're getting into. Do you know what persuaded the captain to let you stay on board? I simply pointed out that if it wasn't you it'd have to be someone else. Do you still have the derringer?"

Ewan nodded. No one had thought to search him after the fracas with Ranald Morrison.

"Good. Keep it secret and keep it close. Now, I want you watching when the passengers go off. If you see anyone who reminds you e'en a wee bit of the fellow who killed MacKay, signal to James, on the bridge. Don't try to take him on alone. Act like a steward, if you remember how. And you *will* report to me, every morning and evening, *everything*, or I'll have your guts for garters. Do ye ken?"

Ewan nodded. "Yes, Ma'am."

She nodded back and stalked out of the cabin. James watched her go, then handed Ewan his steward's cap. Ewan put it on, but now it felt like a disguise.

"Don't worry, Ewan," James said. "She's mad at you, and I daresay she has a right to be, but she also trusts you to learn from mistakes. Otherwise you wouldn't be staying aboard. Keep that in mind, and keep good watch."

"Thanks," Ewan replied. "You watch your own back, too."

Ewan gathered up his other clothes and took a moment to brush off the new derby the count had given him. The steward's cap felt stiff and tight by comparison. He tucked it under his arm and was turning to leave when he spotted Derek's poem, half hidden beneath the pillow. He snatched it up and hurried out, but Derek was already gone.

&

They were made to anchor well outside the shipping channel in the wide mouth of the Firth of Clyde. The closest landfall was tiny Alisa Craig, still a good ten miles away. Kintyre and Galloway were gray outlines to the north and east, and Ireland a distant smudge to the west. Their escort was standing by at the three points of a triangle a mile wide, with the *Isle of Lewis* at its center.

"It looks like they're ready to blow us out of the water at any minute," Daisy remarked.

That's exactly what they want us to believe, Ewan thought.

The weather seemed to have the same idea. The sky was overcast by a low sheet of gray cloud, with a heavy, darker layer coming in swiftly from the west. The wind, fitful at first, became a steady breeze, blowing stronger with every gust. White caps dotted the growing swell. The air was damp, threatening more than just rain.

The coffin for Reverend Curmidge's body did nothing to raise the mood. It came out on the first lighter, was hauled aboard during the hurried breakfast, then taken off first. Mrs. Curmidge followed in black, face veiled, on the arm of Third Officer MacBreive. She went into the lighter's cabin, but the coffin was secured on the small afterdeck, clearly visible to everyone on board the *Lewis*.

Captain Morrison paced the bridge, overseeing the offloading of passengers. The crew had rigged gangways down both sides of the hull, and starboard cabins were supposed to disembark on the starboard gangway, port cabins to port. Aunt Nellie and the chief steward were on deck, trying to play shepherd. Lieutenant Clarke stood braced at the port railing, checking off names while he tried to shelter his flapping list from the wind and damp. Another British lieutenant, sent over with the coffin, was checking them off on the starboard side.

The passengers were their usual contrary selves, going where they willed, huddling with their friends, changing their minds in several false starts, shouting hurried goodbyes and promises to meet again in Edinburgh, and venting a steady stream of complaints when finally faced with the long, precarious climb down the rolling side of the ship to the lighters. The *Lewis*'s deck crew stood by, lending a hand to anyone who wanted it. Given the sudden gusts and ugly swell, most did, but that created two-way traffic and more confusion.

Ewan, meanwhile, went from one side of the ship to the other, watching the passengers closely. He heard Baskins make a noisy scene, complete with threats to have Clarke demoted. He saw King by the funnel, performing some mumbo-jumbo for two of his devoted seasickness patients, then saw him going down the port gangway a few minutes later in company with an older couple, only to reappear shortly afterward on the opposite side of the ship in search of a forgotten valise for the gentleman.

Colonel MacLaren was the last to disembark on the lighters, with a final promise to Daisy to get the ambassador up in arms. That left only the count and his valet.

"*Tu dois débarqer vite, Monsieur le count*," Daisy remarked. *You should debark quickly.*

"*Mais non*, I have a different boat coming," he replied. "*Le voici.*"

He pointed at a low, white hull approaching rapidly from southward. As it raced nearer, they began to hear the noise of its engines, a loud, raw buzz like a deep-throated sawmill chewing up planks of some very hard wood. A tremendous rooster tail of spray arched back from its transom as it skipped across the swells. It drew all eyes, and flags began flying on the *Alexandra*, warning it off. The little ship kept straight on toward them.

"It's flying what appears to be the Union Jack at its stern," Daisy reported, squinting through her little telescope.

Ewan noticed that one of the rotating batteries on the *Inflexible* was swinging round toward it, but couldn't swing fast enough to stay on target. He wondered if they would fire anyway. Then a large banner rose to the top of the little craft's single, slender mast: an elaborate blue and gold coat of arms bearing three hounds, a helmet, a shield, and a crown.

"Those are the arms of my good friend, Victor Grosvenor," the count said. "She is his yacht, *Hornet*, a steam – *quel est le mot?* – Ah, *oui*, same word: *turbine*. She is the fastest ship on any sea, he tells me." He said it as if it were an everyday thing, to be taxied from an ocean liner by the world's fastest yacht, owned by a peer.

The *Hornet* roared up in a matter of minutes, though her captain was seaman enough to slow her to a crawl for the last fifty yards. She was a third the length of the *Lewis* but lean as a rowing gig. Her varnished mahogany topsides gleamed even under the overcast sky. Two sailors in trim whites tossed up lines from bow and stern and held her steady against golden-brown rope bumpers that looked as though they'd never been touched by ship or pier.

The count offered Daisy his hand and murmured something in French. Daisy beamed as she replied, and actually kissed him on the cheek. He bent to kiss her hand in return, nodded kindly to Ewan, then hurried easily down the swaying gangway. Larousse followed awkwardly, laden with their luggage. The *Hornet*'s shrill whistle blew, her sailors pulled in their lines, and she drew slowly away from the side. Suddenly, black smoke belched from her stubby stovepipe stack, and she seemed to leap out of the water and skim across the worsening seas, buzzsaw, rooster tail, flapping banner, and all. Daisy waved. The count waved back, then disappeared into the cabin.

Daisy turned to Ewan, eyes gleaming. "His friend Victor is the son of the Duke of Westminster and somehow related to the Earl of Sutherland on his mother's side. The Queen is his godmother! The count has promised to ask him to intercede on the Skovajsas' behalf!"

"I wondered what that was all about," Ewan said. "Do you really think it'll help?"

"Every protest will help," Daisy replied firmly, slapping her spyglass into her palm. "I would personally call on every peer in the country if I could."

She went below then to join the Skovajsas, who were still being watched over by a marine guard. Ewan escorted her down, checked in with Aunt Nellie, then went back on deck to watch the steerage passengers debark. The wind picked up even more and the seas worsened, slowing the process and making it downright dangerous on the gangplanks. It took three crewmen to help the tuba player down with his instrument, and the bass drummer nearly went overboard.

By the time they were all safely away, it was late afternoon. Another lighter was standing by to take on the passengers's hold luggage, but Captain Morrison refused to open the forward hatches and risk injuring his crew. The ship was pitching and rolling too heavily, and the skies were starting to spit rain.

"There's a serious gale coming," Aunt Nellie said, pointing to the barometer on her wall as Ewan came to report.

"It doesn't take a glass to tell that," he muttered. He shook off his oilskin coat before coming in and closing the door.

"Did you notice anyone suspicious in steerage?" she asked.

"No," he said glumly.

"Not even your friend, Mr. Reed?"

Ewan looked up, startled. "You knew?"

Aunt Nellie glowered. "Only just this morning, going back down the manifest after the cabin passengers were off. The question is, when did *you* find out? And why didn't you tell me?"

"When you gave me the original manifest mid passage," he admitted. "And I decided to keep mum and watch him instead. Though I didn't really think he was the killer. Still don't." He told her about the love poems to Daisy.

Aunt Nellie just shook her head. "*Och aye.* Young love's blind and more than half deaf. Well, he's gone now. You did see him go?"

"He showed up at breakfast just long enough to press an envelope into Dai— Miss MacLaren's hands, then disappeared. But I spotted him among the steerage crowd. He had his disguise on again, floppy hat and long, tattered coat."

Then he had to explain how he'd first run into Derek and later found the disguise in his valise. Aunt Nellie just shook her head.

The ship began to vibrate more heavily. The skirl of a bagpipe sounded suddenly from on deck.

"We're underway," Aunt Nellie remarked, somewhat surprised. "I thought we'd be waiting till morning."

They threw on their oilskins and went out into the spitting rain. Frasier stood under the port wing of the bridge, out of the worst of it, playing *MacCrimmon's Lament*. Across the heavy whitecaps, the British dreadnoughts were showing dozens of flags. Black smoke poured from their stacks. Ewan and Aunt Nellie hurried up the ladder to the bridge, where James was standing watch. The captain himself was at the telegraph in front of the wheelhouse windows. Lieutenant Clarke stood beside him. MacBreive was on the starboard wing, and a quartermaster was setting flags on the signal halyard – all the signs of a busy departure, only now they were heading across the North Channel into a dying day and a rising gale.

"Where to?" Aunt Nellie asked.

"No idea yet," James replied. "All we know is we're to follow *Alexandra*."

"And pray this doesn't turn into a hurricane," Ewan added.

"Don't waste your time on that, Ewan," James said. "It's already made up its mind to."

Chapter 21

Into the Hold

The weather worsened steadily. Aunt Nellie convinced Lieutenant Clarke to let the Skovajsas out of their cabin so they could get some fresh air and have dinner in the relative comfort of the saloon. They welcomed the consideration, though neither of them felt hungry. Daisy, on the other hand, still seemed immune to sea sickness and managed a helping of the pheasant, potatoes, and glazed turnip the cook had prepared. The appearance of the British fleet had ruined his plans for the gala arrival dinner, but neither that nor the weather stopped him from treating the three passengers to his best efforts. Ewan was serving as waiter, but Daisy and Tereza insisted he sit down at his usual place and eat with them. Aunt Nellie, seated at the Captain's place at the head of the table, gave him leave, and he was only too happy to dig in.

Clearing off afterward was a trick, negotiating the heaving passageway to the kitchen laden with plates and glasses. He was on his way back into the saloon with a pot of plum duff when Derek came tumbling down the stairway and nearly knocked him to the deck.

"Ah, there you are!" Derek exclaimed, fumbling with a crystal dessert bowl that had tried to leap off Ewan's tray. "Put that down, quick! There's something going on in the hold!"

Ewan stared at him. Derek was soaked from the rain and dripping onto the carpet, hair plastered to his head, as though he'd just swum out to the *Lewis* from shore.

"How the devil did you get here?" Ewan demanded. "I

saw you sneak off with the other steerage passengers."

"What? Oh, you noticed the hat and coat. Clever, eh? I paid him two bits to wear it off for me. You see, I was fairly sure you'd been poking in my bag, so I—"

"Derek!" Daisy rushed out of the saloon, followed by the others. "You're still here!"

Derek's smile blossomed. "Yes, well, I couldn't very well abandon my friends in this mess, could I?"

"That's all very gallant, but you'd have been wiser to go," Aunt Nellie said. "Lieutenant Clarke will have you clapped in the brig as soon as he knows you're on board. If the captain doesn't throw you overboard first."

"But that's where I've been, you see," Derek said, suddenly serious again. "In the brig, I mean. It's where I hid. Who would think to look there, right? But I was just getting ready to slip out and get a little air, you know, when I heard someone come sneaking down the stairs. It was one of those marine guards, in the red jacket. I stayed mum and spied him out while he worked open the door to the hold – somebody really should grease that thing, you know – and went inside."

"What was he doing?" Ewan and Tereza both asked at once.

"Well, I did peer in, but I couldn't make out much in the gloom. He had a small light of some kind and was poking about among the baggage in the first section there. I thought about calling him out, but decided to recruit reinforcements first. He still has that gun of his."

"For once you've shown a bit of sense," Aunt Nellie said. "Ewan, stay here and keep watch over your friends. Reed, you come with me. The captain needs to hear this."

Derek's face fell. "The captain? Is that safe?"

"Don't worry, I'll make sure he gives you a chance to speak. Come on."

She hurried up the passageway.

Derek hesitated, but Daisy gave him another smile. "Don't worry. His bark is worse than his bite."

No it's not, Ewan thought, but Derek went grinning.

"Professor," Ewan asked, "is that model cannon in your steamer trunk?"

"No," the professor replied, "not with our clothing, if that's what you mean. It's in a separate crate with some of our household things, some books and journals, photos, mementos."

"How is it marked?"

"My name is on it."

Ewan stifled a curse. "He'll find it soon enough then. I'm going down to the hold."

"I'm coming with you," Tereza said immediately.

"No," Ewan said. "It's too dangerous."

Tereza set her jaw. "I know what the crate looks like."

"So do I," her father said. "I will go. You and Miss MacLaren must stay here, where it's safe."

"If they set off your weapon, Professor, is there any place on board that's safe?" Daisy said.

"It's too small," the Professor assured her. "Anything more than, well . . . I suppose its effect could reach the bridge if it were aimed directly—"

"They're hardly going to use it on board," Ewan said. "They just want to make sure it's here."

"We have no idea what they want," Daisy replied. "I think you should go find out."

"Good. We're going." Ewan started up the passageway.

"Wait," Daisy called. "I distinctly heard the purser order you to keep watch over us. You can't do that unless we come along. Tereza? Professor?"

"But Derek said the marine was armed."

"So are we." Daisy reached into her bag and brought out a large revolver. "My father's," she explained, slipping it back out of sight.

"And I have this," Tereza said, hefting her parasol.

"And I'm sure the professor must have something up his sleeve," Daisy continued, "none of which we'll need, because I'm also sure the marine will not shoot at two ladies searching for their luggage."

Ewan shook his head. "I wouldn't be so sure of that."

"You're wasting time," Daisy said. "Lead on."

The shortest route would have been through the engine room, but MacLeod would never have let them down the ladder. Instead, Ewan led them through steerage, empty and dim now, haunted by the faint scent of the passengers who had just left it. They made their way forward as quickly and quietly as they could, given the constant pitch and roll of the ship. They were just above the waterline, and the heavy seas slapped against the wide-spaced deadlights as though trying to break in. The hatch in the forward bulkhead tried its best to pull out of Ewan's hands and bash his face, but he managed to hold it open so the others could pass through. The roll of the ship slammed it shut behind him, but the noise was lost in the racket made by the storm.

The waves almost pitched them down the ladder. They clung to the rail and half slid to the bottom. The hatch to the hold was shut, but the lever wasn't pushed tight to the stops. Ewan signaled to the professor, and together they forced it down till the heavy hatch started to swing free. Tereza threw herself against it just in time. As she and her father held it still, Ewan peered through the crack.

The hold luggage was stacked in racks set on the port side of the central aisle, which led aft into the depths of the hold. Every traveler had a steamer trunk. Couples traveling together often had two, in addition to the suitcases in their cabins. Salesmen often had one or two extra trunks or crates filled with samples of their wares. And there were sacks of mail as well, along with crates of small cargo stacked on the starboard side of the aisle. All this was crammed into the forward fifty feet of hold, the last freight to be loaded and the first to come out at the end of the passage. Every trunk and crate of passengers' luggage and goods was marked with the name of the owner, but they were loaded as they arrived on the pier, with no thought for the alphabet. It was a stevedore's puzzle maze, and finding a trunk while at sea was a matter of time and chance. Bad weather made the search a grueling trial of knocks, bruises, and a heaving stomach.

The marine gave himself away with a loud clatter and a blistering curse, barely heard over the noise of the engine and the storm. Ewan gestured to the others to stay put and squeezed through the hatchway. Timing his movements to the cant of the deck, he zig-zagged from the end of one rack to the next. There were ten of them, and the noise had come from one of the last, on the port side. At the ninth rack, Ewan took out the derringer and cocked it. Aunt Nellie had warned him it was only good at close range; now he wondered just how close. It didn't seem so weighty anymore.

He steeled himself, glanced back toward the hatch, and saw the professor halfway down the aisle, with Tereza and Daisy sneaking up behind him. Ewan shook his head firmly and motioned them to go back. All three shook their heads and moved closer, Tereza gripping her parasol like a sword. Ewan's only thought was to keep her out of harm's way. He stepped around the end of the ninth rack.

The marine was crouched at the far end. His back was turned, his head tipped down, his hands out of sight as he did something right at the side of the hull. His light, a small lantern now wedged between two suitcases on the rack, cast tall shadows onto the painted iron plates, making the marine seem twice as tall and the aisle half as wide. His gun was propped in the corner where the rack met the hull.

Ewan crept forward, trying not to stumble as the ship heaved on the growing waves. There was a shuffle behind him. He glanced back. Tereza had pushed passed the professor, but he'd grabbed her arm. She was trying to shrug him off.

The ship plunged into the trough and they both stumbled forward against Ewan. He dodged the tip of her parasol, but their weight pinned his right arm up against one of the trunks. The hasp bit into his wrist, his hand clenched.

The derringer went off, a sharp bark that echoed off the iron plates. The big bullet clanged against the deck above them and clattered back into the top layer of luggage. The marine spun, went for his gun, staggered as the ship hit the next wave.

"Stop or I'll shoot!" Ewan shouted. He pulled free of the professor as the wave threw them all across the aisle.

The marine didn't stop. He grabbed his rifle and lifted it. Ewan braced himself against the rack and pulled the trigger.

Nothing. He hadn't re-cocked the derringer. He fumbled at the hammer with his thumb.

Tereza stepped between him and the marine.

"Wait, sir!" she cried, pressing the parasol to her chest. "Please don't shoot. I have lost my mother already. Would you take the rest of my family from me? Everything that I love?"

The marine lowered the rifle slightly. "Stay back!" he ordered.

Tereza paused a moment. "Will you promise not to harm them? Shoot me if you must, but please, let that be enough." She was moving forward again, arms outstretched.

"Tereza!" the professor wailed. "Stop! Don't listen to her, sir. I beg you, don't shoot her. She is my only child." He stumbled over Ewan, fighting off Daisy's hands. Ewan grabbed his trouser leg.

"Please, everyone just be calm," Daisy said. "Sergeant, these people have suffered a great tragedy. There is no need to make it worse." She stood beside the professor, one arm in front of him. "Obviously you have the advantage and need only tell us what you would like us to do and we will do it. Isn't that right, Professor? Tereza?"

"Anything!" Tereza agreed, stepping closer. "Just tell us, and we will do as you wish."

Hidden by the women's skirts, Ewan carefully cocked the derringer.

"Damn it, girl, stop blubbering!" the marine snapped. "You there, on the floor! Put down that damn popgun and put your hands out where I can see them."

"Do it, please, Ewan," Daisy asked.

Ewan mumbled a curse and carefully set it on the deck.

"You, miss, slide it to me. Don't pick it up! Just use your foot. Gently!"

"Wait! It's cocked!" Ewan cried.

"Thank you, Ewan," Daisy said. "Excuse me, sergeant, please. For everyone's safety." She stooped quickly, picked up the derringer, and uncocked it. "That's better, isn't it? Here then."

She lobbed it in a gentle arc toward the marine.

He automatically reached out to catch it.

Tereza lunged forward and jabbed the end of the parasol at his neck. A blue-white spark flared. He jerked, stiffened, and fell forward like an oak plank.

So that's what I looked like, Ewan thought. He stifled a momentary twinge of pity, then hurried forward to grab his derringer and the fallen rifle. Tereza stood over the marine, scowling down at him without a hint of pity on her face. She held the tip of her parasol inches from his neck, ready to jab again. Only a slight quaver of the tip revealed her tension.

Daisy bent to check the man's pulse. "Good heavens, Tereza, that thing really does a trick," she said. "He's still alive but out cold."

"It'll pass quickly enough," Ewan warned. "Does anyone have something to tie his hands with?"

"I suppose I could tear the hem off my slip," Daisy replied. "I'll have to throw it out anyway, it's so filthy with soot and tar."

"I fear we have a bigger problem than soiled hems," Professor Skovajsa said. He was kneeling at the side of the hull where the marine had been crouched, examining a gray disk about a foot wide and five or six inches high. "This appears to be a mine."

"A mine?" Ewan hurried over. "You mean a bomb?"

"Mine, bomb – essentially the same result if it goes off," the professor remarked. "We seem to have interrupted him in the act of priming it. At least, I think we interrupted him." He pointed at a knob and latch mechanism mounted on top of the disk. "The knob has been turned, but the key has not been engaged. Unless . . ." He bent over, held his ear close to the mechanism for a moment, then muttered, "*Sakra!*"

"What?" Ewan demanded. "That doesn't sound good."

"It appears to be ticking."

Chapter 22

Into the Storm

The mine had been clamped to one of the iron ribs, right above the seam that joined two of the hull plates.

"How long do we have?" Ewan asked.

"I can't say for certain," the professor replied. "The tick marks on the dial aren't labeled. They're not even spaced regularly. I'm surprised the British would be using such poorly designed equipment."

"Can we get it off?"

"Yes," the professor replied, "although the clamps may be linked to the firing mechanism."

"You mean it might explode if we unclamp it?" Daisy exclaimed.

"It might." The professor shrugged. "That's how I would have designed it, at least; but, as I said, given the crudeness of the dial, we can't be sure they thought of that."

"And we can't be sure they didn't." Daisy sighed. "That's certainly inconvenient."

"I don't think we have to rush," Tereza said. "He wouldn't have wanted to blow himself up, and he can hardly get off the ship during this storm. Let me look."

She handed the parasol to Daisy and went over to her father. Together, they examined the mechanism, pointing at this and that and talking quietly. Ewan realized just how much Tereza resembled her father. Particularly when they argued.

"I'm certain it's safe," she stated, pulling a screwdriver from one of the pockets in her skirt.

"You cannot be certain when you haven't designed it," the professor insisted.

At that moment, James Gilmore and the bosun appeared in the center aisle, followed by Aunt Nellie. The two men carried revolvers, but lowered them when they saw the stunned marine lying on the deck.

"Good evening, Mr. Gilmore, Purser. And you, sir," Daisy added, to the bosun. "I believe you'll want to take this gentleman directly to the brig."

"And get his partner and Lieutenant Clarke, too," Ewan said. "He was trying to blow up the ship." He pointed to the mine and quickly explained the situation.

"The Devil!" Aunt Nellie exclaimed. "How long do we have?"

"As long as we need," Tereza called, turning from the mine and holding up the key. "I've disabled it."

"Tereza!" the professor exclaimed. "I clearly told you not to!"

Said the man who shipped his working brain cannon in our hold, Ewan thought.

&

Captain Morrison was livid. He glared at Lieutenant Clarke.

"Do ye want to explain this, Mr. Clarke?" he growled, accent thick with anger.

Clarke was flanked by the bosun and a bruiser from the black gang armed with an iron cudgel. He stared straight ahead and spoke a single, clipped, "No."

"No . . . what?" the captain replied. His voice was surprisingly quiet, but there was no mistaking the threat in it.

Clarke quailed. Both his men were in the brig, his sword and pistol stripped from him, his ship, a half mile distant, no more than a glimmer of lights veiled by the tumult of the storm. He swayed as the deck heaved beneath him.

"No, sir," he replied.

"Next ye'll tell me you were only acting under orders," the captain said.

Clarke didn't answer.

"I'll tak' that as a yes." The captain leaned back in his chair. "Bosun, throw him overboard."

"Aye, Captain," the bosun replied.

He and the bruiser each grabbed an arm and lifted Clarke off his feet. Clarke's face went white. His mouth opened, but he clamped it shut and tried to look impassive.

"Belay that, bosun," Captain Morrison growled. "I was only thinking out loud. Throw him in the brig with the others. Shoot him if he tries anything."

"Aye, Captain," the bosun replied. The bruiser looked disappointed. Clarke sagged with relief and didn't struggle as they hauled him out of the wardroom.

"What do ye think, Purser?" the captain asked.

"I think the admiralty aren't willing to risk having either the professor or his weapon fall into someone else's hands," Nellie replied. "Their man searched for the crate, didn't find it, and went to the secondary plan."

"I fear she is right, Captain," the professor said.

"Is there such a crate?" the captain asked.

Aunt Nellie went almost as stiff as Clarke had. "Aye, Sir. But it's not with his hold luggage. It came on board earlier and was a wee overlong, so I had it put in the main hold. It's marked with the false name we had settled on: Schmidt."

"And this crate for 'Mr. Schmidt' contains the weapon?"

"Aye, Sir."

"But you didn't see fit to warn me." His voice had gone

quiet again.

"'Tis only a prototype, Sir. Or so I was told."

"It's at one-third scale and produces a small fraction of the resonance," the professor said. "A person would have to be within a hundred feet to experience more than a temporary dislocation of mental faculties. A brief attack of hysteria or paranoia, perhaps, followed by something similar to a migraine headache. Perhaps a brief period of unconsciousness; certainly nothing worse."

They all stared at him.

"We'll discuss this later, Purser," the captain growled. "Right now, tell the Second to put a guard on that crate." He turned to the professor and pointed to the mine. "A few more questions before I let ye go. First, how much time had that *mingin* saboteur given himself to get away?"

"That's hard to say," the professor began.

"Approximately three hours, Sir," Tereza said, "with a potential variance of plus-or-minus five minutes."

"Ye're sure, lass?"

"Yes, Sir. I was able to remove the cover on the timing mechanism before unclamping the mine from the hull."

"Ye did, did you?"

"Yes, Sir. Everyone else was busy at the time."

"Tereza, I told you only to unclamp th—"

The Captain lifted his hand. "It's all right, Professor. It's what I needed to know. Can the mine be set for as little as half an hour, miss?"

Tereza beamed. "Yes, Sir – plus or minus about ninety seconds, but you'll need this." She pulled the key from her pocket.

He nodded. "Keep it till I call for it. Now, ye guests can stay here in the wardroom, if you like. It'll be a wee bit more comfortable than a cabin." He glowered at Derek "And I'll be able to keep an eye on ye, too. Stay out of the rest of the ship, do ye understand me?" He fixed Ewan with his hard glance. "Steward, make sure they do. Ye did good work just now, but we're dealing with more than a puffed-up lieutenant and a pair of red shirts. Someone gave them their orders, and ye can be sure that someone'll be trying again."

&

The gale got worse, but *Alexandra* pressed on, leading them out of the North Channel, then bearing northwest into the Atlantic. Captain Morrison pressed on with his own plans. They could see little of the action from the wardroom portholes, which looked out on the foredeck, so Ewan ducked out now and again to find out what was happening.

The deck crew uncovered the number two lifeboat and loaded it with loose gear and duffle – a sea chair, a life ring, a tarp, some clothing, a half-empty fruit crate from the pantry, even a cabin door – all of it things that would float. Then they fastened it to the davits with spare line, and the ship's carpenter cut through the falls with a saw.

"It's to look like the boat and everything tore free," Ewan explained.

"If this storm gets much worse, they shouldn't have to fake it," Derek muttered. They were all feeling a bit queasy in the heavy seas, except Daisy, who was trying to keep up their spirits with a faltering game of twenty questions.

With the number two boat ready, the crew went to the other side and loaded the number five boat with heavy gear for ballast. Then the captain came and asked Tereza to set the timer on the mine.

"We'll want half an hour please, Miss, plus or minus those few seconds," he said.

Tereza inserted the key, twisted the dial, and turned the key. Everyone held their breath, but all it did was start ticking.

They crowded into the companionway by Aunt Nellie's cabin to watch as the bosun carried the mine out to boat number five and lashed it securely to the center thwart. Then the crew carefully lowered the boat, no easy task in that weather. On every roll of the ship, the peak of the wave came close to the railing, threatening to capsize the lifeboat. Finally, with a hurried drop, they set the boat free and threw off a long bow line to act as a sea anchor. At the same time, the captain veered the *Lewis* to avoid the trailing line and keep from swamping the boat. It trailed into the dark and sheeting rain behind them, still afloat.

"Five more minutes," the professor reported, hands cupped around his watch.

They stared into the raging gloom.

"Four."

"Thre—"

The mine exploded with a terrible flash and roar that was instantly dashed by the wind.

At the same moment, on the captain's command, the electric lights in the deckhouse went out. Five minutes later, the bow light went out. The ship's siren sounded, a long, wailing blast that made them all jump, not just the Skovajsas. One by one, the masthead lights went dark, followed last by the big anchor light on the taffrail as the ship dipped into a deep trough. The crewmen spilled the load from the number two boat and let it drop free into the waves. The captain turned the *Lewis* hard to starboard, rang for more steam, and they plowed at full speed through the open ocean.

Dawn barely came. The storm had lessened briefly during the middle of the night, but soon returned in full fury. The *Isle of Lewis* steamed steadily north by west into the teeth of it, struggling to make slow headway against the looming waves. Ewan moved the group into cabin one, which was closer to the center of balance of the ship and felt the rocking and pitching less. Lying on a berth was easier than staying in a chair, but no one slept. The effort to stay wedged in was too great.

As the light went from black to charcoal to slate, they risked broken limbs by climbing back up to the wardroom. No sooner had they arrived than the *Lewis* plowed into another oversized wave with a rise and a lurch that sent them sprawling. Water washed along the deck as high as the portholes at the front of the wardroom. Something outside rumbled by, then – as they grabbed again for chair arms and the edge of the table – rumbled back forward. There was a clang as whatever it was hit the port rail. Another wave lifted the bow; the rumble came toward them and struck. The walls of the deckhouse rang like a cracked bell. Tereza put her hands to her ears but then had to grab the edge of the table again.

Ewan struggled out into the passageway and fought to open the hatch. Through the noise of the storm, he heard shouts out on deck, curses as the ship heeled and the rumbling moved back toward the rail. He got the hatch open enough to peer out but was almost blinded by the rain and spray. The wind battered the sou'wester tied to his head and flapped the tails of his oilskins like flags. The signal cannon rumbled past, to clang against the railing again, bending the steel bars. The cannon's sliding carriage had torn free of its lashings. Now it was sledding across the wooden deck like a toboggan on an ever-changing hillside. Several of the deck crew chased after it, trying to slip nooses of heavy line over the muzzle.

Ewan took one step out of the hatchway, only to find his way blocked by the bosun.

"Stop gowping and get your daft arse back inside!" the

bosun yelled. "Tend to your own charges. We'll handle this."

"Aye, Sir!" Ewan replied, barely audible above the tumult. He knew better than to argue with a man who could shout louder than a hurricane.

He returned gratefully to the relative warmth and dryness of the wardroom, where the others heard his report with pale faces. The rumbling went on for a few more passes, before stopping. Either the crew had managed to lash the cannon against something solid, or it had taken itself overboard.

Later that morning, the cook managed to produce some hot tea and oat porridge, but only Daisy could eat more than a few bites. It wasn't just the heavy motion; everyone was dead tired and aching. There was only one reasonable human response to the storm: fear. Wedging your resolve against that force took more effort than anything else. After so many hours of it, you found either God or philosophy.

Ewan felt it as much as the others, maybe more. He had been through other storms, but he could tell that this one was much, much worse. He knew how well built the *Lewis* was, and also how fragile.

Now the seas were washing over the deck with every wave. Water was seeping around the portholes and the hatch covers. The cabin door popped free of the latch and crashed back and forth on its hinges until he and Derek managed to wrestle it shut and tie the latch with their shoe strings. The walnut paneling creaked and groaned like a grove of trees being felled by the wind. The ship's steel masts were far stronger than any wooden spars, but the yards and booms were wood, and the rigging was hemp and marlin. The single propeller, he knew too well, was held on by one pin. The engine was assembled from hundreds of parts, all being asked to perform at the limit of their strength, and for who knew how many hours longer. If just one of them went and the engine failed, the *Lewis* would fall broadside to the waves. In minutes, they'd capsize and go down.

"This certainly has gone on for a long time, wouldn't you say?" Derek shoved his spoon into his cooling porridge and pushed the bowl aside. It immediately slid to the far side of the table and slammed against the fender, flipping over it to smash on the deck in a sludge of mush and broken crockery. "I'm sorry," he said, with little energy. "Clumsy of me."

He tried to kneel and mop up the mess with his napkin but popped up quickly and jammed himself back into his seat, white faced. "Don't try that. Head down and it all goes round much worse."

"Stay put," Ewan said. "I'll deal with it." *It's part of my job, after all*, he thought.

He dropped his napkin over the pile and nudged it up against a table leg with the toe of his shoe. It left a smear on the deck, but at least it seemed inclined to cling to the leg and stay out of the way.

"I'll go check with the bridge to see if there's any sign of it lessening," he said.

"Find out where we are, if you can," the professor asked.

"Better yet, find out where he's taking us," Daisy said.

"And how he plans to keep us away from the English," Tereza added.

"I'll ask," Ewan replied, donning his oilskins and tying on his sou'wester, "but I'm guessing he's too busy to answer right now."

He noticed that not one of them offered to come with him. It was a measure of how much the storm had sapped them all.

It was worse in the companionway and hell on deck.

The roar of the sea was horrendous, and the wind blasted his ears with an unholy wail as it sang through the rigging and the railings to hammer spume and spray against his face. It was only a few feet from the hatchway to the bridge ladder, but Ewan had to pause till the roll of the ship swung the hatch away from the side of the deckhouse and then back around so he could slip out, slam it shut, and latch it. The wind tore at his sou'wester, cutting the ties into his still bruised neck, trying to drag him sternward along the slippery deck – a terrible reminder of the garrote. Then the bow dipped into the lee of the next wave and he lunged for the railings on the ladder.

He caught hold and started up as the ship dug into the face of the wave, a huge cliff of gray water, seething like the flank of a monster. The *Lewis* came almost to a dead stop as her bow plowed through the heavy water, lifting slowly till it broke free and rose, shedding sheets of seawater on both sides. The water was four feet deep on deck when the sheet reached the deckhouse, washed against the deadlights, and surged around the side, grabbing at Ewan's boots and pants as he clung to the ladder for dear life.

The *Lewis* reached the top of the wave, broke through the crest, hung a moment as the stern lifted out of the water and the propeller pulled free, whining till the whole ship rattled. Then she sledded down into the trough. Ewan ran the rest of the way up the ladder, now almost flat, before the *Lewis* could plow into the next wave. Water sloshed in his boots. His face was soaked, his arms, even under the oilskins, were wet to his shoulders.

Captain Morrison stood at the center of the bridge by the telegraph, gripping the rail as he stared into the wind. James Gilmore was braced between the port corner of the deckhouse and the port rail, scanning the horizon for stray waves that might come from the southwest quarter.

Fourth Officer MacDonald was braced at the starboard corner, watching for waves from the north. Ewan slid along the rail to James and shouted in his ear.

"How much longer?"

James shrugged. His face was gray, and dark circles hung beneath his eyes, but he managed a quick smile. "It should lessen by evening and blow out by morning at the latest," he shouted back. "Tell your friends the captain says he's seen worse."

When? Ewan wondered, watching the huge waves roll relentlessly toward them. They were as high as the bridge, even higher – forty feet high, some of them, though it was hard to be sure. Wavelets the size of beach breakers broke randomly at their crests. Foam blanketed the entire surface of the sea. He looked across the jagged peaks ahead. The rain and flying spume were so thick, he could barely see four or five crests before they were lost in the gray tumult that fogged the horizon, as though the clouds and the sea were one heaving blanket wrapped tight around the *Lewis*'s small patch of gray daylight.

As he stared, something grew out of the fog, something gray and huge, moving toward them with the waves. Ewan peered through the driving rain, trying to believe what he was seeing.

It was a wave like no other. Twice as high as all the other crests. No, higher. Marching toward them in lockstep with the wind.

The captain pulled on the telegraph, sending a signal to the engine room. Ewan couldn't tear his eyes from the oncoming wave. It loomed higher and higher above the bridge. Above the foremast truck. A vertical wall. The *Lewis* hung at the top of the final crest before the monster, then dipped into the trough. Now the rogue wave, as high as the topsail yard, hung over them like an avalanche waiting to happen.

Chapter 28

The Wave

James grabbed Ewan's arm and yanked him to the side of the wheelhouse as the ship began to roll to starboard.

"Get inside!" he shouted. "That's an order!"

Ewan tried to break free, but James wrenched open the wheelhouse door, and shoved him through. The ship's roll slammed the door and carried Ewan against the binnacle hard enough to knock the breath out of him. He scrambled up, gasping, and clawed against gravity back toward the door. Someone behind him was praying, shouting the words over the roar that pounded the windows.

The *Lewis* began to lift. Then her bow hit the wave, and she shuddered as if she'd struck a building. Ewan slammed forward against the quarter-inch-thick window. He could feel it pressing inward under the battering wind. He peered out through the rain-streaked glass. The bow was buried as far as the capstans and the water kept coming. The *Lewis* began to tip down under the weight of the wave. Outside, Captain Morrison let go of the rail and lurched to the telegraph, yanked the lever down and back up, twice. The water was at the mast and still coming.

The *Lewis* responded, a change in pitch, a heavier vibration as MacLeod and his engineers wrenched open all the steam valves, and the big pistons strained against the propeller shaft, already stressed to its highest torque. The bow began to lift.

The wave swept over the roof of the deckhouse and smashed into the bridge. The captain disappeared in the wall of water, then slammed up against the front windows. The center two buckled and gave, shards of thick glass and a wall of water blasting in on the wheel and the helmsmen and Third Officer MacBreive, cutting his prayer in mid screech. Ewan gripped the handrail beneath the portside window, safe for a moment in the eddy it made, drowned in the fury of wind, waist deep in rushing water that pressed him hard into the corner. The captain sprawled against the front of the binnacle, half afloat, half under, flailing for a grip. The water washed around him, took out both port and starboard doors, ripped off the roof and the starboard wall.

Suddenly Ewan was being pulled to the side. His head went under. He felt a hand – grasping, desperate, clawing at his oilskins. He grabbed back. *One hand for yourself, one for the ship. One for the captain.* He hooked his left elbow through the handrail, wrapped his legs around Captain Morrison's thick body just as the portside window popped free, unbroken, the heavy sheet pressing him against the deck as it slid over his head and the struggling captain and disappeared with the draining water.

Ewan's head broke clear. The bow was still lifting. Or the stern dipping as the water continued its rush down the deck. The *Lewis* rose on the face of the wave, borne backwards but still climbing the impossible slope.

Ewan wrestled the captain closer, gripped him tighter with both legs and his right arm, the left arm straining, almost broken between the rail and what little remained of the front bulkhead. The two helmsmen were still at the wheel, legs stretched back, almost standing on the stern bulkhead, still intact despite all.

Then the peak of the wave curled and fell on them.

Water and foam. Water to the neck, foam so deep it buried their heads six feet under, so thick it choked them. Water ripping again at the rigging, the bulkheads, the wheel. Foam too wet to breathe, too thin to flow, clinging. Ewan held his breath, held on, held the captain, and expected to die any moment.

The bulkhead held. The bow broke through the wave. The water rushed onward, leaving them perched on a ridge thirty feet above all the other waves. Sixty feet above the trough. The propeller wailed in open air at their stern. The *Lewis* tipped forward and began to surf down the back of the wave.

Captain Morrison coughed and retched, tried to break free. "The wheel, laddie!" he gasped. "Tak' the whe—" He broke off with a grunt of pain, doubled over his ribs.

There was only one helmsman still at the wheel, struggling now to keep the ship heading straight down the face. A slew to port or starboard meant capsize. Death to them all.

Ewan let go of the captain and rail and threw himself across the sloping deck, grabbing the base of the wheel. He hauled himself up, took hold of two spokes, and braced his feet as best he could.

"Port a third!" The remaining helmsman, teeth clenched, moved the wheel. Ewan tried to follow his lead: top spoke a third of a turn. Then back. Then starboard. And starboard more. And back quick, as the ship slid into the shadow of the next wave, plunged into the bottom of the trough, through another dowsing, heeling by 20 degrees, then back even farther, straining to rise, the terrible pause before the bow broke free. But break it did, lifting clear, sending another wave down the deck, but not so high, below the remains of the bridge. The next wave was smaller still. And the one after seemed tame, a mere thirty feet high.

Ewan stayed at the wheel. The captain wedged himself in the remaining front corner of the wheelhouse wall, curled over his ribs. He called faintly for an officer:

Gilmore, MacBreive, MacDonald. There was no answer. The bridge wings were gone, torn off and swept away by the monster wave. The officers had gone with them.

Then MacBreive appeared in the chartroom doorway, in the center of the aft bulkhead. The door itself was gone, the portholes blown out, the room a wreck of water and wood and floating paper. MacBreive could barely stand. His hat was gone, his thin hair wild around his pale, balding crown. His mustache dripped. The captain roused himself, ordered MacBreive below to check for damage. To call for the bosun, the carpenter, another quartermaster to stand at the wheel.

Even as MacBreive staggered off to obey, the ship slowed. The vibration weakened.

The captain swore. "I'll tak' the wheel, Ewan Gilmore," he muttered "Get down to MacLeod and find out what's wrong. Tell him we've lost the telegraph. We'll need runners." Ewan hesitated. Blood was seeping from under the captain's sou'wester, running down this face. He pushed at Ewan's arm, recoiled from another pain, then braced himself beside his helmsman. "Go!" he barked. Ewan went.

The engine room skylight was stove in and water sloshed a foot over the grating at the bottom. Hot steam clouded the air, spewing from half-a-dozen hissing joints between the boilers and engine. The lights flickered wanly, barely cutting through the mayhem. The engineers and oilers searched for spilled tools. The black gang struggled on in the filthy water, heaving shovel after shovelful of heavy coal into the greedy fires when they could barely keep their footing on the heaving deck.

MacLeod was unconscious, lashed to a stanchion so his inert body couldn't roll with the ship. Two of the trimmers were dead, crushed by a runaway cart full of coal. One of the stokers had broken his arm. An oiler had been blinded by a jet of steam. The second and third engineers ran from crisis to crisis, shouting conflicting orders, wielding wrenches, pushing their men past the limit.

"We need the doctor," the second engineer told Ewan.

"He went off with the passengers," Ewan replied. "I'll fetch Frasier."

"Get the carpenter!" the third engineer shouted. "Stop up that skylight!"

"We need the light!" the second engineer argued. "The dynamo's failing!"

Ewan raced forward first, where the carpenter was desperately trying to brace the forward hatch, cracked by the toppling great wave and leaking heavy gouts into the hold every time the bow plunged into the next. There was no sign of MacBreive. The bosun took over and sent the carpenter and five men aft to deal with the skylight.

Ewan found Frasier back up in the chartroom. Together, they laid the captain on a makeshift bed of blankets beneath the chart table, then wrapped his head and tried to wind strips of torn sheet around his ribs. The captain ordered them both to the engine room.

"I'll be fine," he mumbled. "It's MacLeod we're needing more now. If the engine—" He slipped unconscious.

A second quartermaster was at the wheel, backed by the coxswain. Two seamen stood watch at port and starboard, scanning all sides for another rogue. There was no need for Ewan there.

"Stay with the captain," Ewan told Frasier, then he made his way down to the wardroom.

It was a dim, wet shambles, six inches deep in water. One of the forward deadlights had been stove in. Derek and Aunt Nellie had managed to cover the hole with pillows, line, and the shovelboard sticks, brought from Aunt Nellie's office. Everyone was helping to bail out the floor in the flickering light.

Ewan went straight to Aunt Nellie.

"The big wave tore off both bridge wings. James . . ." He had to swallow before he could say it. "James went with them. He's gone. I'm sorry."

Aunt Nellie's face went white. She made a small noise, as though a cry had died at the back of her throat.

Daisy moved to her side, Teresa to the other. Each placed a hand on Aunt Nellie's back. The men bowed their heads, all of them clinging to the table or the back of a chair as the ship pitched and heeled, all offering silent comfort as best they could. For a long minute, Aunt Nellie accepted the support. Then she wiped a hand across her eyes and straightened.

"And the captain?" she asked.

Ewan described the state of the ship, the captain, and MacLeod.

"I'll see to the captain," she said. "Frasier'll be better use in the engine room. And we'll need men from the deck crew to help the black gang. Pray MacLeod comes to quickly. If the engine fails . . ." She wiped her eyes again.

"What about the engine?" Derek whispered to Ewan.

"If the engine fails, we'll lose steerage."

"And the pumps," Tereza said.

"If the engine fails, we're all lost," Aunt Nellie said.

Chapter 24

Turn & Turn & Turn About

"I'll go with you to tend the captain," Daisy said. "He's a big man; you'll need a second pair of hands." *And a woman beside you when the storm passes*, she thought, *when you'll have time to mourn for your son.*

"Father and I will fix the dynamo," Tereza said. "That will free the engineers to work on the engine."

"Not you," the purser said. "I'm sorry, Miss, I don't doubt you'd be a help, but that bunch are too superstitious. A quick visit with MacLeod is one thing. With him out of commission . . . No, it wouldn't work."

"I'll go alone," the professor said. "No, Tereza, this time I insist! Your presence would only cause more disruption."

"Derek, go with him and make sure he gets there safely," Daisy ordered. "But don't touch anything unless he tells you to!"

"Yes, ma'am!" he replied, almost saluting. He and the professor left, bracing each other against the constant pitch of the deck.

"A good idea, miss," the purser said. "Keep him out of trouble. We hope."

"Thank you," Daisy replied. "Now, how do we get to the chart room with the bridge ladders gone?"

"There's a ladder by the captain's cabin. Ewan, find MacBreive. He's a *sleekit smatchet*, but he's the only officer conscious, God help us."

Daisy took her arm and they struggled out the door.

The wardroom was at the front of the deckhouse;

Captain Morrison's cabin was toward the rear. The passageway between them was dim and treacherous, four inches deep in sloshing water that pulled at their skirts and threatened to sweep their feet from beneath them. A narrow, difficult ladder just outside the captain's cabin door led up to the chart room, where they found Captain Morrison still unconscious. The purser sent Frasier down to the engine room and took the captain's head on her lap. Daisy struggled back down the ladder to fetch blankets and a pillow to pad his side. They slid him tight against the bulkhead and braced themselves at head and foot. Then they waited, cold and terrified, for the storm to either drown them or abate.

Daisy sang to keep up her spirits, and the purser joined in, humming when she didn't know the words, and sometimes, head turned away as if to watch the weather raging outside their small shelter, weeping quietly. They sang for hours it seemed, while the ship fought on through the waves and sailors brought reports from below: The hatch was covered, the skylight repaired. The pumps were cut back to half strength so more steam could be fed to the engine. MacLeod was still unconscious, but Professor Skovajsa had repaired the dynamo, and the lights were back on all over the ship – those that hadn't been shattered by the pounding of the storm. Now he was devising some sort of switch box to stand in for the telegraph.

The best news of all: The storm appeared to be lessening. Only two things bothered Daisy: Ewan didn't appear with MacBreive, and there was no word from Tereza. She worried they might have gone on deck.

Daisy and the purser had left the wardroom without giving Tereza a task, and that suited her fine. They had refused to let her help in the way she knew best, but she wasn't about to sit idle when there was something else she could do. As soon as the women left, she went to the doorway and, before Ewan could tell her she had to stay put, looked back at him and said, "Where do you think he may have gone? We probably should check his own cabin first, just to be sure, but it's too obvious. If I were looking for a safe shelter in a storm like this, I'd look for a spot near the hull's center of balance. What do you think?"

Ewan stepped closer but kept his grip on the table. "You're right about his own cabin; it's the first place anyone would look, but it's also the closest so I will, and everywhere else here in the deckhouse. After that, I'll work my way downward, deck by deck."

A sudden hard lurch from a quartering wave made them both grab for more support. Ewan gave a grim smile. "And you're right about center of balance, too. The barber's cabin would make the most sense. It's right beside the funnel. The doctor's cabin is right beside it but I'd rule it out – too much chance someone would come in looking for bandages and the like. The cook is in his own quarters right by the kitchens. The saloon is too far aft and too wide open to hide in, and the Ladies Cabin is just as far aft."

"I can't imagine he'd go down to steerage," Tereza added. "Too many stairs to climb if we started sinking."

"True enough, and that's double for the hold."

"So the officers' cabins first, then we'll check the barber's cabin, and then start in on the passenger cabins. Come on."

The ship had just begun a dip into a trough but Tereza didn't wait for Ewan's reaction. She heaved open the hatch and quickly stepped over the threshold into the passageway.

"Wait!" he called, but she ignored him. By the time he had struggled to the hatchway and clambered out she was well down the center passageway leading aft.

Tereza blessed the engineers who had designed the *Isle of Lewis*. The passageways were laid out so you could move between wheelhouse and hold, forecastle and stern, and anywhere in between without ever going outside. With two exceptions: the smoking cabin and the little deckhouse at the very stern. She was ninety-nine percent certain MacBreive would never have taken that risk, but the remaining one percent nagged at her own courage. She gritted her teeth and splashed her way toward MacBreive's cabin.

The only light came through the spray-battered porthole in the hatchway at the far end of the passage. Cold water sloshed over the tops of her shoes. The waves pitched her against the bulkheads on either side, but she hurried on as fast as she could. She came to the first doorway, on the left. There was a second a few feet farther on the right.

"Which one is it!" she yelled, looking back over her shoulder. She wasn't sure Ewan had heard her over the tumult, but he pointed to the left.

"Wait! Let me!" he shouted, and this time she did wait, letting him open the hatch and step in. She peered past him into the cabin.

It was small, with three berths, all of them empty. A slurry of fallen items sloshed forward and back around the bed posts: clothes, books, a briar pipe. Ewan stared at them for a moment, struggling with some emotion. Tereza realized MacBreive must have shared the cabin, most likely with the second and fourth officers, both swept overboard barely fifteen minutes before. One of them Ewan's cousin James.

"I'm sorry," she said.

He nodded. "Aye, there's plenty of reason for sorrow, but we're still afloat and we still haven't found MacBreive."

"The one across next?"

He nodded again, gave one last look around, and stepped back into passage, making sure the hatch was latched behind him.

They checked the other cabins in the deckhouse – MacLeod's, his engineers', even the purser's – but they were all empty. Tereza worried that Ewan might ask her to go back to the wardroom, but he didn't say a thing as they passed it on their way to the companionway. They struggled down, a few steps at a time, and went straight to the barber's cabin and the doctor's too, to be sure. Then they went back forward to passenger class.

"Shall we split up port and starboard?" Tereza asked.

At that moment, another steep wave slapped the hull from an odd direction and threw them together. Ewan managed to grab the door handle to cabin one and put an arm around her shoulders at the same time, holding them upright. He managed a smile.

"Best we stick together, I guess. Less chance we'll take a tumble." He blushed. "I mean, get knocked down."

Tereza suppressed a smile and pretended not to notice. "Yes, we're wet and bruised enough as it is." She didn't pull away until he let go. "Cabin one?" she asked.

"Right."

It was empty too, and so was cabin three and Daisy's own cabin, number five, halfway up the narrow aisle beside the hatchway that led to the forward group of cabins. The pitching of the ship was noticeably heavier, and it got steadily worse as they worked their way forward to number 15, the last cabin on the starboard side. They both agreed that MacBreive would have stayed amidships, but they checked the bathrooms anyway before starting in on the portside cabins. Each step was a balancing act, and they were constantly reaching out for support on an arm or shoulder, maybe more often than needed. The touch was warming, but Tereza was only too glad when they'd worked their way back past the hatchway and the motion got easier. And now there were only two cabins left before they'd be forced to go aft. The probability they would have to brave the deck was steadily increasing.

Ewan was just reaching for the latch to cabin four when Tereza heard a voice. She grabbed Ewan's arm, stopping him, and listened more carefully. The wind was still howling above, the waves pounding on the deck and hull, the wood paneling around them groaning with each surge and heave of the ship, but there! She heard it again, a man's voice, a few words too faint to recognize. She stepped past Ewan to the door to cabin two. The voice spoke again, and another *shushed*. She grabbed the latch and shoved the door open.

MacBreive was there, standing back to. He swung around to face her and stepped close, trying to block her view.

"What are you doing here?" he demanded, voice high and strained. Off balance and off guard, he lurched sideways with the sway of the hull. There were three men behind him. No, four. Clarke, the two marines, and—

Rage gripped Tereza, as though all the emotion she had held in since the Bell Cannon test turned into carnage had finally broken loose.

"Run Ewan!" she yelled. "Get help!"

Then she lunged at MacBreive, thrusting her parasol right at his face. He tried to dodge and stumbled backward into a marine. The other one grabbed for her arm.

"Run!" she yelled again.

But Ewan rushed through the door and into the fray.

When the bosun came up with relief for the quartermasters, Daisy asked after Tereza and Ewan, but he could only say that the wardroom was empty.

Captain Morrison opened his eyes then and muttered something about storm trysails.

"Aye-aye, Captain, right away," the bosun replied.

"Wait!" The captain clenched his side and moaned, but managed another few words. "Run down to Durness. Lay into Loch Eriboll."

"Aye-aye, Captain."

He hurried off, and the captain closed his eyes again

"Captain Morrison?" Daisy asked. "Can you hear me?"

He grunted.

"How is your head? Does it hurt?"

He grunted again.

She held up her index and middle fingers. "How many fingers do you see?"

He squinted one eye and growled, "Don't be daft." Then he drifted off.

"Sounds like he'll be all right," the purser remarked.

"Thank God," Daisy replied. "Where's Durness, Mrs. Gilmore?"

"Just east of Cape Wrath, on the north coast of Scotland. It's owned all about by MacKays. We can lie low there till your father sorts things out."

With a tiny trysail set on the mizzen boom, the sailors at the wheel had an easier time keeping the ship's bow to the wind and waves. Finally, the bosun decided the seas had calmed enough to risk turning tail to the wind. The maneuver was tricky, and the *Lewis* wallowed broadside for an interminable few moments in the trough between two waves, rolling heavily. Everyone held on for dear life while the bow decided whether or not to swing through the turn. Quick work at both masts by the deck crew – striking the trysail and setting a storm jib – brought the bow around, heading due east.

The effect in the chart room was immediate. The

remaining sides of the deckhouse became a windbreak instead of a scoop, and the motion eased from the head-on pounding to a swooping sleigh ride. Daisy could feel her whole body relax. Not ten minutes later, the cook came up with a jug of hot, sweet tea, pieces of honeyed bread, and the promise of warm broth soon.

No sooner had he left than MacBreive appeared at the top of the ladder.

"Where have you been?" Mrs. Gilmore snapped, rising to her feet in anger.

"Attending to matters," he replied. He turned and offered a helping hand to someone on the ladder behind him.

It was Lieutenant Clarke, followed by one of his marines and a squat man Daisy had never seen before.

She stood up, aghast. "What are they doing free, Mr. MacBreive?" she demanded. "Have you forgotten their attempt to blow up this ship?"

The squat man sniffed. "Merely a misunderstanding, Miss MacLaren," he said. "They were not suppose to arm the mine quite yet. I suppose we owe you some thanks for your part in correcting that little error."

His voice made his features all too familiar.

"Mrs. Curmidge!" Daisy gasped.

He nodded in acknowledgement. "In a manner of speaking. You may drop the 'Mrs.' if you prefer."

"MacBreive, what the devil is he doing here?" Mrs. Gilmore demanded.

"We are taking the ship back to England," MacBreive replied.

"'We?' So you're in league with him now, are you? I suppose you helped this imposter sneak his way back on board."

MacBreive actually smiled. "I played my part, yes."

"Unlike some on board," Curmidge said, "Mr.

MacBreive chose to side with the proper authorities."

"And who would that be? The Royal Navy, so you can finish the job Clarke and his *shaan paps* started?"

"I represent the Admiralty," Curmidge said, "though, admittedly, a different office than the lieutenant. Rest assured, ladies, no one on board will be harmed as long as they behave. Lieutenant Clarke and his men will resume their watch over the passengers, and Mr. MacBreive will assume the duties of captain and take command of this ship."

"You're forgetting that Captain Morrison is still quite alive," Daisy said.

Curmidge sniffed. "But hardly able to resume command."

"It was the captain who kept the *Isle of Lewis* afloat," Mrs. Gilmore retorted, "while this *glaikit fearfit* cowered below decks, consorting with spies and saboteurs."

"Yes, well, Mr. MacBreive has shown himself a loyal servant of the Crown. I'm sure he's quite capable of charting a course for Southampton."

"As soon as the clouds break enough to take a sighting," MacBreive replied. He looked down his sharp nose at Aunt Nellie. "I think it would be best if you were to keep company with the passengers, Purser. That's an order."

"What about the captain then? He needs tending."

"I'll have him sent down on a stretcher."

&

Clarke stayed on the bridge, while Curmidge and the marine escorted them down to the cabin. They found Ewan and Tereza inside, under close watch by the other marine. Tereza's left cheek was marked by a large, vivid bruise, but otherwise she appeared to be all right.

"Thank goodness!" Daisy exclaimed, embracing her.

"We were afraid you'd been badly injured or wash— Or worse."

"Or washed overboard," Mrs. Gilmore said. "It's all right to say it, Miss MacLaren. It happens often enough, though we never believe it'll be one of our own." Her tone permitted no sympathy. "Are you all right, Ewan?"

"Yes, ma'am," he replied, though he looked much worse than Tereza, with bruises, a black eye, and a swollen lip.

Curmidge sniffed. "They put up more of a fight than was necessary, I'm afraid. That temper will be the death of him. As for her, quite unbecoming. Now, all of you will stay put while I fetch the rest of your traveling companions. Wandering about this ship in its current condition could be the death of anyone. Mind, the corporal here will be right outside the door, with orders to shoot."

He and one of the marines left. Their guard followed, glaring at them as he shut the door. Daisy noticed he had Tereza's blue parasol tucked into his belt like a short sword.

"I don't believe he's forgotten the shock you gave him, Tereza," she remarked.

"Good," Tereza replied. "Give me half the chance and I'll do it again."

"What now?" Aunt Nellie asked. "Any ideas?"

"If MacBreive does have the captain brought down, we might find an opportunity then," Daisy said.

"Or when Curmidge returns with the professor and Derek," Ewan added.

"We'll need to be close to the door," Tereza said. She studied the layout with sharp eyes and cold anger.

They were discussing tactics when the guard called loudly from outside. "Get all the way to the back wall and stay there."

Ewan slipped behind the door, holding the chamber pot, already cracked during the storm.

But one of the crew came in first, holding the end of a stretcher bearing Captain Morrison. The captain was lashed to the frame and semiconscious, muttering commands that the seamen ignored. The marine stayed outside in the passageway, carbine at the ready. He never gave them an opportunity to try anything.

They had even less of a chance when Curmidge returned a few minutes later. The professor and Derek were crowded into the cabin and made to sit.

Then Curmidge gestured Tereza out. "Come with me, please, Miss Skovajsová."

The professor grabbed Tereza's shoulder and held her back. "Where are you taking her?" he demanded.

"To the hold, of course," Curmidge replied. "To find your model weapon."

"She doesn't know what to look for," the professor replied. "She never even saw the crate. I shall go."

"No, I'll go," Mrs. Gilmore said. "I saw the crate and I know where it's stowed."

"I appreciate your enthusiasm to be of help," Curmidge said, "but no, you shan't, neither of you." He pointed his gun at Tereza. "What you will do is tell us where to look and what to look for. And do please be accurate; the young lady's continued good health depends on it."

They had no choice. The professor and Mrs. Gilmore described the crate and its location, and Curmidge took Tereza away, accompanied by his marine shadow. Once again, they were shut in by the snarling guard.

"There must be some way to entice him in here and get the jump on him," Derek whispered.

"It's much too crowded in here, and Captain Morrison is in no condition to risk further injury," Daisy said. "We will have to make our assault outside."

"But the door's locked," Derek said.

"The door only locks from the inside," Ewan said, pointing to the latch.

"There, you see," Daisy said. "I'll distract him. Watch for your chance."

Derek grabbed her arm. "No, it's too dangerous – I'll do it!"

Daisy removed his hand. "That's very sweet, Derek, but you'd only get yourself shot. Stay back, please, and pretend to be meek."

"But—"

She gave him a quick peck on the cheek, which flummoxed him long enough for her to throw open the door and march out.

"See here, Sergeant, this really will not do."

"'Ey!" The marine jerked alert, raising his carbine.

Daisy went right up to him, laid her hand gently but firmly on his trigger hand, looked up into his eyes, and began to gush. "That won't be necessary, sir, I assure you. I merely wish to request that you bring us an unbroken chamber pot and some rope so that we may arrange a screen." She smiled like her air-headed Charleston cousin, Louella. "I'm sure a gentleman like yourself can appreciate the awkward situation in which we *ladies* find ourselves, being held in a small room with three men, not to mention the invalid captain, who, in all honesty . . ." She leaned in close and lowered her voice. ". . . is in need of some serious hygienic attention in the matter of bathing and . . . Well, you understand what I mean, I am sure."

She lifted her hand to his shoulder and took a step farther into the passageway, turning him slightly with her, speaking quietly, as if she didn't want the others to hear. "Now, I could run to do it myself, but I have no idea where they're kept, and I am fully aware that you do not want to risk letting even one of the men out of your sight. Who knows what they might attempt—"

The guard quickly glanced over at the open door of the cabin, and Daisy cursed herself for even mentioning the men. She leaned even closer, allowing the buttons of her double-breasted Ulster to brush against his forearm.

"I know; they are rather unkempt, are they not? But who among us can maintain proper appearances in such a state of weather? Which brings me back to my growing need to . . . Well, as I said, if you would be so kind as to bring us a usable chamber pot and a bit of twine, I would be so very grateful."

She beamed another Louella smile, eyes wide, brain apparently empty, and let the motion of the ship press her body against his.

The guard stepped back. "'Ere, stay off me, girl. I remember you weren't so sweetsie when your skinny friend stung me with her brolly down ta 'old."

"Come now, sir! I seem to recall you were rather threatening and, shall I say, less than courteous in your intentions at the time. A bomb? Really, sir! That could hardly have been necessary when we were surrounded by a small fleet of armed dreadnoughts. Whatever were you thinking?" She fluttered her hand as though it were a fan. "Besides, the tables are turned, are they not? You have the upper hand now. All I ask is—"

"You can piss in ta corner berth for what I care. Now get back inside!" The marine jammed the carbine into her chest and shoved her off.

"That was completely uncalled for!" Daisy slapped his face, grabbed the barrel and stock of the gun, and jerked it to the side so hard it went off. The bullet tore through the door of cabin number three. But now she had turned him completely away from the other captives.

"You bloody bitch!" he yelled, raising his fist.

Daisy screamed right in his face. It brought him up for just an instant, and Derek, face flaming, launched himself through the doorway.

Chapter 25

The Prototype

Ewan had been holding Derek back, waiting for a signal from Daisy, but the slap was too much. Derek bowled him aside and threw himself into a flying tackle, landing on the marine's back and tumbling them both to the deck at Daisy's feet. Ewan arrived at a flailing tangle of arms, fists, and feet. The marine rolled to the top and landed a solid punch on Derek's face. Ewan grabbed for his shoulders, but a wild kick from Derek knocked his legs out from under him. He fell across their struggling bodies, only to be heaved aside as they rolled and rolled. Someone's fist grazed his bruised jaw on the way by, sending a flash of white pain across his eyes.

"Stop!" Daisy cried. She stood over them, fumbling with the carbine. "Stop it at once or I'll shoot!"

Aunt Nellie grabbed her from behind. "Don't be daft, lass! You're apt to murder them both!"

Ewan dove back in, trying to clamp his arms around the marine, but Derek's body was in the way. But Ewan's hand fell on the parasol. He fumbled for the handle and rolled away, jerking the parasol free of the marine's belt. His finger found the switch. Rising onto his knees, he jabbed the tip of the parasol against the marine's back and set it off.

A blue spark flared at the tip. The marine jerked, arched back, rigid. Ewan clenched his finger on the switch and jabbed again, harder, pressing the tip firmly against the red coat. The parasol hummed in his hand. Crackling sparks flew. The marine made sharp, choking sounds but

Ewan held the switch on. The sparks pulsed for a full count of ten, then faded and died. The marine collapsed in a limp heap on top of Derek.

"Oh dear," Daisy said in a faint voice. "Is he dead?"

Professor Skovajsa bent and felt for a pulse. "No, merely unconscious."

"I meant Derek."

"Well done, Ewan," Aunt Nellie said, "you've clobbered them both with one blow. That's quite the parasol."

"Believe me, I know," he replied. "I'm sorry Daisy. I didn't realize the shock would go right through to Derek."

"Our clothes are still very damp and salty from the storm," the professor said. "It bound them into a single circuit through which the electrical impulse could travel. You're lucky you didn't shock yourself."

"He's young, he'll be fine," Aunt Nellie said. "Now let's get this lobster-back trussed up before he comes to."

Ewan and the professor lugged the man into the cabin, while Daisy took his knife and cut up the curtains for rope. He didn't wake up while they were binding him, and neither did Derek as they carried him in and laid him on another berth.

Ewan found his derringer and the spare cartridges in the marine's pocket. "Stay with them," he said, reloading the upper chamber. "I'll go after Tereza."

"Not alone, Mr. Gilmore," Daisy replied, picking up the carbine. "I'm coming with you."

"And I," the professor said, hefting the parasol.

"I'm afraid I used it up," Ewan said.

"No matter." The professor pulled the metal tip off the parasol and a six-inch blade sprang out.

"I'm for the bridge," Aunt Nellie said, "to take care of Clarke and that traitor MacBreive."

"You can hardly go alone, Mrs. Gilmore," Daisy

protested. "Wait for us."

"Frasier," Captain Morrison muttered.

Aunt Nellie hurried to the inner berth. The captain tried to sit up, but she held him down and added a second pillow under his head from the berth above.

"Find Frasier," the captain said. "He knows where I keep my revolver. Go to MacLeod. Tell him he's in command."

"MacLeod's out cold, Sir," Aunt Nellie replied.

"Then you're in command. Trust the bosun. And send Frasier to me." He sank back. "The Devil . . . Can't stay awake."

"You took a terrible knock on the head, Sir," Aunt Nellie said. "Sleep's what you need. Let it heal you." She gripped his shoulder. "*Dinna faische yer'sel*, George Morrison. We'll take care of MacBreive."

"I know you will, *gel*. Leave me and get to it."

Ewan led Daisy and the professor aft to the saloon companionway, then up to the deck. The change in the state of the sea seemed nearly miraculous. The waves were a mere twenty feet high, long, stately rollers. The foaming white caps had settled to a scatter of white horses, and the cold breeze was clear of spume. They crept close by the side of the steerage companionway and the engine skylights, keeping the broad bulk of the funnel and the tall ventilators between them and the view of the damaged wheelhouse. You could get into the hold through the boiler room; Ewan could only hope Curmidge didn't know it.

They went down the engine room companionway, where the second engineer tried to block their way. When he learned what they were doing, he offered to go himself, with a few of the black gang to back him up. Ewan convinced him that stealth was the only way to save Tereza's life – something else he could only hope was true.

"You do know how to shoot that thing, right?" he whispered to Daisy as they paused outside the hatch to the hold.

"I've a cousin who lives to hunt and begged me to join him a few times." She smiled grimly. "He stopped asking when I kept outshooting him."

"But—"

"Don't worry, it's loaded, cocked, and I have two more rounds."

She pulled them from one of the Ulster's large pockets, a pair of long, weighty, round-nosed cartridges. Ewan's derringer suddenly seemed very small and meek.

"Right. Ready, Professor?"

The look of suppressed rage in the professor's eyes was answer enough. Ewan leaned against the latch.

It was stiff but well oiled. Ewan eased it open, let the others slip through ahead of him, and used the roll of the ship to help ease it shut behind them. The latch sealed with the slightest squeak.

He paused in the dim light, listening and letting his eyes adjust. There was the noise of the engine, the rush of the water against the hull, the creak of the ship's joints as she rolled. An alley led forward between high stacks of crates to port and barrels to starboard. They were roped down tightly with heavy lines, but the storm had shifted them anyway. The alley narrowed and widened on its way forward. A few paces ahead, the wall of crates leaned jaggedly across the aisle to press against the top layer of barrels, creating a dark, narrow archway.

Ewan led the others forward, derringer at the ready. They squeezed through the angled gap and into the open space beneath the number two hatch, then continued forward into a longer, tighter stretch, almost blocked at one point by the butt of the foremast. As the aisle widened again, Ewan could make out a voice, faint above the constant noise of the ship. He recognized it immediately: Curmidge. He fought down the urge to rush to the rescue.

The stacked cargo ended just a little way ahead, and he could see the first rack of hold baggage across the open space beneath the forward hatch. Aunt Nellie had said the professor's crate was somewhere in that space, with several other pieces of luggage and crates too large for the racks.

Ewan stopped and turned to the others. He indicated his ear, pointed to the space, and mouthed *Curmidge*. They nodded. Daisy's face was set and serious. The professor – top hat dented, parasol angled across his chest – looked like a madman.

"On three," Ewan breathed. Then ticked off the count on his fingers. *One. Two.*

On three, he ran into the open space, the other two at his heels.

Curmidge and the marine were both turned away. The professor's crate lay open before them, the top cast aside, revealing a jumble of books, journals, and framed photos. The parts of the Bell Cannon had already been pulled out and laid on the deck: brass, crystal, iron, cables, back boxes – Ewan spared them only a glimpse. His gaze went at once to Tereza. Curmidge was holding her hard against the side of the hull, with his forearm jammed across her neck. She was white as a ghost, her dark hair undone and tumbling around her pale face. Her eyes, almost lost in dark shadow, flashed with tears, but her mouth was a hard line, her jaw clenched.

"You will tell us eventually, my dear girl," Curmidge was saying. He slapped her bruised cheek. "Please spare yourself some pain." He slapped her again.

The professor howled in outrage, and Ewan realized he was yelling, too, aiming his little gun at Curmidge's head. The professor started forward, but Ewan pulled him back, for the marine had spun toward them, raising his carbine. Ewan stepped in front of the professor, shifted his aim, and fired just as the ship lurched into a wave. The little gun bounced in his hand. The shot went wide and rang dully against the iron plates of the hull. The marine's return shot tore into the cargo behind him.

Ewan fumbled to re-cock the derringer, as the marine snapped down the lever on the carbine and expertly slid another round into the breech.

"Stop!" Daisy cried. "Stop or I'll shoot!"

She was braced against the cargo, carbine aimed at the marine. The man hesitated.

"Whippoorwill Station!"

It came from behind them. Ewan turned, and there was Hamilton King, standing in the opening of a tall, black steamer trunk lying among the other storm-tossed baggage. He looked gray and rumpled, tie undone, coat damp and smelling of vomit, but he stood as straight as his stocky frame would allow. In his right hand was a large revolver aimed firmly at Ewan.

Daisy cried out and swayed, the muzzle of the carbine making wild orbits as she tried to keep it aimed at the marine. Suddenly she let it fall, bent over, and retched. She rallied a moment, tried to lift the heavy gun, tried to aim it at King. It was no use; she let the carbine drop to the deck and sank to her knees, retching again and again.

"You despicable traitor!" she moaned.

"You!" the professor cried, pointing at King. "Worse than traitor! You are the devil! You are Denisovitch!"

Curmidge sniffed loudly. He was holding Tereza in front of him now, revolver in hand. "Not hardly, Professor, and consider yourself lucky. Kirill Denisovitch would simply have killed the young lady outright. And then the rest of us. I assume that's not your intent, my dear King?"

King gave a strained smile and nodded politely to Curmidge. "Not at all, *Mister* Curmidge. I know which team to bet on. My compliments, by the way, on your bravura performance as the wife of the late reverend. You could have had a career on the stage." His aim never left Ewan. "Now uncock that little popgun, Gilmore, and drop it to the floor. I think it's obvious you're completely outgunned."

Ewan considered shooting Curmidge first, but knew he had too much chance of hitting Tereza instead. The gun had been no use to him at all. Bitterly, he uncocked it and let it drop to the deck.

"Thank you, King," Curmidge said. "You can relax now. The corporal will shoot the first one of them who dares move. And then I will shoot Miss Skovajsová. Yet, with just the slightest bit of cooperation, none of that need happen. You should be very proud of your daughter, Herr Professor; she has an iron will. Despite repeated entreaties, she has refused to tell me how to connect these parts and operate your marvelous infernal device. I was afraid I was going to have to hurt her. I'm sure that won't be necessary now that you are here to tell me."

"Father, no!" Tereza cried. "You've seen what he's like! You know how he'd use it!"

Curmidge cocked his pistol. "Father, yes," he said, smiling like a well-fed toad. "I am not quite the beast she believes me to be. I overacted a bit, I admit. Despite appearances, I do not wish to see general carnage overwhelm the globe. However, I am indeed prepared to take her life for the greater good of the Commonwealth. You understand me, I'm sure." He pressed the muzzle to Tereza's temple.

Ewan looked wildly for a way to distract him. He measured the distance to the marine. He glanced down at the derringer, lying beside his foot. He willed the professor to tell all.

"I will tell you," the professor said. "On my word of honor. But first, you will uncock your pistol and aim it down."

"Now, why should I even—?"

"My word of honor!" the professor shouted. "If you will not accept that, you can damn well kill us all!"

Curmidge sniffed. "Your honor means more to you than your daughter? Really, Professor. I expected better of you. Still, if your precious honor serves my ends, so be it." He lowered the pistol and uncocked it. "Now, tell."

"I will show you," the professor said. "And mark my words carefully. If you were to connect it backwards, the capacitors would explode."

"Heavens! We wouldn't want that, would we?" Curmidge replied. "Please do show."

It didn't take long: two cables to interconnect the trio of capacitors, and two heavier cables to connect them to the Bell Cannon, through a control box with a switch and three knobs to balance the flow of power.

"That's it?" King said. "This thing is ready to go now?"

"The capacitors must be charged by a dynamo, via the control box, and the resonators must be carefully tuned – that most of all," the professor added, voice breaking. He drew a breath. "I did all that and tested it before crating it."

"Well then," King said, and shot the marine in the head. As the man fell, King shouted, "Rochester Falls! Curmidge, freeze!"

Curmidge went stiff.

King trained his gun back on Ewan and the professor. "If you gentlemen would please stay where you are? Very good." Holding his aim, he walked past them and around the Bell Cannon.

"Now, *Mister* Curmidge, you will let go of the girl."

Curmidge, eyes fixed on King, obeyed.

"Very good. Bring me your pistol. Yes, bring it to me."

Curmidge hesitated, seemed to struggle with himself, but took a step toward King. Then another.

"Give me the gun, Curmidge," King ordered.

Curmidge stretched out his hand and took another step forward.

"Very, very good, Curmidge. You see, I did bet on the right team. The Kaiser will be very pleased."

He reached for the pistol, and Curmidge shot him in the belly.

King grunted and dropped to his knees, clutching his stomach with both hands.

Curmidge sniffed. "Really, Mr. King. Or should I say König? Did you truly believe an Englishman – or woman – would be so weak-minded as to succumb to mere hypnotic suggestion?" He fired again, and King sprawled backward on the deck, face ruined.

"No more acting!" Curmidge snapped. He turned the pistol on Tereza, who had taken a step toward him. "No more heroic gestures! Is that understood? By everyone? You see that I am not afraid to pull this trigger, and you see who will die first."

He glared at Ewan, the professor, and Tereza, each in turn. No one replied. No one moved. Daisy was curled up on the deck, eyes clamped shut. A small moan escaped her.

Curmidge sniffed. "Well, finally we have calm. Professor, Mr. Gilmore, step back against the cargo, if you please. Miss Skovajsová, back against the hull. Remain in place, all of you."

He stepped past King's body to the Bell Cannon and turned it to point at Ewan and the professor.

"Tell me, Professor, how wide a swathe does the aetheric wave cover? Remember your daughter."

The professor glanced at Tereza, still the target of Curmidge's gun, and swallowed.

"At this distance, approximately five feet."

"Stand closer together then, if you would, please."

Curmidge bent to the control box and turned on the switch. The capacitors began to hum. The bulbs topping each of them began to glow. A faint glimmer shone in the crystal rods of the Bell Cannon.

Ewan's ears tingled to a high pitched whine. He felt a small pressure building behind his eyes. Curmidge looked down to adjust the dials on the control box, and Ewan took a quick step toward the derringer.

Curmidge fired his pistol. The bullet rang off the iron plate inches from Tereza's head.

"Step back, Mr. Gilmore. My next shot will not miss, I assure you."

Ewan stepped back beside the professor. The whine in his ears immediately grew louder. The pressure began to grow in strength and size. His heart stuttered, then started to pound. Curmidge played with the dials again. The whine inside Ewan's head became a scream. The pressure was now a pain, round, turgid, swelling against his brain. The professor groaned. His head rolled back and he clapped his hands over his ears.

Fear fed Ewan's anger, yet he felt a growing urge to laugh, to shout, to cry and dance. He fought them all. He stared at Curmidge and focused on anger. He saw the look on Curmidge's face as Curmidge looked at him – fascination, anticipation, even pleasure, an ugly lust to see how he and the professor would die. Ewan realized they would all die. Tereza was as good as dead. Ewan readied himself to die. He readied himself to leap at Curmidge, to give the others a chance to live.

Daisy leaped first, from her crouch on the floor, now much closer to Curmidge, a point she had reached, inch by unnoticed inch while Curmidge threatened and aimed and adjusted and kept his focus on Ewan. She swooped like a dark-cloaked banshee, skirt and coattails flying, arms outstretch to enfold him. Tereza dodged as the gun went off, and the bullet went wide, ringing off the iron hull in a wild recoil.

Curmidge staggered as Daisy struck. She clung to his neck, kicking, tangling his legs, grabbing for the pistol. He grunted like a pig under the assault and fell to one knee, twisting, so that her own momentum carried her around and aside. Her feet hit the Bell Cannon, and it swung away from Ewan and the professor.

Tereza shrieked as the invisible beam reached her. Shrieked and slapped her hands to the sides of her head. Shrieked and collapsed to her knees, then to her side, sobbing, giggling, cursing.

"Mother!" she screamed, and cursed again.

"Eliška!" Professor Skovajsa cried. He scooped up the parasol and charged at Curmidge, point up and out like a lance.

Curmidge kicked Daisy away and fired wildly.

The professor spun from the impact. He threw the parasol as he fell, and the point grazed Curmidge's cheek, drawing blood.

Ewan dove for the derringer as Curmidge fired again. The bullet sang by his ear. He grabbed the little gun, fumbled it around in his hand. Pointed it at Curmidge. Cocked the hammer.

Tereza let out another heart-wrenching shriek.

Ewan shifted his aim and pulled the trigger. The hammer clicked on the empty chamber. Cursing, he fumbled at the hammer to cock it again. Curmidge took careful aim, then Daisy rose to her knees and speared his side with the parasol.

Ewan shot the control box. It jerked against the cables

and sparks flew. One capacitor shattered, the others dimmed. The terrible whining stopped.

Ewan scrambled to his feet and ran past Daisy to Tereza. He pried her hands from her ears and said her name over and over. She didn't respond.

"Look at me, Tereza," he said. "Open your eyes. The cannon's stopped. There's nothing to fear. We're all well, Tereza. Tereza, look at me. Please. Please, look at me."

She opened her eyes, and for a moment they were crazed. Then she saw him, and the madness left her face. She threw her arms around him and pulled him into a crushing embrace.

"It's all right, Tereza," he said, choking back a sob. "You're all right."

She stiffened suddenly and wrenched him around just as shot rang out. A hot line seared across his back. He cried out.

Curmidge was on his knees, pistol raised, aiming again. Ewan pulled Tereza behind him, pressed her tight against the iron hull. She struggled to get in front, to be his shield.

Daisy grabbed Curmidge's arm before he could shoot. He slapped her face with the other hand, wrenched his arm free, and clubbed her with the gun. He turned back to Ewan and Tereza.

"I've two shots left, one for each," he snarled. "Who wants to be fi—?"

Ewan dove at him, pushing the pistol aside as it went off. He shouldered Curmidge in the chest, driving him back and down, onto the parasol stuck in his side. Curmidge stiffened, eyes wide. He gasped once, choked on blood, then slid to the deck and died.

Ewan rolled off him, exhausted. Tereza came and took him in her arms.

Derek dashed in from the aisle, brandishing a huge

wrench. He stopped dead, gaping at the scene, then saw Daisy, lying beside the Bell Cannon. He called her name, dropped the wrench, and rushed to her side, kneeling to lift her head. She opened her eyes, moaned, and threw up.

Chapter 26
The Hornet Stings

The *Isle of Lewis* reached Loch Eriboll just before nightfall two days later. They had taken a long northerly arc, out of sight of the Hebrides and Cape Wrath, steering clear of the few ships they sighted, with the sails set and a Union Jack flying at their stern instead of Old Glory to confuse anyone who ventured near. Captain Morrison, much revived after sleeping nearly twenty-six hours straight, piloted the big ship into a quiet anchorage hidden from seaward view by a high island named Eilean Hoan. As the engine stilled, Daisy finally felt her stomach settle into its proper place. But with that distraction gone, the ache on the side of her head grew to a throb. Derek had staunched the bleeding by pressing his handkerchief against the cut until Frasier could fetch bandages from the doctor's storm-tossed cabin. Face clean, she looked like the hollow-eyed ghost of a turbaned Turk. Derek hovered by her side, constantly forcing warm water and crackers on her. The water she accepted; the crackers she refused. Now she relaxed against the rail, drew in a deep breath perfumed by the nearby land, and considered dinner. Her stomach fluttered.

Perhaps just a few crackers to start, she decided. And a nap, inside, in a bed. She hadn't been off the main deck for more than a few minutes since Mrs. Gilmore had reported the ship was back in their command. MacBreive and Clarke were safely locked in the brig, along with the surviving marine. The Captain was back on the bridge, with Frasier or the bosun always at his side. And here came Tereza, with Ewan at her side. They hadn't been apart for the past two days, except to sleep. Derek went to them and spoke quietly. Daisy smiled – her first smile in many days, she realized. She let the smile grow and felt her knotted muscles yield to weariness. Yes, a quick nap, and then a meal, but first a conference with the captain to plan their next move.

The quick nap lasted till the following noon, and Daisy awoke ravenous. The *Lewis* still lay at anchor in the shelter of Eilean Hoan. The day was overcast but relatively calm. She went to the saloon and found the Skovajsas just sitting down to a hot meal with Mrs. Gilmore. They all looked the worse for wear, she thought. Tereza's cheek was marred by the gray and yellow remains of her bruise. The Professor's shoulder showed the hump of a bandage under his coat, and he cradled that arm in a sling. Both had lingering shadows under their eyes. Even Mrs. Gilmore still looked weary. Daisy joined them eagerly, feeling closer than kin.

"Best tuck in lightly, Miss MacLaren," Mrs. Gilmore warned. "We'll be underway at sundown for the final run. No telling what the seas will be doing through the Pentland Firth, but it's ever choppy at best."

The Pentland Firth, where the Atlantic currents met the North Sea, ran between the northeastern tip of the Scottish mainland and the nearest of the Orkney Islands. Daisy and the others had studied the chart with the captain the day before. He planned to run through the firth during the night, then swing southeast and steam across the North Sea to Cuxhaven, at the mouth of the Elbe River.

It was a bold plan, with plenty of risk of discovery, but it offered the best chance for the professor and Tereza to disappear from the public eye. Hamburg, one of the busiest ports in Europe, lay but a small distance upriver. Riverboats left there daily for Dresden, Leipzig, and Prague; steamers for the Baltic ports, the Mediterranean, the Americas. The professor spoke German fluently. Tereza knew enough to get by, and she could pretend to be shy. Or they could pretend to be British and use English. They could dress down, travel second class. The professor could shave his beard.

Daisy smiled wryly at the thought. The professor would have a harder time acting the role of tradesman than Tereza would acting demure. They might do better to try Derek's ploy and go first class as well-to-do heirs of some banker. Either course was only a chance remark away from detection. Not that Loch Eriboll was a safe haven. While Daisy slept, the captain had met with the local clan leader, and now the *Lewis* was taking on coal ferried out on fishing boats and other small craft. They were in plain view of many small houses on shore. They could only trust to clan loyalty to keep their presence a secret.

After eating, the professor and Tereza went down to the engine room again, where Chief Engineer MacLeod, sporting a bandage much like Daisy's, was directing final repairs from a chair lashed to the railings. Daisy and Mrs. Gilmore went on deck, where the carpenter and crew were building a makeshift front wall for the wheelhouse from the glazed doors of the saloon and ladies cabin. Derek and poor beaten and bruised Ewan were helping Mr. Frasier and another pair of crewmen fasten the signal canon more securely against the front of the deckhouse. Half the black gang were shifting coal. The other half were ashing out the furnaces, pumping the boilers full, and building up the fires, preparing for the departure. There was little time for conversation, but plenty enough for worry.

At 6:00 p.m., the cook served up a generous supper,

though Daisy found it hard to eat. In fact, only Derek seemed to have much appetite. Ewan and Tereza sat side by side, silent, trading frequent glances. By 7:00, they were all on deck to watch the sun as it touched the high walls of the loch. A bell rang in the wheelhouse and the big propeller began to turn. The *Lewis* eased up on the anchor chain while the steam capstan ground around, pulling the big hook free. With no more fanfare than a few growled orders from the bosun and two more chimes from the bell, the Lewis swung away from Eilean Hoan and steamed northeastward out of the loch.

By 9:00 the horizon had disappeared in darkness, with no hint of the moon yet. A few scattered windows shone dimly from the shore, barely half a mile to their right. They had passed one lighthouse already, and another flashed regularly in the distance ahead. They had passed several steamers and sailing ships as well, but that was no longer a worry. No ship could recognize them in the dark, or report a sighting until reaching port.

Derek and Ewan fetched blankets for Daisy and Tereza. They spoke seldom, and in low voices. It was 600 nautical miles to Cuxhaven, far more than one night's steaming. Captain Morrison wasn't planning to arrive off the German coast until late the next evening. His goal this night was to slip past Scotland and be out of sight of land by daylight. Still, no one suggested they turn in. Daisy was certain she'd never sleep, despite the lulling motion of the ship on the calm sea. Her stomach was behaving, and the cool breeze kept her alert. She felt more excited than worried now, in good weather and under the cover of darkness. Derek was standing a bit too close perhaps, but they were well chaperoned by the professor and Mrs. Gilmore. What had been a desperate escape was now an adventure.

They passed the lighthouse at Dunnet Head and

entered the Pentland Firth. The light on the Isle of Stroma gleamed ahead, and Mrs. Gilmore pointed northward, across the broad deck, to the faint light on the island of Hoy, one of the Orcadies. The sea roughened, but not seriously enough to bother Daisy. She wondered if the storm had taught her stomach how to behave. She earnestly hoped it was so.

As they rounded the light at Stroma, the bell rang midnight, eight soft chimes, repeated dutifully by the lookout in the crow's nest. The professor took hold of the rail, and Tereza had her ears covered by the third bell. Daisy stepped closer and began singing, as they had in the cabin during the storm. Ewan joined in, then Mrs. Gilmore and Derek, and by the final bell, Tereza and the professor were singing with them. They kept singing as the *Lewis* bore eastward, following an invisible channel between two more lights that marked the end of Scotland. A bold last-quarter moon rose ahead of them, drawing a line across the North Sea.

Suddenly, Ewan said, "Quiet! What's that?"

The singing shut off, and Daisy listened carefully for something more than the rumble of the engine and the wash of the sea against the iron hull.

Derek broke the silence. "Can't say as I hear any—"

"Shh!" Tereza hissed. She pointed southward. "That way. A whine."

"More like a buzz," Ewan said.

Then Daisy heard it, faint and distant but growing louder. Coming closer. Very quickly.

"It can't be!" she muttered.

"Can't be what?" Derek asked.

"De Beausoleil!"

"The turbine ship!" Tereza exclaimed. "Of course! But how would he know where to find us?"

"A traitor in Loch Eriboll." Mrs. Gilmore spat the

words.

"Never mind how or who," Daisy said. "Professor, Tereza, get out of sight please."

"But—"

"Don't argue. Derek, Ewan, you go with them. Warn the captain and the rest. Mrs. Gilmore, if you would please stay here with me. Follow my lead. I will concoct a story for *Monsieur le comte*."

"You don't think he's just come to rescue his fair damsel?" Ewan asked.

"You flatter me too highly, Mr. Gilmore," Daisy replied, "or think too highly of him. Either way, I'm not going to risk trusting him now. Not after *Mrs*. Curmidge."

"Right," Ewan replied. "Professor, Tereza, if you don't mind."

They began to argue, but Mrs. Gilmore cut them off. "As purser, I'm making that an order. Now be quick about it. That damned *Hornet* is living up to its name." They obeyed.

Already Daisy and Mrs. Gilmore could see the *Hornet*'s bright bow wave and rooster tail, gleaming in the moonlight, the narrow ship itself a dark stain moving rapidly toward them. The aft side of its squat funnel appeared almost to glow with heat. Daisy stiffened her back and waited.

Suddenly, the bright green-yellow beam of a carbon-arc spotlight flared from the *Hornet* and swung toward them. It paused at the name on their bow, then swept back along the broken rail, passing over Daisy and Mrs. Gilmore then jerking back. They were blinded by the hot glare and raised their hands to shield their eyes.

The *Hornet* slowed and swung about, matching their course. The buzzing became more bearable

Captain Morrison came out of the makeshift wheelhouse and stood at the edge of the deckhouse, one hand pressed to his side. A few of the deck crew appeared at the rail forward.

"Stand off!" the captain bellowed.

The *Hornet* matched their speed, standing off no more than ten or fifteen yards, just inside the line of their wake. Daisy peered down through the harsh light. The *Hornet*'s deck was almost twenty feet below her, much of it hidden by Moon shadow.

"Daisy, *mon cœur!* You are alive!" The count's voice carried clearly across the water. He stood at the *Hornet*'s rail near the funnel, waving up at them.

"*Alors, Monsieur de Beausoleil, c'est vraiment tu?*" She affected a great squint from behind her hand. "I'm afraid we can't see a thing with that light in our eyes."

The count snapped an order and the spotlight swung to the side.

"Oh, *merci beaucoup, mon ami*," Daisy called. "That is so much better. Yes, I can see you now. How ever did you find us?"

The count spread his arms wide. "I have been searching from the moment your loss was reported. How could I believe you had drowned? How could I not search? And how can I fully express my great gladness to find you? *C'est un miracle!* But what is that on your head? Are you injured? And what of the others, your friends and companions, *Monsieur* Gilmore, *Professeur* Skovajsa, his daughter? Are they not with you? Surely they, too, have survived."

Daisy lowered her head and wept.

Mrs. Gilmore, taking the cue, stepped closer and put her arm around Daisy's shoulders. "There, there, Dear," she said loudly. "There, there."

Daisy raised her head and smiled a teary thanks.

"I'll be all right," she said, carefully not shouting. Turning back to the count, she raised her voice again.

"The storm was dreadful," she began. "But there was worse." Her voice broken by carefully timed sobs, she told him briefly of the villainy of Lieutenant Clarke and his men, the wreck of the deckhouse and Captain Morrison's injuries, the surprising reappearance of Mrs. Curmidge – now Mister – and the treachery of Third Officer MacBreive. She paused to weep some more and finally forced out the conclusion to her tale.

"The professor is dead, killed with Mr. Curmidge as they struggled over the bell cannon prototype. Tereza was caught in the beam . . ." She choked back another sob. "That, with the shock of her father's death, drove her mad. We tried to restrain her, but she broke out of her cabin and threw herself overboard. Ewan blamed himself. He smashed the professor's dreadful weapon and threw it in after her, and would have followed if Mr. Frasier had not knocked him senseless. We've had to keep him locked in the brig ever since." She broke down, sobbing again.

"Aye, aye, it was a terrible thing," Mrs. Gilmore intoned, shaking her head. "So much death. So, so much death."

"*Mon Dieu! Quelle tragédie!* But what are you doing here?"

"The storm blew us almost to the Shetlands," Mrs. Gilmore called. "We're heading in to Aberdeen. We're in need of coal and food and a good doctor, and Glasgow is too far."

"Then there is no reason for the *mademoiselle* to stay on board with you, *n'est-ce pas?* This little boat is so much faster. Come, Daisy, my friend, let me return you quickly to your father. I have stayed in constant touch. He is distraught beyond imagination at the thought that you have died in the storm. Slow down the ship. We will come alongside."

"Oh, *mon bon ami, tu es si généreux,* but I couldn't

possibly leave now, not after what we have suffered through together, and not without a proper chaperone. I pray you instead to speed on ahead of us to the nearest port and telegraph the news to my father. Then join him in Edinburgh to await our arrival. We can reunite properly there."

"*Mais chére* Daisy—"

The count was cut off abruptly by a sharp command, and his valet appeared at his side from the shadow of the *Hornet*'s funnel. The count answered in a low voice, and they argued hotly. Daisy strained to catch the words, but they were in a language she didn't know.

"Russian!" Mrs. Gilmore hissed. "The *bastarts* are speaking Russian!"

"He's no mute!" Daisy exclaimed. "He's no valet, either. Listen to him tear into the count!" She gasped as the realization struck. "He's Denisovitch!"

Captain Morrison seemed to have come to the same conclusion. He drew his big Navy Colt from beneath his coat.

"Stand off, Count, or whoever you are. We'll have no more of you!"

"*Non*, wait!" the Count replied, but Denisovitch shoved him aside and barked an order in Russian.

A pair of crewmen between the *Hornet*'s funnel and small deckhouse threw off a tarpaulin to reveal a large gun mounted on the deck. One of them swiveled it toward the *Lewis*, and Daisy was staring down at the six barrels of a Gatling gun.

Captain Morrison fired his Colt, but the bullet ricocheted off the *Hornet*'s deck.

The Gatling gun returned the fire. Bullets rang off the side of the hull as the six barrels swept upward. Captain Morrison threw himself back behind the shelter of the wheelhouse. Mrs. Gilmore grabbed Daisy by the arm and dragged her to the deck. Bullets sang over their heads and rattled against the side the deckhouse. Ricochets whined skyward.

"Hard to port! Full ahead!" the captain bellowed, his rough voice almost lost in the endless explosion of the Gatling gun's fire.

The *Lewis* swung toward the *Hornet*, looming over the smaller craft to cut off the aim of the Gatling gun. The deck shook as the engine sped up, driving the big propeller to full speed. The firing stopped a moment, then resumed. Bullets tore through the top of the wheelhouse. The fancy glass in the saloon doors shattered. Mrs. Gilmore pulled Daisy farther back from the edge of the deck. The *Lewis* heeled, veering hard toward the *Hornet*, almost swamping the little ship with her wake.

The whine of the *Hornet*'s turbine rose to a mad scream and the Gatling gun went silent as the *Hornet* sped clear of the *Lewis*'s bow, her rooster tail rising high and silver in the moonlight.

"Get inside!" Mrs. Gilmore ordered. "Before she comes back!"

"Wait," Daisy said. She went back to the rail, watching the gleam of the rooster tail as it raced away from them across the dark water. It swerved though a wide curve and, for a few moments, the *Hornet* cut across the bright, rippled swath of moonlight, a low, sleek silhouette with a silver bone in her teeth. Then she was only a shadow again, marked by the smear of her tail and the biting whine of her turbine, growing louder as she looped back toward them.

Chapter 27

The Lewis Bites Back

Bullets rang sharply against the outside of the hull and echoed unbearably in the small cabin. Tereza pushed Ewan away from the porthole just as the glass shattered. They stumbled back together onto the lower berth. Shards of glass tore splinters from the woodwork. Tufts of bedding and feathers clouded the air, and Tereza felt a sharp sting on her back. Ewan swung across her body, pressing her into the mattress, holding her there beneath him as the clanging fire swept away up the hull. The ringing cut off for a moment, only to sound again, higher up and higher pitched, as though against the funnel or deckhouse. It jarred her ears like a mistuned bell. The sound eclipsed the sting in her back. Her heartbeat sped, her vision began to contract.

No! She railed against it. *Get out of my mind!*

"Let me up!" she cried. "You're smothering me!"

Ewan started to lift himself but the *Lewis* suddenly veered to port. Tereza used the motion to heave him off. He tumbled onto the floor as the Lewis heeled farther. She rolled to her feet, almost stepping on his hand. He groaned.

"Are you all right?" she asked, remembering his wounded back.

"No worse. Keep low. Stay back from the porthole."

She turned away from him.

"Father! Are you all right?"

"Yes, I'm fine," her father replied. "A scratch, nothing more."

He slumped on the berth, gripping his right arm, where a dark, spreading stain showed beneath his clenched hand.

"That's more than a scratch!" she exclaimed. She hurried to him. "Let go. Let go! Let me see it!"

He tried to protest, but she forced his bloody hand open. Beneath, his jacket and sleeve were slit wide, as if by a scalpel. A slice was gone from the side of his bicep. Teresa pressed his hand back down.

"Hold tightly," she ordered. "I'll make bandages." The Hornet's turbine began to shriek. "Ewan, go up and do what you can to help."

"Are you sure you'll both be—?"

"Go!" She was already ripping into a sheet. "Hurry, Daisy could be hurt."

Ewan went.

"Your back," Father said. "You're bleeding."

As soon as he said it, she began to feel the sting again. It was slight, twinging as she moved, as though a splinter were snagging on the fabric of her dress.

"It's nothing," she said, turning back to him with the strip of cloth.

He tried to stand, reaching toward her. "But—"

"You're far worse. Sit down." She pushed him back down on the berth and pressed a wad of cloth under his hand, against the wound.

He hissed in pain, arching back, but she took his shoulder and held him still while she settled the pad into place.

"Hold this," she said, and turned to tear off another, longer strip.

He obeyed, sinking into himself. "Oh, Eliška," he moaned. "*Co jsem udělal?*" What have I done?

Tereza shook her head, blinking back tears. "What have *we* done, father."

"No, Tereza—*Ah!*" He gasped as she began to wind the strip around his arm. "No, the blame is all mine. My theories, my design, my execution."

"I helped you make it. I helped tune it. I made you let me." The tears would not stop. She struggled to see clearly, to make the wrap tight on his wound.

"No," he insisted.

"I mistuned it. The tertiary bell. If I had tuned it right, maybe—"

"No!" He grabbed her hand, squeezed it hard. "No. You did nothing wrong. I retuned the tertiary bell. After you left." His eyes opened wide. He learned forward, more alert that she had seen him since that day. He stared past her, as though watching it play out.

"After I made you leave. I remember it. You had been so upset, I worried you might have made a mistake. I started over on the tertiary bell, from the first resonator. All of them. I retuned them. And . . . And that was the bell that shattered. That hit me. That . . ." He swallowed hard, and tears run unnoticed down his face. "*Drahý Bože,*" he murmured. Dear God. "Dear Tereza. Can you ever forgive me?"

Tereza stared at him, unable to speak. He had retuned the bell. She'd heard him say it, but somehow couldn't understand it. Her mind roiled, as though yet another bell were ringing. Grasping for calm she began to count. *Ninety-seven, ninety-one— No, that's seven times thirteen. Eighty-nine, eighty-three, seventy-nine— Stop! This is just hiding!*

Tereza blinked herself back to the present. Father was staring at her, studying her face.

"It doesn't matter," she said, squeezing back hard on his hand. "I was your willing helper. And even if the Bell Cannon hadn't exploded, its presence would have been known. The general, the secretary, the President – one of them or all of them would have let the world know. A demonstration, as soon as possible. That was always the plan."

"Yes," he replied, "that was always the plan. Someone else was bound to invent one, but we would be first. And look where it has brought us."

The *Lewis* came back into focus, vibrating, rocking on the gentle sea, steaming on through the night. And, in the distance, the whine of the *Hornet*. Growing louder again.

Sakra! Tereza thought.

"They're coming back," Father said, stiffening. He tried to stand.

She held him down. "Keep still," she said, "I need to tie up this bandage." She gave his hand a last squeeze. "Captain Morrison knows what he's doing, Father. We will survive this. And then we will—"

"Yes," he said firmly. "Yes, I know. I agree. We will destroy the Bell Cannon."

&

Ewan came out on deck and almost ran right into Derek and Frazier hurrying toward the bow with heavy canvas sacks.

"Come on, man," Frazier ordered. "We can use another pair of hands."

"How's Daisy?" Ewan demanded, following. "And Aunt —?"

"She's fine," Derek assured him. "Your aunt's taking her below. Grab one if these, would you?"

He shoved one of the bags at Ewan, who grabbed it just as it began to slip from Derek's hands. The weight surprised him.

"Thanks, sport." Derek hefted his other bag with both hands, and they hurried after Frazier.

"What is it?" Ewan asked.

"Ammunition."

They reached the forward end of the deckhouse, and there were the bosun and two of the deck crew, unlashing the signal cannon.

"All right then," Frazier said, setting down his bag and handing the ramrod and swab to one of the crew. "Drag her out and we'll load her up."

"Port or starboard?" the bosun asked.

"Just forward of the hatch till we know which side the *skinkin'* Ruskies will make their approach," Frazier replied. "Look sharp! We won't have time for more'n a round, two if we're lucky."

"If we're lucky, we won't need more'n one," the bosun said. "She may be fast, but I'll wager she's paid for that speed with a thin skin."

We'll need more than luck, Ewan thought.

He threw himself against the carriage to help shift the small cannon; Small but heavy, and the low oak carriage was meant to slide on a track. He, Derek, and the two crewmen had all they could do to start it moving and keep it under control in the gentle swell that was running. They pulled it around the number two hatch cover, halfway to the foremast, and were happy to stop heaving when Frazier said to. Ewan peered out toward the angry whine of the *Hornet* and glimpsed her just as she crossed the path of the moon. He and Derek went over to the rail, watching as the *Hornet* raced ahead of the *Lewis* and then began a sweeping curve back toward them.

"She's coming bow on!" Ewan called, and Frazier ordered them back to the gun.

As he turned from the rail, Ewan noticed Daisy and Aunt Nellie standing aft by the first lifeboat.

"I thought you said they were down below."

"That's where they were going," Derek replied. "I'll go tell her—"

"To your posts!" It was Captain Morrison, up on the forward edge of the deckhouse. "Attend to Mr. Frazier!"

They hurried back to the cannon.

"They can't fire forward the way their gun's mounted," Frazier explained. "They'll steer port or starboard and rake us stem to stern, hoping to clear the decks and take out the helmsmen."

The bosun and crewmen had fixed ropes at each corner of the carriage. Frasier assigned Ewan and Derek to the rear ropes, the two crewmen at the front, and had them swing it back and forth twice to get the feel of it. That was all they had time for.

"She's closing," the Captain called, but they could tell from the *Hornet*'s whine, growing louder and louder as she raced toward them.

"Steady!" the Captain called. "Steady . . . Starboard!"

"Heave to starboard!" Frazier yelled.

They all laid onto the ropes, while Frazier and the boson pushed on the rear. The cannon budged, caught, then suddenly started sliding with the roll of the ship. Ewan hardly noticed the weight. His heart was racing. They crossed the fifteen feet of deck as though it were greased.

"Swing left!" Frazier called. "Again! Stop! Pull forward!"

With one more heave, the muzzle was up to the gap in the railing. Frazier turned the elevating screw, lowering the muzzle. He stepped back and crouched, sighting along the barrel. The bosun took the firing lanyard, stepped to the side, and squatted.

"Get down, you damn fools!" he barked.

The two crewmen were already crouched back from the railing. Ewan and Derek copied them. The *Hornet* sped into their line of view, bouncing over the low waves. Ewan could just make out the bundled barrels of the Gatling gun sticking out from behind the small tower of the *Hornet*'s forward deck house. It was aimed as far forward as it could go. In seconds, it would be aimed right at him.

Suddenly, Derek turned, straightened, and yelled toward the stern. "Daisy! Get inside!" He ran aft.

"Steady on!" Frazier yelled.

The Gatling gun began to fire. Bullets rang off the bow, then the foremast. They whined over Ewan's head.

The Hornet was only a few yards ahead of them, curving outward to get a better angle of fire at the deck.

"Starboard full!" the Captain yelled. He threw himself prone on the deck and fired his Colt. The *Lewis* heeled into the turn. He fired again.

"Steady," Frazier said.

The *Lewis* rose on the next swell. Bullets sang off the railing. One of the crewmen sprawled backward.

Frazier shouted, "Fire!"

The bosun pulled the lanyard, and the signal cannon went off. The carriage skewed back with a violent jerk that tore the end of the rope from Ewan's hands. His ears rang.

An instant later, the aft deckhouse on the *Hornet* crumpled inward around a jagged hole. The small portholes shattered. A body flew outward through the rear, taking the door with it.

The *Hornet* skewed sharply to port, right across their bow.

"You canny dog! You hit the wheelhouse!" the bosun cried.

"I was aiming for the gun," Frazier replied. "Brace!"

The *Lewis* plowed into the *Hornet*. Or maybe the other way, but the effect was the same. The *Lewis*'s bow veered sideways, then rode up over the tiny *Hornet*, rolling it onto its beam end and crushing it into the water. There was a hideous rending of metal, hissing steam, and a dull thump that echoed down the length of the *Lewis* as the *Hornet*'s boiler blew. Ewan was thrown forward as the *Lewis* jerked almost to a standstill, shaking like a wet dog. But she kept going, heeling to port, then rolling heavily back to starboard, throwing Ewan against the rail.

He heard Daisy scream, heard Derek yell her name. He heaved himself upright, clinging to the rail as the *Lewis* rode the length of the sinking *Hornet*, heeled almost to forty degrees. He turned, just in time to see the number one lifeboat rip free from its davits and tumble into the sea, tearing a gap in the railing. To see Daisy topple after it, catch herself on the dangling rail. To see Derek and Aunt Nellie both lunge for her hand, but too late. Daisy fell out of sight. Aunt Nellie teetered on the very edge of the deck. Derek caught her, pulled her to safety, then dove in after Daisy.

&

Twenty-seven feet, Daisy thought, and was surprised at herself for remembering the fact at just that moment. *True, but completely useless. How ridiculous.*

She hit the water feet first, her skirts and coattails flying up over her face from the force of the impact. The water was a tumult of wake, froth, and noise as the dark hull of the *Lewis* swept by. She fought it desperately, water and clothing, reaching toward the surface, struggling against the weight of dress, petticoat, and mostly the woolen Ulster. The weight was winning.

Damn you, Mrs. Ledoux! Daisy fumed. *You never warned that dressing appropriately could drown you!*

She became aware of the throbbing beat of the giant propeller, the grinding of iron on iron. Something struck her arm and she recoiled, only to sink faster. It struck again, took hold, and she realized it was a hand. She grabbed at it frantically with her other hand, found the arm above it and dug in her fingers with all her might.

Don't struggle! she warned herself. *You'll drown both of you!* But she couldn't stop pulling. She needed to breathe now!

She clamped her mouth shut and kicked her water-laden shoes for all she was worth. Her ears rang. A strange light began to fill the space behind her eyes. Her kicking slowed.

Don't breathe, she ordered. *Don't breathe!*

Another hand caught her hair, then groped lower and found the collar of her heavy Ulster. A body swung down beside her, kicking, pushing her up. She began to rise. She kicked hard again, reaching upward, trying to grab the surface, as though she could make it into a handle and pull herself out. The grip on her arm and coat never loosened.

Daisy's head broke into the air. She opened her mouth and sucked in a huge breath, choking on spray and her own soaked hair, come all undone and uncurled, a heavy curtain across her face. The wake from the *Lewis* slapped the side of her head, pushing her down briefly. She renewed her struggle against it. The noise of the engine and sweeping propeller seemed right beside her, punctuated by the screeching and clanging of crumpling of metal, which suddenly stopped, leaving only the wash of water and the beat of the *Lewis*'s propeller, fading as the ship pulled relentlessly away from them.

"Daisy! Daisy, are you all right?"

It was Derek, still gripping her collar.

He put his arm around her, holding her firmly; in other circumstances, it would have seemed scandalous. The shock of the moment made her laugh at the thought, though she could hear a tremor of panic in the laugh that quickly became a racking cough. Derek held her afloat as she hacked and retched up seawater she hadn't even known she'd swallowed. He kept asking if she was all right. She kept nodding and coughing.

"Yes," she finally managed. "All right. Not even seasick!" She laughed again, dizzy and giddy despite everything. She hugged him hard and planted a long, sopping kiss on his cheek. "All right and still very alive, thanks to you!"

"Ah, well," he said. "What else could one do?" He gave a small, self-conscious laugh. "I could hardly let you drown alone."

"The truly brave feel for what their duty bids them do," she quoted softly.

"What? Oh, that's just, well—"

"Byron?"

"Yes, Byron of course, but, well, it hardly applies. I didn't—"

Daisy pressed her fingers to his lips. "Stop. Don't spoil it. Let's just find a way to keep from drowning, alone or together, shall we?"

Debris from the *Hornet* floated around them, most of it too small to offer any support. They found a plank, and Derek helped her slide up onto it, but it tipped and rolled over whenever he tried to get on the other end. They were still flailing with it when the gentle swell brought something larger: The *Lewis*'s lifeboat loomed out of the moon-gray dark and sidled against them like an obedient hound.

"Salvation!" Daisy exclaimed.

"The old girl has never let us down," Derek said. "In you go."

It took some doing. The boat was so laden with water they could tip the gunwale right down to the surface, but Daisy couldn't muster the strength to haul the weight of her heavy clothes over the rail. Derek got behind her and tried to buoy her up, but was finally forced to get both hands right under her buttocks and, with constant apologies, heave with all his strength. He went completely underwater. Daisy pulled and kicked and finally fell over the gunwale and onto one of the seats. Water ran from her clothing into the boat-shaped pond beneath her.

"Now you," she said, leaning down to take Derek's hands.

At that moment, a cry came from the distance.

"*Pomogite! Au secours!* Help!"

"That's the count!" Daisy said, and the call came again.

"Are you sure?" Derek asked. "It sounded like Russian to me."

"And French and English, and I'm sure they all mean the same thing."

"Well, if you say so," Derek replied, and he bellowed at the top of his lungs. "Ahoy there, Count! Hang on! I'm coming!" He pushed away from the lifeboat, striking out across the dark water.

As he drew away, Daisy felt a new twinge of anxiety, but the cry for help came again, and this time fainter. She steeled herself; he had to try of course.

"Help is coming!" Daisy called back. "*L'aide arrive! L'aide arrive!*"

The sound of Derek's swimming quickly faded. The call for help came one more time, and Daisy called back, to both of them. There may have been a reply, very faint. Then she heard a strange rushing and bubbling, a great splashing, punctuated with a sound that might have been shouting. She imagined some part of the *Hornet* breaking free and bobbing to the surface, a life buoy miraculously at hand. A trio of small swells rippled past, rocking the lifeboat, and her heart lifted with them. Then the sounds stopped. She called again, and again, but there was no reply, no sound at all except for the soft, steady lap of wavelets against the side of her half-sunk boat.

Daisy realized then just how cold she was. Her legs, in water from the knees down, grew numb. Bouts of shivering rattled her teeth. Her vision seemed cloudy, her ears clogged. She felt more alone than at any other time in her life, except perhaps when her mother had died. She huddled on the seat and imagined her mother's face and voice, singing nursery rhymes. Daisy tried to sing along, but the shivering made it impossible, so she pressed her lips together and hummed. When she couldn't remember the songs, she still hummed, imagining herself on the deck of the *Isle of Lewis,* vibrating to the rhythmic pulse of her huge engine, the heartbeat of the ship, strong and regular enough to keep her alive. And the others, too. Tereza, Ewan, even Derek. Even the count. But the hum receded as the cold seeped closer and closer to her own heart. Soon she couldn't hear even that.

Nor did she notice when the sound began to grow. She didn't see the ship's lights, approaching from the other side of the boat. She didn't hear the cry of the lookout, the voices calling, the whirr of the davits or the splash of the oars as the *Lewis*'s last usable lifeboat approached her.

She didn't hear anything, until Ewan took her hands.

"It's all right, Daisy," he said. "We've got you now. You're safe."

Chapter 28

Farewells

The mouth of the Elbe was over ten miles wide, more like a bay than a river. Cuxhaven sat a couple of miles upstream on the southern bank. The *Lewis*'s lifeboat, bearing Professor Skovajsa, Tereza, Daisy, and Ewan, approached the small harbor under sail. Dawn was just breaking, but already the wide channel was busy with fishing boats and lighters, freighters, ferries, and canal boats. Soon, it would get even busier, and the traffic would include steam liners, funneling emigrants to the Americas from many inland countries. The *Isle of Lewis* would be noticed at once as a stranger, so Captain Morrison had dropped off the lifeboat well outside the river's mouth. He would keep the *Lewis* far offshore during the day, returning late the next evening to a rendezvous behind a small island some miles south.

Jakub Skovajsa felt half dressed. His chin was bare for the first time since he'd left university. He'd kept the mustache, allowing Mrs. Gilmore to trim it to tidy points. He wore his second-best suit and had replaced his top hat with a derby donated by Ewan Gilmore – ironically, the very derby given to Gilmore by De Beausoleil. Tereza, sitting in front of him, wore her plainest dress, its hem quite shabby after the days of sea and storm, with a suitably mussed hat from Miss MacLaren. She looked older to him somehow, but he supposed that was inevitable, given all that had happened since the Bell Cannon failed.

Jakub stiffened his back. He was remembering more

details from that terrible day. Glimpses, faces, the shrill screams of horses. Eliška's voice, asking if he had seen Tereza. He suppressed a shudder.

"Are you all right, Professor?" Miss MacLaren asked quietly. She sat beside him, as stiff in the back as he.

He was surprised she'd been well enough to come. A few minutes longer in the swamped boat, and she probably would have died. As for the others, well, the captain had continued the search for hours, right till dawn to be sure, but they found only a few small bits of flotsam from the wrecked *Hornet*, and two bodies, both crewmen. Then the realization of losing Mr. Reed had brought such a cry of anguish from her, such a rain of tears. *Good riddance to De Beausoliel*, he thought, *and that zlořečený Denisovitch, but young Reed . . . such a cruel tragedy.*

Jakub swallowed and turned his face from Miss MacLaren, blinking away the prickle of threatening tears. His own grief was, if anything, more volatile than before, as though magnified by all the new grief around him. Or perhaps he was finally allowing himself to feel it. If only it wouldn't leap out and surprise him so sharply.

Amazingly, Miss MacLaren had pulled herself together over the past day and a half. The very day after Reed's loss, she had appeared in the saloon in the middle of dinner, Tereza at her side, bearing between them the cracked and blackened prototype of the Bell Cannon. They laid it on the table with a thump as hard as a slap.

"Professor, what are you going to do about this?" Miss MacLaren had demanded.

Jakub had looked at her face but heard Eliška. He'd heard the shriek of horses. And of men. And when he'd blinked and looked back down at the prototype, he had seen for a moment the full-size Bell Cannon, seen it vibrating, off tune. He realized then that he was seeing the Bell Cannon clearly for the first time. Seeing it for what it was: another weapon, no different at all from a gatling gun, a tool designed and built for the purpose of killing. Strip aside all idealizing and philosophizing, and the end result was death and suffering. By people. Individuals. Wives and daughters. A weapon that kills a single person at a blow is hellish enough. A weapon that can destroy thousands – nay, millions – is infernal. As Curmidge had named it. And he who would use it was damned the moment his finger touched the trigger.

Tereza had come over and placed her hand on his shoulder. It trembled, and he reached up—his own hand shaking—to grip hers. They looked at each other and nodded, in full agreement still. Others would eventually stumble upon the aetheric principles and invent something like the Bell Cannon, but the deaths would be on their souls, not his. Not Tereza's.

"Yes," he said to all of them. "It's time to get rid of the thing. Forever."

Miss MacLaren had gone back to the hold then with Mr. Gilmore to fetch the other components. Then Jakub and Tereza had dismantled every component to its smallest parts, dropping each, one-by-one, into the wake of the *Isle of Lewis* as she steamed across the depths of the North Sea. With each piece, from largest to smallest, he felt a great weight lift from his heart. The others had offered to help, but he and Tereza had insisted on doing the deed alone.

Much as Miss MacLaren had insisted on being allowed to shepherd him and Tereza all the way to the end of this stage of their long journey.

"I assigned myself the role of your advocate, in my father's place," she'd said firmly. "I always finish what I start."

"Professor?" she repeated now.

He pulled himself from his reverie. "I am fine, Miss

MacLaren, thank you. Nervous, I admit. Sad also. I will miss your company. You've been a loyal champion to our cause and a good friend to Tereza when she desperately needed one."

"I'm glad I had the opportunity to get to know her well enough to become her friend, Professor. You and I have both seen how strong she can be. I've learned a great deal from her, and from you."

Jakub hesitated, then took her hand and squeezed it. "We have learned from each other. I will hope to see you again someday, under more congenial circumstances."

"I'm sure we will . . . Herr Weber. You won't forget it this time?"

He smiled wryly, remembering their first meeting. "Yes, Weber we are and shall be for a while. Who knows who we will be next time?"

"I look forward to finding out."

They were approaching the pier now. Mr. Frasier let the wind spill from the sail, and the lifeboat glided against the pilings. Young Gilmore left Tereza's side – for the first time, it seemed, since he had pulled Miss MacLaren from the lifeboat – and went into the bow to take the line and tie it to a bollard. Then he helped them out and brought up their two small valises. Jakub went quickly to the booth at the inland end of the next pier to check on the riverboat to Hamburg. It would be leaving in an hour. He bought two second-class tickets and hurried back to find the others waiting in silence.

As he approached, Jakub noticed that Mr. Gilmore tried to let go of Tereza's hand, but she wouldn't let him. He stifled a paternal urge to frown. Gilmore had certainly earned her affection. He hoped she wouldn't mourn their parting too long, or hold onto vain hopes for a future together. Despite his comments to Miss MacLaren, he knew the odds of any of them meeting again were slim. It would be a wonder if they didn't all wind up in prison somewhere. Or worse.

They said their goodbyes briefly, voices low, because they could only speak English together, and now he and Tereza had to be German. Even the name on the lifeboat's bow had been painted over and replaced with *Gertrude*.

Jakub steadied Miss MacLaren as she returned to her place in the lifeboat. Young Gilmore said one last goodbye to Tereza, then the two of them stood there, fingers touching, apparently unable to pull apart. *Like strong magnets*, he thought. Finally, Mr. Gilmore made to turn, but Tereza grabbed his hand again and pulled him back to plant a kiss on his cheek.

Jakub turned away, wondering again at how much older she seemed, yet how much more like the daughter he remembered. She, too, had shed some weight from her heart. Maybe a time would come when they would both stop jumping at the mere ringing of a bell.

He counted five seconds and coughed. The two reluctantly pulled apart.

"*Danke schön*," Gilmore mumbled, blushing furiously.

Tereza smiled, eyes glistening. "*Bitte*," she whispered. "*Auf Wiedersehen*."

Gilmore swallowed, nodded, and fumbled the line free before stumbling into the lifeboat.

Tereza came to Jakub and took his arm, holding it firmly as Frasier filled the sail and steered the lifeboat away from the pier. They waved until they could no longer see their friends' distant faces, then turned and made their way to the riverboat.

Epilogue

New Futures

A long two months later, Ewan walked down the gangway of the *Isle of Lewis* onto pier 10 in Manhattan, leather valise in hand. He tipped his derby in a friendly goodbye to Messrs. Boyd and Sturgis, whom he had befriended during the passage. Boyd was a banker from upstate New York. Sturgis claimed to represent a brand of lesser-known sewing machines, but he was a well-known card-sharper on all the Northern Ocean lines. Ewan, playing the role of a young heir on a visit to certain financially connected cousins near Baltimore, had managed to keep Sturgis from fleecing anyone during the voyage. It was very possible that Mr. Boyd would lose his wallet in the next few hours, but once ashore he was on his own.

On the pretext of checking rail connections, Ewan made his way through the press of debarking passengers, porters, and longshoremen to the booking office inside the Scots-American Line terminal. He had hardly set foot through the doorway before his mother was on him.

"Ewan!" she cried, squeezing him into a fierce hug. "By God, it's good to see you!" He could feel her tears on his neck and hugged her back, surprised by the lump that suddenly blocked his throat.

She finally loosened her embrace. Holding him at arm's length, she looked him up and down, eyes brimming.

He grinned back. "You see? Still alive."

"God knows how," she murmured.

"Not worth drowning, I guess."

"Nor imprisoning, it seems."

"Colonel MacLaren had us all out in a wink."

She frowned. "You were lucky he had the clout."

He shrugged. "It was easy; he threatened to tell the whole truth." And no one in the Admiralty wanted that. They paid for silence by paying for the repairs to the *Lewis*. The official story that finally went out to the newspapers was the one Daisy had concocted, spur of the moment, when the *Hornet* had shown up off the Pentland Firth, though with no mention of Curmidge. All the blame was laid squarely on the shoulders of one Heinrich Hamilton King and "certain foreign agents."

His mother sniffed, a distressingly Curmidge-like sound. "Well, he should've!" She hugged him again. "But only after you were out. Och, aye, Ewan. Keep this up and you'll give me more gray hairs than your father ever did."

Ewan stepped back, worried. "What's he done now?"

"That's just it," she said, smiling, "he's gone sober. Hasn't touched a drop since the moment we heard the *Lewis* was lost, and when we heard you were safe, he celebrated with spring water and danced me around the pier. He'd be here now, but he's got himself a new job."

"Doing what?"

"You won't believe it – he's dock manager for the West River Air Ferry."

Ewan's mouth fell open. "He's left the line?"

"I told you you wouldn't believe it. He said breaking free was the only way for him. And he says he's going to learn to fly the silly thing, too."

Ewan shook his head, but he couldn't keep from grinning. "He could do it, Ma, if he can just stay sober."

"I know, Ewan." She looked him up and down again. "You've grown."

"It's just the hat. I still wear the same size trousers."

"You've grown inside. I can hear it in your voice."

"That he has," Aunt Nellie said. She came in the door, carrying the lock box from the purser's office, which she promptly handed over to Ewan. "Here, check my tally. And you," she said, turning to Lilla, *"gie's a bosie."* The two women shared a long, teary hug.

"It's good to see you at last, and looking so well," Lilla said, when they finally stepped apart. "You are well?"

"As well as could be hoped," Aunt Nellie replied, blinking hard, "and you can thank Ewan for a good part of that. You should have seen him this passage, Lilla, playing the young sport in the saloon, hobnobbing with the best and the worst, setting Sturgis's schemes *agley*. I think I've found myself the perfect junior purser, if I can just get him to settle down and learn bookkeeping."

He buried his blush behind his counting.

"Any more trouble with that parcel o' rogues in the Admiralty?" Nellie asked then, keeping the subject firmly away from her grief.

"Not lately," Lilla replied, "but this just came from Glasgow."

Aunt Nellie took the telegraph envelope, pulled out the message, and scanned the heading.

"It's for both of us, Ewan," she said, "from one Gertrude Weber. That's Daisy MacLaren," she told Lilla.

Ewan came over, the money forgotten in his hands. "What's she say? Is everything all right? Any news from—"

"Hush! I'll read it. 'Dear Aunt, Good news from Cousin Hilde. All safely arrived Uncle Paul's. Three k's from H to Cousin G.'"

She looked up at Ewan. "Well, H for Hilde means Tereza, and you're Cousin G, and I can guess what the three k's are, but who – or where – is Uncle Paul?"

"South America," Ewan replied. "We worked out a code: Uncle Frank was France, Uncle Peter was Italy, Aunt Isabel—"

"I get it, but where in South America? It's a whole continent, lad."

"Brazil. To start with."

"I thought they were going upriver to Bohemia."

"Too dangerous. Too many people there know the professor."

Aunt Nellie fanned the message in front of his face. "Sending this was too dangerous."

"That's why she sent it to Daisy, as Gertrude, by way of Glasgow."

Aunt Nellie glowered. "Don't you try to reach her, do you hear me?"

"But—"

"No buts! You'll have us all back in jail, ye *glekkit skipe*, along with Miss Daisy and your lady love!"

"She's right, Ewan," his mother said. "And we're not losing you again so easily. Nellie, burn it."

Aunt Nellie raised the chimney on the gas lamp and touched the corner of the telegram to the flame, then dropped it into a wire trash basket held up by Ewan's mother. Ewan watched silently as it burned to ash, wishing he could have touched the message at least. He told himself it was enough to know that Tereza and the professor were safely out of Europe and willed himself to be content. For now. The *Isle of Lewis* would sail east again in another week. He could visit Daisy and hope for more recent news. Meanwhile, he had a box of money to count if he wanted to keep his job.

And he did. Deck crew or junior purser; both if he could find a way. He took off his derby and suit coat, sat down at the desk, and rolled up his sleeves.

—The End—

More Good Books by Dean Whitlock

FINN'S CLOCK – An award-winning gaslight fantasy set in a time when steam is threatening sail, factories are displacing craftsmen, and the immigrants are Irish – unwanted and under threat, but determined to make their place here. It's 1853 and young Finn O'Neill is learning the ropes of a boatman when into fog-bound Boston Harbor there sails a sea-going Chinese junk, bearing mysteries, magic, and a firebrand named An-Ming.

THE ARROW RUNE – An ancient arrowhead found at a Medieval Faire is the key to an alternate world where Anglo-Saxons battle Celtic Britons, and *scops* sing the new saga of Beowulf. Ed Lewis, 17, must cross the world-marches to that middle earth to rescue his kidnapped mother. Facing sword, magic, and monsters with a bow, he finds that skill, friendship, and a healthy dose of fear will solve riddles that reveal the true nature of love, life, and death.

THE CARVER'S WORLD SERIES – Three friends are drawn together by one's misfortune, but each has wrongs to right and a story to tell . . .

SKY CARVER – A talented self-taught sculptor in wood, Carver is trapped in the shadow of his father's painterly genius and his mother's rough talent as a seer. Though they are long gone downriver, presumed dead, Carver is forced to follow his father's trade, until he suddenly shows rare talent as a weather mage. The journey downriver to learn his new craft will challenge his skills, test friendship and honor, and change his life in ways he could never imagine.

RAVEN – Four long years since running away from cruel Baron Cutter, Raven risks recapture to return to

Cutter's estate. She's an experienced bird mage now, but the memory of her escape haunts her. Did her mother abandon her that night, or did Raven desert her mother in an hour of need? To find the answer, she must first learn to control her own erratic talent and temper, to look beyond magic – and herself – in order to save what is most important.

FIREBOY – After a hard year working on the stinking canals of Dunsgow, Fireboy's skill with steamboats has earned him barely half the money he needs to pay off his mother's bond and reunite his family. A chance meeting with a seer sends him to the tangled, bemagicked rapids of the highest reach of the land. Caught up in a battle to control the heartland of magic, he risks new friends and his own free will to discover which bonds really matter.

About the Author

Vermont author Dean Whitlock writes fantasy and science fiction for young and not-so-young adults. His stories have appeared in Asimov's, Fantasy & Science Fiction, and Aboriginal SF, as well as in anthologies in the United States and abroad. In 2019, His novel *Finn's Clock* was awarded First Place in the Young Adult category for the 7th Annual Writer's Digest Self-Published Ebook Awards. An Air Force brat, Dean has lived in a dozen states and three foreign countries, a life of travel that gave him plenty of time to read in the car and now enriches his writing. You can find out more about Dean and his upcoming titles at www.deanwhitlock.com.

This book would not have been possible without the help and knowledge of several special people:

Dorothy Gannon, who kept me honest to the era, particularly in the matter of mores and manners between the sexes.

Pierre-Alexandre Sicart, who helped me put good French into the mouths of Daisy and De Beausoleil (and put great effort into the final proofreading as well).

Sally, Marc, Rich, and Paul who gave me great advice and also chipped in on the proofreading.

The late Kate Reid Ledoux, author of the 1878 how-to book *Ocean Notes and Foreign Travel for Ladies*, a wonderful glimpse of the era, available for free from Google Books.

www.ingramcontent.com/pod-product-compliance
Lightning Source LLC
Chambersburg PA
CBHW051609100726
47898CB00001B/291